This book is dedicated with love and gratitude
In the beginning, for Erin
Through it all, for Caroline and Tonie
And in the end, for all the women whose hearts are buried in the desert sand

ACKNOWLEDGEMENTS

This book was conceived in the midst of a rescue mission. Erin Treanor, thank you for yanking me from the clutches of my mad sadness and inspiring me to write a novel instead of a suicide note.

For encouraging me every step of the way and always saying "More, please!" as you read along, Caroline Marshall and Tonie Knight, there are never enough thank-yous for ALL OF IT. Caroline, you are my gypsy cowgirl life line. Tonie, my lighthouse, always in sight. If it weren't for you both, I may never have passed the open windows long enough to write this book. (And thanks, John Irving, for that reference. It haunts us).

For being, always, a Patron Angel Saint of light and encouragement, Sam Grant.

For making me realize some people will hate this fucking book, no matter how hard I work, special thanks to the now-defunct writers' group in Encino for all your criticism. My ego is in check.

For edits and proofreads and long conversations about writing and creativity, my brother, the formidable writing talent, Kyle Olson. For tireless, tedious, painstaking edits, my red-pen-wielding cousin, Donna Hensley. For even more proofreading after the tons of eyeballs and proofreading software still didn't catch it all, Jennifer Zorbalas. For making sure my crime scene scenes didn't sound like a drunk four-year-old with an IQ of 7 wrote them, thank you to my kick-ass CSI cousin, Triese McDaniel. All mistakes in this final copy are completely my doing.

For my dearly loved and departed Aunt Lois, who wanted a chance to proofread this, I'm sorry. I was worried you would think I was a sex-crazed sicko if you read it. I miss you.

For working something close to a million hours for a "paycheck" of about 11 cents per month, thanks to Joshua Silva, for my beautiful cover design, book layout, website, and your ability to get excited about all of it with me. They don't call you TechMaster Panty for nothing. Actually they don't call you that. I do. And I can't even remember why. It must have been auto-correct.

Thank you also to C.D., for showing me what it means to love a monster. I'm so glad you're gone.

And thank you to anyone who is like me, and actually reads acknowledgements.

Lastly, my deepest thanks to anyone who reads this novel.

For all of you, I am forever Grateful.

Grateful

A novel by MARNIE OLSON

REDHEADED ANGEL PRESS

Los Angeles, CA

Copyright © 2015 by Marnie Olson

ISBN: 978-0-9978122-1-3

Cover Art and layout by Joshua Silva © 2016

Printed in the United States of America

10 9 8 7 6 5 4 3 2 1

"Be careful what you wish for."
-Aesop

ONE

Every Wednesday and Friday at the same time, right around 2:30 p.m., for three glorious weeks he had seen her in the same place. It was pure chance – fate perhaps – the first time Kent laid eyes on her. Maybe she'd recently moved to the area, or had a new routine? Kent had been to the bookstore many times, but on this particular day, that perfect day when he first caught a glimpse of her, he happened to glance out the window at the same moment she walked into the coffee shop across the street.

It was her walk that attracted him, half-glide, and half-bounce, elegant and yet, exuberant. This was a woman who loved life. She wasn't really his type. She was extremely thin. When she came out of the coffee shop, with her extra-large cup, and a huge flowered bag slung over her shoulder, he noticed how lean she was. Slender hips, no arm jiggle, no curves. She had on those, what did women call them? Yoga pants. Yes, and her skin was slightly dewy; the tendrils of curly rose-gold hair clung to her porcelain neck with sweat. Every muscle was lean and taut; she barely had any breasts at all. Normally, he'd be wrestling with a combination of disappointment and guilt while seeing such tiny breasts. He loved big, luscious, full-volume breasts, but then he would chastise himself for being a jerk. How terribly shallow and ungentlemanly! He was above that sort of thing, really. This woman was a goddess, and he could see it. And she was clearly comfortable with herself, small breasts and all. Not one of those vain bitches with plastic shoved in her chest to substitute for tits. "No," he thought, "Give me teeny-tiny titties over sacks of salty water any day."

He stared out the bookstore window at her as her long, graceful fingers curled around her coffee cup. Though there was enough distance between them so that he couldn't make out every detail, his imagination could fill in the blanks. Her strawberry-blonde curls and ivory complexion convinced him that there must be the most delicate, beautiful smattering of freckles across the backs of her hands - freckles that led a tasty path to her tiny, yet strong wrists. The sinews in her toned arms pulled his eyes to rest on her perfect hands. The feminine hand – surely one of the most beautiful sights in nature.

He wanted to approach her, but felt oddly shy. He was afraid his charm would elude him today. He couldn't understand why he was so nervous. And then it hit him. It might seem silly to admit, but it was suddenly apparent.

He was in love. She was The One.

TWO

Grace opened her eyes and stayed very still. She was afraid to roll over. She listened carefully to the silence and glanced at the clock. 7:24. So early. *Why couldn't I just sleep a little longer?* She had to pee of course, badly. Last night's bottle of Sauvignon Blanc pushed at the walls of her bladder with semi-drunk aggression. She'd have to get up. As she started to pull the sheets back, she remembered how naked she was. Totally. Totally naked.

Erick emitted a slight snore. He was still here. He didn't sneak off in the middle of the night! If she was careful, she could slink off to the bathroom, pee, check her face for smeared eyeliner and other morning-after drunk-sex atrocities, and maybe even gargle a little mouthwash, and make her way back into the bed before he woke up.

She crept quietly to the bathroom. Thank god she checked the mirror. Eyeliner smeared under her eyes gave her the appearance of a hung-over raccoon. Combined with eye boogers, foul breath, and fuck-knots in her long brown hair, she was an absolute wreck. She did the best she could as noiselessly as possible. Damn. Why didn't she bring a robe or something in here? She checked out her naked body in the mirror. Whoa. Bad idea. Okay, don't think about it. He liked it just fine. But, it had been dark. Maybe he hadn't noticed the stretch marks, the C-section scar, and the saggy lopsided breasts. So, three deep breaths later, she opened the bathroom door and ran for cover.

"Slow down," Erick said. *Shit.* He was awake.

She stopped in her tracks, naked and vulnerable. She stood as still as she could and took in a deep, pseudo-confident breath.

"What?"

"I just want to look at you."

He stared at her for a moment. She couldn't move. It was weird, and intoxicating.

"You are so fucking hot." He said it as if it was hard to breathe and talk at the same time.

It was hard to breathe. Was there any air in this room? She wanted to open a window, but didn't want to walk over to the direct source of sunlight and give him a view of her dimpled booty. Fuck it. Get over yourself, she said in her usual conversation-with-her-own-mind. You're both adults. You're 36 years old. Okay, 38. He's 36. Okay, 34. Open a damn window. It smells like sweat and cum in here, and it's stiflingly hot.

His stare scorched her skin as she walked to the window, the cool air a relief as she opened it, slightly parting the curtains as she did.

Just as she noticed the gooseflesh springing up on her body, he sucked his breath in.

"Your ass is amazing."

Suddenly, he was behind her. He had his hands on her saggy, dimpled ass, and he was muttering about its beauty.

He kissed her shoulder blades. She had forgotten what that did to her. Her knees buckled. She turned into him. She felt like crying, but grabbed his dick instead.

She was so goddamn lucky.

THREE

It was Wednesday again, and there she was. The Divine Miss Yoga Pants in all her glory. God, the period of time from Friday afternoon until Wednesday at 2:30 was always interminable. He'd wanted to follow her from the coffee shop last Friday, but that was too creepy. That's what stalkers do. And one thing was certain: he was a gentleman, not a stalker. He had been seeing her here for over a month. He'd have to muster the courage to talk to her.

He had observed her long enough to know what his approach should be. He noticed something very interesting about Yoga Pants. She was very open and smiley and almost flirtatious with some men, and downright cold to others. What was strange was that the men at which she chose to beam her radiant smile were the old ones, the awkward ones, the comic book geeks and the fat, balding ones. The better-looking, suave guys she blew off.

This just made him love her more. She wasn't shallow. She saw right through those hipsters and players, those pseudo-intellectuals with their tattered copies of Nietzsche and their presumably for accessory-purpose-only dark-rimmed glasses, that let you know how political, creative and sensitive they were. They were jerks, and Yoga Pants saw right through them.

Now, even though this raised her goddess status considerably, it presented a problem for him, one he wasn't sure he could downplay: his tremendous good looks. What if she saw him as a pretty boy and blew him off like the others? He didn't think he could bear her rejection.

Though he was handsome, he was also quite humble. But what could he do? He never bragged about his good looks to anyone – after all, they were totally apparent – but more to the point, he didn't want to appear conceited.

He would wait until Friday to talk to her. He could dress down, not wash his hair or shave. He had tried to look his best for her today, believing it was the day he would talk to her, but he lost his nerve. Yoga Pants blew off another high cheek-boned pretty boy in skinny jeans, which she did shortly after laughing at some fat slob's joke.

This woman had a lot of admirers. Friday was the day. He couldn't wait any longer than that, or he might lose her.

FOUR

Grace couldn't believe how happy she was. Erick was still showing up. He called her and sent her sweet, sexy little texts almost every day. They wined and dined and made love like they were in a love-making contest and determined to win. After everything she'd been through, she was afraid to let herself wonder,

"Am I getting my life back?"

FIVE

Everything changed when she met the man she would marry. Eight years ago, Grace had been in an extraordinarily low point in her life. She was despondent and exhausted. She'd had a shitty childhood - which was made disappointing by the simple fact that she never really understood how to be a child, and this shitty childhood led right into a shittier, awkward adolescence in which other girls wore lip gloss and had boyfriends while Grace hid in bathroom stalls to cry. She would pray for the day when, as a "grown-up," she would have control over her life, and she would miraculously become happy... somehow. But one thing after another had failed her, disappointed her and broken her heart, and so, when Stan came along, he was a breath of fresh air. A strong, stable, reliable breath of fresh air. A man who wouldn't leave. He was far from perfect, and she'd never be *in love* with him, but she did love him... sort of.

He was admirable in a lot of ways. He was always on time – always. He was proud to be with her. He didn't put her in the shame closet after bedding her – he included her in his life, and introduced her to his friends and family. He called her his girlfriend, then his fiancé, then his wife. Holidays and special occasions were honored with flowers and gifts and romantic dinners. He took her on lovely holidays to beach resorts and quaint bed and breakfasts where they would wine-taste and picnic. He was supportive of her "career" – which really was Grace taking a bunch of artsy photographs and hoping that someday, somebody would give a shit about it. When she got a small showing of her work, he bought her three dozen roses and expensive champagne and gushed about how proud he was of her.

She married him, even though there was something wrong. She knew, from her own experience in life, that the other shoe would drop. She knew this because the other shoe ALWAYS drops. It's the nature of the shoe. Once the first shoe drops, the other shoe feels incomplete, until it too, has dropped.

Less than a year after they met, Grace and Stan were officially engaged. Then things started to change, and not for the better. Grace couldn't put all the blame on him. She was feeling weird. Well, weird was an understatement. It was more like shit-your-pants scared. She told herself that she needed to be smart. When the nice guy shows up, you marry him. Otherwise, you are a stupid bitch. And nobody likes a stupid bitch. Certainly, nobody likes a stupid bitch with metaphorically shitty pants.

But, Stan was acting a little odd too. He got annoyed with her when she wasn't happy enough. After all, he was giving her his best effort, doing everything right, and she just moped around.

Grace's panic would rise as the time for Stan to come home from work grew near. The second he walked through the door, she made every effort to convince him she was in high spirits. It became something of a game for her – a really not-so-fun game that she always lost. She either felt like a fraud when she "successfully" faked it, or she let him down when she couldn't.

He'd enter their house, pensively, and stare at her, searching her face and body language for clues.

"Hey babe," he'd say with the usual trepidation in his voice, afraid to follow with a "how was your day."

Most days, she could pull it off. She'd smile, ask him about his day, and do her best to come up with some bullshit about how awesome her day was, and how glad she was he was home. But, the fact was, some days she just couldn't convince him. No matter how badly she wanted to.

He'd see it on her face immediately. And then it would come out of him, like a warning bell, an ominous toll of his frustration and anger. The deep, heavy Stan sigh. Nobody could sigh like Stan. It was weighty, foreboding, like a big fat "F" on her wife-to-be report card.

Sigh.

His sighs enraged her.

"Let me guess," he'd say, "you had a bad day."

"It was kind of rough, yeah."

Sigh.

Grace, knowing she had no explanation that could satisfy him, would storm out of the room, and then he would stomp around, following her, slamming things down, and ask her through gritted teeth, "So I guess you're having one of your episodes?"

Most assuredly, she was. The darkness always found her, and if she let it take her down, she would lose Stan, and that would be a big mistake.

She decided to grin and bear it. She would be happy. She would be like a bride-to-be was supposed to be. She would beam and glow and radiate bliss. She would show off her engagement ring and plan her stupid fucking wedding.

The very *idea* of marriage was scary to Grace, but the reality of it was pure horror. She became more and more depressed, and Stan became more and more controlling and angry.

When she could fake her happiness, he would calm down and relax, but where was the reward in that? Then she'd have to fake her orgasms because as soon as he sensed even the most lukewarm affection between them, he'd get all frisky and want to have sex.

Grace liked sex sometimes, but mostly she endured it. Not because she didn't like the actual act of it, she just never liked the men she had sex with. They were so tedious. Some were bad lovers, but even the ones who technically "did everything right" still left her cold. She figured something was wrong with her, because something was always wrong with her.

Grace had a dark secret. Something she'd never told anyone. It was so sinister that she just carried it around with her all her life, and hoped no one would figure it out. But Stan was on to her. He was figuring it out. He would learn her secret, and once he knew, everyone in her life would eventually know the truth.

Grace's deep dark secret didn't sound like much at first, but she knew the power of it.

Grace… was… well, Grace was *a lemon.*

She wasn't exactly sure why people started picking on lemons and using them to describe shitty cars that always break down. After all, lemons make lemonade and meringue pie and lovely garnish for iced tea and grilled fish. What was so wrong with lemons?

Lemons are sour, she guessed.

When a car keeps breaking down, it gets dubbed a "lemon." Fix it over and over, pour money under the hood, change the brake pads, the gaskets, the spark plugs, hell, overhaul the whole goddamn engine, but a true lemon will always find a way to break down. It will always let you down. It will always disappoint you, until you wise up and get rid of it.

Grace had faulty wiring. And she'd always known it, even as a child. Other kids laughed and played in a strange and foreign way. She was never really sure what all the fuss was about. And that feeling continued all her life.

She would have "good stretches" when something kind of fantastic or special would happen, and she'd do a little better for a while. When she was younger, she'd fool herself into thinking that it meant things were finally changing for the better. But inevitably, something shitty would happen, and it would completely level her. Or worse, nothing would even have to happen – she'd just inexplicably fall into the deep dark pit and be unable to climb out, sometimes for years at a time.

Two years into her marriage, she accepted once and for all, that she would always break down, and always disappoint the people around her. It was just the way things were. She was doing her best, but Stan was starting to suspect that his wife was worthless and nothing he ever did would make her happy.

Then something truly awful happened that would destroy their marriage, and their lives.

Grace got pregnant.

It was an accident. They weren't ready to start a family. Grace suspected she'd never be ready, but she couldn't very well tell Stan that, because it would just be one more indication of how faulty her wiring was. Even though she didn't want marriage or children, she was *supposed* to want them, and acting like she wanted them could make her appear more normal, and like less of a lemon.

But when she actually got pregnant, her mask slipped, completely. She fucked everything up.

EVERY FUCKING THING.

One day, Stan came home to Grace, curled up in a fetal position on the bathroom floor. The toilet was filled with vomit. There were wads of snotty tissues all over the place. Her eyes were open, but vacant. She was practically catatonic.

"Grace? Grace! Come on, get up. Baby, come on, what's going on?"

Grace lay silent for a while as Stan continued to coax her to snap out of it. He was genuinely worried about her. He was calling her "baby" and being a caretaker. She wanted to stay in that place, because once she confessed what was really going on, he would be angry with her, and it would get ugly. She wanted his sympathy and compassion for as long as she could have it.

Finally, she couldn't put him through it anymore. She had to come clean.

"I'm pregnant," she said, without moving. His thoughts came out in a rush.

"Oh my god. You're pregnant! Oh baby, this is good news. I know it's sooner than we talked about, but that's okay, and… why are you crying? Is everything all right? Baby, talk to me, please…" Stan pulled her up and forced her to meet his eyes.

He was scared. He'd seen some sadness, some darkness, some really terrifying shit in his wife's eyes, but this was the worst. Her eyes were dead.

"Grace!" he was raising his voice now, "Grace! Tell me what's going on. Why are you crying?"

"Because I'm pregnant."

"Okay, so you're scared, I get it. It's scary, but it's going to be okay."

Finally, Grace's eyes began to focus, and she met Stan's penetrating gaze as she admitted her horrible lemony truth, "I don't want a baby. Not now. Not ever. I don't want this baby. Any baby."

There was a horrible silence that seemed to last a hundred years.

Finally, Stan stood up.

"Clean up this fucking mess," he said, and walked out of the room, and then out of the house.

SIX

Kent woke up, barely able to contain his excitement. Today was Friday! He would talk to Yoga Pants for the first time. Her voice would be lovely. He was so excited he had an erection. He contemplated masturbation, but that was such a bad idea. It could sully the beauty of his first encounter with her. Not that he planned on bedding her right away. Quite the contrary. He reminded himself that a true gentleman waits for the right signals from a woman before taking any sexual action. Masturbating ahead of time to thoughts of her was lewd and would disgrace her somehow.

He very rarely masturbated. He deemed it degrading and, frankly, a little wasteful. Being the handsome fellow he was, he got plenty of attention from women, but he prided himself on being choosy. He didn't want to bed just anyone. He couldn't understand men who indiscriminately slept around with any available woman. That kind of behavior disgusted him. He always saved himself for someone special.

He went into the bathroom. He hadn't shaved or showered in days because he wanted to downplay his good looks. He was so worried she would blow him off if she didn't take the time to get to know the real him. He'd seen her coldly dismiss many handsome men in the time he'd observed her at the coffee shop, and those men weren't half as good-looking as he was.

He was disappointed by his face in the mirror. Damn. Instead of unattractive, it was as if he was even sexier. The scruffy facial hair on his chiseled features just made him more rugged and manly. His hair didn't appear greasy, only shiny. He put on his dorkiest ensemble. He kept plenty of dorky things in his wardrobe so that he would seem approachable to women, as he noticed how often women were intimidated by men they thought were "too good-looking."

It made him sad to think of all the women he'd known that believed they didn't deserve him, how insecure they were.

Because of their low self-esteem, perfectly lovely women were always going off with men so beneath them.

As he ran through his mental rolodex of previous lovers, his erection grew more insistent. He needed to focus. He was about to meet someone new. She would be his greatest love so far. She wouldn't disappoint him. He was sure of it.

He moved toward Yoga Pants just as she was leaving the coffee shop.

She was so... *approachable*. She was friendly and open and my god, when she beamed her smile his way, all the achy parts of him melted into the floor. They had an instant connection. He was a hopeless romantic, but he felt that true soul-mate connection with her immediately.

And her voice, her sweet, angelic, tinkling of church bells voice, what could he say about her voice? Well, it buttered his muffin, that's for damn sure.

She had asked his name and knowing he would get a disbelieving giggle at first – he almost always did – he told her.

"My name is Kent," he said, "Last name, Clark." She laughed, asked if he was serious. It was his honest-to-god given name. Kent Clark. In school, he had been teased a lot, especially when last names were listed first because, of course, he was then Clark – comma – Kent. He used to hate it but now he loved it, because it was such a great conversation-starter with the ladies.

"I'm Diane," she said. Diane... Diane... Diane... a true goddess name.

He walked her to her car and made his move. He asked her if he could join her for coffee sometime, and then... something went wrong.

She shut down to him. She got cold and distant. She got jumpy. She started acting really weird, and he couldn't figure out what happened. What had he said to make her change like that? He kept replaying it in his mind, unable to figure out how he had screwed it up.

No, no, no, he didn't screw it up! She's just a cold bitch, like all the others. But he had been certain about this one... so sure.

SEVEN

Stan and Grace did the best they could to stay together and work through her pregnancy and their shitty, stifling marriage. Grace wanted an abortion, but bringing that up would send Stan into insane rages. At the first mention of it, he broke so many dishes that they ate off paper plates for the remainder of their marriage. They fought about that as well. He shouldn't have to buy plates since it was Grace's fault he broke them, because she was an aspiring baby-killer, and Grace couldn't buy new plates because she was too clinically depressed to leave the house, and also didn't care if she ever ate again.

Eventually, they settled into a routine. Stan basically nursed her. He made sure she ate and bathed. He took really good care of her. Once she resigned herself to her imprisonment, she just did what she was told. *Eat your vegetables. Drink your juice. Get some rest. Let's get to your doctor's appointment.* Whatever he told her to do she did, because she couldn't bear any more fights. She wasn't capable of making her own decisions anyway because she was a lemon. She might think she was strong and independent and reliable enough to drive cross-country, but the Stans of the world knew that a lemon couldn't be expected to do that. A lemon will spring a leak in her radiator and blow a tire in the middle of the desert and leave you stranded.

Grace ticked off the days in her mind as her due date approached, or her "doom date," as she mentally referred to it. Her body grew and stretched. It was disgusting. Stretch marks formed on her stomach. She was constipated. She had heartburn. Her feet were so swollen she could barely get shoes on. She was getting fatter every day. She was goddamn miserable. She was plagued by nightmares of slimy aliens that burst out of her stomach and then ate her reproductive organs and her eyes. She would wake up screaming, and Stan would calm her down. They would talk about all the "hormonal changes" she was enduring, but her craziness was no longer mentioned. It was the elephant in the room:

the crazy, depressed elephant with no maternal instincts moping around their house.

Then Grace had a different dream.

Grace was standing in a meadow. Wildflowers were everywhere, as high as her waist. She had on a long, flowing, feminine gown. It was as beautiful as a douche commercial. She had that very fresh feeling.

Suddenly, a young voice called out somewhere in the meadow.

"Mom-my! Mommy? Mommy..."

She followed the voice.

Mommy. Step toward the voice. Mommy. Step toward the voice.

She was standing next to a stream. A small girl, with golden hair, about four years old was sitting on a large rock, crying.

As Grace approached her, the little girl turned and said, "I can't find my mommy."

Grace reached down and pulled the girl up and into her arms.

"Mommy's here," said Grace, "Don't cry, Kaylee, mommy's here."

Grace woke up.

That day she told Stan they would be having a daughter, and her name would be Kaylee.

He was hesitant to believe her at first, only because he knew how unstable Grace could be, but from then on her pregnancy no longer tormented her, so he chose not to question it. He hoped motherhood would be just the thing to soothe his poor suffering wife, and give her something to fill up the hole that so clearly lived in her heart.

EIGHT

The next Wednesday Kent waited at the coffee shop until it closed. He arrived at 2:00 p.m., hoping to see her. He waited and waited, but she never showed up. He kept buying more stupid coffee drinks that he didn't want so the staff wouldn't get annoyed with him for sitting there so long.

He replayed every bit of his conversation last Friday with Yoga Pants… no, Diane… in his mind. He couldn't understand what had gone wrong. What if she never came back here? Was she trying to avoid him? Maybe she was going to a new coffee shop somewhere else.

He was devastated. Heartbroken. How could this be happening… AGAIN? God, women were so damn disappointing. He felt a real connection with this one.

As the punk-ass barista boy came over at closing time to ask him to leave, he held back angry tears and told himself, once again, that there would be others. There would be other women, better women; there would be that one special woman who appreciated a man like him.

NINE

When Grace went into labor, the pain was lethal, and yet she'd never felt more alive. With each contraction, it occurred to her that the massive amounts of pain she had endured in her life had been largely emotional. Sure, she'd had the occasional flu, a headache here and there, but really she'd been pretty lucky in terms of her health. She'd never broken a single bone, not even a toe. She'd never had a cavity. She was not ever hospitalized for any major illness, or endured food poisoning. She had no allergies; in fact, she was so physically healthy that it made her depression even worse – because she felt guilty for being morose when she was in such good physical health. People had cancer and multiple sclerosis and chronic pain, and she was just a whiny little bitch. She especially felt guilty when she got angry that her physical health was so good, because she was afraid she'd have a really long life, and she truly hated that idea. Her soul was what always hurt, not her body, but suddenly her soul was fine and it was her body that felt like shit. She finally understood true physical pain. It was exhilarating.

Grace considered the bullshit about not remembering labor pains that women love to blabber on about as they get all misty-eyed and coo that the moment they first held their baby, they forgot all about the pain. What a load of crap. Grace cherished every moment of it, and she damn well always would. That pain gave her life new meaning.

The only real problem with cherishing every moment of the pain was that, though she didn't know it at the time, she was in an abnormal amount of pain. She tried her best to stay aware, but slipped in and out of consciousness, both keenly and fuzzily aware of the excessive bleeding, the warm stickiness of it. Later, she would be filled in on all the gory details, something about placental abruption, fetal distress, hemorrhaging, emergency C-section, and so on. She didn't care about getting any of the details right. She barely listened to the doctors and nurses. She had suffered, but her baby came out perfect. Kaylee was healthy and beautiful. Grace had done one thing right in her life, and she would wear her abdominal scar proudly. She hoped it was a big, nasty one. She hoped every time Stan saw it, he would realize that she wasn't a lemon after all. She was a warrior. She was a fucking mother. That must count for something.

TEN

If anyone was a prime candidate for post-partum depression, it was Grace. She researched all the symptoms of it before giving birth so she would be prepared for the inevitable.

When she and Stan brought Kaylee home from the hospital, things improved between them. Having someone else to focus on was good for them both, as well as for their marriage. The constant care an infant required gave Grace a purpose she had never experienced before.

When Kaylee was three weeks old, the darkness stirred inside Grace.

You're a shitty mother. You don't know what the hell you're doing.

You're going to fuck this up Grace, you big fucker-upper.

When Kaylee grows up, she'll hate you.

There was the exhaustion, unexplained crying jags, weird obsessive thoughts, anxiety attacks, and just general overwhelming sadness.

But something amazing happened. All those bullshit coping tools she had learned in therapy through her lifetime of depression suddenly came in handy. She just sort of... tackled her problems, faced her fears, and moved through them.

She did it for Kaylee. Someone needed her. Grace intended to be there. Always.

At first, Stan was the dream husband you want by your side when there is a crying baby, a ringing phone, and a stopped-up drain all at once.

But something else happened that was less amazing. Stan began to resent Grace. Being the kind of man who really wasn't interested in digging too deeply into his own feelings, he assumed that there must be a perfectly good reason to resent her.

One night, he came home and Grace was sitting serenely in the big cushy chair by the window feeding Kaylee. Grace was only half-aware of him, and couldn't see any reason to look up from Kaylee when he walked through the door.

"How was your day?" Stan asked.

"Hmm?" Grace was her usual distracted self, never wanting to take her eyes off Kaylee.

"Your day. How was it?" Stan barely held the edge out of his voice.

"Fantastic. She made the cutest gurgling noises today. Let me see if I can get her to do it again." Grace started cooing and cuddling Kaylee while Stan fumed.

"I'll hold her for a minute. You've had her all day."

"I'm good. You need to decompress. You just got home."

He withdrew into silence as Grace stood up and went to the kitchen. She finished making dinner while continuing to hold Kaylee, talking away to her and virtually oblivious to Stan.

They sat down to eat in an appearance of domestic bliss. Stan's quiet and sullen attitude irritated Grace, but she said nothing to him about it. Whatever was going on with him, she'd figured if he wanted to talk about it, he would.

It was a pity Grace couldn't understand what was going on inside Stan because, if she had, she might have had some compassion for him. Instead, she was utterly annoyed. Here she was, smiling, and damn near happy – or as close to happy as someone like her could be – for the first time, in, well... ever, and Stan was moping around and pouting.

Yes, he was pouting.

Grace completely lost interest in him.

Stan could tell.

Grace knew he could tell.

But she didn't care.

She had Kaylee.

During the first six months of Kaylee's life the annoyances and resentments abated, and Grace and Stan reached an unspoken agreement: they would play "house."

They smiled together, played with Kaylee, took family photos and trips to the park. Photos of that time period showed such a beautiful, joyful family. She had a purpose; she was useful. The hole in her heart was filled, filled, filled with love, and more love. She didn't even care anymore that she didn't really love Stan, because she had so much love for Kaylee, who was a part of Stan, that she could love him even though she didn't. And somehow, that made perfect sense to her.

She could stay with him, as long as she had Kaylee. She could live with herself, as long as she had Kaylee. She could even love herself, as long as she had Kaylee to love.

Maybe this could be her life after all. But with that came the same old fear. She was shit-your-pants – no, wait – poopy-pants scared. Poopy seemed like a nicer word to use than shitty, in front of a baby and all.

ELEVEN

Kent Clark had been in mourning for two months, since Diane had rejected him. He needed to buck up and move on. Obviously, she wasn't the girl for him. He'd made another mistake. Now, he was ready to put himself out there again. He applauded himself for his quick recovery. After his last romantic debacle, which had, of course, also ended in ruin, it took him almost six months to recover. He wasn't going to let that happen again. He deserved true love, and he was going to get it.

His favorite diner beckoned him. He hadn't been there in years, because he had been smitten with one of the waitresses, and apparently she quit or got fired, because one day she was just gone. After that, he was too disappointed to go there anymore. It was like the second he felt a real connection with someone, she'd disappear. Maybe women really were just fickle.

He went into Lu's Diner on a Thursday for lunch. Some of these old ladies had been working there for centuries.

Then, there she was, walking toward him, with a spring in her step, her dark-brown curls bouncing. She was luscious; the antithesis of that skinny porcelain bitch Diane who had so coldly rejected him.

"May I get you something to drink?" she said as she put the laminated menu in front of him on the table. He quickly grabbed it from her, hoping to brush his hand against hers. He succeeded.

She caught him and pulled her hand away, but then she winked. Yes, she did; *she winked* at him! Oh my god. Her eyes, her eyes… a deep brown, deeper than the soul of the earth itself, flecks of amber sparkling in them every time she smiled. One corner of her mouth went slightly higher than the other, making her smile the tiniest bit imperfect and, therefore, more enchanting. A dimple formed on that side, where her smile rose higher.

Then, her skin, the creamiest, most milk-chocolate-y skin he'd ever seen. She was magnificent. She was waiting patiently for his answer. What a sweetie.

"Lemonade," he said.

Off she went to fetch his lemonade. When she walked her hips swayed slightly. It was impossible not to stare at her luscious body. She was short and curvy, but solid. He attributed her appeal to the fact that she looked like she could totally kick your ass, but still have vulnerability in her face while doing it. God, he would totally let this chick kick his ass. Yum.

He barely tasted his meal that day, whatever it was. It might have been a tuna melt. Then again, it might have been a bag of sand. He'd hardly know the difference. He had a regular spot again, and a new lovely girl to think about. He made a point of checking out her name tag before he left – which afforded him the opportunity to glance at her ample breasts.

"Cicily," he said. "Thank you so much for your friendly service today."

"You're very welcome," said Cicily. "Have a nice day."

She wanted him to have a nice day! He was! He was having a very nice day!

Cicily... what a romantic name... inscribed on a simple plastic tag, atop those big creamy breasts...

Oh boy. He was going to Boner Town. He had better take a brisk walk home to a cold shower.

TWELVE

As the weeks went by, Kent went to the diner more and more often. He was so excited, but dared not let Cicily get to him. He was afraid of being disappointed again, but his desire for her was quickly trumping his fear of rejection. He did his best not to appear too eager. He wanted to eat every single meal at Lu's, so he could see her as much as possible, but that would be mega-creepy. He didn't want to be mega-creepy. He wanted to be suave and debonair. He wanted to sweep Cicily off her pretty little feet. He was curious about her feet, and whether they were, in fact, little. It didn't matter. Her hands mattered. Her slender, delicate fingers had brushed his hand that first day, and since then he hadn't been able to get another feel of them, and it was driving him crazy.

He loved women's hands. They were the most beautiful part of a woman's body. Yes, there were many, many delights in the female form, but a woman's hands, so different from a man's hands…

Damn, he had another erection. He would not masturbate. He just wouldn't. He didn't want his own stupid clumsy giant man hands on his glorious member. He wanted Cicily's delicate fingers wrapped around it. He had to stop. He needed to calm down. He didn't want to act desperate. Maybe that's what went wrong with Diane. He had come across too needy, that was it.

He went to Lu's for lunch. He knew Cicily's work schedule now. He told himself that it wasn't creepy stalker behavior, it was just romantic interest. He was a regular. She worked there. Nothing creepy about that. He liked their tuna melts. Or whatever.

He loved this place. There was a little bell over the glass door that jingled when you came in. It made every head turn. It was automatic.

Sweet Cicily turned toward him. His heart leapt and, in an instant, fell again. She immediately looked away, as if she didn't want to meet his eyes. He told himself he was imagining it. She had been so friendly to him. She always smiled and chatted, each time she told him to have a nice day. He tipped her well. He was one of her favorite customers. She had said as much, with her soul-of-the-entire-earth eyes.

Maybe she was having a rough day, or the lunch rush had been particularly busy. But it wasn't busy now. He made his way to his regular table, which was in her section. She always worked the same section, right next to the long counter, between the front door and the bathrooms.

Cicily was chatting with one of the older waitresses. He couldn't make out what they were saying, but they were both stealing glances at him. What the hell was going on? He had a bad feeling about this. The old waitress came over to his table. He didn't even bother to glance at her name tag. Her name was probably Mildred. Ugh. Her hands were old.

"Can I get your drink order?" Mildred said.

"Isn't this Cicily's table?" Kent inquired in his most mild-mannered, off-handed way.

"Not today, she's working the other side."

"Oh, well, I want Cicily to wait on me, so I'll just sit on the other side."

"No," said Mildred. "She's busy. I'd be happy to take your order."

Kent was getting annoyed. He knew damn well that Mildred – if that was even her *real* name – wasn't happy to take his order. She was protecting Cicily from him. That was it. She was being protective. But why? He was always nice as pie, to coin a worn-out diner-ish phrase. Why wouldn't Cicily want to wait on him? What was going on? He didn't want a fucking tuna melt, or any other crappy meal this establishment threw together. He didn't come here for the food. He came here for her. He loved her. She was special. And now, she didn't even want to take his lousy order?

He considered storming out. Screw this place. Screw Cicily. Screw Mildred. He considered that he should stay put, out of pride. After all, he wouldn't want Cicily to think she got to him. He should act casual and aloof. Women love that shit. *I'll be all cool and distant. That will win her over.*

Suddenly, Cicily's laugh carried across the diner. As she shifted her weight, he got a clear view of a man sitting at the table. He was smiling at her. He made her laugh, that asshole. What were they laughing about? Were they laughing at him? No, that's paranoid. It couldn't be about him. But she was flirting with him! He was seriously pissed off. She was moving on so quickly. He hadn't even asked her out yet, which he had planned to do today.

He had to stay. He had to swallow his pride and order a stupid meal from goddamn Mildred, if only to be closer to Cicily. He could keep an eye on her and this new schmuck she was flirting with. He'd get a chance to talk to her. He knew when her shift was over. He could meet her in the parking lot, just to talk, and make sure she wasn't mad at him.

He pushed his food around on his plate. He didn't tip Mildred as well as he tipped Cicily. Why should he? Mildred was a bitch, a hovering mother hen, standing between Kent and true happiness.

He was a patient man. That's one thing Mildred didn't understand. Cicily would understand. She just hadn't gotten to know the real him. She would and when she did, she would land her adorable one-dimpled smile on him, and all would be right with the world.

He waited in the parking lot for Cicily. He waited, because love was worth waiting for.

* * * * *

Oh god, it felt so good. It was so good, even better than he had thought it would be. He was grinding in slow, steady rhythm. It was her hands, Cicily's beautiful hands; her long delicate fingers gently stroking him, then increasing pressure, increasing rhythm, faster and faster, until, oh god, yes, there it was. He was exploding, all over her hands, just her hands...

Just her hands! Just her hands! Oh no, oh no, something was wrong, oh shit, her hands.

Her hands, they were on his member – he didn't like the dirty word "dick," nor did he care for the more clinical "penis," or the terribly offensive "cock" – but it was just her hands.

He reached down, terrified, and pulled her hands up and off his body. They were cut off at the wrists, bloody, with jagged flesh and shards of bone, dripping, oozing, severed hands.

His own scream woke him. He was covered in the coldest sweat, as if shards of ice and boiling droplets were fighting it out on the surface of his skin.

He began to weep. Something was wrong. Something was terribly wrong. He wanted to see her. He needed to know she was okay.

It was just a dream. He told himself that over and over. It was just a dream.

He would go to the diner that day. But he already knew she would not be there.

He was starting to realize something about himself, something terribly tragic.

He had a way of stumbling on the most beautiful women in the City of Angels.

And those women had a way of disappearing.

His heart was breaking, again.

THIRTEEN

Grace never knew she could be so connected to someone. She would wake up during the night, before Kaylee even cried. She'd lie still for a moment and, within seconds, there it would be; Kaylee's cries beckoning for her. Grace would get up, no matter how tired she was. Her exhaustion didn't matter at all. She was needed. She felt loved.

Every aspect of Kaylee's care thrilled her: the breastfeeding, the diaper-changing, the bathing, and as Kaylee grew, the playing.

The playing was the best part. The first time Kaylee giggled Grace's heart exploded. When Kaylee learned to walk, Grace burst at the seams with joy. Obviously, every parent believed their baby was the cutest, but they were all wrong. Grace had the most beautiful child on the planet. Though Stan and Grace had brown hair, Grace had been blonde as a child, and Kaylee had these delightful golden curls which made her face truly angelic. By the time Kaylee turned two, her level of adorable was almost unbearable to Grace.

Grace and Kaylee would play this little chasing game, sort of like hide and seek, and to Kaylee, it was the funniest thing in the world, that she could "hide" in plain sight, and Mommy wouldn't be able to find her. She'd yell "Mommy!" over and over and Grace would stumble around pretending she was unable to find her. Eventually, Kaylee would say, "Look at Kaylee, Mommy," and then Grace would "miraculously" find her and Kaylee would giggle and giggle. What Grace had missed out on in her own sullen childhood, her inability to just let go and play, was finally coming over her in full force. Playing was awesome! Playing with Kaylee as a toddler would be one of the great highlights of Grace's life.

Embracing her sense of play inspired Grace to return to photography. Her creativity waned considerably during her pregnancy. She figured that housing a baby inside her was enough work without attempting to be an artist at the same time.

At first, she took copious pictures of Kaylee but, even though her child was the most beautiful child on the planet, other people, stupid people, would think their babies were cuter. She couldn't just keep taking adorable shots of Kaylee. She needed something more artsy, something with an edge.

She used a tripod and a timer, because she would need to be in the photos. Most people would likely describe Grace as a beautiful woman, but where others saw deep chestnut, Grace saw mousy brown hair; where others saw tall and elegant, Grace felt, at 5 feet 7 inches, that she was not nearly tall enough to be statuesque, but too tall to be dainty and feminine.

She had never done any self-portraits, because she didn't really want to sit around and look at pictures of herself. Her work was sometimes portraiture, or landscapes, but rarely anything or anyone "beautiful." She enjoyed shooting abandoned buildings and homeless people and other tragic images. Grace loved humanity's scars. Her own scar was a sign of humanity, proof that she existed.

She showed Kaylee her scar and explained how they had to cut Mommy open to get her out. She believed Stan would disapprove and tell her that she was scaring Kaylee, but Grace knew it would be okay. Kaylee's face scrunched up with concern as she asked, "Did it hurt Mommy?"

Grace explained that they gave her medicine, so she didn't even feel it.

Grace set up the tripod and timer as she was explaining it to Kaylee. She got really cool pictures of Kaylee, up close to the scar, her chubby toddler fingers reaching out in a curious caress. She took a number of photos of the two of them together, almost always with her scar visible. She didn't care if her stomach was ugly or flabby. She didn't care if people thought that what she was doing was "sick."

Kaylee was transfixed. If Grace had any indication that Kayle was unsettled, she would have stopped immediately.

These photos were the work Grace would be most proud of throughout her life. They were beautiful and raw and charged with ragged humanity. They were good.

Stan hated the photos. He told Grace she was sick and twisted. He told her that she was a lousy mother.

Grace wanted to defend herself, but then she remembered something that she had actually forgotten for a while.

Grace was a lemon. And Stan was here to remind her of that.

FOURTEEN

To Stan, Grace was sick and her photographs were creepy, but Grace showed them to her friend Magda. Magda had given a showing of some of Grace's photos in a small gallery on Abbott-Kinney in Venice Beach, back when Grace had been engaged to Stan.

Magda didn't own the gallery, but the owner let her make a lot of suggestions about what should go in there, because she really did have an eye for art and, most likely, the owner wanted to fuck her. Pretty much everyone wanted to fuck Magda.

Magda could make even very beautiful women feel utterly frumpy. She was Eurasian, from the UK, so she had this sexy English accent, and the half-Asian features gave her an exotic beauty. Her dark hair was long, super-straight and sleeker than glass. She usually had a hot pink or purple streak in it somewhere. She had an eyebrow ring. She dressed like an assassin. She was slender and fairly tall for an Asian, her half-Celtic heritage giving her added height. Magda always had some man who was obsessed with her, or some woman who was obsessed with her, or both, or someone who she was getting a restraining order on because he or she wouldn't leave her alone. Grace was pretty sure Magda was a lesbian, but never asked outright. Maybe Magda didn't want to clarify her sexuality, because she was so adept at using it to her advantage. She wanted men and women alike to think they had a chance with her. It was one of the many tools in her arsenal. Another tool was her extensive knowledge of art – paintings, sculpture, photography, any and all. She was like a walking search engine, utterly brilliant.

Grace arranged a lunch meeting with Magda in a little wine bar, and called her best friend Natalie for a favor.

"Nat? It's me."

"Grace! What's up?"

"I'm meeting Magda for lunch tomorrow."

"That's great!"

"It is. Except I can't get a babysitter."

"I'll take Kaylee," Natalie chirped.

"Seriously? Don't you have interviews scheduled every day?" Grace worried that Natalie, being the tremendous friend she was, would do just about anything to help, even at her own inconvenience. Natalie had been searching for work for a long time, and Grace didn't want to jeopardize that with her neediness.

"Every day but tomorrow. So it's your lucky day! Tomorrow, that is. Not today. Well, I guess today's lucky too, since you're talking to me!" Natalie was even chattier than usual.

"You're awfully peppy today, Nat. In a good mood?"

"Yeah. I had a good date last night. This guy I met online."

"Ooh! Tell me!" Grace could stand to hear a bit of sexy excitement, since life with Stan was becoming ever more oppressive, and sex with him was the equivalent of being pelted with damp, used washcloths on a humid day, while hung-over. Then guilt hit Grace. It wasn't Stan's fault. He did a fine job in the bedroom, everything he was supposed to do. Grace just couldn't get all worked up about it, or him.

"Well, don't get too excited. I'm sure he'll turn out to be a jerk. They all do. So what time do you want me to come over for Kaylee? I can just watch her at your place. You have all the baby stuff."

"Yeah, that's perfect," Grace said as her stomach fluttered. She was nervous about this meeting. "Come by around 12:30? I'm meeting Magda at one o'clock at Vino Vidi Vici."

"Oh sweet, that groovy new wine bar? I want to check that place out sometime. Let me know how it is. I assume you'll be sampling the vino?"

"Of course!" Grace now started to get excited about her lunch date. Damn, she was on such an emotional roller coaster. "Magda's a total European – believes wholehearted-ly in day drinking."

"Oh, Grace. We would make such good Europeans. Let's be Eurotrash this weekend, okay?"

"You're on, Nat. I'm buying the brunch, the Speedos and the cigarettes! I owe you one. Thank you so much for watch-ing Kaylee."

"Anything for you Grace. You know that. I'll see you to-morrow."

Relieved, Grace met Magda for lunch the next day, with-out a toddler in tow. If Natalie hadn't saved the day, Grace might have had to bring Kaylee along, and it was highly unlikely Magda would want to be around a child. Nothing about Magda screamed "the maternal type."

Grace was nervous but, after some chit-chat, finally got the nerve to bring up her work.

"So, I don't know if you've heard, I don't know how you would, but I had a baby," Grace began.

Magda said nothing. She did her best to keep her face neu-tral, but Grace could read her thoughts. *Oh god, please don't show me your bloody fucking baby pictures or talk about your baby and its boring fucking things it does that you think are so cute.*

Grace stayed calm and carried on, "So, I've taken some photos, and I just want someone whose eye I trust to tell me if they're any good."

Magda's face remained impassive. *Oh god, it is. It's fucking baby pictures.*

"Stan thinks they're really creepy, but I think... well, I guess I'll just show you."

At the word "creepy," Magda perked up. *Now we're talking.*

Grace had done some black and white and some color shots. She laid them out for Magda.

Magda dug it. She particularly loved one where Kaylee's face was staring very intently at Grace's stomach, and her fingers were right on the scar, as if she were tracing it. She also loved one where Kaylee was kissing Grace's scar.

"I fucking love them Grace. They're raw and beautiful, a stark portrait of the new motherhood, a more feminist, warrior mother. Brilliant, darling."

"Oh my god, really?" said Grace, "I was starting to think I was crazy. Stan keeps begging me to hide them because he thinks they're so disgusting."

"Stan is a cretin," said Magda, then continued, not at all concerned if insulting Grace's husband would hurt her feelings (it didn't). "I'll talk to Bradley about our next photography exhibit, and see if we can get some of them up. It won't be for a few months, but I think they should be shown."

Grace tried to contain herself, but really couldn't stop from gushing out the thank-yous.

"Don't thank me, yet. Wait until Bradley agrees. He will though, even if I have to suck his old dick," Magda half-laughed. Grace wasn't sure if she was serious or not, but it didn't matter. Grace would be happy to suck Bradley's old dick if it meant she could get her work shown, especially this work, the work of which she was most proud.

And then it began; the notion that maybe her life was coming together at last, finally looking up, which always led to the same inevitable dark thoughts.

Shoes were about to start dropping. Shit was about to take her down.

No, thought Grace, *no, no, no, please, please let me have a few moments of peace, of happiness… please don't take me down now.*

FIFTEEN

Kent spent even less time mourning Cicily than he did Diane. After three weeks, he got sick of moping around, wondering why things were so shitty again.

He'd walk around outside, get some fresh air, and clear his head. He couldn't get the image of Cicily's severed hands out of his mind. It was making him miserable. He repeated to himself over and over that it was a dream, but the image still haunted him.

He started to hate Cicily. Who was she anyway? A fucking waitress, in a shitty diner? Who was she to reject him? Seriously, who the hell did that lowly bitch think she was?

He was so angry that he was barely paying attention when he almost ran into a woman, hurrying down the street.

"Pardon me," he said, as he moved out of her way.

"Quite all right," she said, as she moved past him into the juice bar.

He was stunned. The way she spoke. It wasn't quite an accent, but she had impeccable diction, almost like an actress in an old movie.

Her graceful hand pulled open the door of the juice bar, and he followed her inside. She was all class. Dressed in what appeared to be a designer suit, carrying an expensive attaché case, understated jewelry, long shiny dark hair, perfect make-up, and beautifully manicured nails. She was a woman of power, a lawyer or something. She exuded confidence. She was self-assured, and obviously had excellent taste. He imagined her home was a place right out of a glossy interior decorating magazine photo.

He dreamed of what her life was like as he entered the juice bar and stood right behind her in line. She ordered some energy-boosting supplement to her Bananarama juice blend. He didn't know what the hell he was going to order. All this shit sounded the same to him.

He paid for his Razzmadazzle smoothie and made his move. This woman had a busy schedule; she had places to be. He couldn't waste anymore time.

"Hi, I'm Kent, Kent Clark," he started.

"Seriously?" she said, rather coldly.

"Yes, that's my name. What's yours?"

She just stared at him.

"Lauren? Medium Bananarama?" said the pimply kid behind the counter.

"That's mine," said Lauren.

She moved past Kent, grabbed her drink and left. Just like that. She didn't even give him the time of day. She was probably a very busy woman, but she didn't need to be rude!

He took off after her. Pimple-Face called after him that his Razzmadazzle was ready, but Kent didn't care.

She got into a silver BMW and took off. He was on foot so he couldn't follow her, but women like that were creatures of habit. She'd be at this juice bar again. He really should start being healthier. Maybe he'd come here more often, and be lucky enough to run into Lauren again.

Lauren… it had a nice ring to it.

It took quite a few tries for Kent to "accidentally" bump into Lauren again. His second attempt to talk to her didn't go much better than the first.

This woman was cold. But, good lord, she was beautiful. Kent couldn't stop thinking about her, her elegance, her confident stride, and her impeccable, manicured hands.

He had bad moments sometimes, thinking about Lauren's hands, because he would flash on the awful image of the dream he'd had about Cicily's hands, and then they would become Lauren's hands. He got panicky, and sweat beaded on his forehead. He took deep breaths to calm down. Lauren's rejection was making him crazy. What was it about this woman that was driving him to distraction? He didn't usually like women who were so cold and unfriendly. The friendly, accessible ones were more his style. Then again, that wasn't going so well for him lately either. Maybe it was time to step up his game.

Lauren wouldn't be easy to win; she was classic high-maintenance, but maybe that meant she was worth it. Perhaps the prize would be that much greater, if he just put in a little effort.

This time he drove to the juice bar, so he could follow her, to figure out where she worked. He was just curious. He wanted to know her, have a better idea of what to talk to her about. It's hard to strike up a conversation with a woman you don't know anything about.

So on that day, it was a Monday morning; he followed her to her office. As he suspected, it was a fancy high-rise.

He was a patient man. She was the type to work late. That was okay. Kent Clark could wait. He'd been waiting for love this long, what was one more day? What was one more week? One more month? It didn't matter. He could wait.

Yes, indeed, Kent was a very, very patient man.

SIXTEEN

Grace and Stan were hanging in there, their mutual love of Kaylee the driving force in keeping their marriage stable and alive, but Grace couldn't shake the restlessness that settled into her stomach, a foolproof indication that the fan was about to get hit with some shit.

Magda had arranged for Grace's work to be shown at the gallery, and Grace hoped that Stan would be as supportive of her career now as he had been in the past. He was not. He said the pictures she had taken were sick and inappropriate, and as far as he was concerned, it was obvious that Grace was more concerned with being an "artist" than being a mother.

To Grace, becoming a mother only made her a better artist. She could now find the light in the darkness, instead of only being able to see doom and gloom.

But she could feel it coming; the shoe was about to drop. She was being stalked by her own madness, utterly doomed.

The first shoe that dropped wasn't really, in the grand scheme of things, that large a tragedy. However, any reaction Grace had toward negative circumstances was met with a critical eye (and deep sigh) from Stan.

Grace was so elated about the upcoming showing of her photos that when Bradley decided to pull the exhibit because his bitch wife put intense pressure on him to do so – she thought the pictures were in "poor taste" – Grace was crushed. It was utterly unbelievable, since plenty of artists did things that could certainly be considered poorer taste than anything Grace could come up with, even in her darkest moments. Not to mention the fact that Bradley was nearly always more influenced by Magda's opinion than his ice queen wife's. Nothing Magda said could convince him to change his mind. Magda told Grace she would fight to get the photos shown, even if it meant banging down the doors of other galleries, but Grace knew it was all very unlikely. Grace was a nobody, and it was doubtful that any gallery would take a chance on her.

She was completely devastated and, of course, Stan made it worse by gloating. When she told him, he responded with, "I'm sorry, Grace," but the corners of his mouth curled up in a smug half-smile that he fought, unsuccessfully, to pull down. She loathed him in that moment and wished he would run off with Bradley's wife, and the two of them could just sit around in their stupid, unimaginative scaredy-cat banality club and talk about what a freak she was.

Maybe she could have an affair with Magda and become an outrageous lesbian performance artist and humiliate Stan. Then she remembered that Magda could have anyone she desired, male or female, so what the hell would she want with a disaster like Grace?

Grace acted happier than she was so that Stan wouldn't have reason to be smug but, in fact, she was terrified.

This was only the first shoe.

The other shoe dropping is always much worse, because then you're left with no shoes at all.

Unfortunately for Grace, the dark she had experienced in the past was nothing. The dark she had previously experienced was puppies and ice cream and sparkly unicorns riding balloons compared to what she was about to endure.

She did her best to throw herself completely into Kaylee's care, since her career was, once again, or rather still, non-existent. It was getting harder for her to keep it together though, because Stan was always gloating in the background. Once upon a time he had been supportive of her career, but that was no more. Once she had a baby, he couldn't accept her in any role except "mother," and it was annoying as hell.

Grace didn't want to wallow in self-pity, but was she being punished for trying to have a career when she should be more focused on her daughter? Maybe Stan was right, maybe she was a lousy mother.

One day, Kaylee came down with a cold, and Grace took her to the doctor immediately. On the one hand, it was just a cold and a visit to the doctor could be a bit over-protective, but she not only wanted to prove she was a loving, caring mother; she was also really worried, because in her experience, the worst thing she could do was think things would be fine, because things never stayed fine for long.

Things were, in fact, quite far from fine.

Kaylee's "cold" was relentless. For months, it wouldn't go away. She started to run fevers and was often listless. Anytime she got even a slight injury, it would take forever to heal. She bruised more and more easily.

Something was wrong. Grace kept taking Kaylee to the doctor, demanding more tests. She was terrified of what she might learn, but she had to know. She had to know Kaylee would be all right. Kaylee was the only thing that mattered. Screw her ridiculous career, her joke of a marriage and everything else. Kaylee was the only light Grace had ever had in the long, dark tunnel of her life.

When the other shoe dropping is a doctor saying that your two-year-old daughter has leukemia, being negative is not going to improve the situation.

With the diagnosis, not only would Kaylee be in the fight of her life; Grace would be as well. If she lost Kaylee, she would have absolutely no reason to live.

For the first time in her life, Grace would step up to the positivity plate – no more expecting the worst, no more afraid to hope for fear of being disappointed, no more half-empty glassware, and no more doomed outlook.

Grace would reach as far down inside herself as she could. She would seek out some spark of faith, and she would fan that spark until it became a flame, and she would fan that flame until it became all the light and love the Universe could hold. She would live in hope. She would pray to any and all gods who might be listening.

Above all, Grace would believe. Kaylee was the only beautiful thing she'd ever done. She couldn't believe that the Universe, in all its infinite wisdom, would be so cruel as to take Kaylee from her. Nor could she believe that Kaylee would be taken from the world so soon.

Grace prayed a prayer that any parent in this situation might.

Please don't take Kaylee. If you have to take somebody, take me instead.

It was an insane request and leaving Kaylee without a mother would be awful, but although Stan was often frustrated with Grace, he doted on Kaylee. He loved their daughter as much as Grace did, and would take care of her always. Kaylee was perfect. The world needed her to grow up.

Grace was a lemon. The world didn't really need her at all.

SEVENTEEN

Since Erin Taylor had made Detective, she had been on more than a few homicide investigations. It was usually a robbery gone wrong, or a domestic situation spinning out of control that would cause her phone to ring late at night.

She had initially been thrilled about her promotion, but any idealistic notions she'd had about how great it would be to "catch bad guys" had been crushed by the sheer horror of seeing up close the cruelty of which human beings are capable. Taylor was a brilliant woman and these cases, though often gruesome, had rarely been challenging. She could usually walk in, assess the situation, and close the case quickly and efficiently. She also had an excellent partner. With the exception of her father and her older brother, her partner, Dan Garza, might be the only man she could trust.

Convenience store robberies, home break-ins surprised in the act, and domestic violence gone too far usually had one thing in common: men were the perpetrators. Women killed sometimes, but most murders were committed by men. As brilliant as she was, she had a hard time understanding the violent impulses and the desire to kill that many men possessed. In spite of her frequent disillusionment with the system in which she worked, she still had a passion for justice, and perhaps a morbid fascination with the minds of sinister men, which allowed her to keep going, doing the job she did.

She worried that she was becoming cynical and jaded by the sheer volume of blood and gore she saw – the gunshot wounds, the beatings, the stabbings. These things used to turn her stomach; now in the midst of the blood and dead flesh, only clues emerged.

One Saturday, at 3 a.m., she awoke to her ringing cell phone. Crap. She considered beautiful female TV detectives, and how they roll out of bed all made up, and arrive on the crime scene in stiletto boots and sporting mysteriously well-done hair, looking tough and sexy. The cop in Erin was tough, but the woman in her worried that she was going to lose her sexy if she kept up this line of work. The woman in her also worried that one day she just wouldn't care anymore.

She brushed her teeth and pulled her long blonde hair into her customary called-in-the-middle-of-the night ponytail. What the hell. She took a few extra seconds to throw on a little lip gloss and a quick coat – a very quick coat – of mascara.

She felt a little guilty for being vain. There was only one reason she was getting called at this hour. Somebody was dead. And it was her job to find out who killed that somebody.

As she started her car, she experienced a moment of anguish. Her heart fluttered, and her stomach tightened. She had a bad feeling about this one.

She had seen a lot of ugly shit in her career, a lot that made her question just how sick humanity could be, but she had a hunch – she hated that she sounded like a cop, even in her own head – that what she was about to see would trump it all.

Her hunch was exactly right.

EIGHTEEN

Grace was a new woman. She prayed; she hoped; she believed, and she loved with all her might. Kaylee most of all, but she would love all of humanity, just to prove to God that she could be truly compassionate. She was bargaining like crazy and making promises to God to do anything and everything if Kaylee would just get better.

She didn't really earn much money in the time she'd been married to Stan. He had been quite okay with being the primary breadwinner and, in fact, had a bit of an old-fashioned side and actually liked it. They hadn't really had to stress about money, as a CPA he made plenty, but that was changing. With Kaylee's medical care, the pressure was really on. The costs were stacking up.

Grace took a hideous part-time job as an administrative assistant at a marketing firm. She would have normally hated it, but she maintained a positive attitude. She hated the time it took her away from Kaylee, but every paycheck went straight to her care, and Grace wanted her to have the best care money could buy.

Grace kept a smile on her face and stayed determined. She would be a pillar of strength for Kaylee, and even for Stan. He was doing his best to handle it, but he was frightened. They were actually closer than they'd ever been. It was as if they had made a secret pact that no negativity or stress in their less than perfect marriage would be, even on a subtle or invisible level, apparent to Kaylee.

Kaylee would have two loving parents who not only loved her, but loved each other. Kaylee had everything to live for. She had an entire life ahead of her. Grace believed that with every cell in her body, every beat of her heart, down to the core of her soul.

She truly believed that Kaylee would be okay, that she would live.

On February 12, just two weeks before her third birthday,

Kaylee died of acute leukemia.

Grace emitted a guttural scream and then blacked out. She lost three days that she could never account for. The first memory she had after being told that Kaylee was dead, was that she had made a terrible mistake. She had believed, with all her heart, that Kaylee would be all right. She now promised herself that she would never, ever believe in anything or anyone again. She had always suspected that hope and faith were just a prerequisite to disappointment and despair. Obviously, she was right about that.

She would never hope or believe or love ever again, because she could not survive the fall.

The other shoe cannot drop if you accept living barefoot.

She wouldn't pick up the shoe. She wouldn't pick herself up.

On February 15, three days after Kaylee died, Grace crawled out of her bed and curled up on the floor. She would not allow herself a pillow or a blanket. If she slept at all, she slept on the floor. Every night for the next nine months, she slept on the floor. She did not go to work anymore, and bathed only when Stan picked her up and put her in the tub. She ate merely when he forced her, and even then she would only eat broth or saltine crackers. He never attempted to touch her except to put her in the bath or sit her at the kitchen table. He only tried to get her to eat once each day, and sometimes she wouldn't even eat that. He did the best he could through his own blinding grief. He went to work. He paid the bills. He cleaned the house. He did the laundry. He wept in his car on the way to work. He wept in his car on the way home from work. He no longer cried in front of Grace. He only took care of her as best as he could. But how long could he keep this up?

And how many more wretched, dreadful years would Grace have to endure being alive? She refrained from taking her own life only because that would be a real asshole move. Stan lost his daughter as well. And even though they both knew that their marriage was doomed, it was simply too much to talk of divorce when they had already suffered the loss of Kaylee. As much as Grace wanted to die, she couldn't put the burden of his wife's suicide on a man who was also mourning his baby girl. It would be her one act of compassion during those wretched months. Anytime she had suicidal thoughts, memories of her brother Brian would soon follow, and she'd be reminded what it was like to be left behind when a loved one commits suicide. Sooner or later Stan would leave her. Eventually, he would be unable to love her. Once he gave up on her, then she could find a way out. Maybe she could think of a way to make her death look like an accident or a murder, so Stan wouldn't have to feel guilty that he should have stayed, or that he should have done more.

Until then, she would let him take care of her, because it was his way of coping. Stan was a doer. Grace was a lemon. It's just the way things were.

NINETEEN

Kent was driving like a madman. He was hurt and angry and, also relieved. Lauren was, when it came right down to it, a cold bitch. He couldn't believe how icy she had been when he approached her after she left work that night.

Drive, he kept saying to himself, just drive. Get away from it all. Take a break. Take a break from these goddamn women. He was so tired. He should have driven out here before, but he had gotten so angry that he couldn't think straight. He needed to be away from the city.

He headed for his secluded cabin near Joshua Tree. Nothing was going the way he wanted it to, and it was enraging him. He wanted to scream.

So he did. He drove east, screaming, sometimes out loud and sometimes in his head, for two hours. *Everything will be all right. Everything will be all right. It will. Love is possible; it must be.*

TWENTY

Stan had had enough. He wrestled with his guilt but, in the end, he wanted to have some kind of life, and Grace was making that impossible. He simply couldn't take it anymore.

He was afraid of having a big emotional scene, but he wanted out of this marriage so badly that he was willing to face whatever he had to if it would set him free of the tyranny of Grace's sadness.

He came home from work the last Friday in November. Grace was on the floor, under the kitchen table. This was ridiculous. Now she was going to sleep under the table? Jesus Christ, she was getting crazier every day. He should drag her out from under there and force her to meet his gaze, but then he figured there was no real point in that. Why bother looking into her vacant eyes? What could possibly be there?

"Grace," he began, "can you hear me?"

"Yes. I'm sad, not deaf," she managed to say.

"Good. I've got something to say. You don't need to say anything. I don't think you'll have anything to say, but if you do, when I'm finished, I will be happy to hear you out. Okay?"

There was a long pause.

"Answer me, Grace."

"Okay."

"Good," he continued, "I've done everything I can think of to save this marriage. I've done everything I can think of to save you. I did everything I could think of to save Kaylee while I had the chance. I beat myself up every day for feeling like I have failed at all of it. I am seething with resentment toward you right now. I'm sorry, but it's the truth. I'm out of ideas. I can't fix you. I can't fix our marriage, and I can't save Kaylee. It's over. It's more over than anything could ever be. I am a grieving father. I lost my daughter too, Grace."

At this, Stan's voice cracked. The tears would come now, and he didn't care anymore. He didn't care about appearing strong, or being a man. Whatever the hell that meant. Any man who thought "being a man" meant not crying or showing weakness hadn't endured what he had.

"I lost my baby girl," he was weeping as he spoke, "I loved her too Grace, just as much as you did. You have taken so much of my energy that I never really had the chance to just let go, to just grieve. My whole world has been supporting you in your grief. I'm done. It's my turn. It's my time. I need to grieve. I will never forget Kaylee, and I will never stop loving her, and I will never be able to walk through this world without a hole in my heart, but I will walk through this world, Grace, and I wish you would too. You can lie on the floor forever, or you can get up. It doesn't matter to me either way. Either way, I'll be gone."

He waited. And waited. He sat down on a chair at the table, and reached down to Grace. He put his hand lightly on her ankle.

"Grace? Do you understand? I'm leaving. I'm walking out the door right now, and I'm not coming back."

Grace didn't move. He waited for her to say something, anything. After a minute, which felt like an hour, she finally spoke.

"Fair enough."

Stan waited, but he was certain she had nothing more to say. Hot tears burned his face, and the rescuer in him wanted to reach down and pull her up. Some part of him still wanted to fix her. But he walked out the door instead, because he had finally faced the truth. Grace was unfixable.

TWENTY-ONE

Grace stayed on the floor for a few moments after the door closed softly. Stan was gone. There was no one to take care of her, no one to bathe her, no one to feed her.

She was oddly calm.

She stood up and went into the bathroom. After turning on the hot water and stripping off all her clothes, she examined her body in the bathroom mirror. Her C-section scar was still visible; she supposed it always would be. She'd gotten skinny. She felt her ribs. Grace had never been particularly skinny. She hadn't really been fat either, but she had been carrying a little extra post-baby weight before Kaylee... well, before Kaylee left. The additional weight hadn't really bothered her – in fact, she had found it rather appealing; womanly – but it was most certainly gone now, along with quite a few more pounds. Out of morbid curiosity, she stepped on the scale. Yikes. Grace was five feet seven inches tall. She weighed only 108 pounds. She looked like shit. How strange it was to her that women wanted to be this skinny. The woman in the mirror looked horrible and old and sad.

She stepped into the hottest water she could stand, and washed her greasy hair. She shaved her underarms, her legs; she even shaved her bikini line.

When she got out of the shower, she put lotion all over her skin. She reeled at how close her bones seemed to the surface of it.

Once in clean clothes, which hung off her skinny frame, she went into the kitchen. She assessed the situation. Stan really was pretty awesome in the end. He'd completely stocked the kitchen. He probably thought all the food would go bad, but it was an amazingly sweet gesture just the same. He had left her all the foods she had loved when she was interested in eating, and then he had left her.

She was grateful for both. In that moment, she actually loved him.

It took her nearly an hour to prepare a meal. The table, set with candlelight and a glass of white wine was oddly soothing. There was something so normal about it, so human. She sat down and devoured every bite of her food, and as her fork scraped the last bite of pasta with basil, lemon and shrimp off her dinner plate, it dawned on her. Stan had bought her new plates.

After cleaning the kitchen, she put on a negligee Stan had bought her for her birthday one year, and she went to sleep, under the covers, in her bed.

For the first night since Kaylee left, Grace didn't cry herself to sleep. She just crashed and slept eleven hours straight.

When Grace awoke, she had a brief moment of clarity. Perhaps clarity wasn't the right word. It was more like being clean inside. She would do something totally outrageous – go for a walk. She considered a run, but she hadn't exercised in so long, she didn't know if she'd be able to pull it off.

Los Angeles could be really sunny at any time of year and it was warm that day. Maybe it was the first day of December, but she wasn't entirely sure. Things like dates and such escaped her notice since… well, since. No sense repeating it to herself.

She walked for hours, through residential streets, past coffee shops and corner stores, making every effort to smile at anyone she encountered. Eventually, the walking made her notice how hungry she was. She went home and made an enormous breakfast, which she wolfed down.

Then, she called her best friend.

Natalie was delighted to get a call from Grace, finally.

"Grace! Thank god! What's going on? Can we get together? Like, soon?" Natalie gushed. Then she got quiet.

Grace hadn't been very available to Natalie. They hadn't seen each other since the funeral, and that was not even really a memory Grace could grasp. The eager friendliness in Natalie's voice made Grace realize how much she'd missed her. Over the last few months, whenever Nat called, she'd have an awkward conversation with Stan, and he'd tell her that Grace wasn't feeling well. Grace didn't want Natalie to worry anymore, so she charged forward.

"I'd love to get together Nat. How about tonight?" Grace said.

"Tonight? Sure. I mean, I have a date, but screw that."

"No, don't cancel a date, Nat. We can do it another time."

"No, Grace, I've been dying to see you. Besides, I probably won't like him anyway."

"Why not?" Grace asked, though she knew the answer.

"Well, you know, he has a penis, so he's probably a dick."

Grace laughed and then blurted out, "Stan left me yesterday."

"What?" Natalie was shocked. She never really believed Stan would leave Grace.

"It's okay. I don't mind at all."

Natalie choked up, but held back the sound as best she could. If Grace was managing to call her up and finally make plans to get out of the house, the least Natalie could do was hold it together for Grace's sake. Natalie babysat Kaylee a few times for Grace in the past, and she still couldn't begin to absorb the tragedy of Kaylee's death or imagine the pain of what losing one's child must be like. The world was a harsh, cruel place sometimes. Natalie held back her tears with the firm resolve that she would be strong.

She knew how much Grace struggled with depression. In moments of impatience, she had the urge to tell her to buck up, but Grace had been handed more than her fair share of cruel blows in life, so Natalie usually opted for compassion over criticism.

Right now, she was positively giddy about the prospect of spending time with Grace. She hoped that Grace was going to be able to live some kind of normal life. Natalie didn't fool herself into thinking this wouldn't always hurt, or always be a dark place in Grace's heart. This was the sort of thing a parent never gets over, but she would do her best to support Grace through her grief in any way she possibly could. Wine and food would be first though. Well, wine would be first.

TWENTY-TWO

When Detective Erin Taylor arrived on the scene it was a madhouse; the most officers she'd ever seen at a crime scene, so it would be bad. There was already a heavy media presence, and most of the officers had been instructed to keep them out of the crime scene, so now she worried this would be one of those high-profile cases where reporters would want sexy sound bites from her. She was glad she had thrown on a little lip gloss and mascara after all, since the second she exited the crime scene some media whore would be shoving a microphone and a camera in her face.

She flashed her badge to the first officer and bent under the yellow tape.

Her partner, Dan Garza, walked over as soon as he spotted her.

"This is a bad one, Erin. Just giving you a heads up. You may want to slam some tequila or antacids before you go in."

Erin eyed Dan closely. He was pretty shaken up. He wasn't easily rattled, so this made her even more nervous about what was coming. She stared at him a little longer than usual. He was basically a stud. She thought this in a very detached manner of course. He was her partner and therefore, completely off-limits, sexually speaking. He also had a wife. She needed to treat herself to a "ladies' night out" and pick up a man, as soon as she had the time. She worked so hard that sometimes her libido would sneak up on her, and she'd fantasize about someone totally inappropriate, like Dan. Had he always been this tall? Had his shoulders always been this broad?

Stop, she told herself. *Focus. There's a goddamn dead body in there, and you have to go examine it. Get it together.*

She walked over to the dumpster. At first glance, she knew one thing for sure: whoever did this *hated* the victim. A three-in-the-morning dumpster body. No goddamn respect for the dead.

TWENTY-THREE

"Oh, Grace. It's so good to hear you laugh."

"Well Nat, you crack me up. I've missed you."

"I've missed you too. Terribly."

Grace hadn't laughed in so long that it was almost physically painful to do so. She experienced a few twinges here and there during dinner, feelings of guilt that it was dishonoring Kaylee's memory to have fun, but even Grace could only sleep on the floor, cry, starve, and punish herself so long.

"Stay at my place tonight," Natalie said as they paid the check. "We can drink more wine and hang out. Please!"

Nat did her best to keep the worry out of her voice, but if Grace went alone to her empty house, it could turn ugly. Stan had just left the day before. Sooner or later, it was going to hit Grace that even though the horrible pressure of being in a failing marriage was finally over, it was still an enormous loss.

After being back at her place for an hour or so, Natalie excused herself to use the bathroom and left Grace sitting on the couch with a glass of wine. Grace was fine. A few short minutes later, when Natalie came back in the room, Grace was no longer fine. The color had drained from her face, and her eyes were somewhere else, a place far off and unreachable.

"Grace? You okay?" Natalie asked, even though she knew the answer.

Grace burst into tears. And these weren't any tears. It was sudden and violent, a raging torrent, a downpour, an explosion of grief like nothing Natalie had ever seen. It was terrifying. She didn't know what to do.

Grace dropped her wine glass on the coffee table, and it shattered. She absently reached out to clean up the shards of glass with her bare hands. Natalie grabbed Grace's hands and pulled them away from the danger.

Through her sobs, Grace apologized. Her words were barely coherent and Natalie soothed her.

"Don't worry about it, Grace. It's a fucking glass. It's nothing. What's happening? I don't know what to do. You're scaring me."

"I can't... I can't... she's just... I'm dying. My heart is dying. I can't breathe. My heart is on fire. I can't live... I can't... I miss..." and Grace could no longer talk. Natalie sat, helpless to comfort her.

Grace was horrified that she was having such an emotional display in front of anyone – even her closest friend – but she couldn't stop the grief and rage from exploding out of her. It was as if her heart and soul were burning in a horrible fire, melting together in a torment that blinded her. Knives of anguish relentlessly attacked her, stabbing at her. The pain was scorching. Her brain locked up, seized in a single thought that wasn't really a thought at all, but the absence of any coherency. She was scaring Natalie, but she couldn't stop. Panic overtook Grace that this would be her life, forever. That any moment could level her to choked sobs and that there would never, ever be a way out.

"I'm falling apart, Nat, I'm falling apart. I want to die. Why couldn't I die? Why? It's not right. I'm dying... the pain is killing me."

Grace let out a wounded animal cry and then began to pant. She was crying so hard she was unable to breathe.

"Grace, you're hyperventilating. I need you to breathe. Come on sweetie, try to take some deep breaths, please."

Grace couldn't. She hyperventilated and then passed out. Natalie sat, shocked. She needed to revive Grace, but it might be more humane to give her a few moments of lost consciousness. Maybe those few moments would be the only peace Grace would get for a while.

Even though Natalie was not a religious person, she didn't know what else to do, so she prayed out loud.

"God, if you're there, please, please, please give this woman a break. Give her some peace. Heal her heart. Please. So... uh... Amen?"

She sat and waited. She looked around, foolishly, as if God might actually appear and do something, anything, about this mess. Grace stirred. She was calmer when she regained consciousness, but her eyes still had unrelenting grief clouding them.

If God heard Natalie's prayer, he hadn't answered it yet.

TWENTY-FOUR

E rin had acquired a pretty strong stomach in this line of work, but the sight of this body made her nauseous.

The victim, before being beaten, tortured and restrained had been quite attractive. She had long brown hair, beautiful bone structure, and a lovely figure, though little remained of her beauty. Her blouse had been torn or cut open to reveal that her arms and torso were covered in deep wounds, and her throat was severely bruised. Her dead eyes stared up from the bottom of the filthy dumpster in a final, frightened, helpless plea.

"Have we ID'ed her?" Erin asked.

"Lauren McLaughlin. She was 34, single, lived alone, VP at a PR firm," Dan filled her in.

"Shit. A PR firm? No wonder there are so many reporters. This is going to be a nightmare," Erin said. "Who found the body?"

"Homeless woman. She's been interviewed, but we didn't get much out of her. She's completely incoherent. Drunk, probably mentally ill. Nothing she said made sense."

The alley was not crawling with witnesses eager to help, but Erin hoped anyway that someone would come forward with useful information. "I don't suppose anyone else saw anything?"

"No. No eye witness so far, but this shit's going to be all over the news, and I'm sure we will have some people coming forward, especially when they find out Cambridge Public Relations is offering a reward for information leading to the capture of Lauren's killer. Lauren was their rising star, and Eileen Cambridge, the founder and CEO, is crawling up our asses for answers," Dan said.

The body lay battered and broken under Erin's scrutiny. Her partner knew her so well he answered the question on her silent, pursed lips.

"Nothing's been touched."

Erin gave Dan nothing more than a strained half-smile in response. When Captain Jacobs arrived, Erin shared her theories so far.

"The body looks tossed, not posed. My best guess is the killer wanted to get rid of her in a hurry. I wouldn't be surprised if something went wrong. This wasn't part of his plan. The M.E. can tell us how many of these knife wounds are ante or post-mortem, but she seems to have bled a lot, so she was likely tortured ante-mortem. Has anyone found her hands?"

"No," Garza began. "We wanted to leave her exactly as she was, so we haven't done a thorough search of the dumpster. We're combing the area trying to find them, but –"

"But we're not going to find them," Erin said.

"No, the hands are his trophy," added Captain Jacobs.

Erin had a tremendous amount of respect for her Captain. It wasn't easy being taken seriously as a woman in this world, much less a Black woman, and even less so as a policewoman. But Joanna Jacobs was tough, smart, compassionate, and an incredible leader. She wasn't exactly a classic beauty, but her strong, gentle face put you immediately at ease. She was like a female Morgan Freeman. Erin, and all the other officers who worked under her had one thing in common – they'd take a bullet for Captain Jacobs in a second.

The body drew Erin back in. The hands, gone. That was the most disturbing part. Severing a woman's hands at the wrist, and then, presumably, keeping them as a trophy? This guy was one sick bastard, and Erin couldn't wait to hunt him down.

Suddenly, she had one of her hunches. All eyes were on her, waiting for her to speak.

"I don't think this is his first kill. If there are others, and I have a feeling there are, we need to find them. We won't find them in a dumpster. If other women had been found in dumpsters with missing hands, I'm pretty sure we'd have known about it. He must have them hidden somewhere."

Erin continued, "I think it goes without saying that he will kill again. These wounds on her are deep, jagged… no hesitation in the cuts. That's rage, which means he's already accelerating. So that makes me think there were others before and that he's going to need another kill soon."

"You know we can't call it a serial killing until we have more than one body," Jacobs said, ever the pragmatist.

"I know," said Erin. "We don't have to make any official statement. We shouldn't. But I think we should at least consider it as an angle. I have a hard time believing this woman is his first and only victim."

"It could be a pissed-off boyfriend or lover obsessed with her," Dan offered.

Captain Jacobs assigned officers to do the usual interviews of Lauren's friends and family. It would be routine to go through her personal life and possibly eliminate boyfriends and other people in her life as suspects. But Jacobs agreed with Erin. She knew damn well there were more bodies like this one, and that some sicko was out there right now with a collection of women's hands.

Erin steeled herself to meet the press. This was the part of her job she really hated. Garza offered to take one for the team and speak to them.

Captain Jacobs let them both off the hook.

"I'll handle the press," she said, "They need to see that authority, particularly female authority, is making this case a priority."

Erin was relieved. She was totally keyed up. The sun was

coming up already. She wished she could have a nice warm glass of whiskey and a good night's sleep. But there was no time for such luxuries – not with a madman on the loose.

TWENTY-FIVE

Kent was a little calmer when he arrived at his cabin. Finally, some peace and quiet. He took a small cooler and his hastily thrown together personal items out of his trunk.

When he got inside the cabin, the anger rose up again. He couldn't help but talk out loud.

"You cold bitch. Screw you. Screw all of this. I'm through with love. You bitches can't be trusted. I'm a GENTLEMAN! I believed in love! What's wrong with me? Why didn't you love me, Lauren? It could have saved you, if you had just loved me."

Despair consumed him. He had put in so much effort with Lauren, but she was such an ice queen.

He consoled himself with the memory of her, of her elusive beauty.

He went to his duffel bag and took out a bottle of formaldehyde. It was time to get some work done. He hoped he could still salvage some part of her.

He opened the cooler and felt the stirrings in his member at the sight of Lauren's hands. He could still preserve them. He could still save their love.

He could still feel her hands on him.

All was not lost.

TWENTY-SIX

Grace recovered somewhat from her immense emotional display but figured the only reason she wasn't crying nonstop was because she was out of tears. She was in a state of absolute numbness. Sooner or later, she'd have to secure some kind of paying work. Stan had filed for divorce, and even willingly offered to pay spousal support for five years, which was more than he was legally required to pay, considering how short-lived their marriage was. Grace really didn't want his money. There was still some hope in her that she would be able to take care of herself.

Magda continued to try to get Grace's photographs up in a gallery, but so far hadn't succeeded. Magda could do just about anything, but Grace figured even a Magda can only do so much with a lemon. She did, however, come through with a job opportunity for Grace, working at a museum gift shop. It wasn't much money, but Grace had low overhead. She and Stan sold their house and split the profit, so she could get by on a modest income. She moved into a tiny apartment and kept only one small box of Kaylee's things, which she kept buried in the back of her closet. Everything else she gave to a shelter that served abused women and their children.

An outsider would think perhaps Grace was getting back on her feet, or back on that horse, or whatever stupid platitude one tosses out to explain the human impulse to keep on going even though it is really just the motion of life. It is nothing like living. It is only movement.

So Grace did not live; she simply endured. She managed to smile at people and act relatively normal and sane, but her heart was beyond broken. Her heart was mutilated, chewed up, burned to the ground, and torn apart by wild-eyed beasts of grief. A heart without hope can't do much but beat, beat, beat. It would ring loudly in her ears, and she'd will it to stop. With this much despair inside her, why didn't she just die of it? It made no sense. She considered the phrase, *died of a broken heart.* What a thing to die of, but dying of a broken heart sounded pretty damn good compared with the alternative – living with one.

Natalie checked in on her frequently, and Grace would have almost manageable days, where she was kind of okay, but a wave of grief could wash over her without warning.

Grace was so used to feeling numb that she really didn't believe anything would ever change.

Of course, that's when it always does.

Just as she was coming home from her ridiculous job – she'd sold three whole Van Gogh postcards that day! – she got a text from Nat.

Happy hour?

Grace laughed to herself, with only a twinge of bitterness, and thought, *what the hell? Maybe an evening out will do me some good.*

She texted back: *Well, happy is an awfully big word to throw around, but I'd like to celebrate. I haven't had a crying jag in three days!*

She had mild clothing anxiety as she decided what was appropriate to wear to happy hour, but she was sick of being a wreck all the time, so she pulled out a pair of purple velvet pants that laced all the way up one side on the left leg. They only fit when she was at just the right weight – somewhere between post-baby curvy and post-traumatic event emaciated – and when she was feeling brave enough to strut. She hardly felt brave enough, but the pants might fool the rest of her into feeling confident. She threw on a nearly sheer white blouse with a saucy purple lace bra underneath and had one tiny moment where she thought she looked pretty damn good. She ran out of the house before she changed her mind about that.

When Grace walked into the Mexican restaurant, her eyes scanned the dark cantina for Natalie's friendly face. She had a surge of panic. The place was packed with strange faces; faces aglow with alluring drink specials and cheap appetizers, combined with the thrill of being out of work for the day. The Mexico-inspired décor was far too bright, too vibrant for Grace's weary eyes. She also started to feel self-conscious about her purple velvet pants. She looked like a goddamn mariachi. Maybe being around all these strangers was a bad idea. Her coping skills were still only moderate at best. Even two-for-one margaritas might not be enough to make this endurable.

"Grace! Over here!" screamed Natalie from across the crowded room.

Oh my god, thought Grace, *there aren't just a bunch of strangers in this bar, there are a bunch of strangers sitting with Natalie. That bitch. I'm going to kill her.* Nat had purposely not told her there would be other people joining them, because she knew Grace wouldn't come if she'd been warned. Oh well, one drink and she'd be out of there.

Natalie had just started a new job at Cambridge PR, and she was really excited about it. Grace didn't know much about PR, or why the hell anyone would want to do it, but she was glad to see Nat happy. Natalie introduced Grace to a bunch of her new co-workers, but when margaritas are going two-for-one, it's pretty hard to keep them all straight. There was some guy named Claude or something, and he was fabulous and effeminate and wore a purple silk shirt. He squealed when he held out his hand to shake Grace's and exclaimed, "Oh darling, your pants are divine! They match my shirt!" Grace was suddenly glad she'd been brave enough to don her purple velvet pants after all.

Then there was a Laura – no, Lauren – and she was totally gorgeous, and a little aloof until she got a few drinks in her, and after that she got pretty cool. And there was another woman whose name escaped Grace, and she never could quite get it, but then whoever she was, she took off early, so

Grace didn't talk with her much.

Lastly, she met Erick. He kept attempting to strike up a conversation with Grace, but it was very noisy and a lot of it was hard to follow. He eventually maneuvered himself into a seat next to her. As the night wore on she got a little tipsy and might have even flirted a little. He was cute-ish, in a dorky kind of way, but Grace wasn't overly taken by him at first. She mostly flirted because it felt good to do it. She hadn't flirted with anyone in years. *Years.* Probably the last guy she had flirted with was Stan. Ugh, really? Had it actually been *eight years* since she flirted? Well, it was something to do; something to break up the monotony of suffering all the time.

After three margaritas, she felt braver and sexier, so when Erick pressed his right leg against her left one, and when the pressure of him and the slightest tickle of his jeans on her bare flesh fluttered in between the laces on her pants, she pressed back. She was grateful for the noise that covered the sound of her breath being sucked in from the surprise of such a simple gesture affecting her so sensually.

"I love your pants," he slurred.

"Would you like to get in them?" As soon as the words left Grace's mouth, she couldn't believe she'd been so quick and bold. She'd shocked herself and, more to the point, she'd shocked Erick.

"Oh shit," he said, "I can't believe I met you. Where did you come from?" He didn't wait for an answer. He just pulled her ear close to his mouth and said, "Let's get out of here."

Grace had no idea what she'd started. If she had, she would have had one drink and gone the hell home. She would never have stuck around, flirting, getting drunk and following Erick into the parking lot. When he pulled her hips toward him, the electricity stunned her. It was so high school to stand in a parking lot making out with a guy she barely knew, but it was invigorating to experience something for once that wasn't heartbreak, just heartbeats and lips and hands.

She wanted to do a lot more than make out, but he pushed away from her suddenly, so he could throw up in the bushes, and that kind of killed the mood.

She ended up taking a cab home alone and when she got there she was half-elated and half ready to cry. She was suddenly, terribly lonely. Loneliness, in turn, led to terror for Grace. Darkness swirled through her mind… *when you get lonely, you end up letting someone in. And when you let someone in, they leave you.* It's the circle of life; or if you're a glass half empty kind of girl like Grace, it's the circle of death.

She stayed in a funk for the next few days, convinced she'd never be normal enough to maintain even the bare minimum of what could be considered a social life.

"Hello?" Grace only answered the phone because it was Natalie. If it had been anyone else, she would have ignored it.

"Guess what?"

"Chicken butt."

Natalie laughed. Although Grace was feeling down, she could still throw out something silly and because it was coming from someone as dark and morbid as she was, it was somehow hilarious to Nat.

"Well, you're close, but alas, no chicken butt. I have something almost as good!" Natalie was so giddy. She must have gotten a promotion, or a raise, or a hot date.

Grace put as much cheerfulness in her voice as she could. Just because she was miserable didn't mean she couldn't be excited for Natalie and whatever had her so excited.

"Well? Don't keep me waiting, Nat."

"Erick wants your number. Is it okay if I give it to him?"

"Wait. What? Erick?"

"Yea, remember, the guy you made out with last week?"

"Yea, I remember, because he pushed me off him so he could puke in the bushes. It was an epic romance."

"Grace, c'mon, he likes you."

"Well, he had a funny way of showing it," Grace said, dejection in her voice.

"Think about it from his perspective for a minute," Natalie said, "He's horribly embarrassed. He asked me to have lunch with him today and –"

"So, maybe he likes you."

"Grace! Seriously, shut the hell up, let me finish. He asked me to lunch because he wanted to talk about you. He told me that he really dug hanging out with you, and he's totally mortified that he threw up in front of you. He wanted to know if he could have your number, and if I thought you would go out with him."

Grace was dumbfounded. She had been out of the dating loop a long time. She still felt like such a mess, even a year after Kaylee's death she was barely coping. She was like a walking corpse. She really couldn't imagine anyone even being interested in a mess like her.

"Why?" she asked.

Natalie's voice was becoming more exasperated.

"What do you mean, *why*?"

"I mean," said Grace, "Why does he want to go out with me?"

"Oh my god Grace, I am going to kill you."

"Please do."

There was a still moment. Natalie sucked a deep breath in

before she continued.

"Well how about this plan, Grace? I'm going to give him your number. So there. If you don't want to go out with him, then you can tell him yourself. He wants to go out with you because he thought you were smart and pretty and funny, which is all true."

"Yeah, but he met me on a good night. I was having a good hair day. And I got pretty drunk, so I probably seemed like more fun than I really am, and I was faking it, like I always do, trying to act like a normal person, and I've put on like 20 pounds since I started eating again…"

"Oh, so you're like what now? Six pounds above concentration camp victim?"

"Nat, I don't even remember if he's cute. Without the margarita goggles, maybe I won't like him."

"He's cute, Grace. I'm going to hang up now, because I want you to be available to answer Erick's call."

Grace sat in silence, but not for very long. Within the hour, her cell phone rang. She didn't recognize the number but figured it was probably Erick. She stared at the options on her cell phone screen: Answer? Decline? Answer? Decline?

Sorry Erick, Grace hit the "decline" button; *this is for your own good. I'm a mess you don't want to step in.*

After Grace pressed the "decline" button she curled up on her sofa and cried.

After crying, she slept a fitful ten minutes or so on the couch but, eventually, Grace's curiosity got the best of her.

Her cell phone showed two new voicemails. *All right mister, let's see what you have to say for yourself.*

"Hey Grace, this is Erick. We met at Don Pedro's the other night. I work with your friend Natalie. I hope it's okay that I'm calling you. I don't know if you remember me. I hope so. Well, I hope you don't remember the part where I threw up in the bushes. I wanted to apologize for that, and um… I don't know… see if I could make it up to you. Over a proper dinner. Or a drink. But not too many drinks. Well, you can —"

Beep.

"Hi Grace, Erick again. Okay, so I rambled and got cut off. Anyway, I'd really like to see you again, so if you're interested, give me a call. My number is…"

Grace listened to his number, but didn't bother to write it down. If she really wanted to call him, she could pull the number off her phone. A real-live man was calling her, asking for a real-live date. Terrifying.

Grace sat, stunned. She'd been living in some cave of grief for too long, and wasn't even sure what she should do. Should she call him back? Maybe she should wait. Her heart was pounding. Why was this so scary? It was just some dufus-y guy.

Right then, she got a text. It was Erick's number.

I sounded like a total dufus on your voicemail. If you can stop making fun of me long enough to call or text me back, I'd be so grateful that I would cook you shrimp tacos. —Erick

Well, they already agreed upon one thing: he was a dufus. Grace inadvertently smiled. Maybe it was an impulsive act, but if she had stopped to think about it, she never would have done it.

She fired back a quick text:

You had me at "dufus."

TWENTY-SEVEN

From the first night with Erick – well, actually it was the second night if she counted making out with him until he puked in the bushes – Grace wasn't exactly sure what was happening.

Plenty of people had told Grace she was pretty, sexy, gorgeous, or whatever, but it never truly registered with her. It was something people said to women for lack of anything more interesting to contribute to a conversation. She said "you're pretty" to her girlfriends, because they were in fact, pretty, but she might even say "you're pretty" to a woman who really wasn't all that attractive, out of some vapid need to issue a compliment. Grace believed that her friends complimented her because they had to, and total strangers complimented her simply because they had nothing better to say. When men told her she was pretty, she assumed they were saying it because they wanted to get laid, and that was the deal: compliment a woman, get in her pants. That's how it works.

Grace couldn't quite read what it was about Erick that intrigued her so much. He gazed at her with a combination of deep longing and maybe… surprise? Her mind was blown, and his face made her believe that his was too.

Perhaps because of all the grief Grace had endured, she was in a different place when Erick looked at her the way he did. Maybe other men had looked at her that way and she hadn't really noticed, but when Erick did it, she noticed. She saw herself in a completely different light.

The night was a blur. Dinner was too much pressure, so they went to a pub, had a few drinks, made their way back to her place, opened a bottle of Sauvignon Blanc, downed it, and had a night of sex that was oddly satisfying considering they were virtual strangers. And drunk.

And, in the morning, they had round two.

Then, she kicked him out. She wasn't mean, just cold.

She wasn't trying to sound cool or anything like that – she wasn't anything close to cool – she just didn't know what else to say, so she went with a very cagey "see you around" type of thing after explaining how she had so much to do, and so on.

"I'll call you," said Erick as he was leaving.

Grace gave a very noncommittal "yea, sure, cool" type of response as she closed the door in his face.

She couldn't believe what she had just done. It was deliciously electric, and scary enough to entertain the idea of ending it then and there, before it could get complicated and hurt her.

Erick stood on the landing outside her apartment as the door closed in his face. He was smitten.

In spite of all the promises she made to herself, Grace had no real resolve in the face of Erick's intoxicating pursuit. She had never experienced anything like it. Men generally bored her to tears, but something was different with Erick. She could only attribute it to the rawness of her own feelings, coupled with the complete star-struck madness reflected in his eyes.

It was deafening the way he took her in, all of her, without focusing on any one part. And the flaws didn't only leave him un-phased; they turned him on more. The softer parts, the scarred parts, the saggy parts, the scrawny parts were just part of the greater whole, and for the first time ever in her life, Grace felt beautiful. She felt sexy.

It was an intense rush, absolutely frightening and, utterly addicting.

From the moment she realized how stunning she felt in Erick's arms, she began to wish she'd never met him.

There was only one thing that could happen now.

A shoe would have to drop. His shoe, on her heart. It was

inevitable.

And miraculously, he kept showing up. He was attentive, passionate, affectionate. She had never felt anything like this before.

Grace tried as hard as she could to keep emotional distance from him. She had no idea that this was actually what was driving him so crazy for her. He couldn't quite pin her down; he couldn't truly reach her.

But, of course, Grace was making a really stupid mistake. She was falling in love. And love couldn't possibly last for a lemon.

TWENTY-EIGHT

Kent paced the wooden floorboards of his cabin. He was so angry he couldn't stop moving. He had been pacing the floor for hours. Nothing was going right. That arrogant cunt Lauren screwed-up everything. He was a nice guy! He was a gentleman for fuck's sake! He was spinning. His brain hurt from the angry fire burning inside it. He had a way of doing things. He liked to romance a girl. He liked to get her to talk about herself. But Lauren just couldn't be bothered to make the slightest effort. She had called him a fat greasy slob, among other things. She had also called him a repulsive troll and a disgusting balding sack of shit. She was totally unreasonable. Well screw her. Where was her precious pride now? It was in a fucking dumpster, that's where.

He was still angry though. He really didn't like to have his routine messed with.

"I HAVE A WAY OF DOING THINGS!" he screamed to her useless hands. He had tried so hard to feel her hands on him, but it wasn't working. He hated her too much to raise his passion.

Now what? He should have kept all of her with him. That was stupid, throwing her arrogant whore body in a dumpster. She would be found. People would want to know what happened to her. Why? Why had he lost his temper like that? She had infuriated him. She hadn't loved him like the others had. No! They hadn't loved him either. No one loved him. *No one.*

He didn't know what to do. His plan to show that whore waitress Cicily how easily she had been replaced by bringing Lauren back to the cabin was now thwarted. This was all so messed up. It was all going terribly wrong.

He went out to the garage and opened the deep freezer. There she still was. The waitress who had thought she was too good for him. He took Cicily's hands out and threw them on the floor of the garage. He left the rest of her body curled up in the freezer and went to get Lauren's hands.

When he got back to the freezer, Cicily's dead eyes stared up at him, with what he knew was deep regret.

"Well, Cicily, I was going to show you my new girlfriend Lauren, but she turned out to be an even bigger bitch than you are."

He tossed Lauren's hands on to Cicily's body and slammed the freezer shut. He picked up Cicily's thawing hands from the floor and put them in a plastic bag. He would leave them out in the desert with the others and let nature take its course.

He had a way of doing things. He had a ritual. Lauren was supposed to be in there now. She was supposed to replace Cicily but, instead, she was rotting in a dumpster somewhere in Los Angeles.

Things had gone fine before. Cicily had replaced Diane. Diane had replaced Leslie. Leslie had replaced Sharon. Sharon had replaced...

Who had Sharon replaced? He was getting confused. How many women had he tried to make it work with? This was getting ridiculous. Why were women so selfish? They all claimed they wanted a nice guy to love them, but they didn't.

Lauren had broken his pattern. She had been all wrong for him. He should have known it from the moment he met her.

He wouldn't make a mistake like that again. He would find somebody better. Somebody to replace Cicily. She had rejected him in the end too, and he couldn't just let her *stay here*. She had to go, but not until he had a replacement.

He had a way of doing things, but he could adapt if necessary. He was determined to find the right woman even if it killed him.

Or even if it meant killing every last one of those bitches.

TWENTY-NINE

"Triple non-fat latte?"

Erin's head shot up. Crap. She'd fallen asleep at her desk, again. The remnants of a dream clung to her. She must have really been out. A strong desire to call her father pulled on her. It would have to wait. She missed him immensely at times like this, and even though he knew first-hand what the life of a cop was like, it still hurt that she had to work so hard to carve out time for visits. Erin's father had served the force for over thirty years, and had taken a bullet that almost cost him his life and left one side of his body nearly paralyzed. He was mobile, but barely and only through the force of his sheer stubborn will. Whenever she was with him, she would tolerate his protests that he didn't need her help, because it was merely a show to protect his pride, and eventually he'd settle in and let her cook and clean for him. Erin swore he'd be the only man she'd ever cook and clean for. Well, perhaps she'd do it for her brother. She missed him too. Lance and her father had been in her dream. It was already growing fuzzy, but it had been at the beach, a memory of long ago, when she'd been about six and Lance about nine. Lance had been standing up to someone who was picking on her, just like he'd done so many times in reality.

A bit of drool escaped the corner of Erin's mouth. She subtly wiped it away as her partner, Dan, held a coffee out to her.

"Thanks, Dan. Guess I nodded off."

"Yeah? You seem a little out of it," Dan consoled her. "You okay?"

"Yeah. Let's get over to Cambridge and start with Lauren's co-workers. Maybe she mentioned a boyfriend to one of them, or something..."

"You don't think it's a boyfriend, do you?"

"No, Dan, I don't. But we've got to start somewhere."

The clock reminded Erin it was nearly eleven A.M. Damn. She wanted to make it over to the firm before people started taking off for lunch.

"Let's roll," Erin said as she gave Dan a conspiratorial smile. Sometimes they liked to give each other cheesy TV cop one-liners, just to keep things light.

"Let's rock." Dan smiled back.

She grabbed her latte, planning to down it on the way. That would make six shots of espresso before noon. What could possibly be wrong with that?

They made their way to Cambridge PR. It was in a tall, elegant building in the Brentwood area of Los Angeles – the kind of building made of privilege and dollar signs. They found street parking, knowing the garage had already been closed off for the investigation, and made their way into the building and up to the twelfth floor. There, the staff of Cambridge PR and the founder, Eileen Cambridge, were patiently waiting to be interviewed.

Eileen Cambridge was a self-made woman. She ran Cambridge PR like a fair-minded queen. She was an elegant and beautiful woman. No one at the firm was exactly sure about her actual age – somewhere between 42 and 75 perhaps. She was gorgeous, and she clearly had years of experience and the confident bearing of an older woman, but she was either having really great work done or drinking the blood of virgins in her spare time. She was stunning and always well put-together. Nothing but the latest fashions; trendy and yet, age appropriate, tasteful and immaculate hair and make-up. Everyone feared and respected her, and was dying to please her. She could give the iciest stare or the warmest smile depending on an employee's performance, so everyone strived to be on the warm, smiling end as often as possible.

Natalie had been incredibly impressed with her the moment she met her in the interview. She was the kind of woman who younger women hope they grow up to be. Natalie was considerably attractive and well-groomed, but Eileen put most women half her age (whatever that actually was) to shame.

In spite of the grueling hours being a founder and CEO required, Eileen never had a hair out of place or appeared tired.

That Monday was an exception.

Ms. Cambridge called an unexpected meeting in the large conference room. Everyone worried what might be going on – it must be something important; perhaps a big fat juicy client, or some crisis that would require immediate damage control. Natalie loved the excitement of her new job. It was very fast-paced and, like everyone else at the firm, she really wanted to impress Eileen.

Most everyone had assembled in the conference room as far as Natalie could tell, but it was really odd that Lauren was missing. Lauren was Eileen's right-hand man, so to speak, and Eileen would certainly never call a meeting without her. Then again, Eileen hadn't arrived either, so Natalie figured she and Lauren were having a little pre-meeting in her big, elegant CEO office.

Natalie gave her greetings to the people around her. Erick approached her.

"So Natalie, do you know what's up with this meeting?"

Natalie wished she had some inside scoop, but of course she didn't so she just told him no. She was compelled to add, "You look happy."

Erick grinned, and maybe even blushed a little.

"I just can't thank you enough for hooking me up with your friend Grace. She's so awesome. We had such a great weekend."

Natalie was ecstatic. Finally. A good thing for Grace.

No one needed it more than she did. And Erick was really perfect for her. He had a stable job, and he was in the web and graphic design department, so he still had a bit of a creative streak, which would appeal to Grace. She'd seen some of his work, and he was really talented. To Natalie, Erick was a little computer-geeky but for a moment, she saw him through Grace's eyes. He was pretty cute. He had thick, shiny, dark hair and hazel eyes. Yeah, he was kind of hot. Good for Grace. Natalie suddenly felt a little awkward and shy, not because she had any interest in Erick, but because she flashed on some of the sexy stories Grace had told her about the hot, wild nights they had shared. Grace and Erick had some undeniable connection. It was palpable when they were together. Natalie was a bit jealous, because she'd love to feel that way about someone and have that someone feel that way about her, but she was ecstatic for Grace. Every woman should be looked at the way he looked at her.

Natalie was ripped from her reverie when Eileen Cambridge entered the room with two very assertive and official-looking individuals. There was a tall, sexy Latino man whom Natalie couldn't help but steal a glance at, and a rather petite blonde woman. In fact, she was so petite that at first glance, she almost looked like a teenager. However, a closer inspection showed a hard edge in her face that indicated not just a woman, but a very tough one. Her jeans were tight. Her breasts were big, but she was obviously trying to downplay that fact. Her golden hair was pulled back in a ponytail and she had on very little make-up, but large, silver hoop earrings made her appear put-together, as did her totally-unnecessary-in-Los-Angeles, black leather jacket.

Then Natalie really noticed Eileen, and she knew something was very, very wrong. Never had she seen Eileen tired, haggard, or anything but elegant and glamorous. Until now. Had she aged twenty-five years since Friday? Not a hint of make-up, her auburn hair was carelessly pulled up in a haphazard ponytail. Maybe her outfit had been pulled out of the bottom of a laundry basket and her eyes... that was the scariest part. Her eyes were so swollen she couldn't possibly see clearly. They were red – the eyelids, the bags underneath, and what should have been the whites – all red and puffy. She was already a thin woman – no doubt from working out like a fiend – and it seemed she had dropped fifteen pounds over the weekend. The scarcity of her flesh was a jarring sight.

Everyone grew so silent; it was deafening.

Eileen's exhausted voice choked out only a few words.

"I've called you here to... this is...," she indicated the officers, and broke. It was an inside break, as Eileen was the type to hold back tears in front of her employees, but you could see it just the same. Her white face and red eyes betrayed her, as her frail body sank into the nearest chair.

The blonde woman took over.

"I'm Detective Erin Taylor with LAPD. This is my partner, Dan Garza. We are here with sad and unsettling news. Your co-worker, Lauren McLaughlin, has been murdered. She was last seen Friday night, here at this office. My partner and I will be conducting individual interviews with each of you to determine your personal relationship with the victim –" Eileen's face stopped Erin from going on. She concluded, too late, that "victim" was a poorly chosen word.

It was more than Eileen could bear. She practically ran from the room, clutching her mouth as if she was about to vomit.

Garza picked up where his partner left off.

"We also need to know anything you may know about Lauren's personal life or anything that may be helpful to us in determining who is responsible for this tragedy. Please go back to your desks, and we will speak with you individually. Ms. Cambridge has kindly ordered in lunch, so please make no plans to leave. We want to talk to all of you today."

As the employees of Cambridge PR filed out, Dan glanced at Erin. The unshakeable Erin Taylor was absolutely, most assuredly, shake-a-fied.

"I fucked up."

"It's okay Erin; I know why you said it."

"I called her the victim. I need to call her – "

She stopped.

"Yes, you do. They know her. She's Lauren to them."

"Shit, Dan, that was a rookie mistake. I don't do that..."

"Cut yourself some slack."

Then he added, "This is that kind of case," in his faux hard-boiled voice.

They had joked so many times about how different their lives were from the TV detectives. Erin would have laughed, but she felt too sick.

"You're right. This is *that kind of case*. It is already haunting me. Something about this one gets under my skin, Dan. I guess I'm officially one of those hard-boiled, rebellious TV detectives – minus the ridiculously hot and inexplicable sex appeal of course."

Dan winked at her. "Oh, I'd say you've got that part in the bag, too. Don't sell yourself short."

"Ha! I hope that wasn't another one of your short jokes, asshole," Erin quipped. "I'm nearly five feet tall in these boots you know!"

Dan walked out of the conference room, and then, as happened to Erin a lot lately, she flashed on an image of Lauren's hands, bloody and severed. She had never seen Lauren's hands in real life, but they were out there somewhere. She kept those hands in her mind's eye, and would find this poor woman's murderer if it killed her.

* * * * *

Natalie walked quietly back to her desk. She couldn't believe this was happening. Lauren was dead? Murdered? This was the kind of shit that happens in movies, and on TV, not in real life. Erick was walking closely behind her. She stopped and met his eyes.

Neither of them knew what to say. They walked off to their prospective offices.

She wanted to call someone. Grace. She wanted to call Grace, but this was creepy shit. Maybe Grace wasn't the person to tell. She went dark so easily. But Grace was her best friend. Crap. If this could happen to Lauren, it could happen to –

"Natalie Acosta?"

Oh, my God. That handsome detective, Garcia, or whatever, was standing near her desk. Natalie's brain jumped from *Oh crap. He's so cute* to *Oh no it sucks to be questioned by a cop* to *Stop thinking about yourself,* to *Poor Lauren* in seconds flat.

"Yes, I'm Natalie."

Oh this sucked hard. Cops were scary. Even cute ones.

Dan Garza made himself comfortable across from Natalie.

"I'm Detective Garza. So, I'll just get right to it. What was your relationship with Lauren?"

Natalie stared at him for a moment. He really was super cute. Wait, was she in trouble?

"Ms. Acosta?"

"Yes, I'm sorry. I'm just in shock I guess. I didn't know her well, but we would occasionally go for drinks or dinner after work. We may've had lunch together a couple of times, but a group of us, you know. I wasn't really close to her or anything."

"Do you know anything about her personal life? Her family? Was she dating anyone?"

Natalie suddenly felt guilty. She should have been nicer. She should have asked Lauren questions about her family or boyfriends. She just hadn't been very warm at first, and Lauren was so close to Eileen that Natalie had been a little intimidated by her.

"Honestly, sir, I just don't know much about her personal life. She seemed like a really private person, you know? I know she and Eileen were pretty tight. They worked very closely together. I don't know how Eileen's going to manage. She loved Lauren…"

"Yeah; almost everyone can agree on that. Well, if you think of anything, please give us a call."

Dan handed Natalie his card. She took it hoping she would think of something, so she could call him. Oh, a wedding band. Damn. That figures.

* * * * *

Erin and Dan went through the interviews of all Lauren's co-workers and weren't coming up with much. It was time to tackle the big fish – Eileen Cambridge. They would conduct the interview with her together because it was apparent that Eileen, of everyone at the PR firm, would have the most information about Lauren.

Erin took the lead, as she sensed Eileen might be more receptive to her. She knocked gently, and opened the door when a scratchy, faint whisper said, "Come in."

There was no sparkle at all in Eileen's eyes, and they were redder and puffier than before.

"Please, have a seat, detectives."

Erin started to sit and offered, "You know, Ms. Cambridge, if this is too much for you right now, we can come back later."

"No, no, I'm all right. I want to do this now. I know that every second wasted is another moment Lauren's killer walks free. I am in agony right now, but that's not going to change later today, or tomorrow, or the next day, or maybe ever. So, just let me know how I can help."

"Thank you, Ms. – " Dan started.

"Please. Eileen is fine. I'm not your math teacher."

Erin and Dan settled in the elegant chairs across from Eileen's desk. Everything was tastefully decorated. Erin felt the cushions melt up around her ass in a way that said, *I cost more than you make in a month.*

"How long has Lauren worked for you?"

"Almost six years. She is… was… very bright, one of the brightest women I've ever met. She rose to VP in no time."

"Are there any professional relationships she had that you would consider strained?"

"No, not at all. Lauren could come across as cold to people she knew casually, but she really had a way with our clients. She was the best… she…," Eileen took a deep breath. Tears crawled up her throat and Eileen swallowed hard to keep them from pouring out.

Dan kept his mouth shut and let Erin handle all the questions.

"What can you tell us about her personal life? Any boyfriends or lovers we can talk to?"

"You won't find any boyfriends, and as for lovers, well, as far as I know…" Eileen drifted off, and then began to cry.

"Eileen, if you need a break," Erin started.

"No, I can go on."

There was a long pause. Erin didn't want to push, but maybe Eileen had forgotten the question.

"So, you were saying, as far as lovers…"

"Yes. Of course. As far as lovers go, and as far as I know, I was her only lover."

Erin was surprised, but continued, scribbling notes.

"I see… so…" she lost her train of thought. Her instincts told her that Eileen had nothing to do with Lauren's murder, but it was basic protocol to question the significant others. In her mind, she would have been playing bad cop to some shithead boyfriend by now, pushing him up against a wall and scaring the crap out of him. Instead, Erin was pierced by the shards of Eileen's agony.

"So, no, I didn't kill her, if that's your next question. We weren't angry with each other; we weren't fighting. No one got caught cheating. We loved each other. Very much. We only kept our relationship quiet because of the firm. Neither of us wanted salacious gossip spreading around the office."

Eileen couldn't do this much longer. Erin could always come back later. It was time to wrap it up.

"Eileen… all I can say is how very sorry I am for your loss, and that I will not rest until the person who did this is brought to justice. In the meantime, if you think of anything that might help us, please –"

"Of course, I will call you right away. And I'm always here to answer any other questions that come up."

"Thank you Eileen. We'd really like to determine if the kill –" Erin stopped herself. *Choose your words carefully.* "If the individual who did this knew Lauren personally or not. So, even if she wasn't seeing anyone other than you romantically, it is possible that someone was stalking her, or watching her, or obsessed with her. What happened is so tragic, and I have a hard time believing it was just a random act of violence."

Eileen started to say something, but the color drained from her face. *Oh god, what if someone had been watching Lauren? Stalking her? How could I have protected her?*

"I should have been with her."

Erin and Dan stopped in the doorway.

"When?" Dan asked.

"Friday. I have probably said all this before... forgive me; the weekend was a blur, a horrible blur... I'm repeating myself..." Eileen's face became so still it was eerie.

"Maybe not. Anything at all you remember could be helpful," Dan offered.

Eileen took a deep breath before continuing.

"We were going to have dinner together with a client. The client canceled, but I had already left because I had to run home for a change of clothes... I had spilled coffee on my blouse. Lauren was still here, working. She said she'd just meet me there. I called her here, at the office, around 7:15 and told her the client had canceled. I said we could still have dinner together, and she said she was just so tired, that she'd just take the time to go home and rest. If only we'd been together. If only I'd – "

"Ms. Cambridge," Dan inquired, "Is there anyone else that might have seen her leave the building?"

"No, by the time she left, the security guards had all left, and the worst part is –"

Eileen's voice broke again.

Erin's heart broke for this woman. This had been a very frustrating day. They couldn't get one lead worth chasing.

"Yes, we've already talked to the security team. We know."

Places like this always had security cameras in parking garages, but just their shitty luck – or, really, Lauren's even shittier luck – they had all gone on the fritz that Friday night and by the time anyone caught it, it had been too late. The cameras went out at 7:33 p.m. The last anyone saw of Lauren was Eileen, who had left around 6:45.

Lauren's silver BMW still sat in the parking garage, in a space reserved just for her.

THIRTY

Erick, Natalie and Grace sat silently, staring at the garlic fries they had stupidly ordered, fries that sat untouched, fries that were getting cold and creepy-looking.

Strangely, they all picked up their beers at the exact same moment. They shared an identical silent toast.

To Lauren.

Intuitively, they clinked their beer bottles, made eye contact all around, and took deep sips.

"Well, this might be the unhappiest happy hour I've ever been to," Erick said.

Natalie was still in shock, and could only manage a barely audible, "yeah…"

Grace just sat there. She was getting those feelings again, the guilty ones. This poor woman. She'd only met her that one time, the same night she'd met Erick in fact, but this was so awful. Grace experienced the guilt she always did when really, really bad things happened to someone else. She could sink into these horrible episodes of despair, sometimes for no reason, but she was sitting here, still alive. She should be more grateful.

Erick's hand reached out underneath the table and found hers.

Yes, she should be more grateful.

THIRTY-ONE

Los Angeles, with its alluring supply of sultry possibility, called out to Kent. He craved the city lights and, even more so, the city women. It was too desolate out here. He pined for the City of Angels, but it was too risky to go there. He'd made better choices with his previous women, but with Lauren, he'd been too impulsive. His passions had gotten the best of him. She would certainly be found, and he wasn't confident the trail wouldn't lead right back to him. If he'd been so stupid as to leave her in such a public place, he obviously couldn't be certain that he hadn't been seen by anyone. He should let that situation cool off a bit before going back. Perhaps he could revisit his roots. Though he was an L.A. man at heart, he'd actually been born in San Pedro, California. His mother still lived there alone, or rather, with a blind stinky dog and an annoying bird that constantly made these terrifically obnoxious noises. He used to worry about his mother going crazy living like that, but then he remembered; it's pretty hard to "go crazy" when one is already totally nuts.

Kent knew little of his father; he was a longshoreman that knocked his mother up and made a few obligatory visits when Kent was a baby, but Kent had no tangible memories of him. His mother hated the bastard, and rightfully so. Daddy, wherever the hell he was, was no gentleman. Kent had always promised himself he'd be a better man than that.

He didn't know that his mother was much better. She was basically a whore, screwing every guy she could pick up in local dive bars. She barely did anything to take care of him when he was growing up, always dumping him on some pathetic relative until they all got sick of it, and then mostly she just left him alone a lot.

He would sit around reading comic books, and watching old movies when they came on TV, and daydream about the heroic, romantic gentleman he would grow up to be.

The drive to San Pedro was a long one because he was

coming from Joshua Tree, and in that time his mind drifted all over the place. He wasn't sure if a visit to his mother was the right idea or not. His feelings were so complicated. He loved her, but she was a drunk slut, and he hated her for it. He hated his father even more for driving her to such awful behavior. If he had been a decent man, maybe they could have gotten married and raised Kent together, like a real family.

Then again, this pain was part of him, part of what drove him, part of what made him so eager to be a really good man for just the right woman. So he hadn't met the right one yet. It was taking time but when he found her, it would be worth it. Everything he'd had to go through would be worth it.

* * * * *

When he arrived at his mother's house, Kent started having second thoughts. What was he doing here? They were just going to get in an awful argument.

As soon as he knocked on the door, that stupid squawky bird started flipping out, and the stinky, blind dog barked madly.

She opened the door, and he was shocked at her appearance. How long had it been since he'd seen her? Well over a year, most likely. She looked like shit.

"You look beautiful, Mom."

"What the hell are you doing here, Kent? You should have called. I'm really busy." Kent stifled a laugh at the thought of his mother having anything to do besides drink her disability check.

"Oh, so sorry, I just wanted to see my mother and show a little love. Can't I come in so we can visit for a while?"

She walked off, without saying a word, but left the door open. She must have been in one of her better moods.

She sat down on the couch and stared at Kent.

"You look like shit, Kent."

"Gee, thanks, Mom."

"You know your father was really handsome. I'm not sure what the hell happened with you."

"Well, looks aren't everything." He wasn't sure why she was always telling him how ugly he was. Maybe his handsome face reminded her of his father's face, and she was upset by that, so she put him down to ease the pain of her ongoing wound. He hated that he came from that asshole, but he would do better. He would make a beautiful life for himself, as soon as he found a woman worthy of him.

"You got a girlfriend or anything? Can't imagine anyone wanting you, but I know from personal experience how desperate a woman can get and how short she will sell herself for a man, even for someone totally beneath her." She said this with a penetrating stare, which absolutely hit the mark.

Why had he come here? He wanted to punch her in the face, but that wouldn't be a very nice thing to do. Gentlemen don't punch their mothers in the face.

"I just haven't met the right girl, ma. You know me; I'm a hopeless romantic."

She laughed a dry cackle that was more like a cough that could only come from a bitter witch and picked up her glass. She took a small sip of what would be the cheapest whiskey she could get, and glared at him.

"Well, you got the hopeless part right."

She continued to laugh at her own joke, and Kent sat there fuming. He needed to go out. He needed to get out of the range of his mother's wicked glare for a while.

"Ma, I'm gonna go out and see a few friends. I'll come back here later, okay?"

"Oh yeah, you got friends. Whatever. I won't wait up."

He walked out without saying another word. He needed a woman's touch. He needed it soon.

THIRTY-TWO

When Grace and Erick got back to her place after hearing about Lauren, they pounced on each other. The ride home had been eerily quiet, and the moment they walked through the door, they devoured each other.

It was surreal to Grace. Erick pulled her deeper and closer until he was drawing her intensely in, inside his heart and soul. There was fucking, and there was lovemaking, and then there was this. Erick could fuck her and make love to her at the same time. It was a heat that blinded her, shut her off from everyone and everything but somehow connected her to the heartbeat of all humanity. She never thought she could feel this intensely for any man.

She came seven times that night. She fell apart inside and slowly surrendered to him as he put her back together, piece by piece, in a frightening and intoxicating communion. There was no sense of time or place, only a fevered dream.

They were finally quiet and still. Horror at the situation dawned on Grace again.

"What's wrong with us? Is this sick? To have sex like this after hearing about such a tragedy?"

"No," Erick's face managed to be intense and distracted at the same moment, "It's normal. It's funeral fucking."

"Funeral fucking?"

"Yeah, you know, in the face of death, humans embrace life. It's natural. We are affirming our aliveness with the sexual act, the very act that creates life."

Grace quietly pondered what he'd said. She understood it on an intellectual level, but thoughts of Kaylee crept toward her, unbidden, unwelcome, but still determined to strike her down. In the face of Kaylee's death, she certainly hadn't embraced life. She had thought only of her own death, every day, and how long she would have to endure before she'd be free of human form. She'd never really talked about Kaylee with Erick. She suspected Natalie had said something to him, basically to warn him not to ever ask about it, that Grace would talk about it when she was ready, and she may never be ready. The guilt overwhelmed her. How could she allow herself this kind of pleasure when Kaylee was never allowed to grow up and experience life?

Suddenly, the pain washed over her violently. Was she was having an aneurysm? Or a heart attack? She couldn't breathe. Tears began to flood her face, first in utter quiet, and then in choking sobs. She caught her breath, pulling the screams back to keep them from leaving her throat. Her heart was pounding. It was going to explode.

Erick stared, stunned. He pulled her close, but she hit him, though not in anger. She was a wild animal in his arms, a broken creature with injuries she couldn't understand; only reacting violently to being touched. He fought through her panic, holding her close as if he would crush the life out of her rather than let her go.

"Grace. Talk to me. Please. Tell me. Let me help. Grace…. Grace…?"

She finally got so quiet and still that he thought she was asleep.

"I just feel so… guilty. How can I do this?" Grace took a deep, choking breath. "How can I let myself be happy when she's gone?"

"Grace, what happened is tragic, but you barely knew this woman. You don't need to feel guilty for living."

"Not Lauren… it's so sad, but no… I'm just… how can I feel this way, how can I feel so good when my daughter is gone? She's gone, Erick. She's gone. She'll never grow up. She'll never live this, what I'm living right now with you… and she deserved to… she deserved to live, and I don't. I don't deserve to live… or to be happy… or to love you…"

She stopped. Oh fuckity fuck, she had just told him she

loved him. What the hell was wrong with her? Why had she said that? She couldn't look at him. It was so quiet. Why wasn't he saying anything?

"Look at me, Grace."

With hesitation, she met his eyes as he spoke.

"I can't say anything that will make what happened to you okay. It's not okay. But I can say that you deserve to live. You deserve to be happy. When I first heard about Lauren, all I could think of was you. I wanted to hold you so badly. Life is so… well, life is short sounds so trite. Life is uncertain though. I just know that I don't ever want to lose you."

Grace kept her eyes focused on his.

"I don't ever want to lose you either."

As soon as she said it, there was a rising tide of panic. The earth opened up in fiery cracks all around her.

She had made a grave mistake. She had admitted, out loud, that she never wanted to lose him.

In her experience, the things she never wanted to lose were the first to go.

She loved Erick with every last tattered shred of her heart. She loved him with the darkest and lightest, deep-down parts of her soul that she never knew existed. She loved him like being on fire when all she'd ever known was the cold.

She loved him, and she told herself she had better start letting go, before it was too late.

He pulled her close. His eyes were getting heavy. He would be asleep soon.

"Did you say you loved me?" he asked her, with the most adorable sheepish grin.

"I'm sorry; it just slipped out."

"So you don't love me?"

"No, I just mean… I don't want to freak you out, or sound all girlfriend-y or whatever."

"Okay."

He drifted off. Grace watched him for a long while before she finally slept too.

THIRTY-THREE

When Kent walked in the bar, it depressed him. He didn't think of himself as a dive bar kind of man. He would prefer to be in an elegant supper club, dapperly dressed and sipping on a dry martini, with the piano player serenading the back drop, but those days were gone. Men weren't gentle anymore, and women weren't ladies. They were a bunch of ungrateful whores.

He sidled up to the bar and observed the bartender, a slovenly, unshaven man with, really? A flannel shirt? What a pathetic stereotype.

The pickings were slim that night. There would always be the obligatory barfly drinking herself into a blind stupor. There she was. She was probably in her forties, or maybe her thirties and she'd just had a really hard life. She wasn't exactly fat, but she had that thickness that comes from middle-aged spread and a life of hard drinking. She was hardly his dream girl, but she might do for a night of company.

The only other woman in the bar was sitting with a man. She was prettier than the barfly, which wasn't saying much, but the work of getting her away from her boyfriend would hardly be worth it.

Kent ordered a soda. Better to keep his head on straight. He kept hoping another woman would walk in the bar, but every time the front door opened another fat, drunk asshole walked in. They were probably all hoping for a woman to walk in. Any woman.

He approached the barfly. A desperate mess like that should be easy enough to lure out to his car.

As soon as he got near her, he could see she was blind drunk. Just as he opened his mouth to talk to her, she passed out on the bar. What a classy dame.

The slovenly bartender came over and shook her awake.

"Tammy, come on girl, wake up. I'm calling you a cab. C'mon, wake up."

Tammy peeled her aging face off the sticky bar.

"I can give her a ride."

The bartender lost what little patience he had. He was compelled to protect the women in here from tools just like this guy. Even a wreck like Tammy deserved better than this asshole. Hell, maybe even *especially* a wreck like Tammy.

"I don't think so, buddy."

"I don't mind." Kent attempted a smile, but it did not have the desired effect.

"I said," the bartender puffed out his chest, "I don't think so, buddy. Why don't you call it a night?"

Kent was angry. How dare this lowly bartender talk to him like that? He had more class in his little finger than this guy had in his ugly flannel shirt and two-day stubble.

"I haven't finished my soda."

The bartender walked over and picked Kent's drink up off the bar. He poured it in the sink.

"There. You're finished. Get out."

It wasn't worth it. Screw this place. There were no decent women in here anyway. Why was he in this shit-hole? This whole town was filled with drunk whores, just like his mother. He walked out into the night. He considered driving back to L.A., but it was better to stay away from there for a little while. That Lauren cunt was all over the news. He couldn't believe a bitch like that could be missed by anyone. It was ridiculous. He was seething with anger, and his skin burned with the fire of unquenchable loneliness. Gradually, a sound started to nag at him and pull him out of his head.

"Just leave me alone, and go be with your whore, you asshole!"

Across the street, the prettiest girl he'd seen in a long while was yelling into a car window as she walked down the sidewalk, crying. The car was moving slowly, the male driver trying to coax her back into the car.

"Come on, Trish, don't be like that. Get in the car, baby."

"No!" screamed Trish, "Fuck you! Get away from me! Leave me alone. Let your fat-ass ex-girlfriend keep you company! Go away! I hate you!"

"Get in the car, please. I can't leave you out here. It isn't safe. I'll take you straight home; I promise. Just, please, get in the car."

Kent held his breath. *Please don't get in the car, Trish.* She was so lovely. She had the prettiest wispy blonde hair, and she was young, probably not more than 23. She was fresh-faced, even though her eyes were a little red from crying; it just made her more adorable and vulnerable. He wanted to scoop her up in his arms and carry her away. That asshole didn't deserve her. He was cheating on her? What the hell was wrong with him? A girl like Trish was a girl worth your loyalty. She hesitated for just a moment. She was just about to get in the car. Kent stepped back, a bit more into the shadows. They hadn't noticed him.

"Get in the car, Trish, come on."

"No," said Trish. "Fuck off, Greg. Leave me alone."

"Fine. Walk home in the dark and cold if you want." Greg drove off.

Trish started walking down the sidewalk. She was still crying. She was in the prettiest little sundress, and she was shivering. Poor thing didn't even have a sweater. She was walking like her feet hurt. As she bent down to take off her sandals, Kent got into his car and pulled up to see if he could give her a ride.

Trish was so caught up in her anger at Greg she didn't hear Kent's car at first. She got a creepy feeling right as Kent's car pulled slowly up to the curb and kept an even pace with her.

"Hi Trish, I wanted to offer my services as a chauffeur –"

She stopped cold. "How did you know my name?"

"Oh, I'm sorry; I wasn't trying to eavesdrop. It's just that you and your boyfriend were fighting pretty loudly, and I heard him call you Trish."

She continued walking. She was very unsettled. This guy was weird. Bad weird.

"I'd be happy to give you a ride. A lady shouldn't be walking out here alone this time of night. It isn't safe."

"I'm fine. I might just call a cab."

She didn't have her purse. Shit. She had left it in the car. She had no money and no keys to her apartment. She had her cell phone in her hand. She could call a cab, and maybe when she got home she could wake her roommate up and borrow some money from her. This creepy asshole was still driving alongside her. She stopped and leaned in the passenger window, just a little.

"Listen mister, I really appreciate the offer, but I'm all right. I'll call a cab, or walk. It's not that far to my place, so thanks anyway."

"It's really no problem, Trish."

"Stop calling me that."

"But it's your name, isn't it?"

"Well, yeah, but I don't even know you."

"I'm Kent."

"Okay, Kent, please, just go on. I'm totally fine. Really. Please. I just want to be alone."

"I'm sorry, Trish. I didn't mean to upset you. I just hate seeing a beautiful girl like you being mistreated by a man who doesn't appreciate her. You deserve so much better. A gentleman would never leave you stranded on the side of the road like that. It's just not right. You deserve a good man."

Trish did her best not to cry anymore. Her feet hurt so bad. Her new wedge sandals had blistered her feet and now she was walking barefoot on this disgusting sidewalk. Only an hour ago she had been having so much fun, dancing and laughing until that bitch ex-girlfriend of his walked in and fucked everything up. And that asshole just left her stranded. He was probably driving over to his ex-girlfriend's house right now to hook up with her. She was so mad. And this creepy guy, he just wouldn't let up.

"Look, Kent. I mean it. Move on. I'm fine. I don't need your help. Just leave me the fuck alone."

Kent was stunned for a moment. Well then, Trish was no lady after all. She wasn't a damsel in distress. She was a potty-mouthed little tramp. Without another word, he took off down the street and turned right at the next corner, out of that bitch's sight. He turned off his lights and pulled a u-turn to park on the opposite side of the street. He cut the engine and waited.

Trish kept walking. At least the creepy guy had taken off. What the hell was up with him anyway? Did he really think she would get into a car with a strange man? And was he actually hitting on her? Not to be arrogant, but please. She was so out of his league. What was he anyway? Like 40? Gross. And so fat, and balding. And he totally acted like he was all that. He was so ugly and disgusting, and did he really think –

And just like that, everything went dark. Trish felt a sharp pain in her head, and then... nothing.

THIRTY-FOUR

Erin Taylor had a team searching the garage with a fine-toothed comb. They had closed off the garage to everyone else, until they could complete the search for clues, so the only car parked in there now was Lauren's.

All the security cameras and surveillance footage were at the lab, but from the looks of it, nothing had been tampered with. It was just bad luck that they went out when they did.

They knew that Lauren left the office after 7:15 p.m. when she had spoken to Eileen on the phone. There was no sign of her on the security video, so she must have left after 7:33 p.m., which was the last time stamp on it.

Dan arrived to see Erin sprawled on the asphalt of the garage, staring and shining a flashlight under Lauren's car.

"Anything good?" Dan asked.

Erin got up and made a half-hearted attempt to dust off her tight black pants.

"Not really. Her keys were underneath the car, but I don't see anything else under there," Erin said as she waved over another officer and gave him an order.

"Let's get her car to the lab. I don't see anything else we can do with it here." Then she turned to Dan expectantly.

"Well, the house has been thoroughly searched," Dan began, "and still nothing. She couldn't possibly have made it home if her house was locked when we searched it, and her keys were here."

"So, he grabbed her here, hit her in the head and put her in his car? And no blood? Or at least none that we've found. He must have been waiting for her. He had to have been stalking her. He knew where she worked and how often she worked late." Erin continued scanning the garage the entire time she spoke.

"It's hard to believe this guy was watching her and just got lucky. If the security cameras had been working, he wouldn't have been able to grab her unseen," Dan said.

"Kevin called from the lab. There's no evidence that the cameras or footage had been tampered with. If it was messed with, this guy did a good job of making it look like a fluke."

"Crap," said Dan. "I really hope we aren't dealing with someone that smart."

"No shit," said Erin. "If we're up against someone smarter than Kevin, we're screwed."

"If someone was obsessed with her and stalking her, maybe even someone she knew, then there's no real reason to think we are dealing with a serial killer at this point."

"I know, Dan. I know. It's just a feeling I have."

Erin's inner voice was strong. She was smart, observant, and rarely missed a detail or a piece of concrete evidence, but what really made her a good detective was more than just the facts – it was her intuition. And her intuition kept saying the same thing:

There are others. Find them.

She didn't want to scatter the investigation, but she was just sure that if they could find another one of this guy's victims, they would get the answers they needed. But where were they?

"We'll just keep moving forward on this investigation," Erin said. "But it can't hurt to contact law enforcement in surrounding cities. If another body shows up with missing hands, we need to know about it."

THIRTY-FIVE

Trish struggled to open her eyes. The pain in her head was so fierce she felt like she would throw up. The thought led her to another thought, which led her to another, and so on.

I am gagged.

It is pitch black.

My hands are bound behind me.

I am in a trunk.

This car is moving.

Terror seized her in every cell of her body. Everything inside her was running, running away from these horrible realizations.

Blind terror and raging panic coursed through her as she struggled in vain to free herself. Being tied and trapped while the flight instinct erupts from one's deepest core was a kind of torture she couldn't endure, but had to anyway.

Her phone? Did she still have her phone? No way. That man. It was him. That creepy guy. He did this.

Oh my god. Oh my god. Oh my god. Trish's brain roared in a panicky loop.

I'm going to die. Oh my god. Please no. I'm only 24. Please no. I want to live. Please let me live. I'll do anything.

THIRTY-SIX

Grace was freaking out. She was completely horrified that she had told Erick she loved him. How could she have been so stupid? She told herself at first that it was okay. He hadn't wigged out or anything, but it wasn't like he said it back.

She hadn't heard from him in three days, so she was starting to panic. Of course, it was typical of a man to pull away. The heightened intimacy had frightened him off. She'd been an emotional wreck. She'd said too much.

She needed to call Natalie.

"Hi, this is Natalie. I'm not available. Leave a message and I'll call you back."

Shit.

"Hey Nat, it's me. Listen, just… well, call me when you get a chance."

Grace began to pace the floor. It was only two o'clock. She wanted to have a glass of wine, but that was a terrible idea. Maybe she should just text Erick. No. Even worse idea than day drinking. Okay. Maybe he was just busy. But it had been three days! He'd never gone more than a day without contacting her, even when he was busy. It was the love thing. She ruined everything by talking about love. Oh god. Why wasn't Natalie calling her back?

Her phone rang. It was him!

"Hi there." She put on her most casual voice.

"Hey, pretty. Whatcha doin'?"

"Not much. I was just thinking about you."

"Sexy thoughts?"

Grace laughed. Well, it was more like a giggle. *Oh, stop it. You're acting like a silly schoolgirl.*

"Some of them, maybe. Have any plans tonight?" Why did she say that? Stupid, stupid, stupid. She sounded needy and desperate.

"Well… yeah, I'm meeting up with some friends later. I just wanted to check in."

"Oh… so…" Grace didn't know what to say. Obviously, he didn't want to invite her, and she didn't want to invite herself. She was disappointed, but she couldn't let him see that.

"So I'll check in later, Grace, yeah?"

Panic seized Grace. *Don't sound needy. Don't sound needy.*

"Yeah, sure… later then…"

He hung up. Just like that. This wasn't good. Not at all.

Grace swallowed her panic. Why had he even bothered to call? Why was she so disappointed? She poured herself a glass of Chardonnay. This was bad. What the hell? Was she just a raging alcoholic now? Okay, no. It will just take the edge off.

She should have known a good thing like Erick could never last. He was probably going out with someone else tonight anyway. They had never really agreed to be exclusive. She should do that too. Go out with other men. Oh crap. That sounded awful. Dealing with one man was bad enough. Why muddle it up even more?

Besides, she didn't want anyone else. She wanted him. She wanted him way too bad for her own good.

Somehow she endured the long, slow, empty night.

When her phone beeped with his text message, it pulled her out of a drunken sleep. The lights, and her clothes, were still on. She was on top of the covers. It was nearly midnight.

Missed you tonight, pretty.

When she read that she brightened. It was best not to respond. She wanted to sound mysterious, and not at all like the needy drunk loser she actually was.

THIRTY-SEVEN

Erin was scouring missing person's reports for anything that might be a clue to locating more victims of this creep. The big problem was, without a second victim, her search parameters were way too wide. Did this guy have a type? Just searching for missing women was turning up some pretty depressing results. All these missing women. What happens to them?

So, what if he did have a type? Okay, Lauren. 5'8", brunette, age 34, professional, beautiful, slender, athletic… lesbian? Did he hate lesbians? Did he even know she was a lesbian? Lauren's private life had been pretty much that – private. A little digging revealed that she'd also dated a lot of men in the past, so maybe she was technically bi-sexual, or possibly she had only recently come out of the closet. Maybe Eileen would know more about Lauren's romantic past.

Erin, once again, crawled inside the heads of men who killed women. Why did they do it?

They hate them. They desire them, but cannot have them for some reason. She got out her legal pad and wrote at the top:

Possible reasons he hated Lauren:

She's a lesbian

She's a successful professional

She's beautiful

She's unattainable; out of his league

She rejected him, or he perceives she rejected him

She reminds him of someone

There was the possibility that he picked her at random, but she couldn't get over all the signs of rage at the dump site, and on her body. He hated her. He believed she deserved it. Even if he initially chose her at random, he put those shallow cuts all over her arms and torso because he was punishing her. He made her suffer.

Erin was sick and angry. Why did she do this job again? Oh that's right, because somebody had to. And she was that somebody.

Dan walked up to her desk and put the M.E.'s report in front of her.

"Well," he said, "I guess I could say at least she wasn't raped, but that is hardly good enough news to make any of this shit sound okay."

Dan really was pretty cool. He said stupid shit sometimes, but Erin figured that came with his handicap – which of course was having a penis. Even the best of men couldn't help sounding like dumbasses now and then, but Dan had a point. At least she wasn't raped.

"I guess that's something. At least she didn't have to endure that, too. What else? Do we have the cause of death? Was it strangulation?"

"Oddly, no. The marks on her neck were post-mortem."

"Really?" Erin was shocked. Strangling was a common technique with these creeps. *They want to silence us.* Erin appreciated the facts, but also believed in the symbols. Strangling silences her. Stranglers are deluded control freaks. Stabbing her penetrates her. Those who stab are often impotent, either literally or figuratively. If this asshole's signature was cutting off her hands, that meant something.

He's lonely.

Of course. He craves the touch of a woman. He's probably not very good-looking, socially awkward, possibly even disfigured.

Dan gave Erin a minute, as she was doing her retreat-into-her-thoughts thing, and she'd be back in three, two...

"So, if not strangulation, what actually killed her?"

"An aneurysm."

"Are you fucking shitting me?" Erin was pissed. She could just imagine the defense lawyer arguing that it was not actually murder, because Lauren had died of an aneurysm. Damn it. Fucking lawyers.

"Yes, but the aneurysm could have been caused by the blunt force trauma to the back of her head. Most likely, he knocked her out, abducted her, and she regained consciousness. She was still alive when the cuts on her arms and torso were made. Eventually, the head injury likely caused the aneurysm. Her hands were removed post-mortem. Another good thing. She suffered a lot, but at least he didn't do that while she was still alive."

Erin got her pensive face on.

"He got mad at her for dying too soon."

Dan loved working with Erin. She was awe-inspiring at times, but he got a little freaked out when she did this. She went so far away, and her voice got kind of… eerie, like she was channeling or something. Even though she was this tiny, barely-five-feet-tall blonde, in those moments, she reminded him of his rotund grandmother the *curandera*. Obviously, not in the physical traits, just that weird far-away eyes trance thing. He shuddered. He wouldn't be surprised if she started hurling rum and chicken blood at him.

"So, uh… what makes you think that?"

Erin snapped out of her far-away face and did her just-the-facts eye contact face. Dan was instantly more comfortable.

"Well, he wasn't expecting the aneurysm. That just happened. It was probably quite a gift for Lauren in that moment, something merciful. She didn't have to suffer anymore. There was bruising on her neck, so he strangled her, but he could have strangled her moments after she died. Once the heart isn't pumping blood, it gets harder to cause that kind of bruising. He strangled her not to kill her, but maybe to try and wake her back up. He was pissed. He wasn't through with her."

Dan sat quietly pondering Erin's words. It made sense. But it also made things more difficult. If Lauren died by aneurysm, then they couldn't know exactly what his usual technique was. Did he always strangle them? Did he usually remove the hands ante-mortem? If he didn't strangle them, how did he normally kill them?

One thing seemed certain: if this guy had a way of doing things, Lauren took that away from him. He was going to be extra pissed now.

He needed to be stopped.

Some woman could be with him right now.

THIRTY-EIGHT

Trish struggled to open her eyes. The car was still moving. She must have lost consciousness for a while, so she had no idea how much time had passed. Panic seized her. She wished she would lose consciousness again.

How could this possibly be happening to her? She wasn't a bad person. She didn't deserve this. She couldn't stop going down the "if only" road in her mind, the only part of her that could stay in motion. Her mind roared.

If only she hadn't gone out tonight.

If only Greg's ex-bitch hadn't come in and started flirting with him.

If only he hadn't flirted back.

He did that just to hurt me, thought Trish.

He's always hurting me...

And now...

Now, it's all over. Greg can't ever hurt me again, because this asshole is going to kill me.

The car slowed, crunching over gravel, then finally came to a stop. *Oh god, we are in the middle of nowhere. Of course... even if he takes the gag off, no one is going to hear me scream.* The trunk opened up and there he was.

Trish wanted to throw up, but somehow she didn't. Maybe the gag in her mouth stopped it from happening.

Gross. Was that... tenderness on his face? Or his attempt at masking something else?

Trish struggled again, in vain, to free herself.

"We're home, sweetheart."

Home. Sweetheart. He smiled at her, and tenderly scooped her up in his arms. As he did, Trish met Kent's eyes.

The eyes of a gentleman? The eyes of a monster.

Kent carried Trish across the threshold of his cabin. She

was so petite. Light as a feather. She had such delicate bone structure. Not like that Lauren bitch. She had been slender, but sturdy – probably lifted weights or something. But Trish, she was a delicate flower. He could snap her frail frame in half with his bare hands. It was very arousing. She was going to make a terrific new girlfriend. If she could keep her potty mouth shut.

He set her down gently on the couch, and kneeled on the floor in front of her.

"Welcome home," he said.

Trish needed to pee. *Oh god, I'm going to pee myself. No, ask him if you can pee. Maybe you can lock yourself in the bathroom. Crawl out the window. Where the hell am I? How far would I have to run? Why didn't I go to the gym more often? Or, ever?*

Trish's mind was racing so fast it was causing her motion sickness. She scrutinized his every move. He had a brown grocery bag next to the kitchen table. He took a bunch of colorful flowers out of the bag and put them on the table. He went into a cupboard, took out a vase and ran some water into it. He put the flowers into the vase, beaming with pride.

"Do you like them? I got them just for you."

A voice inside Trish said simply, *play nice.* If she cooperated, she could buy herself some time. He had behaved nicely until she told him to leave her the fuck alone. Okay, he doesn't like profanity. Not that she could curse with a gag in her mouth. She couldn't say anything. But she could nod, which she did. She forced a smile, although she imagined, with a gag in her mouth, it wasn't very attractive. She struggled to sit up. It was hard with her ankles bound, and her hands bound behind her back. He was staring at her.

"Would you like to sit at the table, sweetheart?"

She nodded again.

He turned his back on her and reached into the bag.

He took out a bottle of champagne. *How fucking romantic*, thought Trish, *maybe he will at least have the decency to get me drunk before he kills me.*

When the cork popped, Trish nearly jumped out of her skin, which is hard to do when you're tied up.

He was taking his time. He got two flutes, poured champagne in each of them and set them on the table. He took out a box of chocolates and set those down on the table too.

Even though this guy was probably going to torture and kill her, he was already doing more romantic things than that asshole Greg had ever done for her. Not once in the three years they'd been seeing each other had he ever gotten flowers or candy for her. And if he hadn't been such a dick to her, she wouldn't be in this situation now. Trish was going crazy. How could she even be having these thoughts? Maybe it was just her brain's way of distracting her from facing the horror of her situation. Or maybe she needed someone to blame and, for the moment, blaming Greg made her feel better than blaming herself.

Kent walked toward her. Fear had her in a chokehold. Was it possible her heart would explode?

He helped her sit up on the couch, and sat next to her, caressing the saliva-covered cloth in her mouth.

"Would you like me to take this out?"

Trish nodded.

"I'd really like to, but you know I'm going to need something from you, okay?"

She nodded again.

"I need you to be quiet. I can't have a lot of screaming and yelling, all right? Not when I've planned such a nice evening for us. I want us to just have a pleasant, quiet, romantic time together. You understand?"

She nodded.

"It's important that you understand how secluded we are. There is no point in yelling and screaming if you think anyone is going to hear you. No one will. I wanted us to be alone, so we could have a nicer time. All right, sweetheart?"

She nodded, as tears leaked out of the corners of her eyes. She was so fucked.

He took the gag out of her mouth, ever so slowly. She still had the urge to scream, but he was telling her the truth. No one would hear her anyway. If she played nice, maybe she could keep the game going long enough to formulate a plan for escape, or an opportunity to fight back. There must be a way out of this, but she'd have to give him what he wanted. She held back a shudder. Whatever he wanted.

THIRTY-NINE

Grace was calm again. Erick was back to his attentive self, and she was much more relaxed. Things were good, and hotter than ever. Fear gripped her in moments, because her feelings for him were so strong, but she told herself it was worth it. After all, sex had been such a chore with Stan. With Erick, she couldn't get enough. She was learning so much about her true self – that she was, in fact, highly sexual. She'd just never been this… motivated. It was a marvelous and terrifying bliss. Bliss, how rare a feeling it is. Sometimes, when she took a photo, and it would capture exactly the mood she was hoping for, or when it came out even better than she'd expected, she'd have this feeling. And of course, she'd had total euphoria with Kaylee, but she couldn't really dwell on those memories for long, or she'd fall apart. It all seemed like a dream now. She couldn't even believe she'd ever been a mother. She didn't feel at all like one. How could she? She had no child. But would she ever want another one? No. Too risky. Love is a perilous proposition.

Erick was risky. Even if he was a good guy, even if he loved her, even if he wanted her, he could still leave her. He could fall for someone else. He could die. Grace's heart fluttered, but not in a good way, in a fight or flight way. Fight wasn't her style, so she settled on flight.

Leave him before he leaves you. Keep your distance. It's too dangerous. You fought for Kaylee, and you lost. You will always lose, Grace. You are a lemon.

But she'd never felt like this about a man before. Maybe this really was worth fighting for. How would she know if she didn't stick it out? But the pain of loss. It was too much to endure, again.

Grace sat down on the floor. When sadness hit her really hard she couldn't bear to be on furniture, deemed herself unworthy of the simplest chair.

She tried to meditate, but she didn't really know how. *Are you supposed to clear your mind?* Was such a thing even possible? Her mind was cluttered with so many things, so she focused on only one.

Love. She loved Erick, but she wasn't so sure he loved her. He'd never said it.

She couldn't do this. She couldn't love someone who didn't love her back, no matter how good it might feel sometimes.

She would have to tell him.

Go away.

She wouldn't really mean it, but she would have to say it. And she would have to live it if he walked away. Or when. That seemed more likely. When he walked away.

FORTY

After Kent slowly removed the gag from Trish's mouth, he stayed very close to her. If she screamed, he'd have to hit her. He really didn't want to do that. A gentleman doesn't raise his hand to a lady.

They were so close their lips nearly touched. Their eyes locked. Kent relished the stirrings in his member. Trish did her best not to scream or show her disgust. She could see every pore, every broken capillary, every nose hair. He was vile. Beads of sweat glistened on his greasy forehead, and a nasty white film rested in the corners of his mouth. Gross. What was that again? Something random crossed her mind; her Biology 101 professor had said… white film in the corners of your mouth… dehydration. Why was she thinking about that? What good were all those boring college courses going to do her now? She was going to die in this place, and she was thinking about Biology 101? She should have put her energy into designing handbags like she'd wanted to, instead of wasting what few years she had trying to make her family happy, her friends happy, and trying to make some idiot who didn't appreciate her be her stupid boyfriend. If she ever got out of here, she would tell every person she met: *follow your heart. Don't bother trying to make everyone else happy. Be with people who love and appreciate you.* But right now, she wasn't out of here. She was in here, in this horrible fucked-up place, and the only chance she had of survival was to make this guy happy until she could find an opportunity to escape.

Kent picked Trish up and sat her in a kitchen chair, and then worked slowly and methodically on her restraints. Trish's feet were still bare. She had no idea where her shoes were. Maybe in his trunk. Maybe still on the sidewalk where he took her. As soon as her feet hit the kitchen floor, her heart drummed deafening terror. What felt so wrong about his floor? *Oh my god. No. No. This is not good.* A sheer plastic drop cloth covered the linoleum. Why hadn't she noticed it before? He wasn't planning on re-painting the kitchen, was he? *It's for my blood. He wants a nice easy clean-up for my blood.*

Kent tied rope around Trish's waist, securing her to the chair back. This could get tricky. Her ankles were bound together, so she couldn't run, but he needed her hands in front of her. His stare was cold and penetrating.

"Sweetheart, I'm going to untie your hands for just a moment. I know it's not comfortable to have them behind your back like that, but I need you to be a nice girl and not try anything crazy, okay? Do I have your word you will behave?"

With her hands free she could hit him or scratch him, but she still couldn't get away with her ankles tied together, and a chair tied to her back. She'd have to cooperate. Her shoulders hurt really badly from having her arms restrained behind her for so long. To have her hands free for a moment would be delicious.

"I promise I'll be good."

He untied her hands and pulled her arms gently to the front of her body, resting her hands in her lap.

"Does that feel better my darling, sweet girl?"

"Yes," Trish said, "thank you."

He gently caressed her hands. Trish willed them to stop shaking. He moaned with desire and she retched inside. This guy was a sick, twisted pervert, and she was trapped all alone with him.

"Your hands are lovely, so delicate, Trish. You have such dainty, feminine bone structure."

Was she supposed to thank him? What did he want to hear?

"Thank you," Trish murmured.

Kent's excitement began to rise. She had barely whispered, and he knew she was feeling it. Everything was just right.

She was so sweet, so perfect. He loved her. And she loved him. She was so much better, so much purer than those other whores. Everything was going to be all right with her here.

"Everything's going to be alright," he said to her.

Trish wanted to believe him, but surely his version of "all right" and hers were very different things.

FORTY-ONE

Melissa woke up late that day and went into the kitchen for some orange juice. She took the carton out of the fridge. Damn it, Trish. Always putting empty cartons back in the fridge. Where was she anyway?

Melissa walked over to Trish's room. It was empty. She hadn't come home. Probably went home with her boyfriend. Melissa hated that guy; she really couldn't understand what Trish liked about him. Such a phony douche-bag. And he treated Trish like shit. She didn't think she could listen to one more of their stupid break-ups, or even worse, their loud make-up sex.

Melissa suddenly felt something bad in the pit of her stomach. It was odd, Trish not coming home. She didn't really spend the night at Greg's place very often. Occasionally, but usually, they came back here. And even if she had spent the night at his place, wouldn't she have come home by now? It was almost 2 o'clock. Maybe they went to lunch or something. It was silly to worry. Everything was probably fine.

But it couldn't hurt to check. Melissa got her phone and fired off a text message to Trish.

Hey girl, just checking to see if you went home with Greg last night.

Hours went by; Melissa showered and got ready for another exciting night of bartending at the local shit-hole. Trish did not respond. That was weird. Trish was a texting fiend. She never let her phone out of her sight. Melissa called Trish repeatedly, but it went straight to voicemail every time. Maybe her battery died.

Melissa wished she could call Greg. She remembered something her mother used to say to her.

You girls need to look out for each other. Get each other's friends and boyfriend's phone numbers, and check on each other. It's a crazy world out there.

She, like many other girls, should have listened to her

mother.

If she left early, she could stop by the bar where Greg worked. He probably had a shift tonight. He would know where Trish was.

Melissa left her apartment, unable to shake an ugly, sinking feeling.

FORTY-TWO

Erin ordered another bourbon, neat, from the bartender. She didn't like ice in her bourbon. It broke up the taste of the booze, and cold made her teeth hurt. The bartender was cute in an overly L.A . metro-sexual kind of way. Not really her type. Not that she even had a type anymore. Someone was staring at her from the end of the bar. Oh boy. Another George Clooney wanna-be pretending he wasn't married. Well, she didn't just come here for the drinks. It was the bar closest to Lauren's office, and a lot of people from Cambridge PR stopped by this place right after work for a drink, including Lauren. If any of these patrons were regulars, they'd have seen her.

She hated these kinds of bars. They were cropping up all over L.A. now. Over-the-top interior design, music that somehow always sounded a little contrived, hipster patrons of the excessive accessory persuasion, and of course, the utterly ridiculous drink menu. The bartender (or mixologist as he was probably called) handed her a menu when she sat down. It was designed to look like a brown paper lunch bag with "hand-written" drinks on them. Each of the drinks cost about $12, contained fresh organic ingredients from the Farmer's Market, and had names like Rosemary's Baby's Bibb (featuring fresh muddled rosemary and garnished with a leaf of Bibb lettuce) and the Raspberry Beret (containing sprigs of lavender and a fresh raspberry skewered on a specialty cocktail sword with Prince's male/female symbol for an extra-retro vibe). One glance at the menu nearly elicited a snarl at Mr. Underwear Model Mixologist – "Just put some whiskey in a glass!" But that wasn't fair. Poor little Fancy Pants was just trying to make a living. Erin showed him Lauren's picture, but he didn't recognize her. He'd just started working there a few days ago after the Barre Bar (no doubt with ballet barres and floor-to-ceiling mirrors to remind you to maintain your eating disorder) had closed.

So, back to George Clooney. He was still giving her the stare-down. Erin walked up to him. He immediately turned on the smarm.

"Hey, gorgeous, can I buy you a drink?"

"Sure," said Erin. No sense turning down a free drink. She wasn't technically on-duty. She was working overtime, in her free time, which she would do, night and day until she caught the sick bastard who killed Lauren.

Fake George Clooney ordered whiskey from Fancy Pants, and Erin sat down next to him. She glanced at the tan line on his ring finger. She inadvertently glanced at his pockets to see if the faintest bulge of a wedding ring was buried there, in his tight pants. Big mistake. *Oh boy, he actually thinks I'm checking out his package. What a tool.* He leered at her.

"So, I haven't seen you in here before."

"No," Erin began, "This really isn't my kind of bar."

"Really? What's your kind of bar then? Maybe we could go there."

As tempting as it was to throw up in her mouth and spit it in his face, she might get more out of this douche-bag if she worked a little of her petite, but feisty, magic on him.

"Well, I heard the best-looking men hang out here, so I thought I'd check it out," she said with all the charm she could muster.

"Is that so?" he said, as he moved closer to her, with a grin that said he was sure he was getting lucky tonight.

"Yeah, a friend of mine told me about it. She comes in here a lot. Lauren. You know her? Tall, pretty, long brown hair?"

"She a *close* friend of yours? Maybe if we find her all three of us can have a little fun."

This guy was ridiculous. He was seriously the worst cliché she'd ever come across, and she'd seen a lot of them.

"Actually, I've been kind of worried about her. I haven't seen her in a while." Erin took a photo of Lauren out of her jacket pocket and held it up for him.

"This is her. Have you seen her in here?"

He admired the woman in the photo. Lauren's beauty was obvious, but there was slight recognition in his eyes as well.

Fake Clooney picked up his drink. He took a slow sip before answering Erin.

"Yeah, I've seen her in here a few times."

"Alone?"

Fake Clooney got a mischievous grin on his face.

"Ooh," he oozed, "Jealous much?"

Erin smiled coyly.

"Just curious," she said, "If you've seen her in here with anyone in particular."

"I've seen her. Not in a while. She'd come in here alone, sometimes. Sometimes with an older woman – attractive, you know like a Helen Mirren type. Older, but you still wanna bang her."

Erin twitched. Wow, this guy was a class act. It took everything in her not to kick his face in.

"Really? You ever talk to her? Lauren, that is."

"I tried to chat her up at first, but she definitely wasn't interested. She seemed pretty reserved. She kept to herself, or talked to whoever she came in with, but she never really talked to anyone else, except to order a drink. Why are you so worried about her anyway? Why don't we talk more about you?" He put his hand on her knee.

Erin tensed up. She wasn't getting anywhere, and this guy was starting to get annoying. The game was getting less fun. She discreetly showed him her badge.

"The truth is, I'm really worried about this woman, so anything you can tell me would be sincerely appreciated,"

Erin said with a smile that was only slightly condescending.

"Hey, oh… I'm sorry, Officer," Fake Clooney fumbled as he quickly removed his hand from her knee.

"It's Detective Taylor. So, I'm just curious if you ever saw her talking to any men," Erin said.

"Well, I think… I mean, I'm not saying this because she rejected my advances, I just… well, I think this woman may have been, you know, um… not so into men." He was desperately uncomfortable.

"A lesbian?"

"Yeah, but not because –"

"I know. Got it. We know that already."

"Did something happen to her?"

"Yes," Erin said quietly, "And I need to figure out what."

Fake Clooney longed to slam his pansy drink, if the absurdity of "slamming" a drink with Chambord in it hadn't stopped him.

"There was something," he began.

Erin brightened.

"Yes? What?"

"Well, nothing I saw, just something I heard. This guy came up and hit on her, and she blew him off, and –"

"What did he look like?" Erin couldn't help but interrupt.

"He was this young kid. Good-looking, probably a trust fund kid. Had that frat boy look about him."

"Did he get angry or anything when she blew him off?"

"No, not at all," said Fake Clooney, "he just moved on to the next female. I don't think there was anything dangerous about him. It was just the conversation between this woman –"

"Lauren," offered Erin.

"Lauren," he said, "and her lady companion. She said something like 'what is it with these guys today?' And the older lady said something about how beautiful she was and, of course, men would constantly want to talk to her, and then Lauren said, 'but they can be so creepy, like this guy who always shows up at Franklin Berry and tries to chat me up. He never gets the message.' Something like that. I could only hear parts of it. Then they asked for their check and left soon after that."

"What's Franklin Berry?" Erin asked.

"You know, that organic smoothie place on Franklin Avenue."

"Right," she said, even though she had no idea such a place existed. What the hell ever happened to drinking coffee? Or bourbon for that matter? Had the whole world gone soft?

"I'm sorry I don't have more. I wish I could help. I'm sorry I was... you know. I didn't realize."

"It's all right. Look, do me a favor, okay?"

"Yeah," said Fake Clooney.

"Go home to your wife."

Erin threw a few extra bucks on the bar for the underwear model/mixologist and walked out. Finally, a solid lead. First thing in the morning, she would get herself a nice delicious organic smoothie, chock-full of antioxidants. Or whatever.

FORTY-THREE

When Erick asked her to go have sushi with him one Friday night, Grace accepted even though she was feeling really shaky. It made her so happy to be with him. Her heart pounded with excitement whenever he was near, but the panic was overwhelming her. She couldn't stop thinking about how much danger she was in.

They had an amazing night, but Grace was really far away. She had a feeling this might be their last night together, so she embraced it as best she could.

They had never again spoken of Grace's "love slip," but it might be better if things were out in the open. She loved him. And if he didn't love her, he would have to go.

She was on top of him when she said it.

"I love you, Erick."

He said nothing. He brushed her hair back from her face, just like men do in romantic movies when they want a girl to know how much they care, and he kissed her. That was it. He never said another word. They made love. He slept. Grace lay awake most of the night, fighting back tears.

When he finally woke up in the morning, he immediately started to fondle her. He was ready for their usual morning round, but she couldn't do it. Her brain was spinning; her blood was cold, and her body was unable to respond. She pushed his hands away.

"I can't do this," Grace quietly said.

Erick offered only a pensive, "Okay..."

Grace took a deep breath. This was so hard. But she had no choice. If he didn't love her, she couldn't go on seeing him. It was going to hurt too much.

"You know I love you. I've said it," Grace ventured.

He said nothing. She lay there waiting, but the bastard said nothing. This was torture.

"Obviously, you don't love me. You've never said you did."

"I never said I didn't."

Grace waited, but nothing more came.

"What does that even mean, Erick? Look, I think we have a great time together. I don't know how many other women you're seeing, and I'm really shaky here. I'm shaky about what we're doing, and how you feel. But I know how I feel. And I know I can't be with someone I love if he doesn't love me back. If you don't love me by now, maybe you're never going to, but I can't invest anymore of my heart in you, hoping and waiting."

Again, she waited. Why couldn't he just say "I love you too," and then they could make love, and go to brunch and then make love again, and then drink champagne and lounge around all day? But he said nothing. He was quiet for a while, and then he actually reached out and touched her left breast. She moved away from him and sat up.

"No," she said, "I'm serious, Erick. I can't be with you. I can't do this anymore with you. I need you to go."

"You don't mean that, Grace."

"Yes, Erick, I do. If you can't love me, and say it, then walk out the door."

There was a horrible pause. He actually attempted another caress, and she recoiled. He said nothing as he got out of bed. Calmly, he dressed and put his keys and cell phone in his pocket, each banal movement meticulous, deliberate and in sharp focus to her. Knives of fire plunged into her when he brushed his hair away from his eyes, only to let it intentionally fall back down. He did this just the way he always had, opening and closing to her all at once, his sweet cocktail of present intensity and imminent escape. Her eyes ached with eager tears, but she was done giving him anything else. This was done. Fuck this. Fuck him.

"I understand," he finally said. And he left.

Grace broke down then, choked by sobs. She cried for hours, or maybe for centuries, but when she finally stopped crying, she felt better, clean and strong. She had stood up for herself in a way she never had before. She had invariably settled when it came to men. Always, she had settled for men she couldn't love. Now, she wasn't about to settle for a man who couldn't love her.

FORTY-FOUR

Melissa stopped by the pub where dickhead Greg worked. She still hadn't heard from Trish, and she was really starting to panic. He wasn't there when she came in, and she couldn't wait around or she'd be late for her shift, so she left a note with her number on it and asked the bartender to give it to him when he came in, and that it was extremely important.

Later that evening, she was completely swamped at work. Her phone vibrated in the pocket of her jeans, but she couldn't stop to answer it. She was having one of those nights. She'd go home and smell like beer and gin and bar rot, but at least she'd make some money. Busy was always better than standing around. She was a little concerned though. When she had a moment, she checked her phone. She had a missed call from a number she didn't recognize, as well as a new voicemail. It was probably Greg, and she really wanted to listen to his message. She desperately hoped he would tell her Trish was with him, and everything was all right.

It was after midnight before she had a chance to listen to his voicemail.

"Hey Melissa, it's Greg. I got your note, and no; I haven't heard from Trish today, but she was kind of pissed last night and said she was going home. So, uh… I guess call me later… and let me know if you've heard from her. I'm working tonight too, so call me even if it's late. I'll be up."

As it got closer to 1 a.m., Melissa had a moment to breathe and asked her fellow bartender if he could handle everything while she took a little break. She went out back and called Greg.

"Hello?"

"Hey, Greg, it's Melissa."

"Oh hey. Any word from Trish?"

"No. What about you?"

"No. Nothing. I texted her a couple of times today, but when she didn't respond, I figured she was still pissed at me. She didn't come home?"

"No," Melissa said, with a pounding heart and a sick stomach.

"You know what?" started Greg, "Maybe she doesn't have her phone. Maybe she left it in my car. I'm going to check. Hang on."

Melissa impatiently waited through the muffled outdoor noise and then, a car door opening. There was a brief silence before Greg returned to talk to her.

"Shit."

"What? What is it? Do you have her phone?"

"No, I don't see it. I don't know, maybe she had it in her hand when she got out of the car, but her purse is here."

"That's bad," said Melissa, "No matter how mad she was at you, she'd call you back to get her purse. I mean, her wallet and everything is in there, right? And her keys?"

"Yeah," Greg was disheartened. He sat down on the passenger's seat of his car with Trish's purse in his lap. He started to panic. He had let her go. He let her walk off into the night, alone. If something happened to her, he'd never forgive himself.

Melissa needed to take charge of this situation. She had to find Trish.

"You closing tonight, Greg?"

"Yeah, but I might be able to get out early. I can see if Valerie can close up."

"Okay, I'll try to get out too, but either way, can you come here and get me? I didn't bring my car; I walked. We should call the hospitals and stuff like that. What time did you drop her off? Maybe if she didn't have her keys, she couldn't get in, and I just didn't hear her knock or something. If her phone was dead already, and she couldn't call either one of us..." Melissa's brain roared with possible scenarios. Greg's stomach plummeted.

"Melissa, I didn't drop her off at home."

There was a long pause.

"What?"

"I didn't take her home. I tried to, but she wouldn't let me. She was really mad. We were fighting in the car. She got out when I stopped at a stop sign. I kept trying to convince her to get back in the car so I could take her home, but she wouldn't. She was so mad... I can't believe this. I should have dragged her into the car. She just kept screaming at me, and I drove off."

"You drove off and left her?"

"Yes... I know. It was bad... I kept saying, get in the car."

"You asshole. You drove off and left her?"

"Stop it! I know, okay? I know. I fucked up. Please. I'm freaking out."

Melissa stopped and took a deep breath. She needed to calm down. Everything would be all right. It had to be. Trish had to be all right. If Greg was the last person to see her, they needed to cooperate, and stay calm. They had to find her.

"Okay, I'm sorry. I am. Can you pick me up?"

"Yes," Greg quietly said.

"Cool. Just get here when you can. I'll get out of here as soon as possible. I'll start calling hospitals, and we'll drive back to the place where she got out of the car. Do you remember where it was?"

"Yeah, I remember." Greg would never forget. He could still see Trish's beautiful, but angry, face as she walked down the sidewalk. Where was she? *Oh god. Please let her be okay,* he silently prayed.

They drove to the stop sign where Trish was last seen. Melissa had been calling hospitals from her cell phone with no luck. It would be hard to find Trish this way. Even if she was in a hospital, she didn't have any identification on her, so they might not know who she was. Detailed descriptions of her had so far produced no results. Their panic was rising.

Greg pulled the car over and parked, and they both got out and walked around. Melissa spotted it first.

One of Trish's wedge sandals lay on the edge of the sidewalk. She had just bought those shoes a few days ago. She got them on sale, and was really excited to show them to Melissa.

Melissa reached out to the shoe, and then thought better of it. It might be evidence. As the word "evidence" entered her mind, she began to cry. She slumped down and sat on the curb and began to cry. Greg walked toward her.

"Melissa? What is it?"

Melissa pointed to the shoe. Greg wasn't overly observant about women's footwear, but he still knew.

"It's hers, Greg. It's Trish's shoe." Melissa began to sob. Greg sat down next to her, and tentatively reached toward the shoe.

"Don't touch it. We have to call the police. We have to…" Melissa was losing control of her emotions.

Greg put his arm around her. He'd screwed up, bad. Melissa probably hated him, but none of that mattered. The only thing that mattered was finding Trish. He picked up his cell phone and dialed three digits. He had never needed to dial these numbers before. He had never had to hear these words in real life. He could not hold back his tears as those words assaulted his ears.

"911. What is your emergency?"

FORTY-FIVE

Trish was having thoughts she'd rather avoid. She had managed to keep her brain off these tracks, but she was losing hope that she would ever get out of here. She had seen this guy's face. She knew his first name. He would never let her go, no matter how much she begged, no matter how hard she worked to cooperate and make him happy; she knew in her heart that he intended to kill her, whenever he was through with his sick little game. Maybe there would be an opportunity to escape, but she doubted it. He was tying her wrists together now. Her hands were in front of her, which was at least more comfortable than having them behind her back, but her wrists were tightly bound; her ankles were tightly bound, and her torso was tightly bound to the chair on which she sat, thinking of her mother, and her big sister, Lillian. Her beautiful mother, who had worked so hard to raise her and her sister all alone after Trish's father died. She wished there was some way she could call her mother now and tell her how much she appreciated everything she'd done, and everything she'd sacrificed to raise her and Illy. Lillian was her grandmother's name, and her sister was named after her, but everyone called her Lilly. Everyone except Trish, who couldn't say "Lilly" when she was learning to talk, so when she wanted her sister's attention, she would say, "illy, illy, illy" over and over. Illy stuck, and Trish still called her that. She wanted to be with her right now. She reached out to tell her mom and her sister, with her mind, how much she loved them, and that she'd be home soon.

Her roommate, Melissa, wouldn't miss her at first because she would assume she'd gone home with Greg. Greg wouldn't miss her because he would think she was ignoring him out of anger, even if he did call her. Besides, he was probably already banging that fat-ass ex-girlfriend of his and not even giving Trish a second thought. By the time anyone missed her, it would be too late. Unless... *there must be some way out of here.* Wasn't that a song lyric? Her brain was starting to hurt. Searching every angle, every window, hoping against hope there would be a way out. She had to get out of these ropes.

She had been lost in her own head, avoiding too close a look at her captor. What was up with this guy? What had made him so crazy that he would do something like this to a helpless woman? How many women had he done this to already? Would he be caught? Would he get away with this? How many more would he get before he was caught? *My mother and my sister will never rest until they find out what happened to me, you son-of-a-bitch*, her brain screamed, as her face forced a smile. He left the room.

Trish struggled in her ropes even though it was hopeless. Furtively, her eyes scanned the kitchen. There must be a knife in there somewhere, but even if she could get to it, what then? She could free her ankles, but he wasn't going to leave her alone long enough to actually free herself, would he? She scooted her chair closer to the drawers in the kitchen. The plastic drop cloth bunched up underneath the chair legs and made a harsh dragging noise, amplified by her fear. *Shit.* She'd have to be careful. She could stand up, but she'd have to hop, bent over, with her ankles bound.

"What are you doing, sweetheart?" He was back. His voice dripped with a fake sweetness. His anger was thinly veiled. He was holding a large bottle of lotion. *Oh shit. What the hell is the lotion for?*

She stopped cold and sat the chair back down.

"I'm sorry, I just…"

"You're not thinking about leaving me are you? I'm doing my best to make you happy."

"No, I'm not trying to leave; I'm just…" Trish needed to think fast. Suddenly, it hit her, mind and body. She still needed to pee. The adrenaline had made her forget, but she really needed to go. "I just, well, this is so embarrassing, but

I really need to use the bathroom."

He stood in front of her, so close his legs touched hers. He peered into her eyes for some sign of deceit.

"Do you really need to go, or are you just playing around with me?"

"I really need to go. Like really, really."

Kent untied the rope around Trish's waist and pulled her to her feet. He didn't believe her. She didn't really need to pee. She wanted to leave him. He couldn't take that. He couldn't take another one leaving him. She had to stay. He would make her stay.

"You're trying to ruin our nice evening. I worked so hard to plan a romantic evening for us, and you're going to ruin it with your lies."

He was shaking her now. He would make her stay. Trish was crying. She didn't want to be, but the terror was taking her over. Suddenly, she felt the warmth on her legs and the shame in her face. A dripping noise drew Kent's eyes to the puddle at Trish's feet. Trish was angry and scared, and she couldn't believe this was happening. The humiliation of it all was unbearable. She wanted to be brave and strong; she wanted to fight, and she was standing here whimpering and pissing herself.

"Well, I guess you really had to go, sweetheart. You weren't lying after all. I'm sorry I didn't believe you."

He left her standing there and grabbed a towel off the kitchen counter. He was gently wiping her legs, and she was having a hard time standing with her ankles bound together. This was horrifying.

"I'm sorry," Trish blubbered, "I'm sorry. Please. Please, can you just let me clean myself up? Please? I promise I'll be good."

"Shhhh…" was all he said as he sat her back down in the

chair and calmly tied her to it once more. He wiped the tears and snot off her face with the same towel he had used to wipe the urine off her legs. She almost retched, but managed to hold it down.

Poor thing was such a mess. Maybe all the excitement of being with Kent was too much. The champagne, the flowers, and the candy, his rugged good looks – she was overwhelmed that was all. Something was missing. Damn, how could he have forgotten candlelight? He left the room once more for a moment.

Trish could search the drawer again for a knife, but the consequences if he caught her in the act could be dire. She wiggled a little, and felt a small relief. The ropes around her waist weren't as tight as before. In fact, they felt really, really loose. In fact, she could turn her upper body just enough to see he had forgotten to double-up the knot, and she could bring her hands around just enough to pull the rope…, and she could feel it. One good wiggle and her body would be free. She could stand up. He was coming down the hall! She put the rope as close to her body as she could, and very carefully turned the chair toward the direction he'd be coming in the hopes he wouldn't notice her waist was free.

He entered the kitchen. Her chair was angled differently. He eyed her suspiciously. Trish beamed a big smile at him, and forced cheerfulness.

"You're back!" she said as if she'd never been happier to see anyone in her life.

He swelled with pride. She was really starting to take to him!

"So, my beautiful girl, you missed my handsome face?"

Trish would have loved the opportunity to laugh in this guy's ugly face, but that would be a really bad choice. Did this guy actually think he was handsome? Was he utterly deluded? He must be. And she must play along. She swallowed hard.

"Yes, I guess I did."

Kent put a candle in a brass holder on the table and lit it.

"Would you like to hear some music?"

She really didn't. If there was any chance she would ever hear anyone coming along, she wanted the opportunity to scream. The last thing she wanted was music drowning out any sounds from outside that might give her clues to her whereabouts, or a chance of rescue if anyone could hear her scream.

"I thought it would be nice if we could just sit quietly and talk. Get to know each other a little better." Trish shifted uncomfortably in her seat. She was still wet from peeing herself. Disgusted, she realized wiggling wasn't such a good idea. He might notice the loosened ropes on her waist.

"Oh, I think a little music would be romantic."

Kent made his way over to a very out-dated looking stereo system. Was that a record player? Trish couldn't believe anyone still had one of those. He put on a record, and this classical-sounding music started to play. Trish had no idea what it was, but whatever it was, she would always hate it. It would probably be the last music she ever heard, but she pushed that thought out of her mind.

He came back over to the table and picked up the champagne flutes. He handed her one, which she did her best to hold with her bound hands, but if she drank it, she would spill it. Oh well, better covered in champagne than piss.

"Here, sweetheart," Kent took the glass from her, "let me help you."

He held up the two glasses and proposed a toast.

"To us!"

He held one glass to her lips, and she drank it. She actually didn't want any alcohol in her system, because she wanted to keep her wits about her, but she was also dying of thirst, and imagined he would get angry if she refused him. He took a small sip of champagne and put the flutes down on the table. He fed Trish a piece of chocolate, which tasted like ashes in her mouth. She loved chocolate, but this was the worst thing she'd ever tasted. *I guess when it's a piece of chocolate fed to you by a lonely psycho who plans on killing you, it kind of loses its sweetness.* She wanted the horrible taste out of her mouth.

"May I have another sip of champagne?"

"Of course, my princess."

He gently held the glass to her lips, and she drank just enough to get the ashy taste out of her mouth.

"Thank you," she said.

"You're so pretty," Kent said as he leaned closer to her. He considered kissing her, but it might be too soon. A gentleman should be patient.

"Thank you," Trish said again.

"This is the part where you compliment me," Kent said, with a hint of danger in his voice.

Trish stared at him. What did he want her to say? She was afraid if she said the wrong thing, he would get mad. He had told her she was pretty. Did he want her to tell him he was handsome? She searched for one attractive thing about him. Even if he wasn't a psycho who had tied her to a chair, he'd still be ugly.

"Tell me how handsome I am."

Okay, well at least she knew what he wanted to hear. Be a good actress, Trish, you've got to make this believable. She remembered a drama class she had taken, just for fun, her sophomore year in high school. Her friend Tiffany had talked her into it. She didn't really get all that excited about it. Maybe she should have paid more attention. She passed the class because she did what was asked of her, not because she had any talent. What had her teacher said to her after a particularly painful attempt at performing a monologue for the class?

*Trish, stop acting. Acting isn't really what we need to do to be believable. Stop acting. Just **be**.*

Just be. Suddenly, it made sense. Just be. Right now, in this moment, her very survival depended on *being* with this man. He had power over her life, whether she liked it or not. She met his eyes.

"You're so very handsome," Trish said. "It takes my breath away."

Kent was pleased with that answer.

"I desire you very much, my darling," Kent said to her. Since they'd been here, he hadn't used her name once. He called her pet names, but he hadn't called her "Trish" since he talked to her on the street. He was creating distance. He was de-personalizing her. On TV shows, cops were always telling grieving parents and loved ones to appeal to killers and kidnappers by making the victim real. She needed to be real to him. She was playing out some sick fantasy, and when that fantasy started to deteriorate, as fantasies always do, he would kill her.

"Trish," she said.

"What, my sweet?"

"My name is Trish. You know that," she started nervously. She sensed his rage growing. He didn't want her making the rules. She had to play this carefully.

"I just like the way it sounds, Kent, when you say my name. It makes me feel special. I want to be special to you."

"You are special. You are. You're the one," he said.

"So tell me, Kent," she used his name again, "Tell me I'm

special and say my name."

Kent was unsettled. What was she doing? She was acting strangely. She really wasn't like the others. She wasn't begging to be let go. She was talking to him. He didn't trust her though. He'd been hurt before, by so many women. They always let him down. They always disappointed him. He was afraid she was up to something. He wasn't going to fall for it. She wasn't going to manipulate him into letting down his guard. He was the man. He was in command. He was going to make the rules. He needed to trust her first. He needed to know how much she cared, how much she loved him.

"Do you love me?" he asked her.

Trish didn't move a muscle. She worked to keep her face expressionless. She had to tell him. She had to make him believe it. But what was the point? No matter what, no matter how many insane things he made her say, he would never let her go. *He's going to kill me, and he wants me to tell him I love him first.*

"I love you," she choked out the words. Well, screw it, she was no actress. She'd known that since she was 15 years old. She eyed him icily. He didn't care. He didn't care if it was true or not, he just wanted to hear the words. He was standing and swaying back and forth with his eyes barely open.

"Tell me again how much you love me," he said.

Trish's face was damp with tears and fear-filled sweat.

"I love you," she said, with bitterness and hatred in her voice.

"Tell me what a nice time you're having, how I'm such a gentleman, how much you desire me, that you love me; you want me..." he trailed off as Trish stared in dismay. Was she even supposed to remember all this drivel? And then what? Just keep parroting his own stupid words back at him, until... until what? Until he killed her?

Trish was sick of this. *Let him kill me. Waiting to die has got to be worse torture than actually dying.*

"Do I need to remember your list of amazing qualities in any particular order, or can I just rattle things off at fucking random?" Trish said sarcastically.

Kent went blind with rage. *I knew it! I knew she was a potty-mouthed little whore.*

The sting was harsh when he slapped her face. She was afraid she'd fall out of the chair, and he'd see... he'd see that the rope was not tied around her waist. She planted her bound feet firmly on the floor and willed her body to stay in the chair.

"I'm a gentleman! And a gentleman never raises his hand to a lady! So what does that make you? Are you a lady, *Trish*? Are you?"

Warm, sticky blood oozed out of her left nostril. He'd said her name, but it didn't sound like such a good thing. He didn't want to have a real-life woman in here; he wanted his fantasy. She wasn't it anymore. She was just Trish, potty-mouthed little whore who was going to die.

"No, Kent, I guess I'm no lady."

Kent sat down, unbearably sad. Things had been going so well. What went wrong? Trish's face, with so much blood on it, and under that blood her fear, was entirely his doing. How could he have raised his hand to her? He was a gentleman! This was no way to behave. It was all so horribly distasteful.

"I'm so sorry, baby; I'm sorry I raised my hand. That was wrong of me. I need to be more patient with you. You still love me, don't you? Don't you? Tell me, tell me you love me."

Trish didn't think she could do it one more time, but he was coming closer to her. He stood up and he was getting so close. He picked up the bottle of lotion off the table.

"I love you," she said, hoping he would just sit back down and not do whatever he had planned for her next.

But Trish had no such luck. He came toward her, and she could see his erection. *Oh no, he is going to rape me first. Please just kill me. Please don't rape me too. Please just kill me. No, I can't die. I want out of here.*

Kent grabbed her hands and squirted a generous glob of lotion on them. He set the bottle back down and started massaging the lotion into her hands. He was moaning and moving his pelvis back and forth.

Trish's brain was screaming in silent shock. What the hell was going on? He was in his own world now, and she wasn't really a part of it. She was nothing but hands. He saw nothing else, no other part of her. She was only a pair of hands.

"Oh, yes, you love me so much, oh your hands feel so good on me," he moaned as he continued to massage lotion into her hands with his left hand.

His right hand moved to his pants zipper. Trish began to heave aching sobs as he pulled his small, but erect penis out of his pants. He moaned again and continued to tell her, finally, exactly what he wanted.

"I want your hands on me; it feels so good, just put your hands on me…"

He told her to put his hands on him, but he did it for her. Kent was so excited. This felt so right. He pulled Trish's tightly bound wrists toward him and put his stiff member between her soft palms. Finally, he would get the sweet release he had waited for. She was so special. He could feel how much she loved him, how much she wanted him. He was grinding against her soft sweet flesh, sinking into the exquisite touch of her feminine hands. He was in such a state of bliss, he didn't notice the rope had completely fallen away from Trish's waist.

Just as she was thinking, *I hope I die so I don't have to live with this memory,* she noticed it. The rope from her waist was on the floor. She could stand.

She just didn't know if she should.

FORTY-SIX

Grace's strength lasted for only a matter of hours after Erick had left. Eventually, the pain and tears came in their typical, relentless fashion. She called Natalie every day for weeks, for moral support. Natalie was her usual fantastic self, but Grace didn't want to bug her all the time. Nat had finally met a guy whom she actually liked, and they were really hitting it off. Grace fantasized about Erick showing up and saying how sorry he was, and that he'd been an idiot, and, of course, he loved her. And then she and Erick, and Natalie and her new boyfriend whom she refused to call her boyfriend (it was too soon), would all go out on a double date, and after that everyone would go home happy and have crazy (but loving) sex. *The End.* However, of course, Erick didn't call. Or text. Or e-mail. Or smoke signal. Or concoct elaborate schemes to chase her through an airport or buy her a submarine that was also a hot-air balloon filled with flower petals and champagne. The hours crawled into days, days into weeks, and Grace forced herself to face the truth. She had given him an ultimatum, and she was having a hard time dealing with the consequences. She told herself it was better to go through this now. If she had continued to see him, she would have just gotten deeper in, and it would hurt even more when it ended.

She sat across from Natalie at a trendy wine bar having overpriced wine – only $9 for four ounces during happy hour! – and lamenting her loss as best she could while feeling horribly guilty that she was raining on Nat's shiny new love parade.

"I'm sorry," Grace said as she fought back more tears, "I need to talk about something else. I made my choice. He made his. It's for the best. I need to live with it, and move on. Let's talk about you. How's it going with Zach?"

Natalie smiled pensively.

"I'm afraid to like him too much."

"Well, it's scary. Like leads to love. Love leads to despair and isolation."

Natalie laughed.

"Ah, Grace, the hopeless romantic... I can always count on you for inspiration!"

"I'm sorry. I was trying to sound joke-y, but I'm afraid everything sounds bitter and cynical coming from me."

"So, I guess you haven't heard from him?"

"No," said Grace as she looked out the window, almost as if she was hoping he would be there, even though he had absolutely no reason to be. "He hasn't contacted me. And he won't. I shouldn't –"

Natalie's phone beeped. Her eyes darted uncomfortably toward it. Grace could spot a lover's text message a thousand hundred million miles away, through dust storms and fog and cumulus clouds, through the smoke of a burning city, surrounded by burning villages. She knew the expression that Natalie hurriedly pushed off her face – the furtive glance, hopeful, then happy, next the moment when you tell your heart not to appear too eager, and your sense of proprietary manners dictates you not be rude to the people around you. Grace sensed Natalie mentally chewing her fingers off not to read it, not to respond. She knew that feeling, missed it, grappled with the jealous pangs and the guilt that follows because you want your heart to be happy for your friend, and not bitter about your own loss. Grace acted like she was interested in the hors d'oeuvres, which were really pretty pathetic, so pathetic, in fact, she was glad she had no appetite. Natalie pulled her focus to the moment in front of her, and off Zach's text message.

"So, a tiny bowl of Kalamata olives really constitutes an appetizer? And what are they charging for this shit anyway? Probably seven dollars. Do you want to order some real food?" Natalie's eyes unwillingly darted toward her phone.

"Just check the message, Nat."

"I don't want to be rude. I want to focus on what you're saying."

"I have nothing new to say. It's the same, old tired shit. Just text him back."

Natalie put on her best *okay-if-you-say-so* face and texted Zach.

"He wants to meet me later for dinner."

Grace smiled. She really was happy for Natalie. Natalie deserved a great guy. She hoped this guy Zach was a great guy, and not a giant ass-face like Erick. He should never have led her on. No, it was her fault. She was a mess. Why would someone like that, hell why would *anyone*, love Grace? She was a lemon after all.

"Grace… are you okay?" Natalie's words pulled on Grace. Grace struggled to come back to Natalie's voice, but the undertow dragged her down. The same-old grief; grief that was always waiting for her… sink or swim… Grace could do neither. The current pulled her down, tossed her about, threw her onshore, dragged her out to sea, pulled her under and yanked her back up. She had no control. There was Grace, and there was Grace's Pain, and her Pain would always win.

Grace! I'm losing you! Come back!

Was Natalie yelling? Was she yelling out loud in this trendy little wine bar in Culver City? Was Grace crying in public again? Was she making a scene? *Pull back, Grace. Come on, you can do it. Come back.*

"I'm okay… am I crying or something?"

"Or something," Natalie's voice was weighted with worry.

"He doesn't love me." Grace wasn't sure if she was crying. She couldn't feel her face. She wasn't sure if it was even still there. She must be fading into oblivion. *That must be what happens when no one loves you.* You just fade away. You become nothing, because you are nothing.

"Yes, he does. He just doesn't know it."

Grace laughed in spite of herself, but it was a bitter laugh.

"Well, it doesn't do me any good if he doesn't know it."

"I don't get it, Grace. I really don't. I've seen the way he looks at you. If that's not love, then I guess I don't have the slightest clue about what love looks like. And maybe I don't."

Natalie's phone beeped again. She kept her eyes on Grace, but with some effort. Grace let her off the hook.

"Go to dinner with Zach."

"Come with us!"

"Oh yeah, that'll be fun. I'm sure Zach would love that. 'Oh, hey baby, I know this relationship is new, and therefore, super hot and sexy, but I brought my mopey friend Grace along. See how she can turn a simple evening out into tear-filled misery in three easy steps!'"

Natalie promised to call Grace later; Grace insisted Nat not worry or ruin her romantic evening, and Grace headed home. She no longer had the energy for tears. Nothing really mattered anymore. *So what? So I met someone I'm crazy about, for the first time in my life? It doesn't mean anything. It does me no good. Love cannot exist in a vacuum. Love needs love to breathe, to live. Love needs love. My love has nowhere to go.*

She was so distracted that she didn't notice the shadowy figure waiting on her doorstep.

FORTY-SEVEN

Erin Taylor managed her temper as she navigated the shitty L.A. traffic. L.A. didn't have normal rush hour. It seemed that nobody in L.A. really had a job. "Executive" and "corporate" positions didn't mean you worked 9 to 5. It meant you were working in PR, Marketing, Advertising, a Law Firm or a Talent Agency. It meant if you were a loser, a bottom feeder who worked in the mailroom or had to suffer the indignities of being some pompous asshole's personal assistant, you were in the office at 7 a.m. and left at 10 p.m., or maybe you were running around all day, dropping off scripts, or picking up dry cleaning, or getting your boss' Shih-Tzu groomed. Which meant you were in the car. All day. And if you were, in fact, the Big Shot Executive? You could go into the office whenever you wanted. "I have to be in the office in the morning," if you were somebody, meant you had to drag yourself in by 10:30 a.m., right after your sunrise meditation and morning yoga class that you didn't actually make it to, but you tell everyone you did, as you tell yourself you'll drop last night's vodka-cran calories with a high-colonic later.

Take Fountain. Bette Davis' famous words about how to navigate L.A. Yeah sure, Ms. Davis, maybe in the 1940's Fountain was a lovely street to take, but now, all the pathetic kids fresh off the bus from Ohio, their résumés plastered with their college theatre roles, were taking Fountain, and it was becoming just as bad a cluster-fuck as any other street.

Erin knew her city, and she loved it, but she hated sitting in traffic at all hours simply because so many idiots wanted to be actors, and they had auditions *all day. All over town.*

She navigated her way on various side streets, up and over, up and over, don't go there; you'll never get your left turn there, try that one, until she finally made her way to Franklin Berry Organic Smoothies. Looking for a place to park was almost as fun as needing to take a left on Melrose after 3 p.m., but it was worth it. She couldn't let it get to her. She had a murderer to catch. She took a deep breath, and did one of her nearly foolproof tricks for finding a parking place in L.A.: she manifested it. If she said that to any of the other detectives she worked with, they'd probably laugh their asses off, but by shit, it worked. It really did. Good advice she'd give anyone trying to park in L.A.: if it looks like an open spot that means it's probably illegal to park there. If you see what looks like a vacancy, you will discover when you get closer, there's not a space to park in after all. Perhaps there's a tiny Smart Car parked there that you didn't see until you got nearer, or there's a fire hydrant, or a valet-only stand (yes, you even have to valet to go to the gym), or best of all, a stack of parking signs so ridiculous and confusing not even an L.A. native can be sure they are correctly interpreting them. No Parking Wednesday from 8 a.m. to 12 p.m., except by permit 6 p.m. to 8 a.m., Two hour parking only from 9 a.m. to 6 p.m., No stopping 4 p.m. to 6 p.m., Passenger Loading Only 7 a.m. to 9 a.m. except Sunday, Valet Only 6 p.m. to 12 a.m., all on the same parking spot. It's nearly impossible to navigate, so the general rule of thumb: if it was legal to park there, somebody already would have. Erin focused her mental powers on Franklin Avenue, outside the Organic Smoothie shop. She cruised the street slowly enough that she could slip into an available spot before anyone else noticed it, but fast enough to keep douche bags from honking and screaming – like they had someplace to be other than at their Recurring Guest Star on an Inaccurate Cop Show audition.

I need a parking space to appear... right now...

Just then, a smallish SUV pulled out into traffic. Perfect timing. Yup, it worked.

Erin pulled into the spot, and saw the green light on the meter (still money in it!) and assessed the bullshit of the parking signs. *All good.*

She put on her best power-strut and went inside for her first ever organic smoothie experience, which, of course, would not in any way involve ordering, buying or drinking pro-biotic yogurt blended with hydroponic raspberries served in a seven dollar recycled cup.

She walked like she was on a mission, which she was. She walked like she wasn't disgusted by corporations throwing around words like "organic" to make a buck, which she was. She walked like she was going to solve a murder, which she was.

Okay, so it wasn't horrible inside. It was just trendy. All right, maybe it was horrible. Live green algae??? In a shot??? Four fucking dollars? An ounce? What the hell ever happened to tequila shots? Good god, the world was doomed. Holy crap, heroin was cheaper than this shit. Well, bad heroin anyway.

Erin shifted her mind to the task at hand. She assessed the room. Lauren came here a lot. She'd called Eileen Cambridge to confirm that detail. Yea, Lauren loved this place; swore by the healing benefits. Sadness washed over Erin – the kind of sadness she'd have to dismiss to stay focused. Lauren was a gorgeous woman. The kind of woman who wanted to stay that way; who spent hours at the gym, getting facials, putting on sunscreen, and drinking live green algae. All of that work to stay young and beautiful and some maniac comes along, cuts off her perfectly manicured hands, and throws her in a dumpster.

I'm coming for you asshole, she thought, as she approached the pretty, pink-haired, nose-ringed girl at the counter.

"How can I improve your life today?" she chirped.

Erin stared. *What. The. Fuck. People couldn't just ask to take your order? They had to improve your life?*

She flashed her badge at pixie nose-ring girl.

"Detective Erin Taylor; I need to ask you a few questions."

If a pixie could get any paler, Erin had never seen it until now.

"Um… okay… officer… I really tried to get the phone back. I called, like a bunch of numbers in it, and everything, and I guess it was already reported or something, and I only used it for like, a couple of texts, and then…"

Erin spotted her name tag. *Raynebough*. Of course. Even Rainbow was too trite now.

"Raynebough… I'm not here for you, specifically. I just need to talk to anyone who works the weekday morning shift, normally. How long have you worked here?"

"Three days."

Probably a long career for Raynebough.

"Okay, who can I talk to then?"

"Well, Shad is like, the manager, or whatever." *The Manager, or Whatever*; Erin wondered if that was his official title.

"Great, can you get Chad for me, and get back to your customers?"

"It's Shad. With an S."

Of course. Erin considered responding, but a tired half-smile would more than get her message across.

The terrified pixie scurried over to a skinny guy with bad skin and whispered to him. Chad – no wait, *Shad* – gave Raynebough his toughest *I'll handle this* look and sauntered toward Erin.

"Can I help you, Detective?"

Erin tried to think of something more fun than interviewing a 6-foot-two, 95-pound 20-year-old that looked 15 and thought he looked 30, but a lot of things were more fun than that.

"I hope so," said Erin, turning on the teensiest bit of older-but-still-hot-because-I'm-experienced-enough-to-blow-your-mind charm, only because it would work wonders on a kid like this. It did. He was over 6 feet; she had to lie to get to 5 feet, and she towered over him.

Shad gulped. He had seen enough detective shows on TV to know that when a cop came to interview you, you either got the handsome guy, the ugly guy, or the hot badass chick. He was so excited he got the hot badass chick.

"Do you know this woman?" Erin held the picture out for Shad. Immediate recognition in his eyes.

"Yeah, yeah, she used to come in here a lot. I haven't seen her in a while."

"Did she come in alone?"

"Yea, always alone. Well, a couple of times with this older lady. But not in a long time. Mostly, she was alone. I overheard her on the phone a couple of times, or saw her texting, you know, I guess getting another person's order, cause those days she'd order two things. But mostly, she was in here alone, always ordered the same thing."

"Did you ever notice any other customers talking to her? A man, for instance?"

"Say," Shad said with genuine concern, "Did something happen to her?"

"Yes. And I want to find anyone who can help me figure out what."

"Well, she's really pretty, so a lot of guys, some girls too, would smile at her, and say 'hi' and stuff, but she was kind of... I don't know. She wasn't mean or anything. But kind of intimidating? I guess. You know, I only talked to her to take her order. There was this one guy though... creepy dude used to come in here. Haven't seen him in a while either."

"Really? And he talked to her?" Erin's heart raced as she took furious notes.

"Yeah... well, he tried. She didn't look too... what's the word?" Shad grinned sheepishly. "Receptive."

"Did you hear anything they said? Did they leave together?"

"No, I didn't hear anything. Early morning is kinda crazy in here and whatnot. He was just clueless… you know. She was totally out of his league, *like totally*, and he still tried to talk to her."

"What did he look like?"

"Average Joe. No, wait… Below Average Joe." Shad chuckled a bit at his own joke. Erin was too excited to lose patience with him. She might really be on to something here. This could be the guy.

"Go on… height? Hair color?"

"Not tall, not short. I don't know. Shorter than me, I guess, but not a little dude. Brown hair, what was left of it… balding… you know, and a comb-over. Dude, that shit was sad," Shad caught himself, "Oh man… I mean ma'am… I'm sorry."

"It's okay, Shad, just go on."

"Well, he was a big guy. I don't know if it's cool to call people fat. Is that cool? Is it like un-PC or whatever?"

"Shad," Erin said with as much patience as she could muster, "I don't give a shit about bad words or being politically correct. I just need to know what he looked like. You're doing great. This is really helpful. So, he was fat?"

"Yeah, dude was pretty fat. Well, like a big belly, you know. Not in shape."

"Got it. Listen, would you be open to coming down to the station and talking to one of our artists? You could describe this guy, and we could maybe get a sketch."

"Oh man, I can draw him!"

"Really?" Well, it probably wasn't Shad's dream to work at Franklin Berry forever. Of course, he had hidden talents.

"Yea, I can draw him. I mean, it won't be perfect, 'cause

I haven't seen him in a while, you know; I do better with a live model. But I can go a bit from memory."

"How fast can you do it?"

Shad scanned the room nervously.

"Well, can I get it to you later? I mean, I really need to get back to work. I'm the Manager and stuff." (Manager and Stuff was probably a higher position than Manager or Whatever).

"I understand. Could you possibly draw it on your break?" He probably didn't want to spend his break drawing some creepy guy, but Erin couldn't bear to leave here without more information. Every cell in her body was sure this was their man.

"Yeah, sure I can do that, Detective… or Lady Detective… I have a fifteen-minute break at 11. I was going to use it to smoke, but smoking is bad, right? It's probably better to help the police."

"Yeah, Shad. Smoking is bad. Helping the police is good. I'd really appreciate it if you could do this for us. I'm happy to wait here until then." Erin smiled with the slightest hint of flirtation.

"Cool, cool," said Shad. "Hey, since you're gonna be waiting, do you wanna have one of our Bee Pollen Blasts? I can give you my employee discount. Bee pollen's really great for your brain and everything."

"You know what, Shad? I'd love to try a Bee Pollen Blast." She wouldn't really love to try a Bee Pollen Blast, but Shad was an angel, and she could tell it would make him happy to blend up a ridiculous hippie smoothie for her.

Erin sat in a corner as the Angelenos came in with their money and left with their overpriced cups of trendy antioxidants. The bright California sun beamed through the window, and the condensation from her cup dripped onto the warm surface of the table. She sipped her smoothie.

Hell, this Bee Pollen Blast isn't half bad. It just might give me the energy I need to catch a killer. She caught Shad's eye, raised her cup and smiled a "thank you." He blushed and went back to his duties as Manager and Stuff.

FORTY-EIGHT

He was getting frustrated. Usually, a woman's hands were enough to get him to the point of bliss, but Trish was all wrong. She was all wrong. He could see it in her eyes. She would leave him. She didn't love him. He knew it. Why? Why did this keep happening? Why wouldn't she stop crying? She was getting less pretty. Blood and snot ran out of her nose, and her make-up was smeared from all her unnecessary tears. He had done so many nice things for her, and she didn't appreciate it. Not one bit.

He kept trying though. He pulled hard on the ropes on her wrists. She yelped.

"What's the matter?" No sweetness remained in his voice. Trish was starting to panic. It was as if she could see a display... digital numbers on a clock... no, it was a timer... like when a bomb is set to go off. *She knew.* She was living in the last moments of her life. There was no way out. She would never marry. She would never have children. Suddenly, the only thing she wanted was to grow old. How lucky are women who get wrinkles. They get to live. Trish would give anything for wrinkles. She would give anything to live. She would pay any price. But she knew. Tick. Tock. The numbers ticked off, as if on a giant movie screen; her heart raced. *Please get here in time. Please save me.* Who was she talking to? No one was coming.

Kent kept tightening the ropes. He was yanking her hands harder and harder.

This would never end. Maybe it would be better to die. Better than going on and on like this. At this thought, her mind spiraled into a rage, red and black at once, and blinding, the brightest darkness she could ever imagine, could never imagine. She was so fucking angry. How could this be? How could this be how she would die?

She screamed. SHE SCREAMED. She screamed a scream so loud she hoped her mother would hear it, all the way across the miles that separated them. She screamed for her sister. She screamed for the daughters and sons she would never have. It was one moment, miniscule and infinite in one. *There is no time. There is every moment I've lived and every moment I will never have, right now.* She stood up.

Fuck this shit. Fuck him. I will die fighting.

Kent could not believe the screams. Unlike any of the others. They all cried. They all begged. They all screamed, eventually. But not like this. There was no fear in it. There was only a defiant rage piercing the air around them. He had a moment of panic, terrified someone might hear, terrified of what she might do, but then he remembered. He was in command. He was the man. He grabbed the filthy dish towel and crammed it in her mouth and held it there.

She was still standing. Her bound hands clawed helplessly at his stupid dick. His stupid idiot dick, getting more flaccid by the moment. She could taste her own blood, her own tears, and her own urine on the towel he shoved in her mouth. It didn't matter. The screams were already out there. She could see them, whirling in the air around them, whirling like angry dust mites hell-bent on revenge. *You have killed many. You will kill many more, but you will never forget me. I will be the one you feared. I saw it in your eyes, asshole.*

She was falling to the floor, greeted only by the sticky plastic underneath her. He was off balance. She spat out the filthy towel. She pulled her bound ankles up to her chest and thrust them out as he came down on her. Her left ankle wrenched, a snapping noise, a bone, fractured, but she made it, landed her feet square into his chest and pushed with everything she had. She felt the anger of all of them, every woman he had taken. She saw them. She felt them, and she kicked for them too. He fell back on to the floor, stunned. In that moment, she twisted her broken ankle harder, on purpose, using the brokenness to free it from the restraints. With her feet free she went for him. She was no match for his weight. She cursed her fragile 115-pound frame. She was on top of him, clawing at his face with her bound hands, wrenching her wrists at the same time. *Break your wrists; get your hands free.* But it was too late. He was getting his wind back. He shoved her off of him and rolled on top of her. Her ribs could crack under the weight of him. She spat in his face.

He put his hands on her throat. Was he crying?

"How could you? I loved you, loved you so much, you were the one…"

She struggled, but the pain that came was the blackest, most horrible thing she could ever have imagined, could never have imagined.

Air. Please. Air. Please. Air.

His pleading words were getting so far away, and she pushed them further.

NO! Your voice will not be the last thing I hear. Your face will not be the last thing I see.

The pain. Air. But there is no air.

Please… make it stop.

Please… mommy… Illy… I love you so much.

She could see her Daddy now. He was there. He'd be there for her. He was waiting.

"I will always love you, Trish."

Kent was saying it, but Trish heard her father's voice. She saw her father's face.

I'm so sorry, Daddy, she told him, *I fought as hard as I could.*

I know, said her Daddy, *so did I. It's okay.*

It's okay, Trish said. And then it was.

It was done.

FORTY-NINE

Kent sat for a moment. He missed her already. He always missed them when they left. But he still had a part of her. He still had her warmth.

He reached out and untied her hands. Her wrists were raw and bruised, but the palms of her hands were still soft and warm. That wouldn't last. He didn't have much time left with her. Soon, she would be icy cold. It's what happens; the whole of them eventually became as cold as their hearts had always been.

He went out to the garage for his supplies. He returned and made sure the plastic drop cloth was evenly spread out. He hated to make a mess, but there was no other way.

He held her hands again. He wanted to hold those hands forever. He'd always loved a woman's hands. They were the most beautiful part of a woman's body.

His member stirred. He anticipated the release that would come, once her hands were free to pleasure him.

Everything was delicious. Everything was warm.

FIFTY

"Hey you."

Grace shrieked.

Erick stepped out of the shadows, right outside her front door.

"Shit. You scared me."

"I'm sorry. I didn't think... I was just... I don't know, Grace. I miss you, I guess."

Grace stared at Erick for a moment. She held back tears of frustration, of anger, hope and anticipation. She didn't know what to say.

"Why are you here, Erick?"

"I don't know, Grace. I miss you. I..." Erick stood there, dumbfounded, like he wasn't sure why, in fact, he was there.

Unspoken words hung in the air. She had told him to leave if he didn't love her. If he couldn't say it. So he could say, "I..." but he couldn't choke out "love" or "you." How very typical.

"You look beautiful."

Grace stared at him. She had no idea how she looked. She didn't really care all that much, which surprised her. In a mixture of numbness and excitement, she wanted to grab him and pull him inside, or push him down the stairs, but she couldn't decide which. Finally, she couldn't stand the awkwardness anymore.

"I'm going inside," she said, pointedly not inviting him.

He stood there, staring, as she unlocked the door and went inside. She turned to him; he was standing like a sheepish little boy, but more dangerous because she loved him so much her heart seized up when he was near. She considered just shutting the door in his face. Normally, that would be a rude thing to do. But when you love someone, really love someone, like a field of wild fires and an ocean of forever, all at once, and that someone doesn't love you back, then it's probably all right to throw social protocol out the door and down the stairs and protect your heart.

"Grace. Please." Was he whining? Maybe a little. He was pathetic. Pathetic, and really, really cute.

"Please what? What do you want from me?"

There was silence. Erick really hadn't planned out anything beyond the part where he showed up like a romantic stalker and made things awkward. Maybe in his mind Grace would have taken him in her arms by now and made him feel... whatever it was he felt when he was with her... terrified safety.

"I don't know. Do you have any chili?"

Grace supposed he felt awkward and scared, that he was deflecting from real intimacy by making a joke, but it wasn't good enough. Whatever he'd been feeling, even if he'd missed her, she had been dying. Her heart died a little bit every day that he didn't call to tell her he loved her, and that he was stupid for leaving. Her heart had been dying bit by bit, for seventeen days, six hours, and she wasn't sure how many minutes. *I mean, who's counting?*

"Erick... I've said it already. I love you. Now, fuck off."

His face fell with hurt for a moment before he muttered, "You don't mean that."

"Chili? You want chili? Well, I'm fucking out of chili, Erick. And I'm out of patience."

She shut the door in his face. She considered crying, but held it back. She didn't want him to hear that. He was most certainly still lurking outside the door.

She set her purse on the couch and sat down, shaking. It was killing her to do this. She was an idiot. She wanted to let him in. She could. She could just open the door...

He'll hurt you Grace. He'll hurt you so motherfucking bad.

Beep, beep. Grace's phone alerted her to a text. She read it with blurry eyes.

Knock. Knock.

Of course. He just had to act cute. She was furious. And thrilled.

She went to the door and opened it. He was staring at his phone, waiting for a beep back. The expression on his face was one she'd never seen before. She couldn't describe it. She'd never be able to. Later, when she reflected on this moment, she still wouldn't know what his face was saying.

I do love you, but I'm a coward?

I don't know what the hell is going on?

I am trying really hard – ha ha – hard – not to get a boner?

I really do just want some chili?

She'd never know because he'd never really give her the truth. He'd tell her things. Things that were true for her, but not really anything but words that got tangled up in feelings, which lay trapped below the surface of the things that kept him safe.

"What do you want, Erick?"

"You. I just want you."

It's romantic in the movies. But in real life, being wanted wasn't enough. She wanted to be loved.

"I really need you to go. I meant everything I said before. I'm tired, Erick. I don't want to get into this anymore. We have nothing more to talk about."

"Please, let me come in. Please. We can talk. Just talk. I promise I'll be good."

"It's not about being good..." Grace paused. Her resolve was wearing thin. "You hurt me. I've been hurt so much... enough. I can't do anymore. I can't do this if you're going to hurt me. And you will. It's the nature of love. Love, and I'm the only one in it."

"So I can't come in? Just for a few minutes?"

This was infuriating.

"If you can tell me what you want – and I don't mean chili, or some stupid shit you use to deflect intimacy – I mean tell me really and truly what you want from me, I'll let you in."

Erick took a breath. He told her what he wanted.

"I want you, Grace. I want to be the reason you smile. That's all… I just… I… you should have a reason to smile…"

Grace relented.

"You can come in, but there will not be sex. Got it? You're going home. You're not sleeping here."

"Okay. Of course."

They sat down next to each other on the couch. It was quiet. He reached for her hand. She gently withdrew it.

"I'm sorry. I just miss you so much," he said.

"I'm sure you do. I miss you too. But it's worse for me."

"I doubt that, Grace."

"How so?" Grace was exasperated. Pathetic and confused silence was all he gave her.

"Erick, I told you how I feel. I'm done now. If you don't love me, there is nothing more to discuss. All the missing and wanting aren't enough. I'm not trying to pressure you. I don't want you to lie, and say things you don't mean. I just need you to respect what I'm saying, and what I'm asking. I cannot be with someone I love who doesn't love me back. I just can't. It's excruciating."

"You don't have to be with someone who doesn't love you."

"I know. I don't have to be, so I won't."

"No," Erick said, "That's not what I mean. I mean, be with

me. Be with me, because I love you. I do. I just have a hard time with this stuff. It's…"

He trailed off. Grace waited, hoping he would keep talking. She wasn't sure if she could trust this. He could just be saying he loved her to get her back, not because he really felt it. But really? That was so junior high. Would he really sink that low? She searched his eyes for clues. It looked a hell of a lot like love to her, but maybe she was seeing what she wanted to see.

"It's scary. I know," she consoled him. "It takes a lot of courage to love. I think I can't help loving you, then I think I should stop it somehow, but I tell myself to be brave… but I'm not brave. I'm a mess."

"You are brave, Grace. You are one of the most amazing women I've ever met. And one of the most beautiful too, inside and out. It isn't brave to love you… it's… just there. It makes sense. *We* make sense." He paused; always unable to resist being silly. "Am I making sense?"

Grace smiled for the first time. It affected him. She could see that. He was leaning closer.

"I don't know if we make sense… we make senseless maybe…" Grace trailed off.

He kissed her.

"Can I fuck you senseless?" He said.

What's a girl to do? Romance is hard to resist.

FIFTY-ONE

Melissa and Greg had been at the police station for so long, she had run the gamut of emotions. Panic, frustration, terror, confusion had coursed through her; until now, Melissa was mostly just angry with Greg for letting this happen. He would be grilled really hard by the cops; she figured. After all, he was the boyfriend. Didn't they always suspect spouses and lovers first?

Sooner or later, she, or someone, would have to call Trish's mom. Melissa really hoped it wouldn't be her that had to make that call, or that Trish would just come home, and no one would have to make that call. This was a nightmare. Something was wrong; she was sure of it. This wasn't like Trish. Not at all. No matter how hard she tried to convince the cops that Trish wouldn't just take off, and not tell anyone, they kept insisting it was a possibility. It wasn't a possibility. Not anymore. Too much time had passed. Trish was in trouble. Talking to these cops was starting to feel like a monumental waste of time, but what else could they do? Trish was nowhere, or nowhere where it would make sense for her to be. That could only mean she was somewhere, somewhere where it made no sense.

Someone took her. Someone bad.

Melissa kept turning that over in her head, and every time she did, her stomach would clench like a fist, and she was certain she'd throw up, or cry, or both. She had to stay calm, for Trish's sake. It wouldn't do any good to panic. She needed to keep a clear head. There could be something she was overlooking. Melissa shifted her weight in the uncomfortable plastic chair in the cold hallway. She had been questioned already, and now she sat waiting for Greg to come out. He'd been in there a while. He was a suspect. *Could he have done something to her?* Melissa asked herself. It just didn't seem possible. *I mean, he's a loser, but he's not violent. Hell, he's probably too lazy to do anything violent.* Melissa just couldn't wrap her head around that possibility.

He came out of the interrogation room like a beaten dog. His skin was ashen, and his eyes were red-rimmed.

"Hey," he said.

"You all right?"

"Not really. They think I did something to her." Greg sat down suddenly, as if he would faint if he didn't, as if a huge invisible weight pressed him down into the ugly, yellow, plastic chair next to Melissa. She didn't say a word. What could she say?

"You know I wouldn't do anything to her, don't you?"

"Of course," said Melissa, with more conviction than she felt. Unfortunately for Greg, he didn't really have much in the way of an alibi in the time after Trish got out of his car. He went home, and his roommate was out of town, so no one could vouch for him. He was a wreck. He kept running through every word of the argument, every shitty and inconsiderate thing he'd ever done to Trish, and discovered it was an even more substantial list than he cared to admit. *What an asshole I am.*

"Come on," Melissa added some tenderness to her voice, even though she was angry and scared, "Let's go and get some rest, and then we can start searching a few more places."

It won't matter, said the voice in Melissa's head, but she pushed it away. She had to try. Even worse, she had to muster the courage to call Trish's mom.

*   *   *   *   *

Jillian Morris was quite the looker. She kept a nice figure by using the treadmill in her condo five times a week. She had long blonde hair and elegant features. She looked at least ten years younger than she was. She received plenty of male attention, and she dated some, but she kept her distance more often than not. Certainly, she kept her distance while she was raising her two daughters, all alone, after her husband died. She was perhaps one of those rare breeds, a woman, who really, truly, had been madly in love with her husband. The devastation she felt when he died was only made manageable by her love for Lilly and Trish. She struggled to support them and herself, be a good mom, and had been determined not to be one of those women who re-married simply because she needed a man to help her, or to have a surrogate father for her children. Jillian was a romantic – albeit a rather broken-hearted one – but a romantic just the same. As far as she was concerned – and this was in no way a religious belief, but rather more spiritual in nature – one should marry for love, for no other reason, but only for love. A woman who married for position or possessions was nothing more than a prostitute, and although Jillian was generally kind-hearted enough not to judge women for doing just that, she couldn't live with herself if she did. Her daughters were everything to her. She had maybe been a bit too overprotective when raising them, but she just couldn't bear the thought of losing either one of them. They were very good girls, hadn't really given her a lot of trouble, even when they were teenagers. They had been quite a threesome, in fact. So when Jillian got the call that her beautiful Trish was missing, it was a combination of sheer terror and disbelief that gripped her heart. She simply could not endure anything happening to her baby girl, so she disregarded the nagging fears, the horrible nightmares she'd been having, even before the call came, and spent all her energy creating positive, protective light around her daughter.

She was, immediately, on a plane to California, and she had steeled herself to do whatever it took to pressure the police to find her daughter. She would call every media outlet, max out every credit card, and stop at nothing until Trish was found.

FIFTY-TWO

Grace was in a blanket of euphoria. She and Erick were closer than ever. She couldn't believe how incredible it felt to be with someone whom you actually loved, someone whom it wasn't a chore to talk to, certainly not a chore to have sex with – in fact; every facet of their relationship was better and stronger. Fear still stalked her, because it was too good to be true. She dared not think of that pesky "other shoe" – and how much it enjoyed dropping. And, maybe she could become something other than a lemon. Perhaps she could be a pomegranate or a raspberry, or she could finally learn how to make lemonade with the lemons life threw her. She hadn't been truly happy since the brief time once Kaylee was born, but before Kaylee had gotten sick. This was a distinct kind of happy, not better, just different, and she rationalized that maybe Erick was a sort of consolation prize for all her past suffering. She was truly grateful for him, and for all the unbelievable things he made her feel. So sometimes they were one of those really annoying, totally "in love" couples, but she figured it was maybe her due. Though a nagging voice told her she shouldn't get too attached, she did her best to push it away. Erick loved her, and she loved him. She would have followed him to the ends of the earth, and all that other romantic drivel. No matter what happened, she told herself it was worth the risk to feel like this right now. To have this kind of love, to be this desired merited the risk. Or so she told herself, as she rolled over onto Erick's chest while he slept. She breathed him in. He was asleep, and couldn't hear her, but maybe he would still somehow feel it if she told him.

"I will love you for the rest of my life," she said, and though she was tired, she fought off sleep as long as possible, so she could enjoy a few more minutes in the quiet stillness of love.

FIFTY-THREE

"I got something!" Erin nearly pounced on Dan.

"Great. What is it?" Dan said, with a good-natured grin. He liked to see Erin this excited.

"Well, the kid working at the smoothie shop where Lauren liked to go is an artist, and he did a sketch of a creepy guy who tried to chat her up a few times."

Erin was thrilled with Shad's drawing. So the kid had real talent that went far beyond blending up wheatgrass smoothies. She triumphantly placed the sketch down on Dan's desk. They both stared at it, and a quiet shudder ran between them.

"He looks like… like I thought he would look. You know?" Dan spoke just above a whisper.

"Yeah," said Erin, equally quiet. "This is the guy, don't you think?"

"Maybe," Dan said, as he peered at the drawing. "Well, he's no Ted Bundy, that's for sure."

"Jeez," Erin laughed, "This guy isn't even a John Wayne Gacy."

"Harsh, Taylor, very harsh. But accurate. So, you ready for something else?"

"Yeah. When am I not? Spill it, Garza."

Dan dropped a piece of paper onto the desk next to the sketch. Before Erin could read it, he was already explaining, "BOLO for Patricia Morris, AKA Trish, 24 years old, Caucasian, last seen by her boyfriend Friday night in San Pedro."

"It's the same guy," Erin said.

"Her boyfriend?"

"No," Erin held up the sketch. "This guy. He took this girl Trish, too."

"Taylor, Trish Morris disappeared from San Pedro. That's what? Twenty-five miles south of where Lauren was found?"

"Right. The heat is on him up here. Maybe he headed out of his comfort zone to get away from that. It's the same guy."

"How can you be sure?" Dan asked, though he knew better. She'd say she just knew.

"I just know."

"Of course you do," Dan smiled.

"Don't patronize me, Garza."

"I'm not patronizing you; I just had a – what do cops call that again? Oh yeah, a hunch – that you would say that."

"Go eat a doughnut, asshole." Erin walked off toward the Captain's office with the bulletin and the sketch in her hand.

"Hey! You know I don't eat that crap! It's not politically correct to stereotype! Some cops eat salads!"

* * * * *

Jillian Morris called in a favor to an old friend – well, "old friend" as in a guy she dated for a while two years after her husband died. There hadn't been much of a connection with him; probably she had still been grieving too much, but he had been smitten with her. She kept in loose contact with him via e-mail, and suspected he still carried a torch for her. He had worked for a small paper in New Mexico where they both lived, and eventually got an opportunity to work in Los Angeles and moved there. The career opportunity was once in a lifetime, and he proposed to Jillian before he left. He offered to stay, or take her with him to L.A., but she turned him down. He hadn't been angry with her, and he still hadn't married. Jillian wished he would. She wished him happiness. But right now, she was willing to use any leverage she had to get him to use his media clout to put pressure on the police force. L.A. would probably have a slew of unsettling cases involving missing women, and she wanted Trish to be top priority.

In a sleek and modern office, the intercom buzzed on Marcus Carlton's desk.

"Yes?"

"There's a Jillian Morris on the phone for you, sir."

Marcus Carlton's heart leapt in his chest. The beautiful, elusive, Jillian Morris… the One That Got Away. This was better than a crotch-shot on Oscar Night.

"Jillian!" He nearly squealed, not caring how silly he might sound.

"Marcus. It's so good to hear your voice," Jillian barely managed to say, her own voice catching in her throat, "I'm in Los Angeles, and I need your help. You always said if I ever –"

"Jillian, my love. Anything. Anything at all for you."

Jillian breathed a deep sigh. Maybe there was hope. With enough pressure, maybe the police could find Trish before…

She stopped herself from thinking "before it's too late." It just couldn't be too late. It just couldn't be.

* * * * *

"Taylor," Captain Jacobs said as Erin rushed into her office. "Tell me you've got news. Tell me you've got anything."

"I do. A kid working at a smoothie shop Lauren frequented did a sketch of this guy who tried to chat Lauren up multiple times. " Erin put the sketch down on the Captain's desk. Captain Jacobs took her time absorbing it.

"This is good," said Jacobs. "Kid's got talent."

"Yeah, he does. Maybe we should hire him as a sketch artist," Erin offered, only half joking, before continuing, "Captain, I have a hunch about this BOLO on the Morris girl –"

"I have that hunch too. We don't have much to go on. No body, no hands. No witnesses who saw anything actually happen to her. I've got the media breathing down my neck on Lauren McLaughlin, and now on Trish Morris as well. All we need is for someone to decide there's a serial killer out there – of which there is no proof – and we will have a media firestorm and panicked citizens."

"I know," said Erin. "I think Dan and I should get right to interviewing Lauren's friends and co-workers to see if any of them have ever seen this guy."

"Perfect, Taylor. Do that. I'll send this sketch down to the Pedro office and have the officers there show the sketch to Trish's boyfriend, her roommate, and any other witnesses from the bar Trish and her boyfriend went to the night she disappeared. I don't think we should release the image to the public right now. We've got to finesse this one carefully. Maybe we could release it without incriminating him in anyway. Only say we want to find him because we believe he might have information for us about Lauren. Once he sees his face on TV, or in the papers, we'll be dealing with a whole other ball of crap."

"Yeah," Erin agreed wholeheartedly, "If he does have Trish, he could panic, become enraged. We don't know how reactionary he is, or what kind of ego we're dealing with. Seeing himself in print might change his pattern, and I don't know if that's such a good thing, since we know so little about him."

"Get to those interviews and let me know how it goes."

Erin turned to leave. Just as she hit the door, her hand stopped before touching the knob. She stood perfectly still. She held back a shudder.

"Taylor? You all right?" Joanna Jacobs was genuinely worried. Erin was even more tense than usual.

"I just know we're too late. Trish Morris is already dead. We're too late."

Captain Jacobs swallowed hard, "Maybe not."

Erin turned into Joanna's warm brown eyes. They maintained a soft, liquid look, a look that hoped for Trish's life. But Erin's blue eyes seemed lighter than ever as the glare of the afternoon sun hit them; her eyes were frozen in resolve. They were the eyes of relentlessness. She knew in her heart that Trish was already dead, but she'd find her anyway. Even if she couldn't save Trish's life, somewhere another woman was walking around living her life, not knowing how close she was to death. Erin hoped that maybe she could save that woman. If not her, then maybe the next one. Or the one after that. She would never, ever stop. And neither would he.

FIFTY-FOUR

Grace savored a bite of warm cheesy pizza and then chased it with an icy swig of draft beer. Food was a funny thing. In her dark moments, it was something she could barely choke down. But food that she ate across from Erick was a divine bounty, every morsel a shared sacrament, more sublime than anything she could taste alone. Food eaten solo was merely fuel, but this pizza before her now was one of the finest things she'd ever savored, simply because Erick's eyes were watching her eat it. He loved to watch her eat. There was a time that might have made her self-conscious, to be stared at like that while she ate, but she was relishing it now, simply because of the way his eyes sparkled across the table from her. He wasn't eating, which was strange, because he usually wolfed down food like an animal, but tonight, he just stared at her.

"You don't want any pizza?" she said carefully, hoping she didn't have mushrooms in her teeth.

"No, I do," he said, "I just enjoy watching you."

He raised a frosty glass of beer and locked his eyes tight with hers. She picked up her glass, and they had an unspoken toast, the tinkling of the glasses as they met rang in Grace's heart. She was so *happy*. She didn't really even know what to do with this feeling. She'd had it so rarely in life; she felt like she needed to carry it around in a tightly-woven basket, or a lock-box, or put it in a safe that only angels held the combination to, and she felt this way because she was scared that somehow, having this feeling inside of her, it could get twisted and tainted; it could get ruined. Happiness got ruined when it came in contact with her. Other people knew how to hold on to happiness; Grace didn't. She couldn't really bear it, because she couldn't bear losing it, watching it go, and being unable to stop it from leaving. She couldn't endure the fleeting, elusive nature of it. Why couldn't it just stay? Why did a moment like this run like sand through her fingers, and why did moments of pain paralyze and isolate her in a vacuum of eternity? There was absolutely no way that one minute, sixty seconds, of sitting across from your lover, eating warm pizza and drinking cold beer and staring into each other's eyes was the same amount of time as one minute of lying on the floor, wretched and broken-hearted, crying for your daughter's tiny lost soul. It just wasn't possible. Time made absolutely no sense to Grace. It wasn't just pessimism. It wasn't a debate of whether the glass was half-full or half-empty. It was a matter of whether you were drinking the delicious contents of the glass, or simply drowning in its putrid liquid.

Erick took another swig of beer and put his hand over Grace's.

"Grace?"

She froze. There was something frenzied about him that scared and titillated her.

"Would we still have this much fun if we were married?"

Grace was stunned. Married? This was extremely out of character for Erick. She didn't know what to say. She had no real desire to marry again. She had been pretty miserable when she was married to Stan, but she wasn't sure if that was because she didn't love Stan, or she just didn't like being married. Suddenly, she had no idea how she really felt about it, about the concept of marriage. It had always seemed pointless and, after experiencing the horror of going through a divorce, she never wanted to go down that road – or rather, that aisle – again. But this was different. This man was different. Her feelings were different. Could she marry him? He wasn't really asking. He was doing the cowardly man thing, and gently putting his toe in the water to see how cold it was. *Yes*, said her heart. She'd marry him. She would. If he really asked, she would. She wouldn't be able to say no, because she was smitten. Smitten. The word rolled around in her lemon brain. Wasn't "smitten" the past participle of "smite?" To smite meant to strike down, to injure, to slay, to hit hard. So, when one was "smitten" by love, one was already slain. One was already dead.

"I think we'd have fun no matter what," she finally said, trying to get out of her head and into his heart forever.

He wolfed down more than half a pizza after that, and they anxiously left the restaurant, ready to crawl into bed and not sleep.

FIFTY-FIVE

K ent woke up on the floor of the kitchen in his quiet cabin. He must have dozed off after…

He hated this part. The part where he had to clean up the mess of another lost love, another broken heart. Trish was ice cold, and her hands no longer brought him comfort, but he wasn't ready to let go of them. He stood up, still clutching her dainty hands. He kissed the hard, icy flesh on each of them and opened the freezer door. His refrigerator was old, and the doors stuck. He had to tug hard to open it. Maybe he was just exhausted. He took out a frozen pot pie and set it on the counter for his dinner. He wasn't sure that he loved Trish anymore, but he missed her. He felt the overwhelming loneliness that always came when yet another woman left him. *How many more? How many until one stays?*

He shrugged off the sadness. He coped with it the way he always did, with ritual. There were steps to follow. There were procedures. He had a way of doing things. Lauren had disrupted his flow, but that no longer mattered. That cunt no longer mattered. *She never existed*, he told himself; *she was just a bad dream.*

Go back to the ritual. Trish's hands will go in a fresh baggie and into the freezer. Trish will be wrapped in her plastic sheet and go in the deep freeze in the garage. Cicily will have to come out of there, so there will be room. Cicily will see Trish, and she will see where she went wrong. Stupid bitch, so easily replaced. Cicily will be driven out to the remote spot in the desert and left with the others. Lauren's hands still rested on top of Cicily's body in the deep freeze. They would have to go too. He couldn't bear to keep her hands around anymore. He felt nothing but hatred for Lauren and Cicily, and soon the hatred would come for Trish too, but he would keep her around for now so she could see. Trish needed to see how easily replaced she was. She never really appreciated him and all that he'd done for her, but the right woman would. Trish would regret not loving him. They all did.

He went through the steps, and felt more hollow than usual. He was tired, but he didn't know how to stop. A myriad of thoughts coursed through his brain as he followed the ritual. *How can you just give up? How do you give up on love, on hope, on the dream that somewhere out there is the right person, the one who will really, truly, "get you;" how do you give up on The One? She will love you, Kent. She will. She's out there. You just have to find her. Never stop searching for her. She's out there, waiting to love you. She won't be mean to you. She will be nice, and love you no matter what. She will give you endless, unconditional love.*

The hunger for a new love was coming faster. It used to take him so long to get over a woman who broke his heart, but already Trish was fading from his memory, and his desire quickened for someone new. Trish was not mature enough to appreciate him. She was a young silly girl. She'd had a delicate frame, light as a feather; her bones seemed almost bird-like. It was so appealing to him at first, so delightfully feminine, but now it started to repulse him. He needed someone more ample, someone with more meat on her bones, and more years on her face. A woman who'd been out there, and had experienced first-hand what jerks men can be – a woman like that would appreciate a gentleman, and she wouldn't be a stuck-up, superficial, little bitch who thought she was too good for him.

He coped with his exhaustion by fantasizing his new woman, and how pleasing she would be; how warm and comfortable her body would feel; how delicious her plump fingers would be as they caressed him.

Later, he sat down to a microwaved chicken pot-pie, in need of a good night's sleep. Tomorrow he would have to venture back to the city. He really needed to visit his apartment and take care of a few things. He figured he should call the handyman company he freelanced for and see if he could pick up a few days of work, so he could pay some bills and have enough money to buy flowers and candy for his true love, wherever she might be.

He hoped the Lauren hype had died down and considered listening to the news for updates, but he was just too tired. A broken heart takes a lot out of a man.

FIFTY-SIX

Joanna Jacobs was a patient woman, but dealing with certain members of the press was just the thing to stretch her patience so thin she worried it would snap. She was deeply empathetic for the terrified family members of missing people, but would become very frustrated when their attempts to be "pro-active" or "put pressure" on the police force resulted in actually slowing things down and making them much more difficult.

Marcus Carlton really didn't strike Joanna as a bad guy. In her previous dealings with him, which had so far been few, he actually had been pretty decent, and he was highly intelligent. She respected what he'd done since taking a position at *TV-zine*, a hip Hollywood "news" show designed for self-important, self-indulgent people more concerned with the drug problems of starlets than world events. However, Marcus had started to change the dynamic of the show by including local news that wasn't celebrity related, and also added a segment called "The World in Your Pocket," where the ridiculously attractive hosts would pull out their smart phones, use them as reference tools, and fill in their viewers on global news in quick, funny bites for the short-attention span viewers. It improved the reputation of the show by expanding their audience without alienating their current one. Marcus had only contacted Joanna a few times for information on local crime stories, but when he contacted her about Trish Morris, she sensed something was different. This was personal. There was something in his voice that brought Joanna's compassion out in full effect, and she agreed to meet with him on the condition that he would not put anything out there in the media that could create public panic or in any way hinder the investigation. He was extremely cooperative. Marcus Carlton was smart enough to know that panic wouldn't find Trish any faster and the last thing he wanted to do was anything that could further endanger Trish. He had only met her a few times when he'd been dating Jillian, but he knew how much her daughters meant to her. They were the most important part of Jillian's life, something he could never compete with – that, and the memory of her dead husband. But he would always be in love with Jillian Morris, that he was quite sure of, so if he could do anything – pull any strings, call in any favors – he would. He would not let his ego fantasize about being the hero who helped bring Trish home safe, when a grateful Jillian would embrace her daughter and then fall passionately into his arms for safekeeping, forever. He pushed aside all of that, and thought of poor Trish, and what she must be enduring. She wasn't just somebody's little girl; she was Jillian's little girl, and they all needed her home safe and sound.

Joanna sat across from Marcus and sized him up. She could easily sense that he was very distraught.

"So what can I do for you, Mr. Carlton?"

"Please," he said in a shaky voice, "Marcus is fine. I just want to know if there is anything you can tell me about the search for Trish. If there is anything delicate, anything you don't want me to talk about, I promise you mum's the word. This isn't about getting a story for me. I know Trish, and I have a personal relationship with her mother, and I just want to know whatever there is to know, and if there is anything I can do to help, I will do it. If there is anything you do want on our show, you let me know. I will work out any programming issues, give you all our airtime…" his voice cracked slightly, "…just anything I can do."

"Mr. Carlton – Marcus, unfortunately, I don't have a lot of information. I'm sure you know interviews were conducted with her roommate, Melissa, and her boyfriend, Greg."

"I know Jillian is talking to them as well."

"Yes," Joanna agreed, "I'm sure she is. But honestly, we don't have much to go on. We have her purse and her keys, as well as the shoes she was wearing that night. We haven't really found much else in the way of clues. I wish I could be more helpful. I really do. Believe me, we are using every resource to find her."

Marcus stared at her. He had a strong suspicion there was something she wasn't telling him. He'd seen this woman, Lauren McLaughlin, plastered all over the news. He suspected – or at least, he suspected that the police suspected – a connection. Was there a serial killer on the loose, and was that why they were being so secretive?

"Captain Jacobs, do you think there is any connection between Trish's disappearance, and the death of that woman, Lauren, from the PR company?"

Joanna met his eyes head on. In her personal life, she never lied. She was a strong believer in honesty. *Thou shalt not lie.* She believed that, but often times her job required a little more finesse, and things weren't always so simple. Sometimes, thou *shalt* in fact, lie thine ass off, if it might save a life, or keep an investigation from going horribly wrong.

"We have no reason to believe there is a connection at this time," Joanna stated diplomatically.

Marcus didn't buy that. She was definitely not telling him everything, but he certainly didn't like the version of the story where there was, in fact, a serial killer, and he had Trish hostage, or had possibly already killed her. He much preferred some other scenario, something less sinister, but he couldn't quite figure out what that scenario might be. Trish was not an irresponsible girl who would just go wandering off into the night without her keys, or her purse, or her shoes. It didn't add up. Maybe it was time to have a talk with that punk boyfriend of hers.

"What about the boyfriend? Is he a strong suspect?"

"Well, off the record, he doesn't have an alibi for the night she went missing, but he really doesn't seem good for it. If he did anything to her, there is no evidence of it anywhere in his car. There's no blood, no real sign of a struggle. They were fighting, but according to him, it was all verbal, an argument, and we have no proof of anything physical happening. It seems unlikely that he would do something with her, and then go driving around with her purse in his car, but we are going to continue to press him, simply because he was the last person to see her. As far as a strong suspect goes, he's all we've got. We're keeping close tabs on him, but we also don't want to waste time on him if he's not responsible."

Marcus' phone vibrated in his pocket. It would be Jillian, but he checked to make sure. He gave a quick gesture to Captain Jacobs so as not to appear rude, and then answered.

"Jillian? Just hold on one second okay?"

He stood up, muting his phone for a moment.

"Captain Jacobs thank you so much for taking the time to meet with me. Please, will you call me, directly on my cell, if you find anything at all? I know you're busy, but –"

Joanna stood up and shook his hand and took his card, on which he had written his cell phone number.

"Of course, Marcus. I will. We will all do our best."

Marcus thanked her and walked out of the office, un-muting the phone as he left, partially elated to hear Jillian's voice, but mostly dreading the news he had for her, which was basically, that he had no real news for her. No information, no leads, and no hope to give her.

After Marcus Carlton left, Joanna stared once again at the sketch of the man they believed had killed Lauren, and abducted Trish. Her eyes followed every line of the pencil marks in the drawing. A cold chill ran up her spine. She instinctively reached for her own hands, grabbing each wrist with the opposing palm, in a gesture like prayer. She massaged her own wrists one at a time. How much bigger, older and sturdier they were compared to Lauren's or Trish's. Was Trish without her hands? Was this man really the one who had her?

She coldly shuddered, stopped staring at her hands and went back to the drawing of his face, almost like a caricature – a face of the mild-mannered neighbor whom everyone ignores, but senses is a little creepy. He was the pudgy, unkempt, lonely guy who comes into your head when you think of a homely serial killer. He certainly wasn't the suave, handsome charmer who could possibly lure women into his car. He hits them over the head, because he probably has no other option. He was a man who was dying of loneliness. How many women had died, and might still die, of his loneliness as well?

* * * * *

Erin and Dan made their way over to Cambridge PR with the sketch and showed it to every single person that worked in the firm, as well as the security guards that worked the garage. No one recognized him. There were a few other friends outside of work they made the rounds to as well, but it started to turn very quickly into a dead end. Part of the problem with guys like this was that they were exactly the kind of guy no one noticed – or no one noticed until it was too late.

Erin had been driving quietly after the last pointless interview, and Dan was also silent; he just stared out the passenger window. Night was falling over the City of Angels, as a devil ran free somewhere out there. Erin suddenly pulled the car over to a red zone on the side of the street. Crap. Dan had a bad feeling about –

"Motherfucking cocksucking ball-face BITCH!"

Dan jumped out of his skin for a just a moment, and then he couldn't help himself. He laughed.

Erin was still pounding the steering wheel and making weird "grrr" noises. She stopped when he laughed at her.

"What the hell is so funny?"

Dan couldn't stop laughing now, and couldn't explain it. It was that partner thing. Good partners have an unspoken agreement – one panics; the other calms; one gets angry; the other brings it down a notch – it was all about balance, and Erin and Dan had it. Laughter seemed the best diffuser in this moment.

"I'm sorry Taylor, it's just – ball-face bitch? Is that what happens when you suck too much cock? You get ball indentations in your face?"

Erin stopped. What had she said? Ball-face? How stupid. She laughed too, and then, predictably, the tears came. God damn it all. Not now. She put her forehead down on the steering wheel. She hoped Dan wouldn't notice, but she knew he would. He'd also be smart enough to act like he didn't.

"Come on, Taylor, we're doing everything we can. You know that."

"I know Dan, I just – I'm frustrated. He's killed her. He's the one that got Trish Morris; I know it. And I know she's already dead. I can feel it. I don't know what to do. Do we release this sketch? Will it help us find him? What if he sees himself on TV? Will he accelerate? Go deeper into hiding? Leave the city? Is he even still in the city? He took Trish from San Pedro; that's still L.A., but kind of a hike. If he went there to escape the heat from Lauren's death being all over the news, he could be anywhere now. He could have a place, but –"

Dan had been waiting for Erin to get to whatever point she was trying to make, but something was bugging him, and when she said "he could have a place" he knew.

"Erin. You said you thought he had the other bodies somewhere else, right? And we haven't found any other bodies in any other dumpsters. It's not likely we'd miss that – parts maybe, but a whole body? This is L.A. Dumpsters are the shopping malls and food courts for the homeless."

"Yea, exactly. So where are the others? What does he do with them?"

"Well, like you said, he could have a place that he takes them. He's not going to want anyone to hear a woman scream, and he strikes me as the kind of guy who's gonna want some time with his new lady friend. So maybe he does have a place, way out somewhere, but Lauren doesn't add up. If he took her somewhere far, why would he drive her body all the way back to L.A. just to dump it? That's too risky. He killed her, and he needed to get rid of her quick, so he had to have killed her somewhere nearby."

"Exactly. Lauren's house is clean. No way he killed her there. There was absolutely no evidence of that, or of a clean-up job, and her keys were still in the parking garage, and there was no sign of breaking and entering. He probably wouldn't take her back to his place – assuming he has a house or apartment here in L.A . – because again, too risky. He could be seen bringing her into his place, and when she shows up dead on the news, he's suspect number one."

"Exactly," said Dan, "So let's think, right around the spot where we found her – what options do we have?"

Erin peeled her car out onto the street.

"Sepulveda Boulevard," said Dan.

"Yup," agreed Erin, "seedy motels just south of Venice."

Los Angeles' west-side – which boasted such clean neighborhoods as Beverly Hills, Culver City and Brentwood – had some pretty dodgy pockets as well. From one block to the next, the urban climate could change drastically. Motels often put things like "spa" or "suites" into their name to make it sound palatable, maybe for the tourists because locals knew that places like this were frequented by stars on drug benders and local politicians banging one out with prostitutes of various genders.

They started at the Sun Dial Spa & Suites (it has Spa and Suites in the name, so you know it's nice) and got nowhere. The guy at the front desk spoke a language that was a version of English and something that even Erin and Dan had a hard time figuring out, and they'd interviewed just about every nationality one could name. Finally, they left a copy of the sketch, and gave the usual, "please call us if you think of anything that might help us" and moved on.

The next stop was so close they could walk to it. The Starry Moon Motel wasn't any better looking, but the guy at the front desk had a more intelligible accent. Dan showed him the sketch.

"This guy look familiar to you? Maybe one of your customers? Would've been here Friday before last?"

The unkempt guy stared at the sketch half-heartedly.

"I don't know. Maybe. Lotta guys look like that."

"Just take your time. Really look at it."

"Could be. Man, I don't know. I'm not here every night."

"Okay," Dan said, keeping his temper in check, "Is there someone else we can talk to?"

"This guy Fred works here some nights."

"Does this Fred have a last name? A phone number? An address?"

"Probably."

"Well, can we get it?" Dan was getting frustrated, but Erin would be ready to grab this guy's throat by now, so he shot her at look that said, "I got this." She kept a short enough distance to hear, but took deep breaths to keep her temper from flaring up. She was starting to worry Dan. She'd been extra pissed off lately.

"I can give you the owner's number, and he can tell you

how to contact Fred. I mean, I think he still works here."

"Great, thanks," Dan said as he took the number, and left the sketch. "If you remember anything else, please call us."

Dan immediately walked away, dialing the owner's number from the card the clerk had given him.

"Starry Moon Motel," said the clerk upon answering. Dan turned around and – yes, sure enough – the clerk had just given him the motel's front desk line.

"Are you kidding me?" Now Dan was losing his temper.

"I'm sorry. I'm sorry. I wasn't thinking. I'll check for his home number."

The clerk rummaged around and eventually produced a tattered index card with a name and number scrawled on it. He rewrote the information on a scrap of paper and handed it to Dan.

"Thank you for your cooperation," Dan said, doing his best to hide the sarcasm, but not really caring if he failed. He handed the paper to Erin.

"Maybe you should call him, and use your best warm and sultry I'm-a-smoking-hot-cop voice, not your angry man-hater voice."

"I'm not a man-hater."

Dan started walking back toward the car with a slight chuckle. Erin yelled after him.

"I don't hate *you*, Dan!"

"Not yet you don't. But believe me, I do what I can to stay on your good side."

Dan said it with as much humor as he could, but he was only half-kidding. Erin Taylor was a feisty little thing, and she just might need a vacation from chasing women killers. She left a message for the motel's owner.

The darkness of the L.A. evening descended on them and,

even with a sketch in hand of a guy who may or may not be Lauren's killer and may or may not have abducted Trish, they were no closer to saving the women of the city from a madman, and no nearer to redemption. But they walked side-by-side back to the car, with an unspoken language between them. Eventually, Dan spoke.

"I think we need to release the sketch to the media. We're getting nowhere."

"I completely agree," Erin said.

They headed back to the station. They needed to see the Captain. And there was always more to do. So much more to do… the exhaustion and frustration settled into Erin's bones and into Dan's as well; it was as if their shoulders slumped in unison, and then once again, in the unspoken language of their partnership, and in the shared urge to be relentless in their pursuit of this man, wherever he was, they found their second wind. They knew that serial killers operated on compulsion – hell, everybody knows that. They had to be just as compulsive in their pursuit of him as he was in his pursuit of his next victim, or he'd win. They couldn't let him win. They wouldn't let him win.

"Garza," Dan said as he answered his ringing cell phone. He immediately put it on speaker for Erin's benefit.

"We've got a connection between these cases," began Captain Jacobs. "A bartender in San Pedro kicked a man out of the bar where he works on the night Trish disappeared. He said the man he kicked out looks just like the man in the sketch, and he kicked him out for trying to give a drunk woman in the bar a ride home. He was kicked out only blocks away from the place where Trish's boyfriend said she got out of the car. The timing makes sense too. It's the same guy."

Erin met Garza's eyes long enough to know they were both thinking the same thing. *We have to find this guy before he takes another woman.*

FIFTY-SEVEN

Kent drove back into Los Angeles and made his way back to his apartment. He had a lot to take care of, but it was getting more and more difficult to focus on mundane tasks. He picked up a couple days of work, paid some bills, and did some light cleaning in his place, but then there he was, pacing the floor, frustrated, lonely and bored. He was getting angrier at Trish. He choked on bitter disappointment. She had seemed so sweet, but she was a crazy, selfish, little bitch, just like all the others. He wanted love, but he also wanted revenge. He'd get someone new, someone better, and show Trish her mistake. She had been cruel to him, and now she would see just how easily replaced she was. And she'd be replaced with someone better. He couldn't wait to show her how happy he was without her, and how joyful he would be in the arms of someone new.

He had to stop pacing. He turned on the TV to catch up on the evening news. Hopefully, everyone had lost interest in that Lauren bitch by now. He was hardly able to focus on anything that was being said. He was going crazy. These women were making him insane. Why were they all like this? There had to be one good one out there. There just had to be...

He snapped to full attention at the voice coming from the television. "The ongoing investigation into the murder of Cambridge PR's Vice President, Lauren McLaughlin..."

He turned up the volume, and just like that; he appeared onscreen. Or what appeared to be a sketch of him. The sketch itself didn't really do him justice. He was better-looking than that, but it was him... wasn't it? He peered harder, and leaned closer to the TV screen.

"...trying to determine the identity of this man. Authorities think he may have information about Ms. McLaughlin, and are hoping to bring him in, to answer a few questions..." the newscaster's voice droned on as Kent rushed to the bathroom and stared in the mirror. That sketch... it was him...

wasn't it? He looked at himself, really stared. Something felt wrong. He couldn't see himself clearly. Where was he? Where was his face? It was there; he could see it, but it was becoming... transparent... was he fading away? No, it was all an illusion. He was still there, still his old self. He had to be there. He feared he was melting away, disappearing. He was fading off into nothing. He needed someone to love him. If no one loved him, would he just disappear, cease to exist?

He needed to make a change, just in case someone could recognize him, even from that inaccurate sketch. He got a fresh disposable razor out of the drawer next to the bathroom sink, pushed the stopper down, and ran warm water into the basin. He picked up the shaving cream and covered his head. It was hard to get the back, but he took his time and shaved his entire head. From the other room, the evening news droned on, but it was just background noise, until the words, "a reward is being offered for information leading to the location of Patricia Morris, AKA Trish, last seen..."

He ran out into the living room. Fucking Trish, crazy little psycho bitch that she was, smiling in a photograph, bright and beautiful onscreen, with a number listed at the bottom to call. A reward? For that bitch? God, people were so stupid. She wasn't worth a reward. She wasn't worth shit. He was so angry. He grabbed a pen and wrote down the phone number.

He went back into the bathroom and studied his new freshly-shorn head. He hadn't bothered to shave his face in days, so he shaved what facial hair he had into a tidy goatee. As he cleaned up the mess, drained the sink and rinsed or wiped away all the hair, he checked his appearance in the mirror. He liked his new look. The shaved head made him feel sexy – dangerously sexy. Women love that shit. Women love a tough guy, a badass. That's what he looked like.

"Hello, handsome," he said. It was time to find her. The

One he could love; The One who would love him back.

He grabbed a light jacket and considered a hat. No, maybe not a hat. His freshly-shorn head might feel good in the night air. He needed to take a walk. One didn't find love unless one went out and took a few risks. Love doesn't walk up and knock on your door. Love has to be sought out. Love has to be found. Love has to be conquered, captured. You have to make it stay. Sooner or later, he'd find a way to make it stay.

He walked out into the L.A. night, which was a little chilly, as it often was, year-round. He walked for what seemed like hours, even though his watch told him it wasn't nearly that long. He made a stop in a store to pick up a disposable cell phone. Walking off his anger wasn't working. When he dialed the number he'd written down from the news program, a woman's voice answered and Kent immediately cut her off. He didn't give a shit what she had to say, some lackey bitch answering phones for the stupid police. He had something to say, something much more important.

"They'll never find her. They'll never find Trish. She's gone. I never knew what true happiness was until she was gone." He wished Trish could hear him say that.

He hung up before the idiot on the other end of the line could say anything. Then he smashed the phone and tossed it into a gutter.

He walked past an alley, and a noise made him stop and turn his head. He got that tingle that only came when Love was near. There she was. She was loading cleaning supplies into the trunk of her car. She dropped a bucket and some cleaning products fell with a light rattle, and a barely audible, "shit" escaped her mouth. He couldn't see her face. He peered down the alley. She must have left one of the businesses that had closed for the evening. A simple cleaning lady, that's what she was. She was delightfully chubby – not fat, just deliciously squeezable. Her long, dark, wavy hair was pulled up in a slightly unkempt ponytail. She was dressed in gray sweats and a T-shirt. Excellent. This wasn't a woman who put on airs. She worked hard for a living. She appreciated the little things in life. She would appreciate him. He should help her. She was in distress. Anyone could just come along and take advantage of her. He walked down the alley toward her.

His steps grew nearer and louder, and Rose hurried to gather her things and put them in her trunk. He picked up his pace. She still needed to lock up the travel agency's office. A voice inside her said, *Leave it. Just get in the car and go. Now.* But she needed this job. Cleaning small offices after-hours was the only way she could put herself through nursing school, the only way she could change her life. If she didn't lock up, she could lose her job. The keys shook in her hand as she hurried toward the door of the office.

"Can I help?" Kent offered, as he picked up a bottle of glass cleaner she had missed and set it in her trunk.

"No, I'm fine, thanks," Rose said, hoping against hope that he would just leave.

"Are you sure? It's late, and this alley is dark."

"I'm fine. Really. Just need to get home. My husband is expecting me." She wasn't sure why she lied. It made her feel safe to think of some man waiting for her at home. Some man who would listen to her, and rub her tired feet. Someday, she hoped to meet a man like that. Every instinct in her body told her this man was not that man. Something was off about him. And his head? It was so... weird. There were fresh scabs, and bizarre patches of hair here and there. It looked like he'd shaved his own head, and done a really bad job of it.

"Your husband? He's a lucky man. You're quite adorable there... what's your name?"

She wanted to lie again. She stood still. She should run.

Could she outrun him? She wasn't in great shape. All the work and all the studying didn't leave much time for getting to the gym. She promised herself to get in shape as soon as she could complete these last few courses. Maybe she could take a self-defense class or something. Kill two birds with one stone.

"I asked you your name. It's a little rude not to answer."

Rose panicked – true panic, not silly panic you might have if you didn't study hard enough for a big test, or forgot to pay the phone bill, or were running late for work – no, this was primal, frozen panic. A gazelle that knows she is lunch for a lion kind of panic. This was wrong. Rose knew it. She ran. But he was already so close. Neither of them was in great shape, but there wasn't much distance between them. The second she took off, Kent was ready. He knew when a woman was about to bolt on him. They always try to get away. They never wanted to give him a chance. It was only a few paces, and he was grabbing her dark-brown ponytail and shoving her into a wall. A sharp pain in her nose shot straight into her brain. She saw stars. Literally. Shards of terror rushed behind her eyes. She didn't need to finish nursing school to know her nose was broken. She tasted the warm metallic blood of her newly split lip. He had her arms pinned behind her. She screamed. He kept one arm on her wrists and put the other hand over her mouth.

"Don't scream. I just want to know your name; that's all. If you tell me your name, I'll leave you alone."

He turned her face toward him and met her eyes. His erection grew when he saw the fear there. The fear started to appear more and more like love to him.

"Tell me your name and I'll let you go."

Rose didn't know why she said it. She was such a little liar tonight.

"Debbie," she whispered, as soon as he took his hand

away from her mouth.

Kent wasn't sure how he knew. It was something in her eyes. He was so angry.

"Liar!" he screamed, and bashed her head hard into the bricks. Rose was out cold. He was surprised no one had seen or heard anything. One of the extraordinary things about living in a big city was that no one gave a shit about anyone. People just walked on, minding their own business, or being self-absorbed assholes. Who knew what people would notice if they only looked up from their lives, from their egos, took out their earbuds and stopped checking their smart phones for cat videos.

He moved quickly anyway, just to be safe. He took rags from her cleaning supplies, tied her wrists and ankles and gagged her, put her in the trunk, and picked up her keys. He would just take her car. Even better.

Her name wasn't Debbie. He'd seen the lie in her eyes. She was just afraid to love him. She would though. She would love him. He just had to get her alone. He drove. Going home was dangerous. He'd stop for supplies when he got out of L.A. and into Riverside County.

When he stopped the car later at a gas station, he searched for information. Her wallet, with her driver's license, gave him just what he needed. Rose Santos. What a name. He would buy her roses.

Rose tried to distinguish the noises outside from the darkness of the trunk. The blinding pain in her head made it impossible to open her eyes. Her nose hurt; her eyes hurt, her mouth hurt, and she couldn't figure out where she was. She couldn't remain conscious. She slipped away again, not knowing what a blessing it was to disappear from the terror she would feel when she learned where she was, and what was going to happen to her.

FIFTY-EIGHT

Erin and Dan worked late, night after night. The calls coming in on the hotline since they'd released the sketch to the media had mostly been from obvious nut-jobs. The only one with any promise was a man's voice saying, "They'll never find her. They'll never find Trish. She's gone. I never knew what true happiness was until she was gone." Unfortunately, the call had come from a disposable cell phone and there was no way to trace it; most likely it had been destroyed and dumped by now. Various officers followed up on some of the other calls, and thus far nothing of substance had turned up.

Erin considered the possibility that the sketch was inaccurate, or that this guy was so far below the radar that no one had ever noticed him, or he'd already altered his appearance.

They sorted through the other missing women's pictures to see if there was anyone else that could be one of his victims. They worked on the assumption that it was, in fact, the same guy who had taken Trish and killed Lauren, because the connection between the bar in San Pedro and the smoothie shop in Los Angeles seemed to point to the same guy. Examining Trish and Lauren hadn't really turned up much of a type. They were both pretty, and both white, but that was about it. Trish was 24; Lauren 34. Trish was blonde; Lauren brunette. Trish was extremely thin and slightly built; Lauren was fit, but not small-boned. Trish was heterosexual; Lauren was gay, or possibly bisexual. Trish had a low-paying job at a clothing store; Lauren was a successful professional. As far as the investigation had led them, it was very likely that Lauren was stalked, whereas Trish was probably a crime of opportunity. Or, maybe Trish's boyfriend had killed her and dumped the body, and the two cases were completely unrelated, and he was just getting away with it while they all spun their wheels trying to force a connection that wasn't even there. Erin would interview him personally as soon as she could, but for now she'd give one more look at the missing persons. They had already eliminated everyone male, all children, and all senior citizens. They focused the range on women 18-50. Erin sought out the pictures of the prettiest ones. Serial killers almost exclusively go after the pretty ones, not just because they're prettier to look at, but because they hate attractive women more. Beautiful women were there *for* men, and when they didn't give up the goods, men like this asshole got good and angry. Pretty women had no business being pretty and not sharing it. Or at least, that's how Erin believed men saw it. She sometimes didn't like when men told her she was pretty for just that reason – she always thought they believed she owed them something now: a giggle, a smile, a kiss, a lay. If you were pretty, you were property.

Erin laid out the images of the most attractive women between 18 and 50 in front of her. She didn't know if she should focus on only the white women. Serial killers usually killed within their own race and the sketch they had was a white male. Maybe Trish wasn't his normal type either, and he'd just nabbed her because she was available. Erin's anger built again. Even if Trish's boyfriend hadn't actually killed Trish, Erin couldn't help but blame him for abandoning her. If he hadn't abandoned her, she might still be alive. How long could Erin do this work and not become a complete man-hater?

Dan came back with two cups of crappy, vending machine coffee, which they would both drink out of a desperate desire to keep their eyes open. Erin knew he'd gone to call his wife, Veronica, and disappoint her once again when he told her he'd be working late. Sometimes she envied him because he had someone who actually cared when and if he came home, but then she'd remember how much easier it was to stay single and not disappoint anyone. Every relationship she'd ever attempted had ended for pretty much the same reason – men couldn't handle playing second-string to all the murderers who kept Erin out late. She debated whether she should ask Dan about how things were with Veronica, but figured he'd talk if he wanted to, which he did.

"I really don't want to be one of those cops whose marriage ends because the job is taking too much out of us. It's so trite. But I can feel Veronica's anger, even now."

"So go home to her, Dan. I've got this. We're spinning our wheels on this anyway."

Dan sat down, and his face twisted. It was the face of a man whose life was falling apart, but sure as hell wasn't going to cry about it.

"I'm losing her. Veronica's going to leave me."

"She's not going to leave you, Dan. She loves you. She just misses you. Go home."

"I can't go home. She told me not to."

Erin was surprised. She could see how much Veronica and Dan loved each other. If any marriage had a shot, it was theirs.

"Really?" said Erin, attempting to keep her face impassive.

"Yeah, she told me if I wasn't home to have dinner with her last night, not to come home the next night. Well, I didn't make it home for dinner last night, and it's now the next night, and I thought I could smooth things over, but she said not to come home. That I should crash on someone's couch, or go to a hotel, but not to come home."

Erin pretended to sort through the pictures of the missing women. She didn't know what to say.

"Well, you can crash at my place if you need to, but I really think if you let her cool off a little, you can fix this. You're going to have to spend more time with her though, Dan. I'll handle the late-night shit. Don't worry about it. I got nobody that cares when I come home." Erin's voice cracked a bit when she said this, and she cleared her throat to cover her tracks. She was falling apart. She was so tired. Erin took a deep breath and pulled her focus back to the task at hand.

"Okay, so I guess we can focus on the attractive Caucasian women. I don't know if he has a preference, but we've got to narrow our focus, so let's eliminate the women who aren't white. Ignore hair color, since we've already got a blonde and a brunette, so he might not care about that, though he could prefer brunettes since he probably stalked Lauren. Let's stay focused on women who've gone missing in the last five years."

Dan and Erin sorted through the profiles and came up with quite a few names. They started with the women who had disappeared from the west side of Los Angeles, or San Pedro, because Lauren and Trish had disappeared from those neighborhoods.

They came up with over thirty women.

It was a start. A very depressing start. Wasn't there anything that could connect these women to each other? By two a.m., both Erin and Dan were exhausted, and frustrated, having come up with almost no useful information. Once at Erin's condo, she directed him to the guest bedroom. They both collapsed into sleep, ashamed of their own perspective loneliness. By six a.m., bleary and worn out, they would have to be up and back to work. They desperately needed a break in this case. Anything. Anything at all.

* * * * *

Erin put fresh towels outside the guest bedroom door for Dan and went back into her own bathroom for a quick shower. She had already brewed a pot of strong coffee to jump-start their morning. Oddly, she was calm and it was a little weird, but she liked having Dan there. It was nice to have a night once in a while with someone else around, even if he was in the other room. He knew exactly the stress she was under because he was under it too. Veronica would be waking up sad and alone today, but Erin quickly dismissed her concerns. She had enough on her mind without worrying about Dan's struggling marriage.

Dan and Erin barely spoke to each other as they poured coffee in travel mugs, gathered their things, and headed to their cars. It wasn't awkward silence at all; in fact, they shared the feeling that they were acting like an old married couple that just didn't have much to say to each other anymore, day in and day out.

They were in the station by 7 a.m. and, fortunately, they were about to get a break in the case, finally.

The pressure from Cambridge PR, and from Jillian Morris and Marcus Carlton, as well as countless other media outlets, fell on Captain Joanna Jacobs, which trickled down to Erin Taylor and Dan Garza, as lead detectives, and then on to every cop in the station. Everyone was aware that if anything of any real substance came in from someone who had actually seen the man in the sketch, Erin or Dan needed to be immediately notified and, if possible, be able to talk to the person with the information.

* * * * *

Nancy Bauer had watched the news with a sick feeling in her stomach. Looking at the sketch, she knew it was the same guy, and suddenly other things started to make more sense. She called the police station and couldn't get through. She was on hold for quite a while before she gave up. First thing in the morning, she would visit the station and talk to someone.

"Can I help you?" said the officer behind the reception counter.

"Yes, my name is Nancy Bauer, and I saw a sketch on the news last night, and I've seen that man, and I'd like to talk to someone about it."

"Absolutely, I'll bring an officer over to talk to you directly." The officer made a quick call and then said, "Ms. Bauer, an officer is coming right away to take your statement."

A pudgy Latin man came out to greet Nancy and took her back to his desk. He introduced himself as Officer Martinez and immediately asked her name. He wrote down everything she said, hoping to determine whether or not she was another crackpot, but they didn't get far before he said he would need her to wait just a moment. This was something Taylor and Garza would want to hear. He called Dan Garza's desk.

"Detective Garza, there's someone here I think you and Detective Taylor would be interested in talking to."

Dan instructed Officer Martinez to take Ms. Bauer to one of the interview rooms right away. He went straight to Erin.

"Taylor, we've got a woman saying she's seen him." Erin grabbed a copy of the sketch, and they went straight away to meet her.

Nancy Bauer looked like she was well into her 60s, maybe even her 70s. She was thin and wiry; there was a bird-like quality to her. She looked like she'd smoked thousands of cigarettes in her lifetime, and that she'd always had to work really hard to survive. Deep lines were etched in her face, and her claw-like bony hands just accentuated the bird-like quality she possessed. All of that aside, she was an angel to Erin, because she had seen this man, and she was a responsible citizen showing up to talk about it.

Erin immediately put the sketch in front of Nancy.

"Officer Martinez tells us you've seen this man."

"Absolutely." Nancy peered at it again. "Yes, that's him. I'm sure of it."

"Where? When?"

"Lu's Diner. That's where I work. I've been a waitress there for 24 years. He used to come in, on and off, a few years ago, and then he stopped for a while, and then came in again, but he hasn't been there in a while, but I'm sure it's him. I don't forget faces. That's how I remember my tables. I remember a face; I know where you're sitting and what you've ordered. I've got a system. I hardly ever make a mistake on an order. He orders tuna melts, every time. And lemonade."

Dan and Erin both listened patiently to Nancy's story, and as soon as she took a breath, Erin was ready.

"So, when was the last time you saw him?"

"Well, I think it's been quite a few months – time's a little fuzzier for me than faces – but it's the circumstances that were interesting. Now, there are quite a few of us veterans there. We've been working there for years, but a lot of the young girls – they're usually actresses or something – they don't normally work there long, so there's a lot of turnover. I see a lot of young ones come and go. Don't think much of it. Some girl doesn't show up that day, well one of us vets just works a little harder 'til they hire another one." Nancy worried she sounded like an old rambling lady, so she added, "I know this seems like I'm rambling, but there's a point. I want to be clear why I'm just now realizing the possible connection between him, and… well; look, I don't know what you've got on this guy and that poor woman Laura or whatever that's been all over the news, but I think this man –" Nancy aggressively put her bony finger out and tapped the sketch, in the space precisely between his eyes – "this man right here, I think he took that poor sweet girl Cicily, and maybe that other one too… Jenny."

Erin's heart was pounding. This was something. This was really something, and they both knew it. Dan wanted to pick Nancy up and twirl her around and plant a big kiss on her bony cheek. Erin pretty much felt the same.

"Do you remember the last names of either of these young ladies?" Erin gently prodded.

"Oh no, I can tell you what they look like, but I can't remember last names. We only have our first names on our tags, but I'm sure the owner will have that information in her company files."

"What makes you think this man had something to do with these women going missing?"

"Well, like I said, a lot of young girls come and go, but when Cicily was working there, well, she's a pretty little thing. Brightest smile, cute little dimple on one side, and the customers loved her. She'd be really friendly with everyone. But this guy got a little too attached. He always wanted her section, and I understand some men would rather be waited on by the pretty young girl than by me, but one day, Cicily asked me to take her table, to wait on him for her. She said he was making her uncomfortable, you know, making up reasons to touch her, complimenting her a little too much, and staying a little too long. He wouldn't even eat his food half the time, so she felt like he was just there to talk to her. So I waited on him for her, and yeah, he was kind of nasty. Just wanted Cicily, kept glaring at me, and staring at her. He left in a huff that day. Cicily was off the next two days, but then when she was scheduled to work again, she didn't show up. Police came by and asked some questions. I mentioned something about this guy, but I didn't really put too much into it, and neither did they. After all, lots of men tried to chat her up. She's really pretty; that happens. Not every guy who flirts is up to no good. Just most of 'em I guess... wasn't really sure what happened to her. I thought maybe she just got sick of the job and stopped comin' in. Like I said, happens all the time. I hope I'm not wasting your time. I know you're busy. I just thought it might be worth mentioning, and if he did do something terrible, and I didn't say anything, well, I'd feel bad about that. Wouldn't be right."

"You're not wasting our time at all, Ms. Bauer," Dan gave her a warm smile, "so you said there was another girl, Jenny?"

"Oh yeah, Jenny… she was a there a few years ago. I don't know how many. Three? Four? Time is tricky for me, at my age… she was a cute little thing too. I think she was a student at UCLA. She was real friendly too, kind of a studious girl, responsible and hard-working. I was kind of surprised when she stopped showing up, but maybe the pressure of it all just got to her. She would say her parents were always on her about her grades and wanted her to quit the job anyway, but she liked feeling like she was contributing or something. Pretty unusual for a young person, but maybe stereotypes are there for a reason." Nancy gave an uncomfortable laugh.

"What do you mean, stereotypes?" Dan asked.

"Well, Jenny was an Asian girl. Chinese or something. Well, back in my day, everyone called all of them Chinese, but I know that's not really polite. I don't honestly like that sort of thing, hurting people's feelings or being rude. But I do believe she said she was Chinese. Oh, I'm not sure. I don't want to sound ignorant or anything; I just really can't tell the difference. I know that sounds awful, but I can't tell. So that's what I meant, you know the Asian parents putting pressure on the daughter, who's a good girl and studious and everything. I just remember now, that he used to come into the diner back then too. He was shy though, he didn't really chat her up so much, but when she stopped coming in to work, he still came to the diner for a few weeks after that, and one day he asked about her, if she still worked there. He didn't ask me; he asked this other woman, Ellen that works there, and she said no, and I happened to hear it. Then, when I saw his picture… well, what if there's a connection? I mean, the same guy, same tuna melt and lemonade, very interested in these two girls, and they both end up gone. My late husband Bill, God rest his soul, always used to say that a coincidence was just a fancy word for a pattern you should pay attention to."

"Were there any other women you can think of that might have disappeared?"

"Well, like I said, a lot of girls just stop coming in, but Jenny and Cicily are the only ones that did during the times when he was coming in a lot."

"Ms. Bauer, we can't thank you enough. This is very, very helpful. We'd like to come by and see if we can't get more information on these women from the company records." Erin was elated. This was incredible information.

"I'm sure that will be fine. I don't know how stuff like that works, with privacy and things, but I can mention it to the owner when I see her."

It did seem odd that Jenny was Asian. Had they been wrong to limit their focus to Caucasian women? Maybe physical type wasn't a factor at all. What if it was something else that attracted him? Nancy had described both women as friendly, accessible. Lauren was described by most as kind of cold and distant until you got to know her though. Nancy moved like she was ready to leave.

"Ms. Bauer, you said Jenny was Asian. What about Cicily? What does she look like?"

"Oh, she's a Black girl. Real pretty, curly brown hair. Very light-skinned. I think she might have been part white, but I'm not really sure. You don't ask those things, you know."

"Any other physical traits about either of them? Height, body type?" Erin prodded.

"Oh, Jenny was petite, like a lot of Asian girls are. Really tiny. Don't think she could have been even five feet tall. Slender, small-boned. Cicily was taller than that, but not real tall, average height I guess. Very curvy body, you know, stuff…" Nancy shifted with discomfort and trailed off. Erin kicked Dan under the table.

Dan immediately made an excuse to leave.

"I'm sorry Ms. Bauer. I'm going to let Detective Taylor finish up this interview. I just remembered I have a meeting I need to get to. It was a pleasure meeting you."

As soon as he left, Erin urged Nancy to continue.

"You can be frank with me, Ms. Bauer; we need to know everything we can, so don't be shy."

"Well, Cicily had large breasts, and kind of… well, an ample, um… behind. Jenny's body was more girlish, narrow hips and a bit flat-chested. It sounds like a stereotype, but it is what it is, I suppose..." Sadness passed over Nancy's face, like she was disappointed in herself for saying these things. "I just know they were both really nice, sweet girls, and I'd be real sad to hear that something bad happened to either one of them."

"Ms. Bauer, thank you. You helped a great deal. And you don't need to feel bad about anything you've said here, okay? These women looked how they looked, and you've done an incredible job giving us these details. The more we know, the better. If you don't mind leaving us your phone number, then if we think of anything else we'd like to ask, we will call you. I don't suppose you ever got this man's name?"

"No, he always paid cash, and he never told me his name, and I certainly never asked. I remember faces, and I remember orders. I give my customers nicknames to help me remember sometimes. He was always Lonely Tuna Melt to me."

Erin emitted a laugh that was barely a laugh. Lonely Tuna Melt. It was funny until she thought of all the women he'd hurt and killed.

Kent would never know that Nancy called him Lonely Tuna Melt, and Nancy would never know that he thought of her as Mildred. Mildred, with the Old Hands.

FIFTY-NINE

Kent arrived at his cabin, and weariness washed over him. He rested his forehead on the steering wheel of Rose's car. He wasn't even sure he had this in him right now. He was starting to have doubts about Rose. He hadn't really gotten to know her very well. He hadn't had time to court her. His face had appeared on the news. This was worrisome. Here he was, searching for love, and now he was under all this pressure. He had to keep going, as quickly as possible. He considered just going to bed and leaving her in the trunk. Women were so demanding. A man has to jump through all these hoops, buy them flowers and candy and compliment them, and how do they repay a guy? They don't. They never even appreciate it. They just want more. More, more, more, more, more. They were impossible to please. He would be turning thirty-nine soon. He was getting too old for this. He should be happy with someone by now, but he was starting to think that was just a dream. Maybe what he was doing was... well, maybe it wasn't right. He was killing these women. *Killing them.* He buried that, deep. It wasn't real. Perhaps he should just let Rose go. *No.* His face had been on the news. He was going to have to end it. But he should at least give her a chance first. Maybe she really would love him, and then everything would be okay. *Love me, Rose. It's your only chance.*

Rose came to when the car stopped, and she struggled to get her hands free of the rags he had tied them with. Every part of her body ached with injury and terror but, with her hands free, she removed the gag and the ties from her ankles. Her first instinct was to scream, but she stopped herself. *I'm in a trunk, but I don't know where I am. I could be anywhere. He will probably open the trunk soon. I will kick him and spray him with...* she grabbed some glass cleaner with her newly freed hands and hoped it would sting his eyes bad enough. Bleach might be better, so she quietly fumbled around in the dark trunk, but there wasn't a lot of room to work with. She and all her cleaning supplies were crammed in there. The car door opened, and his heavy steps hit the ground. No more time for thinking. Only time to act.

Kent approached the trunk and opened it. A harsh sting filled Kent's eyes as Rose sprayed glass cleaner in his face. She kicked him as hard as she could with both legs and took off running. As soon as she did, she realized her mistake. She should have kicked him and hit him hard with something while he was down. There was nowhere to run. She was out in the desert.

Kent furiously rubbed at his eyes. Everything was blurry, but he could make out Rose's shape as she ran. She had nowhere to go, the dumb bitch. *There's a reason I brought you out to the middle of the desert, you ungrateful whore.*

His footsteps falling behind Rose drowned out everything else – her rushing blood, pounding heart and her own desperate steps through this brutal landscape. She needed a weapon, anything she could use to fight him off. A rock! Its unyielding surface gave her a second of hope, which was crushed as soon his arms wrapped around her from behind. With her last effort, she whirled around, knocking him hard on the head with the rock.

"You little bitch!" Kent yelped at the sharp pain on his temple, and the warm blood trickling down the side of his face. The blood dripped toward his eye. Rose tried to get a second hit in, and he grabbed her wrist and wrenched it so fiercely, the rock dropped out of her hand. He stared at her, and the fear came off her skin in electric currents, rippling into him and through him, charging him, propelling him into a highly erotic state. *Oh god. This feels good. I love her so much for giving me this. This feeling.*

Rose clawed at him and he reached out and grabbed the sides of her face and wrenched her head to one side as hard as he could. Her neck snapped, and he felt her go limp as the life force abandoned her. At the same moment, his life force exploded out. He came. He collapsed onto the sand with her in his arms. Just one moment. One moment with her, and then he would need to take her inside. Just in case someone came out here.

He took a few deep breaths and stood up. He bent down to lift her; she was lighter than he expected. He took her inside the cabin and placed her gently on the sofa. He went back out to the car and grabbed the supplies he'd bought, shut the trunk of the car and re-entered the cabin. Rose lay there, still warm. He could spend more time with her. It was sweet like this. She was nice and quiet, not spewing her vicious lies and cold cruelty. He carried her into the bedroom and laid her down on the bed. He lay down next to her, and stroked the stray strands of hair that had escaped her ponytail.

"Oh Rose, you look so beautiful, and so peaceful. Thank you for being here with me."

He reached down for her hands. Poor Rose. She had worked hard. Her hands were rough and dry. He got a bottle of lotion and lovingly massaged some into her palms, becoming more aroused as he did so.

He groaned with pleasure and pulled his still-sticky member out and put Rose's hands on it. They shared a beautiful moment. He made love to Rose's hands. This was much better. Just shut them up right away and get to the good part. These bitches have nothing to say, and everything they do say is just more lies anyway.

He fell asleep in her arms and when he woke up, she had already gotten cold. They always did. Women always went cold, and it always made him angry. Then he remembered that little whore, Trish. It was time she saw Rose and learned her lesson.

He sighed a deep sigh and gathered his supplies. He calmly spread the plastic drop cloth out in the kitchen and put Rose on top of it. He got his lightweight handsaw and got to work. It was ugly work, but it was worth it. Rose had given him so much pleasure. He still loved her. He started to think, even though he hadn't gotten to know her well, he might love her more than all the others.

He finished up with Rose, and got her ready to replace Trish. Trish went into the trunk of Rose's car for her trip to his favorite remote spot in the desert, his graveyard of broken hearts.

SIXTY

Grace was giggling again. Erick sat across from her, tipsy and sloppily pouring more champagne and orange juice into her glass. He was making a mess of everything, and they should have quit before they caused a worse scene, but they were having so much fun. The only thing better than this, would be the part where they stumbled back to her place and attempted to make love. They would probably pass out before they could do a very good job at it, but it would be fun just the same.

On the walk back to her place, they stopped at a liquor store and bought another bottle of champagne, which Grace knew damn well they wouldn't be able to finish, but it felt so good to throw caution to the wind, to be bad, to be free, to be in love, to be... happy. All days couldn't be as outrageous as this one, so she forced herself to stay in the moment and not worry about anything else, certainly not worry about what horrible things may befall her later.

As they stumbled into her apartment, and then into the bedroom, tearing off each other's clothes, Grace stopped for a moment at the edge of the bed, as Erick tumbled onto his back and stared hard at her.

"Whaaat?" Grace slurred.

"C'mere..." he slurred back.

She climbed on to him and met him body-to-body, face-to-face.

"I fuckin' love you, Grace."

"I fuckin' love you too, Erick."

"You know what else? You know what's what?"

"What's what?" Grace asked.

"You're gonna marry me someday Grace Elliott. Someday, you're gonna marry me."

"You think so?" she asked.

"Yup," said Erick, just as he passed out. Grace rolled over and off of him, curled her back close up to the side of his body, and began to cry.

"Please don't take this away from me," she said to whoever might be listening, "Please let me have this."

She was grateful for the drunk because it knocked her out, and took her to the sweet oblivion where Erick would always love her.

SIXTY-ONE

Nancy Bauer left and Dan immediately entered the interview room where Erin was standing up, ready and excited to follow these new leads.

"Hold tight there, Taylor," Dan motioned for her to stay put. "I've got something."

After excusing himself from the interview with Nancy, he had gone back to the missing persons' files to find information on Cicily and Jenny. He put two files down on the table in front of Erin. She closely examined the contents and the photos of the two women.

"Jennifer Chan, age 20 when she disappeared nearly four years ago. Worked at the diner a few days a week, studied microbiology at UCLA. No boyfriend. Originally from Seattle. According to her parents, Jenny had already put in her resignation at the diner, and not much was done in terms of questioning anyone she worked with. They were extremely angry and not very cooperative with LAPD." Dan took a deep breath and continued.

"Cicily Masters. She was a struggling actress, age 27. Moved out here from Alabama five years ago. Some discrepancy about when she was last seen. One witness said she was at the gym on a Friday, which would have been after her last shift at the diner on a Thursday, but there wasn't a record of her using her membership card. So either she got by the front desk without using her card, or possibly it was a computer glitch, or maybe she wasn't actually there, but she had a shift at the diner on Sunday, which she never showed up for. She could have been missing for a few days at that point."

"Holy shit, Dan, we've been going through all these files, eliminating women just like this. It's got to be the same guy, don't you think? I mean, this is the most solid lead we've gotten."

"Yea, we need to re-interview everyone we can about

Jenny and Cicily, and I think we also need to consider that physical type and race aren't motivating factors for him at all, which means we have a lot more potential victims on our hands. Shit," said Dan, "that leaves us with a lot of possibilities."

"Yeah," said Erin, "shit indeed."

SIXTY-TWO

Kent became depressed after he put Rose in the freezer. He had let her leave too quickly. Sure, it had been a very erotic encounter, but he was starting to feel dirty. It was like a one-night stand. He hadn't gotten to know her. He just took her out here, and everything happened so fast. It had gotten out of control so quickly. The experience had cheapened him. Rose was a tramp. She didn't know what love was. Total despair washed over Kent. He needed to get back to the city. The memories of this cabin were plaguing him. He convinced himself that the next time, the next woman, would be different. However, the doubts still gnawed at his brain and crawled on his skin like ants.

He needed to get back to his place and get his car, and he needed to get rid of Rose's car. What should he do with it? He started to get overwhelmed with all the technical problems. His fingerprints were all over the car, and on some of the other things in the trunk. He couldn't abandon the car in too conspicuous a place, where it would draw attention, but how was he going to get back to L.A.? It was too risky to drive her car all that distance. What if he got pulled over, and the cops ran the tags? Maybe he could take a bus back to L.A. That could work. He would wipe the car down of all prints and, with gloves on, drive her car into Palm Springs and leave it parked somewhere. It would take a while before anyone noticed it and towed it, or reported it. From Palm Springs, he would take a bus back to Los Angeles, and he would re-group. He would find a woman. He would take his time. He needed to stop making rash decisions. He was acting desperate. Love is not desperate. He would take his time finding her, and he would take his time loving her when he did. He knew; he just *knew* the next one would be very, very special. He couldn't wait. But he would. Because she was going to be worth the wait.

SIXTY-THREE

Erin and Dan suddenly had more work than they knew what to do with. The process of re-interviewing any family members or friends of the missing women would be difficult; they had no real information, or hope to give anyone, so it was quite a bleak fishing expedition.

Erin drove down to San Pedro to interview Trish's boyfriend, Greg. She still wasn't too sure he should be let off the hook as a suspect and, at the very least, maybe there was something he had overlooked telling the cops at the San Pedro station. It wasn't all that difficult to track him down because he was one of those pathetic losers who spent part of the afternoon drinking in the very bar where he worked. When she walked into the dingy, dark pub, she spotted him immediately. A hangdog expression reluctantly pulled away from the draft beer to the blonde with purpose in her stride. Great. Another cop.

"Let me guess… you have a few questions for me," he said.

"Good guess. I'm Detective Taylor," Erin said as she put the sketch of the suspect down on the bar, "He look familiar to you?"

Greg glanced at it and shook his head, "No. Not at all."

Erin pulled a stool up and sat close to him. She actually felt some compassion for this poor guy. He really didn't seem like a killer, but one never really knows for sure.

"Did you kill Trish, Greg?" she bluntly asked.

"What? God, when will this end? No. NO. I didn't kill her. *I don't kill people.* I love her. I fucked up, okay? I'm an idiot. A selfish, stupid idiot. But I'm not a killer."

"Okay."

He just stared at Erin and, with confusion said, "Okay? That's it? Do you believe me?"

"Yes," she said, "Actually, I do. But I needed to be sure. I wanted to look in your eyes. How well did you know Trish?"

"What? We've been seeing each other for… I don't know, like three years. I know her."

"Would she just take off somewhere and not tell anyone?"

"I don't think so. That doesn't sound like something she would do. I think someone hurt her. And it's my fault. I left her there on the side of the road. I'm a dick."

Erin wasn't going to argue with him. It was a dick move to leave a woman stranded on the side of the road late at night. She stood up to leave. He had no information for her, so she'd do a quick walk-around the area where Trish disappeared, and then she'd head back to L.A.

Just as she was about to turn her back, Greg asked her in a broken whisper, "Is she dead?"

Erin paused for a moment and stuck to the facts. "We don't know."

She turned and headed for the door but, even with her back to him, and even with Greg's voice so low and cracked, it still pierced her, louder than if he'd screamed.

"Yes, you do."

She didn't need to turn around to know he finished his beer in one swallow.

* * * * *

Erin wandered around the city blocks where Trish had been taken. She didn't think there'd be any real clues conveniently left behind, but she could get a feeling, something. She wasn't sure what she was hoping to find. She traced all the steps, all the details in the report. Where Trish got out of the car, how long Greg drove along side her, where he remembered taking off and leaving her. Pictures of tire tread. The inventory of items found: Trish's wedge sandals, one on the sidewalk, one thrown into a grassy area near the sidewalk, her cell phone was also found in the grassy area, flung a further distance than the shoe. The shoes were brand-new, according to her roommate Melissa, and there hadn't been much wear and tear on them. Maybe they were hurting her feet and she was holding them as she walked. She only had a few blocks to go to get home. A few short blocks, and she'd have been safe.

Erin walked along the sidewalk, ignoring the noise of the traffic around her, imagining it was dark, late, and she was walking alone. A car pulls up, possibly offers her a ride. Maybe she takes it? No, she was grabbed. If she had taken it, her shoes and phone would still be with her. So she declines the ride. She continues walking and he... he what? He takes off and hides. The tree on the corner is large, nearly obscuring the stop sign. That was the corner. He'd taken off and parked his car there. He got out and waited for her there. They'd found a few drops of Trish's blood on the sidewalk, not far from one of her shoes. If he hit her hard enough to knock her out, which he obviously did, her other shoe and phone could have been flung a good distance, which they were. Erin stared back at the faint traces of tire tread on the road. Something clicked.

She took out the photos of the tire tread. She read the interview notes again. The tire tread was attributed to Greg, when he said that "he got mad and drove off." Though, what if he hadn't left the tire tread? What if the killer had? Erin looked up Greg's phone number and called him and was surprised that he answered.

"Hello?" His voice was despondent.

"Greg, it's Detective Taylor. Listen, I've got another question for you. When you took off that night, you said you were angry, would you say you peeled out? Left tread on the street?"

"I guess. I don't know. There was tread there, I mean in the pictures the cops showed me. One of them kept saying, 'You were angry, right? You took off and left her? And then what? Did she get back in the car with you around the corner?' Come on, I know they told me there was blood around the corner from where I said I left her, but I didn't go in that direction. I didn't take a right there. I kept going straight. But I guess I could have left tire tread. I don't know."

"Can you drive over here now? I need to examine your tire tread, exactly where you left Trish." As soon as Erin said it, she realized he couldn't drive.

"No, I have to… I have to work. My shift starts soon."

"When?"

"In a little while," he said, with caginess in his voice.

"You're drunk," said Erin.

"Well, I have had a few beers, and I can't get in my car and drive over to hang out with a cop. Sorry, that seems like a bad idea."

"Fine. Sit right where you are. I'm coming to get you. Then I'll drive your car over here. You'll be back in time for your shift."

Erin rushed back to the pub as quickly as possible.

"You ready for a little experiment?"

Greg's perpetual confusion elicited nothing more than a half-hearted nod.

"Give me your keys," Erin said, and he did. She and Greg got in his car. She drove them right back to the spot where Trish had gotten out of the car.

"Now, this is the spot where she got out when you two were fighting?"

"Yes. I'm sure of it. She didn't get out while the car was moving. We were at this stop sign. I drove slowly, trying to get her to get back in the car, and she wouldn't."

"Okay," said Erin, "I'm going to drive, and you tell me the point where you think you took off and left her."

"Well, I'm not sure. I can't be 100% positive about something like that."

"I know. Just do the best you can. I'm going to drive, slowly. Close your eyes if you need to. Try to remember the argument. If you need me to speed up or slow down to match the speed you remember going, just tell me. Tell me if I need to stop."

Erin drove. Greg leaned back in the passenger's seat and closed his eyes. He didn't want to cry in front of this woman, this cop. He wished he could go back to that moment. He'd get out of the car, and he'd make her get back in. He'd kiss her. He'd reassure her. He'd do anything. *Focus.*

"Slow down," he said. Erin slowed the car. "Now, stop." She did, and he opened his eyes and looked out the window. He was quiet as Erin waited patiently. "Back up, just a little." She motioned to a car behind them to go around her, and then she backed up slowly.

"Here," he said, "stop."

She stopped the car. "This is where you took off? You're sure, Greg?"

"Yes, give or take. This is as close as I can estimate."

"All right, I don't suppose you know how fast you were going when you took off?"

Greg slumped into the passenger's seat. "I don't know. I just don't remember."

"This fast?" Erin said as she peeled out fast enough to leave tread.

Greg gasped, "What the – no! Not that fast."

"You're not going to get a retroactive speeding ticket or anything. I just need the truth. That fast? Faster? Slower?"

"Slower, much slower."

"Like this?" she said, as she took off again. Not the tiniest squeak out of the tires.

"Yeah, about that. Maybe a little faster, but not much."

Erin lurched the car forward again.

"Yeah," Greg said, "I guess about that fast."

Erin put the car in park and checked the road for tread. Unless Greg was lying about how fast he was going, there was no way he could have left tire tread like that at the speed he claimed to take off. They also weren't near the spot where the original tread had been photographed. To be sure, Erin got her phone out and took detailed pictures. There was a lot of room for human error, coaxing someone who'd been upset, angry, and possibly drunk to explain exactly where and how he'd stopped and started, but the distance seemed too great between where he left her, and the spot where she was abducted. Unless he was just lying, or had driven around the corner and waited for her and hit her over the head there..., but it still didn't make sense. There was absolutely no evidence of blood in his trunk, and there had been evidence of Trish's blood on the street. If her head had been bleeding, she would have left some in the trunk of his car. She was starting to think the cops had overlooked a lot in the hopes of pinning this on the boyfriend and closing the case.

She sent the pictures of the tire tread to her favorite lab tech and called him right away.

"Hi, Kevin, Taylor here," she said as soon as he answered.

"Hey beautiful white woman, what can I do for you?" Kevin said the weirdest things, but he was the smartest lab tech she'd ever worked with. He made these bizarre jokes that weren't politically correct, but he got away with it because he wasn't afraid to joke at his own expense. He would quip that it was only his smarts at science and math that let people know he was Asian, since he was pudgy, didn't know kung fu, and had white, hippie parents who had adopted him and raised him on rock and roll and positive reinforcement.

"I need you to access the Trish Morris case and pull up the crime scene photos of tire tread taken right after she disappeared. I just sent you shots of tire tread that I made with the primary suspect's car. I need to know if they match. I have a hunch they won't. If they don't, I'm wondering if you can tell me anything about the tire tread from her file."

"I'll call you back in five minutes," Kevin said. If anyone could really come up with something like that in only five minutes, it was Kevin.

Greg was standing sheepishly outside the car and staring at his phone.

"Let me take you back to work," Erin said. She dropped him off, parked his car, and gave him his keys back. Before she headed to her car, she put her hand on his arm, just to stop him.

"Thank you so much for helping me today."

"Yeah, sure, I just hope..." he trailed off as shame washed over his face.

"We will find her Greg. We will. Now, maybe don't drink too much during your shift. I'd hate to think of you driving home tonight all liquored up."

"Yes, Officer. Sorry. Detective. I promise I'll be good."

"Listen, I know you're upset. I know you feel bad about what happened, about your part in it. But beating yourself up isn't going to change anything. The only thing that changes anything is the next step you take, and the next, and the next... you know what I'm saying, Greg?"

Greg's eyes drifted to the ground, and he stared at his feet.

"Yeah, I guess I do know what you mean." He went inside the bar. That was that. He'd never see Trish again, and she suspected he already knew that.

Her phone rang.

"It's been well over eight minutes lazy ass," Erin said to Kevin.

"It's actually been eleven minutes and 13 seconds," he replied.

"Are you just putting numbers together to sound smart?"

"Yes!" Kevin said, delighted that she knew. "So, you're right, Erin; these tire treads aren't the same. The size is different. That I can tell right away just by matching the photos, proportionately. The tire tread you made today is slightly wider than the tire marks from the crime scene photo."

"Is there any way to track down make and model?"

"I'm working on it. I'll see what I come up with, but I can surmise one thing; these marks weren't made by the same car, or at least not by the same tires, on the same car, probably not the same tires on a different car..."

Erin laughed, "I'll let you worry about the scientific details Kevin. Just find me the kind of car this asshole *might* have been driving, and I'll love you forever."

Erin jumped back in her car and took off, heading north to L.A. Her phone rang just as she got on the 110 freeway.

"Dan, what's up? Got anything exciting?" she said as she kept her eyes on the road and put her phone on speaker.

"We've got another missing woman."

Erin's stomach turned over.

"Who is she?"

"Rose Santos, 37, worked evenings cleaning offices after hours, was studying to become a nurse. She cleaned a travel agency night before last. Owner came in this morning and found the back door unlocked. He called her to berate her and could hear her phone ringing. He stepped out into the alley and found her phone on the asphalt. Then he found blood on the brick wall near the back door, and immediately called the police. I'm heading over there now. I'll text you the address if you want to meet me there."

"You bet. Shit. You think it's him?"

"Could be, Erin. She's a little older than some of the others, but as far as physical type, it's hard to say. He doesn't seem to have one."

"Yeah, I know. This might have just been another opportunity he couldn't resist."

By the time Erin got to the crime scene in West L.A., a lot of the work had been done. However, Erin wasn't there to take blood samples, or put fibers in baggies; she just wanted a feel for whether or not Rose had been taken by HIM, by Lonely Tuna Melt. She headed straight for Dan.

"Officers are already canvassing?" she asked.

"Yup," said Dan, "We've got them loaded up with our sketch, asking everyone around here. I really think he must live somewhere close to here."

"Yeah, could be. Lauren, Cicily, Jenny, and this one – Rose, they were all taken from the west side of L.A.," Erin said.

"This has got to be his comfort zone. But what about the connection to San Pedro? We can't be absolutely certain this same guy took Trish, but if he did, was it a coincidence that he was in San Pedro? Or does he have a reason for being there? A job, or a family member? Wasn't there another missing woman taken from Pedro years ago?"

"Yeah… I think a Samantha something…we should look into that some more." Erin's eyes scanned the alley. She walked around, out to the sidewalk, walked by the alley, and then down it again.

"Did Rose have a car? Where is it? If she had her own cleaning supplies, she must have a car."

"Yeah," said Dan, "We've already checked on that. There's

a good chance he took her in her own car. There's no sign of it around here, so we're doing a thorough search of the area, in case he dumped it somewhere, and we also need to release all the information to the public, so that if anyone spots her car, we are notified immediately."

"Is it a common car?"

"Not really. White '97 Buick Riviera."

"So we report it stolen? In case an officer runs the tags… or if he's already left L.A., we want CHP to know we're on the lookout for this car, too. Have you gotten a picture of Rose?"

"Let me check on that," Dan walked off to talk to another officer as Erin stood staring down the alley. Where was this asshole? Did he get Rose too? Was this a random act of violence, or was it him? If it was him, then there was no longer any doubt. If he had taken Trish, then Trish was dead. Rose was her replacement.

SIXTY-FOUR

Kent had followed his plans exactly. Ditching Rose's car had been easy. Riding the bus back to L.A. was not the biggest thrill he'd ever had, but it was the smart thing to do. He rode all the way to Hollywood, and then took a cab back to his apartment. He was exhausted by the time he got home. He immediately felt such an extreme combination of fatigue and restlessness he didn't know what to do. He took a shower and paced around. He considered going out, but when he turned on the news and saw Rose's picture, he felt sick. *Damn. I've got to get out of here.*

He was running out of money, but he needed to get the hell out of Los Angeles. There was too much pressure here. Then, he noticed the strangest thing. The red light, blinking on his answering machine. Most people didn't use these anymore. Most people had fancy voicemail systems and cell phones that went on the internet, but Kent had little use for things like that. Every so often, he'd get a call from Gene, the guy who called to offer him handyman work, and some years his mom would remember to call him on his birthday, but he rarely got any other calls. He almost never had messages, so he really wasn't in the habit of checking his machine too often, but there it was, blinking like a beacon of loneliness in his dark, depressing apartment.

He suddenly felt nervous. That blinking light. It could be anyone. Probably just Gene, with a job. Or someone wanting to sell him carpet cleaning or something. It was just a message, but he still felt a strange social anxiety about listening to it. He tentatively pushed the button.

"Hi Kent, it's your Uncle Roy. Listen, I need to talk to you right away. It's important. Please call me. It's… it's about your mom… she…"

Kent's brain went blank before he could listen to the rest of the message or write down his Uncle Roy's phone number. He sat down on the floor. His upper lip started to sweat. His palms started to sweat. His breathing was labored. This couldn't be good. He needed to call Uncle Roy, but every time he tried to listen to the message, he couldn't get through it. He felt sick and scared. It took him five or six tries to get the information down, and then a few more tries to gather the courage to call his uncle.

"Hello?" came the gruff voice that Kent hadn't heard in years – many, many years. Kent had lived with Uncle Roy for a few years, off and on, as a child. Of all the relatives Kent's mom had tried to dump him on, Uncle Roy had been the kindest, and had put up with it the longest. Roy had compassion for his mess of a sister but, eventually, even he couldn't take it anymore. At one point, he had even offered to legally adopt Kent, but Kent's mother had gone through the roof, and taken Kent back home to live with her, for good. He had been about 11 years old, maybe 12, by then, and she realized he was old enough that she could leave him alone, so she did just that, and stopped dumping him on other people. That's when the real loneliness started for Kent. Things were never the same after that. Before, his life had been hard, but there had been a kind of adventure to it, not ever knowing if he'd be staying with an uncle, his grandmother, an aunt, a cousin. But then it was just him, and his mom, and she was never there. And even when she was there, she wasn't really there.

"Hi Uncle Roy, it's Kent."

"Kent, I'm so glad you called me back. Listen, I think you'll need to come down to San Pedro. Your mother has… well; she's gone, Kent. She died…" Roy paused and gave Kent a moment before continuing.

"It might have been a stroke. We're not sure yet. A neighbor heard one of her dogs barking incessantly and went over to check on her. She knocked on the door for some time, but your mother didn't answer, so she called –"

"It doesn't matter, Uncle Roy. I don't need the details. Can I come down and see her?"

"Well, there's a lot we need to take care of, and yes; I think you should come down here. I am the executor of her will, and I – well, how soon can you get here?"

"I'll leave now. I'll be there in less than an hour."

Kent hung up the phone and packed a duffel bag with a few things, because it might be a while before he came back to this apartment. If he ever came back to this apartment.

As he drove down to his mother's house, the house he sort of grew up in, the house that loneliness built, he rode a roller coaster of emotion. Numbness, then anger. Numbness, then anger.

That numbness, like pins and needles, fought its way to the surface of his skin, and in those moments, he did not care that his fucking mother was dead. She had never been much of a mother, and now she was gone, and the nothing that was there wasn't much different than the nothing he'd felt sitting on the floor when he was six, wondering why she never bothered to look at him. He could have lit himself on fire, and she wouldn't have noticed, wouldn't have cared.

That's when the anger would come. He fought to keep from speeding his car down the freeway, and the rage pushed against his eyes until he was sure they would explode from their sockets. *That bitch.* She went and just died. She died without hearing him yell in her face how much he hated her. He should get that chance. He should get to tell her. *It's all your fault. Love is impossible, and it's all your fault.*

She never believed he would find someone to love him. But he would. He'd show her. Even in death, she'd know. *Love conquers all. Death is but a shadow in Love's light.*

It was then that he cried. Believing in the possibility of love was draining the life out of him. He was worn out from pointless, fruitless hoping. He drove, and he cried. He finally stopped crying when he parked in front of his mother's house. How strange it was to see so many people there, and with so many lights on. It had been a very, very long time since that house had so many people inside it, and been warmed by so many lights. He looked to the shadows for his mother. She was there and, also not there, just like she'd always been.

SIXTY-FIVE

When Grace got Magda's call, she felt a mixture of excitement and guilt. She really hadn't been too focused on her career. Her past disappointments and failures had discouraged her from really working on anything new or trying to get any of her previous photographs shown. When she was honest with herself, she knew that was only part of it. Erick had been a distraction – a lovely distraction, but a distraction nonetheless. She had been schoolgirl-silly for letting a love affair sidetrack her from her higher purpose. Then again, maybe she really had no higher purpose. Perhaps not everyone was here for some grand reason. Still, Magda's confident voice on her voicemail was a welcome reprieve from daily despair. Grace immediately called her back.

"Hi Magda, it's Grace."

"Grace darling, I got you a showing."

Grace couldn't believe it. "Oh wow, really? Did Bradley have a change of heart?"

"Not at Bradley's gallery. Screw that asshole. Actually no, I wouldn't screw him with someone else's vagina. I've got this great hook-up with this up-and-coming kick-ass feminista named Gretchen. She just opened a gallery in Venice called Re-Vag-Olution and she's kicking it off with a series called 'Warrior Priestess.' Anyway, darling, she absolutely loves the shots of you and your daughter and is dying to see if you've got anything else that might fit with the theme."

Grace ran through her mental files and knew she had more stuff. She was so excited she nearly squealed, but she tried to sound cool because she was still intimidated by Magda.

"I can put some stuff together and show you… or Gretchen… however you want to work it."

"Fabulous, Grace! We're moving quickly. Can you meet tomorrow?"

Grace was supposed to work her crappy job at the museum in the morning but screw it. An opportunity like this doesn't come along every day. She'd call in sick.

"Of course! Name the time!"

"10 a.m. at her space. I'll text you the addy. Bye, love." And just like that, the elusive Magda was gone. Grace was so excited. She wanted to call someone. She wanted to call Natalie. She wanted to call Erick.

She called Nat and left her a message. She called Erick, and he didn't answer either. Damn. She wanted to share her news with someone.

"Hey, Erick, it's me... Grace. Give me a call. Got some good news today and wanted to share."

She hung up and paced around. She pawed through all her photos, some that she had taken quite a long time ago, before she was married to Stan. She had been obsessed with the seedier parts of downtown Los Angeles for quite a while back then. She would go down early in the morning, around six or so, and she would bring hot coffee and donuts and toiletries, and she would approach the homeless people and ask if she could take photographs of them. Some of them would freak out and yell at her, but many of them were very nice and would happily take whatever goodies she had. Grace would tell them just to go about their business and ignore her, and she'd take pictures. There was one woman, in particular, Grace befriended and had captured quite a few great pictures of her. Could this woman even still be alive? She had said her name was Tilda, and Grace was never sure if that was really her name or not, but Tilda told Grace one day that she loved jelly beans. So Grace would visit Tilda once a week and photograph her and bring her big bags of jelly beans. Tilda told Grace many stories that rambled here and there and sometimes contradicted each other, and Grace always wanted to know (as she did with all the people she met on the streets) what had happened to Tilda to get her to this place – this hard life. Tilda couldn't really say, she would only offer "oh, you know how life can happen to you," but she showed Grace her only real possession – a sort of scarf or chain that Tilda had crafted out of found things such as plastic six pack rings, soda cans, bobby pins, random pieces of broken plastic that were often unidentifiable, as well as broken sunglasses, socks too tattered to wear, even a used condom here and there. None of the stuff was very useful for if it were, it would likely have been stolen but, somehow, it was beautiful to Grace. Forgotten, useless objects... just like these people here. She wanted to document it all. No person, no pair of broken sunglasses, should be forgotten, useless, discarded.

Grace asked Tilda why she did it, expecting a rambling or incoherent answer or no answer at all. Much to her surprise, Tilda answered her.

"I find one thing each day, and I tie it to one end. Every day I add a piece. It helps me count."

"What are you counting?" Grace asked, again assuming she'd get no real answer.

"The days. It's the only way he'll know."

"He? He who? And know what?"

"My George. He'll know how many days."

"How many days of what?" Grace remembered her eyes tearing up when she asked Tilda that, and she wasn't sure why.

"He knows," Tilda said as she caressed a little girl's barrette that had lost its sparkle in what Grace could only imagine was some kind of grief chain, "My George knows. He knows how many days."

And that is all that Tilda would ever say on the matter.

Grace had taken quite a few pictures of Tilda. The strange grief chain of objects Tilda wore over her dirty, layered clothes was featured in many of them. The deep lines of street-living etched in her face were featured in all of them. But beneath the dirt and lines, some faded Eastern European beauty, some past with George lingered. A son, a lover, a friend, a father? Grace would never know. Each photo, laced with the mysteries of one more hard-luck story, made its way back into the folder she had labeled so many years ago, "Skid Row Priestess."

Grace was moved to tears, but not for her own pain. There was a certain pride swelling in her that she had done all this, captured such beauty in all that ragged suffering. Why wasn't she still taking pictures? And why had she never shown any of her work to Erick? She had seen some of his graphic design work, but she'd never shown him any of her photography. Had she been too shy? Maybe it was because he'd never really asked about it. She'd take a chance and show him some. Maybe tomorrow night they could go out and celebrate her success.

Grace was giddy. She had a showing! She had an amazing man who loved her! She had a fabulous best friend, and they would both be there on the opening night of her show! She was a real-live artist, a real-live human being, which sounded weird, but to Grace it meant so much. Maybe she could do this. Maybe she could do this human thing, after all.

The voice crept around the edges of her, slinking up to her, resting on her shoulder, whispering in her ear, "Remember: you're a lemon Grace, always a lemon."

Grace pushed it away. She was not going to let her old negative thinking ruin this. No, she had suffered enough. She had suffered the death of both her parents in a car accident when she was 14, then she had suffered being raised by her passive-aggressive aunt and alcoholic uncle. She had suffered her schizophrenic brother's suicide when she was twenty-two and he was only eighteen. She had suffered a divorce, and worst of all, she had suffered the death of her beloved daughter, Kaylee. Enough was enough. It was *her time*, her time to be happy. She just knew it. She was finally getting a break. The Powers That Be had seen fit finally, to let her live. Grace was going to live. She was going to live like nobody's business. She was going to live life like life was supposed to be lived. There would still be hard times ahead, there would still be disappointments, but she could do something she hadn't really been able to do before. She would roll with the punches. She was going to be grateful. Life had given Grace more than her fair share of lemons, but that was okay. Grace was going to make some sweet-ass motherfuckin' lemonade.

SIXTY-SIX

Yolanda Flores used her master key to enter room 17 at the Starry Moon Motel where she'd been working for almost a year. She had cleaned every one of these rooms many times over. She did her best to stay positive in spite of the filth she was often witness to. The pay wasn't great by American standards, but she was so happy to be here, away from the vicious husband she had left behind in Mexico City. She did her work, made her money, took care of her beloved son, and was doing her best to become an American citizen. She didn't like to get too involved in people's business as a general rule but, on this day, when she went in to clean the room, she would have to decide just how involved she should get. She hadn't cleaned this room in a while. She'd mostly been cleaning second floor rooms lately, but today she was doing the ground floor.

She always did the vacuuming last, because it made more sense that way. She could wipe everything down, and onto the floor, and then mop the bathroom tile, and vacuum the area around the bed. As she pushed the vacuum under the edge of the bed, something small and shiny rolled out from under it. She stopped and turned off the vacuum cleaner and knelt down to see what it was. She must have knocked it with the edge of the vacuum. It was an earring – a small gold hoop with what looked like diamonds to her, set in three places in the gold, but she had never seen real gold or real diamonds, so she couldn't be sure. But it looked nice, expensive. As she went to pick it up, her mind raced. What if it was expensive? Could she sell it? Pawn it? Maybe if she looked hard enough she could find the other one. As soon as her hands touched it, she dropped it and recoiled. She peered closer. There was something on it... was it flesh... dried blood? Now, she was afraid to touch it. It had probably been violently ripped from someone's ear. Maybe she should turn it in to the owner of the motel. Or call the police. That scared her. She couldn't go back to Mexico. She couldn't go back to her angry, abusive husband. He'd be really mad now because she left him. He might kill her. He might kill their son. No. She couldn't go back. But what if this woman, who owned this earring, what if something had happened to her? Maybe she had an angry husband, or boyfriend. So what if she was a fancy, rich, white lady with expensive gold earrings? Some man might have hurt her. No amount of money can keep any woman safe from a mean man. Yolanda grabbed a tissue, picked the earring up, and set it on the dresser. She decided to move the bed and see if there was anything else under there. The bed was positioned between two nightstands, so she couldn't move it very far without moving one of those too. She moved the bed as far she could toward the window. What was that, on the carpet? A very dark stain. Her heart began to pound. Could it be blood? She dragged the nightstand all the way across the room, so she could move the bed further. Yes, there was a stain on the carpet. It could be blood. She didn't know why she did what she did next. It was like some voice inside her was telling her what to do. She lifted the bed up and leaned it against the wall. The bottom of the bed was covered in blood spatter. She screamed, and dropped the bed back to the floor. She would have to call the police. She needed to tell the manager. Mr. Fred was here today. She hated talking to Mr. Fred. He talked in that rude, slow voice white people sometimes used with her, as if she would understand his English better if he talked to her like she was stupid. She wasn't stupid. She was learning English, but some words she still only knew in Spanish. She was so scared. She considered taking the earring and putting the room back in order and not saying anything. No one would ever know. Or some other maid would eventually find it. IF she happened to lift the bed. But what about the woman who had worn this earring? Yolanda didn't know who she was, of course, but, in a way, she felt connected to her. Yolanda knew what it was like to be afraid, to be terrorized by a man. And she had to do the right thing. She wanted to be an American, and she needed to be a good citizen and tell the police. She went to the motel office.

"Mr. Fred, I think we call the police."

Fred stared at her through the window. What now? He really didn't want to have the police crawling around here, but once Yolanda showed him what she'd found, he didn't have much choice. Something pretty bad had happened in that room. He went back and retrieved the slip of paper where he'd written down that detective's number. He'd almost thrown it away, but, fortunately, his own laziness had prevented that.

"Detective Taylor," Erin said when she answered the phone.

"Detective Taylor, my name is Fred Watson. You left me a message about a sketch of some guy. Well, I don't know anything about that guy, but I think there's something here you might need to see."

* * * * *

Fred hung back, miserable, as cops and crime scene investigators poured over the motel room and every part of the grounds. He had searched the records for any indication of who had rented that room and couldn't really offer much. He was getting a little nervous. Cash transactions were kept under the radar for the obvious reason of avoiding tax on all the income, which meant if someone paid cash, any paperwork with their information on it was "lost" – as in, never filled out. There were no surveillance cameras on the property, and really no way to learn the identity of the person or persons who had rented that room on the night in question. Fred looked at pictures of Lauren McLaughlin. He'd seen her on the news of course, but he still had the same answer. He'd never seen her at the motel. Every staff member was questioned. She didn't look familiar to anyone.

Eileen Cambridge was contacted and shown the earring. She broke into hard tears. It was most definitely Lauren's earring and, in fact, those earrings had been a gift to Lauren from Eileen. There was sufficient DNA on the earring to confirm that it was Lauren's, and that it had been ripped from her ear, or maybe she had been hit hard enough at just the right angle for it to rip out of her ear, taking tiny bits of flesh and blood with it.

The investigators examining the bed and carpet suggested that the bed had been picked up, and the killer had leaned it against the window, maybe to cut down on sights or sounds coming through the window into the parking lot. Strangely, there was only the one stain on the carpet, but it may be that he had covered the floor in plastic to prevent blood from leaking into the carpet, and the stain had been a mistake, or the plastic had torn in one spot. Perhaps moving the bed had been done on purpose, so that it could be moved back to the center of the room to cover any stains. Every fiber they could bag, they did. They took the vacuum cleaner bag as evidence. They snaked the drains for any hair, blood or other DNA. The blood had been cleaned off the walls as well. A good enough clean-up job had been done by the killer that none of the cleaning staff had noticed anything. If it hadn't been for the earring, the evidence could have gone unnoticed indefinitely, or until an extreme clean or re-model occurred, which, obviously, wasn't too often in a place like this.

Erin spoke decent Spanish, but Dan was fluent, so he got the task of interviewing Yolanda Flores. He reassured her that her cooperation and help meant a great deal to them, and that she didn't need to worry that she was in any trouble, or at risk of being deported. He didn't get much information from her other than the obvious – what she'd found, and how she'd found it. When asked why she had lifted the bed like she did, she told Dan she didn't know why, she said a voice inside her head told her to, so she did. It reminded him of things Erin would say. "I just had a feeling…" was a perfectly reasonable explanation, and Dan knew exactly what Yolanda meant. And he was so glad she'd just "had a feeling" that she should pick up that bed.

Lauren's blood was in this room. They had their abduction site, the murder site and the dump site, and maybe they were finally a few steps closer to catching this guy. His DNA was in this room somewhere too. It had to be. Maybe he wouldn't be in the system if he'd never been convicted of a crime, but they'd have a sample. People think they can clean up after themselves well enough to avoid getting caught, but that was virtually impossible. A piece of this killer was in here somewhere, and they were going to find it.

SIXTY-SEVEN

Grace adored Gretchen on sight. She was a solidly built woman with dark-brown skin and silver dreadlocks. Everything about her screamed "strong woman," and Grace always liked being around women like that. She admired that strength and wished she herself could possess it. It was so easy for life to level Grace, and she was so quick to tears that she couldn't help but perceive herself as a weak woman. Her newfound lease on life, where she was going to truly live and all that, made her think that attracting someone like Gretchen into her life was a good sign, and part of the new journey. She could learn a lot from Gretchen and Magda about feminine strength. They were very striking together; Magda with her elegant and tough Eurasian beauty and Gretchen with her stunning dark skin, silver hair and powerful confidence. Grace felt frumpy by comparison – boring, milky, like a bowl of vanilla pudding, but she reminded herself that these two women thought very highly of her work; enough that Grace's pictures would be part of the "Warrior Priestess" exhibit. Grace told herself it was okay to be happy, and proud of this. Grace told herself she was a Warrior Priestess too.

The night of the opening was a blur to Grace in many ways, because it felt so surreal. Natalie came with her boyfriend Zach, and they were awesome and supportive, gushing over how much they loved it. Natalie was so happy for Grace. Grace was beaming at first but as the night wore on, Natalie could see her fighting off some pain around the edges of her eyes, and it was obvious what it was. Grace attempted to be covert, but the number of glances towards the door, and the discretionary checks of her cell phone said it all. Erick was late. And as the evening ended, it was worse than "Erick was late." It was "Erick never showed up."

Grace got home very late that night, wrestling with a combination of exhilaration and disappointment. She had gotten a text from Nat asking if she was okay, and she texted back she was happy, because everything had gone so well.

She was disappointed that Erick never showed and hadn't responded to her last text when she asked him where he was, but she didn't say anything about it to Natalie because she was determined not to give in to negativity. Erick had a reasonable explanation for missing the opening and right now, she hoped he was okay and that nothing bad had happened to him. She sent him one more text just before she fell asleep, and hoped there would be an answer forthcoming.

It was two in the afternoon the next day before he responded with the message: *I'm so sorry, Grace. My mother was rushed to the hospital last night. I had to go and be with her, and I didn't get home until this morning.*

Grace felt awful. She had been so selfish; only thinking of herself and her opening, wanting attention from Erick and here he had been at his sick mother's bedside. She called him right away.

"Hey, babe. Is everything okay? Is your mother all right?"

"Yea," Erick said, though his voice was really tired, "She's okay now. I'm so sorry I missed your opening. I totally suck. I'll make it up you, somehow."

"It's okay. Don't worry about it. Hopefully, there will be others." Grace waited for a response, but Erick said nothing, so she continued, "What happened with your mother?"

"Well... I don't know... it might have been a stroke. She fainted, or fell or something. So, they're testing some stuff, but she's going to be fine."

A voice inside her said: *he's lying.* But, why would he lie about something like this? She dismissed his perceived dishonesty and put the blame where it belonged – on her bottomless insecurity. Grace took deep breaths to calm the uneasiness in her gut, to stay in the moment and be grateful. He was sorry, and it was a circumstance beyond his control.

"Well, my photographs will be up for the entire month, so maybe we can go over one day, and you can still see the exhibit. It's a really cool gallery."

"Sure, babe. That'll be fun. So, how about I make it up to you tonight? Dinner, drinks and dancing in the sheets?"

Grace's heart leapt. Everything was fine. It was all going to be all right. This was her new life. Gratitude works.

They had an exquisite night together. He apologized repeatedly for missing her opening, and they made plans to go to view the exhibit the following weekend. He spent the rest of the weekend with her, and when he left for work on Monday morning, he kissed her forehead and told her he loved her. Grace stayed in bed as long as she could, relishing the deliciousness of it until she had to go to her job at the museum gift shop, and she didn't even care how boring it was there because she was happy. She felt loved, and safe, and successful. She felt so good that she managed to tune out the voice telling her that she was still, and always would be, a lemon, and that the other shoe simply couldn't wait another minute to drop. After all, it's the nature of the shoe.

* * * * *

Grace felt great that week, though, as it wore on, she started to have that uneasy feeling again. She shrugged it off, and told herself it was ridiculous to let insecurity consume her. Things were going well. She didn't hear from Erick all week, and she told herself that he was just busy. They would be going to see her exhibit on Saturday, and they could both use a little space anyway, so she chose not to bug him with messages. By Friday, when she still hadn't heard from him, she started to get annoyed. He had said, "I'll call you, and we'll figure out what time to meet up on Saturday." But he still hadn't called. She was being too high-maintenance.

Natalie called on Friday afternoon and asked her to meet up for happy hour with her and Zach and some people from work, and Grace accepted. Maybe Erick would be there too. She should text him and see, but decided against it. She told herself she was being too needy, and she could just talk to him later, or tomorrow.

As Grace walked into the bar, the same cantina where she'd met Erick, she scanned the room. Her eyes passed quickly over everyone she expected to be there until she spotted Erick. He didn't see her at first, as he was engrossed in his phone, probably sending a text. She walked up to the table and there were all the customary greetings, but Erick hadn't noticed her. She stood behind him and then leaned down to kiss the side of his face.

"Hey, babe, glad to see you here." To her shock, and humiliation, he flinched.

"Shit, Grace, you scared me," he said. Grace's face burned. What the hell was going on? Why was he acting like this? He furiously put his phone away. He was hiding something. "I didn't think you'd be here. Natalie didn't say anything about you being here." It came out like an accusation.

"Well, Erick, I'm so sorry I surprised you, but I guess I stupidly thought you might be as happy to see me as I am to see you."

"Grace," he lowered his voice as he noticed everyone else at the table starting to stare, "Can we please not do this here?"

"Do what here?" Grace demanded. When Erick offered no response, she added, "Would you like to go somewhere else?" She already knew what his answer would be.

"I... I can't," he said, "I have to go. I have to meet someone."

"Who? Who are you meeting?" Grace could not keep her voice from going into an all-out panicky shriek.

"Really, Grace? You have to know everything? Come on, I just have to go is all. I'll call you later." Erick stood up and headed for the door.

"Tomorrow? You'll call me tomorrow? About the plans we already made to go to the gallery?" They were making a scene. She was foolish, and desperate and insane, but she didn't care anymore because she was watching him walk out the door, without answering her question, without turning around to even look at her. Grace's tears came – hard and fast – and the explosion of them, so close to the surface made her face feel bloated, ready to burst, and she swallowed giant hard lumps of confusion and rage as she followed him out of the restaurant.

"Hey!" she screamed, no longer caring at all how angry she sounded because her rage was all there was right now.

"What, Grace? What?" He finally turned to her. He looked… inconvenienced by her, by her pain. The expression on her face was far worse than him walking away.

"I don't understand what's happening. Please… just talk to me." Grace quelled her anger and hoped he would only see how hurt she was. Maybe if he understood how vulnerable and defenseless she was, he would warm up. This coldness was killing her.

"I'm sorry, Grace," he said, as some forced tenderness returned to his face, "I'm just going through some stuff, and I need to go right now. I need to be alone. Please. Can we please talk tomorrow?" He reached out to her and pulled her close.

"Okay," Grace said, warily. Something was wrong. She was terrified she was losing him. What had gone wrong? What had she done? She searched his eyes, hoping for some clue as to what he was feeling.

"You'll call me tomorrow, then? Please? I'm going to be worried until then."

"Yes, Grace. I'll call you tomorrow." He released their embrace.

"I love you," Grace said, as she looked into his eyes, past

her confusion and hurt, and past whatever he was going through, and right into his heart and soul.

"I love you, too," he said, but his eyes were already on the horizon.

He walked to his car, without a single backward glance to Grace. She went straight to her car and let the tears flow. She texted Nat, *I'm sorry. I can't come back inside. I'll check in with you later,* and then she drove home so she could be alone with her pain. He wouldn't call her tomorrow, but she allowed the futile hope anyway, to help her manage her escalating anxiety. She did her best to distract herself, but it was hard to think of anything else. He was avoiding her, and it was obvious. She just didn't know why. She waited it out all day Saturday and never heard a word from him. She had a long conversation with Natalie, who desperately tried to reassure her. She went to see a movie, and had absolutely no idea what it was about because she couldn't concentrate on any of it. She had only wanted an excuse to turn her phone off, so she could stop compulsively checking it for calls or texts from Erick. She drank an entire bottle of wine alone in her apartment on Saturday night and cried herself to sleep. When she woke up on Sunday, she had a momentary lapse of reason and thought everything would be okay, and then she remembered that it wasn't okay. It was far from okay. She needed an answer. She finally broke down and called Erick, and of course, she got his voicemail.

"Erick, it's me. Just wondering what's going on. We were supposed to talk yesterday and get together. I still haven't heard from you. What's going on? You need to talk to me."

She hung up, and she waited. Time was a ridiculous illusion. A minute was more like a year in a prison of isolation and confusion. After three excruciating hours, she got a text from him. Her heart flew to the very edge of the cliff of hope and was instantly dashed to the jagged rocks below when she read the message.

I can't do this anymore. I don't have the strength for a relationship.

Grace screamed, or rather something foreign to her poured out of her, unrecognizable to her own ears, because it was not exactly like a scream. It was a scream she suppressed that came out more like a yelp. She whimpered and growled like a wounded Chihuahua with her leg in a trap, or at least, that was the bizarre image that entered her mind. It took her a second to realize the awful noise had come from her. She had been standing near the kitchen counter, and her legs buckled beneath her. She lay down on the floor and curled into a fetal position. She cried in a way that was more like dry-heaving. Grace had cried so much in her life that it must be impossible for her body to produce any more tears. Surely there must be a limit on tear production. Surely there must be a limit on human suffering. Grace had reached it. She had reached her limit. She was filled with a rage that consumed her, burning out of control, unstoppable and unrelenting. How could this be happening? How could he go from loving her to not wanting to be with her at all? She retraced every step she'd taken. There must be someone else. That's who he'd been texting at the restaurant. There was someone else. Someone better than her. Of course, there was. It wouldn't be too hard to find someone better than her. After all, she was useless. She was a lemon. A stupid, broken, ugly lemon. She should have known better. She wasn't the kind of person who could keep a hold on things like happiness and love. She was here to suffer, and she had stupidly forgotten that. She had once again let someone into her heart, and he was gone. He was gone, just like her parents, and her brother, and her daughter. Her life was a graveyard. There was nowhere to go anymore. Everything was death and decay. Everything was heartbreak. Everything was flesh, which rots down to the bone which crumbles to dust and is nothing anymore, nothing distinct or separate from the ground we walk on without a second thought about it.

She waited two hours to respond to him because she simply didn't know what to say. It wouldn't matter what she said or did at this point. She had lost him. It was there, in his words, "I can't do this anymore." It wasn't that he didn't love her – he *couldn't*; he was incapable of it. But he had loved her before, hadn't he? Or had he been lying? Or did he just realize with each passing day how very unlovable Grace was? She had tried so hard to believe, to open her heart, and to be good to him. Oh god, she was so stupid. She had made a promise to herself. She remembered now that she had promised never to believe in love again after Kaylee died, and she had gone back on that promise. This was her punishment. She had betrayed Kaylee's memory, desecrated her grave with her silly, selfish love affair, and now she was being punished. It seemed harsh and unfair, too extreme a price to pay. Why couldn't she just be happy? Why did everything have to get taken away? Why does everyone die? She was surprised Erick didn't die too, just to get away from her.

She called Erick and left another message rambling on and on about how she didn't understand and who the hell was she, who was he fucking, and that she had a right to know.

Later that night, he texted her one last time: *There's no one else. Please don't make this any harder than it needs to be.*

Well, if being dumped for this mysterious woman who was presumably superior to her was bad, the thought of being dumped because being alone was better than being with Grace was even worse.

Grace didn't bother responding to him, since he had clearly told her not to "make this any harder." *What an asshole.* As if it could be any harder for her. Few things are harder than discovering just how unlovable you are.

Grace went through the very basic motions of her virtually non-existent life. After four days of not eating or sleeping, she collapsed at work and woke up on the floor of the gift shop with her boss hovering above her. He told her to take a few days off and had one of the other employees drive her home.

Grace hadn't told Natalie what had happened. She was dreading telling her that Erick had dumped her with a text message because then Natalie would be worried. Grace suddenly hated herself even more than she ever thought possible. She hated being the crazy, fragile friend whom Natalie always had to worry about. She also didn't want to bother Nat, who was having such a great time with Zach. Other people had a real shot at happiness, and Grace was sick of dragging everyone down around her. She considered suicide, as she had many times in her life, but she had promised herself, no matter how bad things got; she wouldn't do that. She wouldn't do what her brother had done. She remembered how bad she wanted to kill herself after Kaylee died, and she somehow gotten through that. She hadn't wanted to put Stan through it. She understood, first-hand, what damage suicide does to the people left to pick up the pieces. She was already a shitty, selfish person. She couldn't bring herself to be even more selfish. Then again, who would care if she died? Natalie would. And then Natalie would have to feel that horrible guilt and wonder if she could have done anything to stop it. Grace ruled out suicide, but she didn't rule out dying.

If Erick didn't love her, then fuck him. Why would she want to be with someone who didn't love her? She didn't. Grace's mind raced. She felt like a caged animal, the cage her own life, and there was no escape. Not even death. Where was death when you needed it?

After numerous blurry days of repressing suicidal thoughts and fantasizing about running over Erick's face with a bus, Grace got a call from Natalie.

"Grace, are you okay? What's going on with you and Erick?"

"Nothing is going on with us, Nat. Not anymore. He's done with me. He text-dumped me."

"WHAT?" Natalie wanted to run over Erick with a bus too. She listened to Grace tell her everything, and she dreaded adding to it, but she had to. Grace was her best friend. She had to tell her the truth.

"So that asshole told you there was no one else? That shithead."

A crack ran sharp and jagged down Grace's heart. *That's gonna leave a mark.*

"Just tell me, Nat. I need to know so I can start hating him some more."

"This chick came by to have lunch with him today. They were... well, let's just say, they weren't just friends. They were all over each other. It was sickening. I was horrified, and I didn't want to say anything, you know in front of her. But after lunch, when she was gone, I confronted Erick. Apparently, she's an ex he was with years ago, and he reconnected with her at some party, and now he's all in love, and when I asked about you he said it wasn't about you; it was just he'd never really gotten over this woman, Stephanie –"

"They're always named Stephanie," Grace interjected.

"No shit. Aren't they? Remember when Lizard Man blew me off without a word and then was engaged to a Stephanie like the next week?"

"Seriously, men suck," said Grace, "That was horrible. I hope someone shoots an arrow through that guy's skull."

Natalie laughed in spite of herself. Her ex getting an arrow through the head was a hilarious image.

"So, I know it's petty and stupid but I have to ask, is she prettier than me?"

"No, Grace. Not at all. Not even close. So, when I asked him 'What about Grace?' he just started rambling about this chick and how he saw her with her dog, and he just knew she was the one because she was so tender and open-hearted with her dog, and it just didn't make sense, none of it, and I said, 'I hate you for hurting Grace, Erick.' And then I stormed off, but I wish I could have done more. I didn't know what to do, Grace. I'm just… I'm so angry. I mean, what the hell is up with him? Is he insane?"

"No, Nat, he's not insane. I'm the crazy one. He wants a nice normal girl, with a dog. See if only I'd gotten a dog, I could have love, but I can't take care of a dog. I can't take care of myself. I couldn't take care of Kaylee… I'm useless, Nat. Useless." Grace couldn't do more than cry as Natalie listened helplessly.

"Grace, why don't I stay over at your place tonight? Or you come to mine. I don't think you should be alone."

"No," Grace pulled herself together. She couldn't bear being around anyone. She wished there was some way she didn't have to be around herself, but she hadn't quite figured out how to pull that off. "I'm fine, Nat. I'm not going to do anything… you know; I'm not going to kill myself or anything… not tonight."

"Not tonight? What's that supposed to mean? Maybe tomorrow? Maybe next Wednesday? Come on, Grace. Think of Brian."

"I do, Nat. So you know… I won't do that… but just… just check on me… tomorrow I mean, and the next day. And… well, I'm okay, but I'm not you know? I just need… right now; I need to lie down, and try to sleep. I'm worn out from this shit."

"Okay, I understand. But I'm calling you every day, Grace. You're officially on suicide watch. Just remember: Erick is a complete douchebag. He's obviously, totally unworthy of you. I know that doesn't take away the hurt, or the sting of rejection, but he's the worthless one – not you. I know, okay?

You can trust my opinion more than his right?"

"Of course I can, Nat. I love you."

"I love you, too, Grace. Call me any moment of any day, any night if you need to."

Grace had tried to come off stronger than she felt because, if there was any way to put into words what she was feeling and thinking, Natalie would never have left her alone. She'd probably have her committed.

Grace stumbled through a nightmare, a personal hell, the graveyard of her life and downed three sleeping pills with a glass of wine. She woke an hour later, rushed into the bathroom and vomited up the wine and sleeping pills. She could never keep those things down without something in her stomach. The idea of food made her feel like rusty nails were swimming in her gut, so she got the bright idea of drinking more wine instead. What could possibly go wrong with that plan? And even though drinking it straight from the bottle and keeping said bottle on the nightstand next to her bed was probably an indication of unhealthy levels of self-medication at best, and crippling alcoholism at worst; nothing could stop her from chasing the sweet oblivion of passing out.

She woke up at four in the morning. She distinctly felt a heaviness that she couldn't shake, as if a demon were sitting upon her chest, gradually suffocating her. She knew this demon well. This demon was Despair, and he wasn't going anywhere. He was going to sit on her chest but never have the decency to kill her. Stupid, asshole demon.

She indulged a memory of being in bed with Erick, and the tender way he would caress her hip when he first woke up. She pushed the memory away– actually shoving at the air with her hands and growling out loud. She hated Erick, despised him for doing this to her. She didn't know if she would even want him if he wanted her back. She just didn't want to endure another grieving process. She simply couldn't bear the grief of her existence.

She had trusted his heart to love her. She had trusted herself to open her heart to him, and now she was utterly lost. She'd never be able to trust herself again. And if she couldn't trust, if she couldn't open her heart, how could she ever have love again? She couldn't. There was no hope. She couldn't even kill herself because she didn't want to be a selfish jerk. Erick was a selfish jerk, why couldn't he kill himself?

Her heart hurt. It pushed at her chest. Her heart was trying to escape, but the demon pressed harder. Her heart beat louder, faster, and stronger. She willed it to stop, or to explode. She focused all her energy on it. *Just stop beating. Just stop. It's burning so much. It will burn up in my chest.*

Grace spent hours wishing she would have a heart attack, and failed. She wished someone would break into the house and murder her. That would be a tragedy, but then no one could be mad at her for committing suicide. She could leave her doors and windows unlocked from now on. She considered putting on a revealing outfit, with some cash sticking out of her pockets, and stumbling drunk down a dark alley in a bad neighborhood in the hopes she'd be attacked and, hopefully, killed. This was dark even for Grace, and she could never really tell anyone she'd considered it, but it offered her some sick, strange hope. A fantasy of release.

Grace was a lemon. She didn't know how to live. She only knew how to suffer. She was sick of always landing back in the pit of her despair. So she hoped, with all her heart, that someone would give her the most magnificent gift of all. Grace wanted someone to come along and put her out of her misery.

SIXTY-EIGHT

Kent was miserable. Once the initial shock had worn off, and the funeral was over, and the distant relatives had gone and left him all alone, he sat by himself in the house that loneliness built and felt like a lost little boy, all over again. It was over. His mother was gone for good this time, and he'd never see her again. He'd never get the love from her that he'd been waiting for, and he'd never get the love from any woman that he so desperately needed and deserved. What if there was no one out there for him? What if no one would ever really, truly "get" him? Every woman he met ended up being a selfish, crazy bitch that didn't appreciate him, didn't love him. He felt more lost than ever and didn't know what to do next. He had messed everything up with Rose. He hadn't really given her a chance.

He should get out of the house and meet someone new. It was a gift in a way, having this house. He could let his apartment go and, between this place and the cabin in the desert and the little bit of money his mother had left him, he'd do all right. It was all still in his mother's name, and since she'd gone back to using her maiden name, he and his mother didn't even have the same last name. So for now, with everything still in her name, he could fall off the radar a little, which might be a good thing considering all the news coverage about Lauren, Trish and Rose. The media had also released his sketch in conjunction with two other missing women – Cicily Masters and Jennifer Chan. It was maddening. Being repeatedly broken-hearted and betrayed by these bitches was bad enough, but now it was on display for everyone to see. Maybe it was good that his mother wasn't around to see what was happening. He should lay low for awhile. All this attention was making him nervous. He'd never allowed himself to spend too much time worrying about what would happen if he got caught. He didn't think he would anyway. He couldn't even fathom he was doing anything wrong. But the media plastered these women's faces all over the place, glorifying them, treating them as if they were somehow the victims of some dreadful tragedy. He was the real victim here. These women were shallow, vain, arrogant creatures. They glided around in their soft skin, tossing their flowing hair around, luring men with their luscious scents and then castrating and humiliating them, and getting indignant when men treated them like sex objects. Underneath the beautiful exterior, they were all icy, snake-like devils.

Kent sat at the dining room table in his mother's kitchen, which he supposed was his kitchen now. It was a lost cause, looking for love, but he'd been doing it so long that he didn't know what else to do. He couldn't live any other way. His mind raced with images of devil women luring him in and then rejecting him, but his heart kept whispering the same promise to him: *she's out there, Kent. The one woman who can love you, who will understand you, understand all the pain you've endured, is out there. She's just waiting for you. You have to find her.* Knights in shining armor don't sit at their mother's dirty kitchen table drinking tepid, flat soda. Knights in shining armor rescue damsels in distress. He could almost hear it now… a low, soft coo at first that built up to a cry; a damsel sobbing, trapped in a tower of grief, waiting to be rescued.

"I am coming my love," he said out loud to her. He hoped her heart would respond.

* * * * *

Grace woke up with a start, gasping for air. She'd had another nightmare about Erick. She kept having these gruesome dreams where he'd be really sweet and tender, and then he'd strangle her or stab her, and she'd wake up, unable to breathe, and she'd have to turn on all the lights and pace around the room for hours before she could get back to sleep. She was cracking, utterly falling apart. Sometimes a noise would startle her from sleep and when she'd wake with her face soaking wet, she'd realize it was the sound of her own sobbing that was waking her, her entire face soaked with tears. When she wasn't sobbing in unmanageable grief, she was consumed with rage. She incessantly fought off images of Erick with his brand new dog-loving woman, happier than he could ever have been with Grace, and she'd see them in her mind's eye, frolicking in the park, holding hands and playing with New Awesome Girlfriend's dog. She wished Erick would die. She couldn't bear living in a world that had him in it. Unless he was miserable and suffering, which he wasn't. Of course he wasn't. He got to be happy. Grace got to be miserable. It was just the way things were. *Of course I'm miserable, because I actually have feelings! And a heart! What the hell does Erick have? Besides an awesome new girlfriend and a dog? He's a fucking liar. Telling someone you love them when you don't is a mortal sin. It's about the worst thing you can do, and you will pay!*

But he wouldn't pay. The Ericks of the world never do. They leave a wake of misery and heartbreak behind them as they skip off to their next conquest, their next bright hope of true love. It's the Graces of the world that pay, and pay, and pay. Grace figured she must have done something horrible in a past life or something, and now she was doing penance. She didn't have a life;, she had a sentence, and all her belts and shoelaces had been taken away so she couldn't even end it. She just had to endure it. Every day, when Grace woke up, she got a red marker and made a big red 'X' on the day before on her calendar, showing herself that she could do it, that she had survived another day.

Grace went out as little as possible and lived a barely functional existence. She learned how to make things sound better than they were to people that asked, and how to smile a passable smile, and talk about the future like it wasn't a prison sentence, even though to her, that's exactly what it was.

She was enraged that she had been this immensely wounded, again. All the arguments she had with herself about how Erick was a jerk and unworthy and good riddance to him, and that he wasn't worth it, felt hollow. She could still remember his hands on her skin, his eyes locked with hers. She recalled with harsh clarity how real it had been to her, and worse, that somehow, in spite of herself, she had believed in it. She had believed in love. She had been duped.

Now, there was nothing to look forward to, no one to rescue her. Grace sat in quiet mourning, her battered mind coped by drifting to dramatic images of herself, dressed in widow's weeds, enduring sunless days and nights of terror, living a half-life, locked in a tower of grief.

SIXTY-NINE

Erin was running on fumes. With the new evidence from the motel room, she could believe that they were, in reality, closing in on this killer, and still... nothing. Or not enough to get them any closer to actually arresting someone. DNA confirmed that Room 17 was, in fact, where Lauren had been murdered. The killer had done a good job cleaning up – but not good enough. There was male DNA in some of the root-attached hair they recovered, but there were no hits in the system. All they had was what they already knew – an unidentified male was murdering women. They couldn't even be sure all the crimes were connected. It was just a feeling Erin had, riddled with too many coincidences to discount. She pored over all the missing women's files again, and again, trying to find some connection between them. Blonde, brunette, redhead, white, Black, Asian, 20s, 30s, 40s, professional, working-class... it just didn't make any sense. What connected these women? Were they all just crimes of opportunity? No, Lauren was stalked. She had to be. He knew where she worked. He waited for just the right moment. He had frequented a diner where both Jennifer and Cicily had worked. Trish had been walking down a sidewalk, maybe just in the wrong place at the wrong time. There had to be a thread, only Erin couldn't see it. It was like a spider-web; translucent in this light but, if she could get the sun to hit it at just the right angle, she would see it.

This guy didn't seem to have a physical type. So, it was something else. It wasn't accessibility and friendliness. Lauren wasn't approachable. Cicily and Jennifer were. Trish could have been completely random, or not; maybe he followed her from somewhere else.

Serial killers escalate.

He's looking for something... no *someone* to complete him. He's lonely. He's searching. Each woman is a reaction to the one before. Erin considered the act of dating, even on the non-psychotic level. It doesn't work out with someone; you think you'll never be with someone like that again, so the next person you date is the antithesis of the one in the past. The out-of-work musician drove you crazy, so your subsequent boyfriend is an insurance salesman, but he bores you to tears, so your next one is a puppeteer who surfs. It's an endless cycle if you're bad at dating, which Erin was. But this guy was worse, because when it didn't work out, when he was disappointed in someone, he just killed her and moved on to his next conquest, his latest hope for true love.

Erin went into a meeting room, where she could spread everything out, and asked Dan to join her.

"Let's put these in chronological order, from when they went missing."

"Uh-oh, Erin's got an idea."

"Yes, I do, Dan. Let's go back four years – no wait, more. Five?"

They set the files out in chronological order, with Rose's file being the most recent. There were so many missing women in Los Angeles. Most of these could be totally unconnected to this killer. Some of them were too close together on the timeline to both be taken by him. Erin was fairly certain he only took one woman at a time. Taking two women at once was far too risky, and it didn't fit the profile she had been working in her mind. He was a one-woman man, every single time.

"Okay, Dan, you're a man."

"Last time I checked. Don't ask my wife though; I'm pretty sure she's still referring to me as a hairy slug or something equally charming."

"All right. Male reaction, quick off-the-cuff, to the woman I show you, imagine you're going to ask her out, and tell me why, or you're describing her to your bros –"

"*My bros?* Seriously?" Dan had to laugh.

"Okay fine," said Erin, "whatever. You know what I mean.

It's that 'bros before hoes' crap I'm looking for. Gross male interpretation of a woman as an object of your – ahem – affection."

"Fine. I will play your twisted game, Taylor. But I'd like to state, for the record, that I have never – and hopefully will never, this instance notwithstanding – used the term 'bros before hoes.'"

Erin gave him a petulant half-smile. He was being playful, and she needed to lighten up and have some fun too. This case would make her angry and humorless if she got any more obsessed.

"Okay, this is just a gut instinct, but I'm going to start with this girl. Disappeared five years ago from San Pedro, grew up there. Samantha Alexander, age thirty-two when she went missing. Worked as a groomer in a pet store. First impression?"

Erin held up the picture. Dan peered at it. He winked at Erin, just to let her know he was "checking Samantha out" and not thinking about this poor woman's tragic end.

"She's adorable. Girl-next-door type. Wholesome, brunette. Average build, not fat, not thin. This is the girl you bring home to mom. If you're smart, this is the girl you marry."

Erin put the picture down and moved forward in her timeline. She eliminated a few women because they went missing too soon after Samantha had. He probably took more time off between kills back then. Nearly always, as killers escalated, their kills got closer together. Erin picked up another photograph.

"Emma Burke. Disappeared almost five years ago, 23 at the time, near Santa Monica. She was putting herself through college by stripping. The autopsy revealed high levels of cocaine in her system."

Dan stared at her. She was pretty. And... dangerous.

"Don't think it, Dan! Say it!"

"Sorry, Erin. Okay, she's gorgeous. Has the coloring of a natural redhead, but looks like she dyes it a deeper color. Very dramatic. Sexy. Dangerous-looking though. In spite of her youthful face, there's a toughness behind the eyes. Kind of an angel-face, devil inside vibe. Hot. But…"

"You don't take this one home to mom, then?" Erin teased.

"Not my mom, anyway."

They continued through the photos, and Erin was sure she was on to something. Samantha, the girl-next-door, Emma, the stripper. Jennifer, the hard-working Asian student and waitress, Sharon the white trash crack-head. Isabel, the voluptuous Puerto-Rican nightclub singer, Diane, the slender and pale strawberry-blonde yoga teacher, Cicily, the friendly Black waitress/actress, Lauren the cold, yet elegant, professional, Trish the waifish young blonde… and lastly Rose… nothing like Trish. Older, heavier, years of hard work on her hands and figure. There were many more, but again, no way of linking them all to one killer, but it made Erin think she was on the right track.

"It's almost like a porn site," Dan offered.

"Gross, Dan. Aren't you the noble feminist who avoids phrases like 'bros before hoes'?"

"No, what I mean is… if you go to a porn site, with lots of options – not that I would know except from doing work-related research on sick bastards who do that sort of thing – shut up, Erin – I mean, you get all these options. Asian hotties, big-titty lesbians, college girls, dark chocolate, naughty librarian – basically, whatever turns you on, you can find it. It's almost like, if this guy is really going after all these types of women… well, it's like he is sincerely searching. He doesn't really know what, or who, he's looking for."

"I think he does," Erin said, "I think he's looking for love. Each woman is erasing the disappointment of her predecessor. Each woman is idealized, disappoints him, and then she's summarily discarded. He moves on to someone completely different, in the hope that she will also be better. It's a theory."

"So we're looking for a guy, who's looking for love..." Dan trailed off.

"And I'm afraid his search for love is leading us to a pretty big graveyard."

Dan and Erin sat quietly, staring at the sea of women's faces. Women who had met untimely ends, probably at the hands of a man, some maybe even the same man. Women whose only crime could have been disappointing a man who was certain he knew better than they did what love was.

* * * * *

Erin woke with a start. She caught her breath as she sat straight up in bed. She'd had a dream that was already fading around the edges. She couldn't remember any of it, but one name kept crashing through her brain over and over, like an angry locomotive with a roar that drowned out everything else.

Samantha Alexander.

The pet groomer from San Pedro. Dan had said it. *The kind of girl you take home to mom. If you're lucky, the kind of girl you marry.*

She was from San Pedro, grew up there. *The killer knew her.* Maybe went to school with her or worked with her. Had a crush on her, obsessed on her for years. She may have been his first kill.

Erin went into the office. Sure, five a.m. was an early start even for her, but there was no way she could sleep now. She needed more information on Samantha.

Samantha Lynne Alexander. Born September 10, 1973, to

Ronald Alexander and Lidia Avalos Alexander. Graduated San Pedro High in 1991. Attended USC in Los Angeles, graduated in 1995, English Major. Earned her teaching credentials and then taught in the Los Angeles Unified School District until 2003, when she quit teaching and relocated to San Pedro, where she held a few odd jobs before discovering her true passion, working with animals. Began working as a groomer at a large pet store chain in 2004. She left work on June 25, 2005, and was never seen again. Her car was discovered less than a mile from the pet store, parked on a dark suburban street with the keys locked inside. No usable prints were found anywhere inside the car, not even Samantha's own.

Erin considered that Samantha knew her killer. Maybe they had even been friends. Maybe he'd been that guy Samantha pitied so she was nice to him, and he got the wrong idea. He probably followed her around for a while, and then just went over the edge. When she couldn't give him what he needed, when she couldn't love him back, he killed her.

Erin started searching for males who graduated San Pedro High between 1990 and 1992. Unfortunately, there were quite a few to choose from, close to a thousand. The high school had an enrollment that was more than 60% Hispanic, and other non-whites composed about another 10%. The man in the sketch was white, so that narrowed it down, but it was still too high a number to be sure. The sketch showed an exceedingly dumpy, middle-aged looking man. He had probably changed a great deal since high school. Maybe this was a long-shot, but Erin's heart raced the way it always did when she was getting closer to the truth.

She could also be feeling something else – HIS racing heart. After all, Rose Santos was missing, but there was no way to know if she was still alive. She might already be dead too. If she was still alive, then she was suffering at this guy's hands right now. But if she was dead, then he was starting to feel lonely. And if he was feeling lonely, then it was only a matter of time before he found his next victim – or perhaps his next "true love" as he may be so inclined to call it.

SEVENTY

Kent couldn't stand it any longer. He was so cooped up in this house. It was making him crazy. He would just go for a drive. He was lonely, but he reminded himself that his last attempt at finding love had gone very wrong. He needed something that would last, and that might take time. He needed to be patient.

He got in his car and drove aimlessly around San Pedro. It made him even more depressed. He really hated being in his childhood town. He wished he could go back to his apartment in Los Angeles. Maybe he could, but it was really risky. He drove down near the water and cruised Tuna Street over to Wharf Street.

That's when he saw her. Kent had once fallen for a woman down on her luck, but he hadn't thought she was a prostitute; he had believed she was a damsel needing rescue. This woman… or girl maybe… she was definitely a prostitute. Really young possibly, but heavily made up, so it was hard to determine her exact age. He'd never hired a hooker in his life. The very idea of it was so distasteful. He believed in love, and connection. A prostitute fabricated these feelings, for a price. Maybe it would be worth it. He could just pay her, and she'd tell him she loved him. She'd play a role, but he could pretend, just for one night. She was pretty. She had nice full lips and a luscious curvy body – not too fat like that useless bitch Rose had been. This girl was perfect. She had dark curly hair and olive skin. She might be Mexican, or Columbian, or Puerto Rican… he fantasized about her exotic beauty. He had sat in his car staring long enough. She approached the car. He rolled down the passenger window, and she leaned in.

"Hey there handsome, do ya need a date?" she asked in a sultry voice, with the slightest hint of an accent… Spanish. Delicious.

"I'm looking for love," Kent said. Would she laugh at him? She had better not.

"All right, a man who knows what he likes... a romantic," she purred.

She got him. She understood. They could play this game all night.

"Yes, I know what I like. I want a woman to love me. I want to love her, too."

"You know love can get a little expensive, daddy."

"Don't call me daddy!" Kent let a sharp bite of anger slip. Her face got a little paler, and she averted her eyes. "Wait, I'm sorry. I just... have a complicated relationship with my father. You can call me Kent. What's your name, beautiful?"

"Luz," she said, still more than a little nervous.

"I know what that means," said Kent, "It's Spanish for 'light.'"

"Very good, Kent." She said his name with purpose, with delicacy, with love. But she started to back away again.

"Wait! Luz! Don't go!"

"Sorry Kent, I'm on the clock tonight. You have to pay to play. It'll be worth it. I promise."

Kent stared at her for just a moment. He was so lonely. And she was so pretty. They could just talk. He'd pay her just to talk to him. She put her hands on the edge of the door, where it met the rolled down window, and where her fingers curled over it, he stared. Her hands were lovely. He did not, would not, think of how many men they'd already touched. He pushed it from his mind and made a decision.

"How much for the night?"

"The whole night? Oh, that's expensive. Why don't we start with an hour and see how that works out?"

"But I want to spend the night with you."

"I charge five hundred for that."

He stared straight out the windshield. Five hundred dollars? That was an awful lot of money. Maybe he could just pay it. He had gotten a little money from his mother's life insurance policy – which he was shocked she even had, but then again, he wasn't really earning much these days. He should be careful. But, once she was with him, and she saw how nice he was, how well he treated her, she might decide not to charge him. She was probably used to really bad, insensitive men taking advantage of her, hitting her, raping her. She might truly enjoy being with a gentleman like him.

"All right, let's do it. Where do we go? Do you have a place?"

"You got the money?"

"Of course." He reached into his wallet and started pulling out money. He always carried a lot of cash because he didn't like to use credit cards. They made him nervous. He only had a little over three hundred dollars on him.

"That's only three hundred Kent."

"I know. I thought I had more on me. How much time can I get for three hundred?"

"Three hours. My rate is a hundred an hour."

"Then why is the whole night only five hundred?"

"That's the wholesale rate. You know, you buy five hours, you get a couple extra free."

She would stay with him the whole night no matter what Kent paid her. He was sure of it, so he opted not to argue anymore.

"Okay, so you know, it's only three hours then?" Luz needed to play hard ball, just so he didn't get any ideas, but she was pretty happy already. Three hundred was a good night, and she normally had to do at least three guys to earn that, sometimes more. She'd get this ugly asshole off, and send him packing.

"Yes, darling, whatever you say," Kent slipped into romance-mode.

"Darling, huh? Okay then. I'll tell you where to go. I have a room we can go to."

Luz directed him to a seedy motel where she had an arrangement with the owner. He let her rent by the hour, and she always paid cash and cleaned up after herself.

Kent was glad she took charge of talking to the front desk clerk because he was very nervous about being recognized. He still kept his head clean-shaven and maintained his goatee. He had even dyed the hair in his beard black, to alter his appearance even more. It was quite striking, very bold. He should bring his duffel bag inside, but decided against it for now. Maybe he wouldn't need any supplies, and he did have a knife in his jacket pocket, just in case she needed some convincing. Maybe she'd be really loving, and nothing bad would have to happen to her. Maybe he could rescue her from this horrible life on the streets. He could propose to her. That was silly. He didn't even know her, and he didn't have a ring. He was getting ahead of himself.

They went into the room together, and he hid his disappointment at how dingy and unromantic it was. He had a gorgeous girl with him, and they would make it beautiful in here, with their special love.

As soon as they were in the room with the door shut, Luz sat on the edge of the bed and gave Kent her sexiest stare.

"Come here, handsome," she said, not even choking on the words. Luz was a pro.

Kent sat next to her on the bed and immediately felt uncomfortable when she started touching him. This was not at all right. She was too aggressive.

"Luz, I want to just talk first, okay?"

Oh shit. These lonely sad sacks are the worst. Luz preferred dealing with the ones who just wanted fast, uncomplicated sex. She reminded herself of the three hundred dollars resting in her purse. *Give him what he wants.*

"What do you want to talk about, baby?"

"I just want you to tell me you love me."

Luz was revolted, even for a hooker. God, this guy was pathetic. She could do it, but why was it so much easier to talk dirty lies than it was to lie about love? Lying about love seemed… profane to her. She had no issue with telling these assholes how great they were in bed, how big and hard their dicks were, but when they wanted love talk, that's when she really felt like a whore. *Well*, she reminded herself, *that's what you are. A whore.*

"I love you," she said, meeting his eyes, making him believe it.

"Say my name when you say it," he whispered.

"I love you… Kent." She pronounced his name with intent.

This was nice. Kent felt good. He had found the right girl.

They were sitting side by side on the edge of the bed. He reached out for her left hand.

"Let me see your hands, Luz."

She offered her hands to his and waited patiently while he caressed and examined them. He was getting an erection, and she was grateful. Maybe they could get this show on the road.

Kent continued caressing Luz's hands with his right hand, while using his left to unzip his pants.

"Sit behind me," he said, in a voice that made Luz think twice. It exuded something sinister. She brushed it off and sat behind him on the bed. He grabbed her hands and brought them around to the front of his body. Luz had done a lot of crazy stuff in her career as a hooker, but even for her, this was kind of weird. It wasn't entirely comfortable either, having her arms wrapped around this big guy as he was tugging really hard at her hands, and using her hands to jack himself off. *What the hell?* Luz knew it took all kinds, and just did what he wanted. In a way, it wasn't as bad as what some guys wanted to do to her; just weirder.

"Keep telling me you love me," he said.

Luz leaned all the way up against his back; her arms wrapped around him in a backwards embrace, letting him yank her hands up and down on his dick while saying she loved him over and over. Anytime she stopped saying it, he'd tell her to say it again.

This was dragging on forever. All her normal seductive tricks were useless. He could only see her hands. He wouldn't let her say anything except that she loved him. He showed no interest in any other body parts – and she had some good ones – and her arms were starting to cramp up from the awkwardness of the position.

Kent was getting frustrated. He had to keep yanking at Luz's hands to keep them where he wanted them. He was angry with himself for paying her so much. This wasn't love. She didn't love him. She was lying. She loved his money. This was so beneath him. She was beneath him. He just wanted her to go away, but he couldn't stop. He wanted release, but her hands were her own; *he'd never get it this way.*

He took one hand off of hers and reached into his jacket pocket.

"Everything okay, baby?" Luz asked.

"Yes, just keep going." Kent took the knife from his jacket pocket and used his left hand to pull her hands off his member and hold them still.

"What's wrong Kent? You want to try something else?" Luz sweetly inquired, unable to see the knife he held.

"Yes, I want to try something else," Kent said, all pretenses of sweetness and charm vacant from his voice.

Luz had a moment of panic, which was quickly interrupted by extreme pain in her right wrist and total shock and fear washing through her body like a tidal wave.

Kent dug the knife deep into the flesh of her wrist and began sawing away at it. It wasn't the right tool for the job, but he was acting on impulse. All his good tools were in the trunk of his car.

Luz screamed in agony. Kent released her arms and whirled around, smacking her across the face with the back of his hand. The knife grazed her face in the process, and a bright-red gash appeared across her cheek. She screamed again, and Kent panicked. He needed her to shut up. He grabbed her by the hair and yanked her head back. In one sweep, he slid the knife across her throat.

For them both, a slow-motion movie began to unfold. The shock and horror on Luz's beautiful face, the blood spewing from her neck, as she futilely reached her hands up to the fatal wound. Kent, consumed with sadness and desperation at another failure. Another lying bitch had made him do something he didn't want to do. Love had failed him once more.

Luz collapsed, her warm blood seeping into the cheap, worn bedspread. Kent had to get the hell out of here, fast. He couldn't leave her like this though. He needed her hands.

He went to his car for his duffel bag. Back in the motel room, he picked Luz up and put her in the tub. He removed her hands with a hacksaw and turned on the shower. He put her hands in a plastic bag and put that inside his duffel bag. He wiped down all the surfaces and left.

He drove away from the hotel, angry. He wanted to take Luz out to the desert, but it was too risky. He'd have to let her rot in that filthy motel room bathtub.

Later, after putting Luz's hands in the freezer in his mother's house, which was now his house, he sat down on the kitchen floor and let the emptiness wash over him. San Pedro was a horrible place to be. This house was a tomb. He missed L.A. He'd go back. Just one more time, and then that would be it. If he didn't find the right woman, maybe he'd leave town for a while, start over somewhere new.

He felt the old anger at his mother wash over him again. This was all her fault. If only she'd been a real mother to him. If only she'd loved him. He grabbed a trash bag from the kitchen and tore through the house, searching for pictures of his mother. There weren't very many recent photos, but there were some she had saved of herself when she was still young, still beautiful. Time had not been friendly to his mother. All the years of hard drinking and whoring around had taken a toll on her once beautiful face. He only came across one picture of him and his mother together. She was still beautiful then. He was young, maybe two or three. They were sitting on the ugly plaid sofa they'd had then. Kent was looking at his mother with total admiration and love, and she was looking somewhere else. There had always been that distance in her, and that pain behind her eyes. Even when she was near, she was never near. She was never there. Her long, straight, shiny brown hair swept down below her shoulders, falling over her innocent-looking peasant blouse, her beautiful, but vacant, green eyes scanned some unknown horizon searching for something she'd never uncover. It was far too late for her to find what was missing from her life because her life was done. This photograph was the only one he saved. The rest he put in the trash bag which he shoved in the living room closet.

The picture he kept, he folded neatly and put in his wallet. He told himself it was sentimental and stupid to keep it, but he couldn't bear to let it go. He wished he could go back to that moment in the picture and tell her, warn her, that if she didn't pull him into her lap, right then and there, and hold him, and love him the way a mother was supposed to, that she would live to regret it. She wouldn't live to regret it though. He had never mattered to her, and he never would. The only thing that could make everything okay again, would be finding HER. The one. The one he could love forever. The one that could help him forget his mother once and for all.

Kent was exhausted. He took a long time falling asleep. Every time he closed his eyes, he saw the shock and horror on Luz's beautiful face as the blood poured from her neck. He couldn't figure out how things had gotten to that point so quickly. At last, he fell into a fitful sleep and dreamt of his mother. Maybe it was a blessing that she was finally free of that pain behind her eyes.

SEVENTY-ONE

Erin and Dan drove down to San Pedro, a little after two a.m., as soon as they got the call. The dingy motel was crawling with cops, and they made their way to the room where she'd been found.

The body of nineteen-year-old Luz Ramos still rested in the bathtub. The shower water had been turned off, but her body was still wet from it. Erin boiled with frustrated anger that crucial evidence had been washed down the drain. That had been a smart move on this guy's part. Lifting for prints wasn't going very well either. Many surfaces had been obviously wiped down. Another prostitute who worked the same area Luz worked identified her, and though Luz's prints were in the system, her identity could not be confirmed by those since her hands were missing. Her mug shot showed a young, but hardened, Latina woman with full lips and curly hair, heavily made-up. The woman in the tub, upon close examination, resembled the mug shot. Except all her make-up had been washed away, there was a huge gash across one cheek, and across her neck a fatal wound. Her eyes were still open. The water may have washed away blood and other evidence, but it could not wash away the vacant terror still in her eyes.

The bed was soaked with blood, so it seemed obvious the fatal wound had been delivered there, and the body moved to the bathtub for the severing of her hands. After close examination of the room and the victim, Erin and Dan went to interview the prostitute who had identified Luz. She was a tall Black girl who called herself Charmaine.

"She got into a car with this dude, a white dude," Charmaine drawled.

"Anything else?" Dan asked.

"Well, Luz and me, and some other girls, we watch each other's backs you know, in case something... well, like this shit. In case somethin' go wrong like this. We pay attention, and we listen – to *everything*. We talk to the john, use his name a few times. She called him Kent. But a lotta johns lie, you know. They married and shit. But this guy, don't know who would marry him. It was dark, but I think he had a beard. And his car was blue. Dark blue. I think it was like a Honda or something. And I know part of his license number."

Erin was shocked. This was too good to be true. She wanted to hug Charmaine as she asked, "Are you serious? Part of a license number?"

"Yeah," said Charmaine, "I seen it and I remember the numbers, cause they my birthday. 229. February 29. I'm a leap year baby," she purred at Dan, "that's how I stay so young, honey. Only have a birthday once every four years."

"And you're certain? 229? You remember any of the letters?" Dan gave his most charming and information-gathering smile.

"No letters, but I'm sure about 229. Like I said."

Dan showed Charmaine the sketch of the alleged killer. She eyed it closely, but she couldn't be sure it was him, and said as much. The man in the sketch was clean-shaven and had a receding hairline. The man she saw was bearded, and he might have been wearing a cap, too.

They were getting close. Erin could feel him. He was so near. Her stomach tightened.

They would release an altered copy of the sketch with an added beard to the press, as well as adding the information about his car. They had a possible first name. And part of a license number. It would be easy enough to search DMV records for a full name and license number.

SEVENTY-TWO

Kent saw his bearded image on the news the next day, and the announcement about a dark-blue Honda. He felt very grateful that his mother had such good timing when she died. He left his dark-blue Honda Accord parked in her garage, and transferred all his supplies to her car, a tan-colored Oldsmobile.

He shaved his goatee down to a mustache and headed for Los Angeles. Driving up the 110 freeway, he knew this time would be different. This time he would find The One.

Grace barely knew what day it was anymore. Each one dragged by in a haze of pain, confusion, and anger. She welcomed the bleak, empty, numb feelings when they came, because when the rage came, she didn't know what to do with it. In her angriest moments, she just wanted to kill Erick for putting her through this. It was either that, or die herself.

She wanted to get away, but had nowhere to go. Anywhere she went, she'd still be there. She'd still be in pain. She'd still wish she was dead. She told herself to be grateful. Grateful that she still had a job, that her exhibit had gotten such great reviews, and that if Erick was this big an asshole, that he was out of her life.

The worst part wasn't even that he was gone. It was that he had taken everything from her. After all she'd been through in her life, she had still managed to open her heart to someone, and believe in love. He had taken even that. She'd never believe in anyone again. She'd never trust another man. She'd never trust herself to make a smart decision about a man. She'd just be a lonely, miserable recluse, counting down the days until her death, which she hoped wouldn't take too long. Her thoughts were bleak and unhealthy, but she couldn't stop them. The Dark was finally and completely taking her down. There was nowhere to go. Nowhere at all. She was already dead. She just needed her body to catch up.

The smallest tasks nearly pushed her over the edge. As she drove home from work, she was filled with relief that she no longer had to maintain an appearance of normalcy, but she was also filled with the dread of going to her apartment where she would be alone with her craziness. She glanced down at her gas gauge. She was nearly on empty. She yelled out loud.

"God damn it!" Grace was definitely losing her mind. The slightest thing made her fly off the handle. Her life had given her post-traumatic stress disorder. Or maybe she had post-traumatic Erick disorder.

A seemingly simple task, like gassing up the car, is no easy feat when you're crazy, depressed, and on edge, and you live in Los Angeles. Just finding a gas station that is conveniently located on the right side of the street (because taking a left can be such a chore) is frustrating as hell.

Grace pulled into a station and had to think for a moment which side her gas tank was on. Her brain was so foggy from grief that she doubted every move she made.

When she got out of the car, she noticed how windy it was. The Santa Anas were blowing in, and the wind had a life of its own. The wind was warm, but there was a strange chill on her skin.

Kent pulled off the 405 freeway and wasn't exactly sure where he was going. He had no real plan, just wanted to be near the city.

He sat patiently at a stop light and weighed his options. He considered all his old haunts and dismissed each one in turn. He was right next to a gas station. He'd gas up while it was convenient. He mustn't push his luck and risk running on fumes with no accessible options. How could such a large city have such long stretches of road with no convenient gas stations?

The Santa Ana winds were blowing so loudly they banged against his eardrums, even with his windows rolled up, and the skinny palm trees bent in submission to the will of the wind. A large palm frond crashed onto a parked car on the side of Venice Boulevard. The car alarm went off. He pulled into the gas station.

Kent saw the most beautiful woman he had ever seen in his life. There was something about her that set her above all the rest. It wasn't perfect features or anything like that. To some, she might just be a reasonably pretty woman, but to him, she was so much more. She was a goddess of sorrow.

Grace didn't even realize anymore how often she cried in public. She never noticed people staring at her because of it. She was utterly oblivious to how raw and on the surface her pain was. She thought she was invisible to the world because she was so useless and empty, but her pain was so visible, anyone with any humanity could bear witness to it, wailing off her skin. The warm winds blew a chill through her and brought a memory of Erick's touch, of cool air brushing her skin, of tiny little hairs standing up in eager anticipation of more caresses. She started crying, as the numbers on the gas pump climbed ever higher, not caring how expensive the gas was, only mulling over why everything had to hurt so much, all the time. Tears didn't daintily drip from her eyes; they poured out in sheets down her face. Her grief strangled her.

Kent couldn't take his eyes off her. The wind blew her long, straight, brown hair around her tear-covered face. Strands clung to her wet cheeks, then blew up and around, and settled back again in the tears. She wore her pain like a cloak. It enveloped her completely. Her eyes were bright green, made brighter by the strands of red surrounding her irises. She had on a simple, feminine peasant blouse and jeans that were just a little too big. She was magnificent. She would know him. She would understand. She would get him.

He wanted to approach her but hesitated. He watched her as he put gas in his own car. She hadn't noticed him. At one point, she glanced his way, and he couldn't tell if she had seen him, really seen him, or not.

Grace could barely see anything through her tears. It probably wasn't even safe for her to be driving, but she had no real choice. She got into her car, but she hadn't put her gas cap back on, so she got out and did it, and once back in her car, drove down the street to the grocery store. She would get some wine. She was self-medicating, but she didn't care. How else could she survive? She could buy some food too. She would probably end up throwing a lot of it away, but she would buy it, so she could feel normal. So she could feel human. She pumped gas, and bought groceries, just like a person. If she kept acting like a person, she might eventually be one again.

Kent watched Grace get back in her car, and was ready to approach her to tell her she had forgotten to put her gas cap back on. It was the perfect opportunity to strike up a conversation with her, but she caught her mistake and had it back on before he could make his move. She was leaving. The impulse to follow her overtook him. He desperately needed to talk to her.

He pulled out on to the road, right behind her, and followed her as she pulled into a grocery store parking lot. This was perfect. He could talk to her in the store.

When Grace arrived at the store, she pulled herself together. If she was going to buy wine, she was determined not to be crying while she did it. That was just too pathetic, even for her.

Once inside, she made herself wander up and down the aisles, holding a small basket and pretending like she was a normal woman, doing an ordinary thing. She was buying groceries. She was a person. She wasn't even sure what she was putting in her basket. The only conscious decision she made was two bottles of red and two bottles of white. The rest of her purchases were a confusing mess.

She got suddenly paranoid. It was obvious she was crazy. Four bottles of wine, a can of corn, a bundle of cilantro, a bottle of mustard, one piece of string cheese, and some pre-packaged Asian noodle dish. Maybe she should put all this shit back. This was weird. No, she really wanted the wine. The rest of the stuff was her cover. It was her humanity. Okay, maybe it wasn't much of a humanity to make mustard-cilantro-corn for dinner, but it was a start. Maybe she should get a bag of potato chips. Something she could actually eat. She wasn't sure when she'd last eaten, but figured it had been a while since she was a little light-headed.

She stared at the bazillion varieties of chips. There was so much weird shit to choose from. It was terrifying and utterly stupid. How could she be scared of chips? *Just pick something, anything.* Salt and vinegar, jalapeño cheddar, bacon ranch. It all gleamed like a beacon of her insanity. It was too confusing. Just plain potato chips. Just plain, with nothing on it. Nothing. Nothing like her. She was nothing. She deserved nothing. She was starting to tear up. She had to get out of here. She grabbed a bag of something; she wasn't sure what, and just as she turned to go, she nearly bumped into a man.

"Ah!" she yelped, a little louder than was normal, "I'm so sorry. I wasn't paying attention."

The pain upon her face was so beautiful; it inspired absolute awe in Kent. He wanted to reach out and touch her, but stopped himself. He'd made too many mistakes lately. He told himself to take it slow. She was special.

"Oh, it's all right."

Grace turned to go. He had to stop her.

"Wait," Kent said, "Can I ask you a question?"

Grace stared at him. He was so odd-looking. She stepped out of her crazy brain for a moment. This man was... she couldn't put her finger on it. His loneliness was palpable.

She really didn't have the emotional energy to chat with some lonely sad-sack, but then again, she was a lonely sad-sack herself, so maybe she should be compassionate.

"Yeah, sure," Grace said tentatively.

"Are those any good?" Kent asked, pointing at her basket of groceries.

"Are what any good?"

"Those chips. I was thinking of buying them. Are they really spicy?"

Grace was utterly confused by the contents of her basket. What were these chips? Nacho Blast Tortilla Strips? What the hell? She had wanted plain potato chips. Plain! She definitely could NOT handle Nacho Blast in her life right now.

"These? Oh, I don't know. I actually grabbed these by mistake. I wanted potato chips. Just plain ones." Grace took the Nacho Blast monstrosities out of her basket and stared at the aisle of chips. She couldn't see where she'd gotten them from. Her confusion must have been obvious, because the man reached out to take them from her.

"Here, let me help," Kent offered. As he reached out for the bag of chips, he let his hand slightly touch hers, and said, "I'll put them back for you."

When his hand touched hers, one word echoed in Grace's head. *Danger.*

She pushed it aside. She just wanted to be home, alone.

He put the tortilla chips back and got a bag of plain potato chips off the shelf.

"Here, are these the kind you wanted?"

Grace took the potato chips, in a daze.

"Yes, thank you." She turned to go.

"Wait," he said. A really awkward moment passed between them as he carefully chose his words.

"I'm glad I met you. I'm Kent," he said, as he offered his hand, "Kent Clark."

Grace half-smiled, but it was a pained and confused expression more than anything remotely resembling an indication of joy.

She tentatively shook his hand, and the word *danger* appeared again in her mind, but she didn't brush it aside this time. She let it sit and rolled it around in her brain. What did it mean? What was danger anyway? It was dangerous to be alive.

"I'm Grace," she offered.

Kent held her hand as long as he could until it became too awkward to keep doing so. *Grace.* He loved her more than ever now. She was Grace. She was glory. She stood there, staring at him, and he believed she must feel it, too. They were connected. All the suffering they'd endured up until now, it would all fade away once they were together. He would do anything to have her, to be with her, forever. She was in beautiful agony. He was in agony too, just being so near her, *Her,* Grace, so elegant in her pain.

"Well," she started, "I guess I should get going. It was nice to meet you, Kent." She said it as a show of her humanity, to prove that she could be polite and normal, more than any real feeling of it actually being "nice" to have met him. It was just something humans say, and she was doing her best to be one.

She was leaving. Kent couldn't bear to let her go. As she walked to the check-out, he picked up a bag of plain potato chips. It was a good sign that they both liked the same kind of chips. They probably had a lot in common.

He went to the express lane, bought his chips, and made his way to the parking lot. He got into his mother's car and waited. Grace came out of the store and got into her car. He pulled out and followed her, at a reasonable distance. He was giddy. He was head over heels in love.

It was corny to think so, but he was a hopeless romantic. Everything would be all right. He was in a State of Grace.

* * * * *

Grace made her way home and immediately poured herself a glass of wine. She told herself she could have wine if she ate five potato chips for dinner. She ate the chips, which tasted like greasy cardboard, but that wasn't the chips' fault. It was hers.

Natalie called.

"How you holding up?" She chirped.

"I'm fine. Just having dinner."

"Wine and potato chips?"

"Yeah…" Grace considered defending herself, but it wasn't worth the effort. Natalie wasn't judging her. She just knew her really well.

"You want me to come over? Or you wanna go grab a drink or anything?"

"No, I'm tired. I'm going to have a little wine and pass out. I mean, sleep."

"Okay, get some rest. Call me if you need me."

Grace was grateful for Natalie, but was embarrassed that Natalie seemed more babysitter than friend these days. When had Grace let herself become so pathetic?

Grace distracted herself. With normal things. *Tasks*. She spent an inordinate amount of time washing a coffee cup in the sink. She was empty. What if she lived another 40 years? Another 50? How many more of these days could she do? *Tasks*, she said to herself again, *pick a task*. Check the mail or something. She probably hadn't checked it in days. She sometimes got curt little notes from the postal worker to please empty her over-stuffed mailbox, as it was impossible to fit any more mail in there. She set her wine glass down on the counter and grabbed her keys. She would get the mail. Maybe pay some bills. A lot were probably overdue by now.

Grace walked down to the front of her apartment building to the row of metal mailboxes. Hers was so overstuffed that the key would barely turn in the lock. She took deep breaths through her frustration and finally got it open. The mail was folded, creased, stuffed, and crammed inside. So much of it was crap anyway. She sat on the edge of a brick planter after tossing the bulk of it in the community trash can near the mailboxes. Why carry it upstairs just to throw it away and then bring it back down to throw it away again?

Kent couldn't believe his luck. He had been sitting outside Grace's building, hoping for another chance to talk to her, but figured she was in for the night. At least he knew where she lived now. But then, there she was, sitting on the edge of a brick planter, sorting her mail. He had to play this carefully. He might frighten her if he walked up to her right now, but he was growing impatient. He wanted to be with her, and he wanted it to be now. He was so tired of waiting for the right woman. *She* was the right woman. He was sure of it.

Grace formed two stacks of mail on either side of her, resting them neatly on the worn bricks of the planter where she sat. One side for the stuff to keep and the other for stuff to toss. Her stomach clenched. A sick feeling twisted inside her, and she choked back nausea. Erick, and his newer, better woman and the life they had together was all she could focus on. How happy Erick could be now that he didn't have a lemon like Grace dragging him down. A deep sense of foreboding washed over her. Phrases like "it will get better" were useless, hollow empty words. Utter bullshit people tell each other and themselves to dismiss the present pain in the hopes that someday something wonderful will happen. But something wonderful never happens. Because something wonderful is always something awful in disguise. "If you love something set it free" was bullshit too. *If you love something, just wait. It will leave you.*

Then it hit her, hard. The envelope in her hand wasn't the usual crap. Bills and fliers and credit cards offers receded away in their utter banality, and this envelope sang a dirge of foreboding. It was handwritten, addressed to Ms. Grace Elliott, and made of nice paper, eggshell colored linen stock, or whatever the hell invitations of stupid shit you don't want to go to are made of. Sick to her stomach, she turned it over, and did not recognize the return address at all. Somewhere in Illinois, and Mr. and Mrs. Barrera. There was nothing familiar about this, and yet, there was.

She opened the invitation, and as she read, the anguish swam around her, angry piranha snapping at her skin, tearing off enough flesh to pain but not to kill her, a tunnel of darkness where the world used to be, narrowed into a tiny pinprick until nothingness. She was on the ground; her head bent into the planter, and she was throwing up.

Mr. and Mrs. Barrera request the honor of your presence at the marriage of their daughter Stephanie Marie. And, just like that, she knew. Erick was not just a jerk who had dumped her. He was a sick, twisted sociopath who found it amusing to discard her, and then invite her to his goddamn marriage to the woman who had replaced her. The woman who had bested her at life, at the pursuit of happiness, and most of all, at love.

It was too much. The sobs and vomit and rage spilled from her in a roiling shit tide of despair. There was nothing more. *Please,* she begged to a god she knew was no longer listening, *please stop. Please. I cannot do anymore. I cannot hurt anymore. It is a lie to say that we do not get more than we can handle. This is more, way more.* This was the end. Grace would never be able to take another step. Not one more. She would lie here with her head in a planter until she disintegrated. Her heart was burning at the stake.

Suddenly, there was a hand on her shoulder, and a tentative utterance of her name.

"Grace?"

She couldn't register what was happening. It was him. The weird guy from the grocery store... his name... she searched the sludgy mess where her brain used to be. He was familiar. Of course he was familiar; she had just seen him at the grocery store. But no. There was something else familiar. Something was very off about this. What the hell was he doing here? She willed her mouth to speak the words, to ask him just that, but her throat was closed up. She pushed, but no words came out. She was dumb-struck by her life. It was absurd. Everything was blurry. It was hard to see anything through the veil of tears, but this man, Kent, that was his name, was still standing there. She was hallucinating. This couldn't be happening. A bright light on the outside of the building came down at such an angle that she couldn't see him clearly. There was a hazy halo around him made of the radiant light and her tears.

"Are you okay?" Kent asked, reaching out to her. "Here, let me help you up."

Grace just sat there. This was wrong. Very wrong. Very bad. *Danger.* Again and again. *Danger.* But she couldn't move. She was paralyzed. She wished someone would come out of the building and see this. She needed a sane person to tell her what was happening. Why was he here?

Kent shifted his weight from one foot to the other, and back again. Grace still stared up at him through her foggy wet eyes, and as the light shifted as well, from too bright, to gone, then bright again, then to haze, as Kent's weight shifted in front of it, she suddenly knew what was familiar. He wasn't just some guy. He was *that* guy. The one from the news. The one who had killed Lauren. Had she really been so self-absorbed in her stupid pain, she hadn't noticed it before?

"You're him," was all Grace could say. She should run. She should scream. Why wasn't she running and screaming? *Run. Scream. Run. Scream.* Her body would not obey. Her voice would not abide.

Kent panicked. Did she recognize him from the news, or just from the store? He didn't want to hurt her. He loved her. But he needed to get her out of here. He fingered the taser gun in his jacket pocket. He would only use it if he had to.

"I'm who?" Kent asked.

"Him. From the news. Lauren…" Grace said.

"I'm not going to hurt you, Grace," Kent said, "I love you." He kept his voice calm, though the mention of Lauren's name sent a surge of angry fear through his whole body. Grace knew who he was. He could NEVER let her go.

He reached down to her, poised and ready to use the stun gun. He always had to use something. No woman ever willingly went with him. They had all been such disappointments. To his amazement, Grace started to stand up on shaky legs. Her skin paled with the effort. He would rescue her from this. She was in so much pain – the weight of it was all around her. He made sure no one was watching, and then pulled the taser slowly from his jacket pocket.

Grace met his eyes.

"Save me," was all she said as the dark tunnel returned, diminishing the entire world to a pin prick, and then she left. She simply fainted.

Kent, like the gentleman he was, caught her in his arms. He would save her.

SEVENTY-THREE

With the name "Kent" and a California license plate with "229" in it, it was only a matter of time before Erin and Dan were able to get a full name for Kent Clark, owner of a 2006 dark-blue Honda Accord. He had no prior arrests and owned no real estate. He rented an apartment in a run-down area of Culver City.

As soon as this information was released to the press, a media firestorm erupted in full force. The city was in a panic. Everyone knew Kent Clark's name and face now. There was no escape for him.

The cops on the case were in a frenzied state of anticipation. Surely, they were closing in on this guy. The people personally affected by his violence lived heart-pounding lives, hoping and praying for some kind of justice.

A team of officers, led by Dan Garza and Erin Taylor, paid a visit to Kent Clark's apartment. Erin knew he'd be gone. He'd been so many steps ahead of them so far, and she knew he still would be, but maybe his home would have some clues that could lead them to where he might be, and where he might take his victims. There had to be an out-of-the-way place to which he had access.

They scoured every inch of his apartment. There were no severed hands in his freezer. No creepy pictures of women he'd stalked. No diaries or journals detailing his sick obsessions. No newspaper clippings mentioning this story. In fact, it was as if someone barely lived here. There was very little in the way of food inside the refrigerator, and what was there was mostly spoiled. The mail was piled up. There were few toiletries in the bathroom. The drawers and closets had the appearance of being picked over. It looked as if he'd packed up and left for an extended trip. There were few family pictures or personal memorabilia. The only prints they could find were his. His life was a very solitary one, which was not surprising.

Erin's mind was racing forward to the moment when

she caught this bastard. She knew his name. She knew his face. She knew how dark his soul was. She just didn't know where he was, right now. She didn't know if he was alone, or if he'd already grabbed another woman.

There must be someone, somewhere, that knew where to find him. Erin's stomach clenched into a fist. She knew better than to think they would have found Kent casually sitting around in his apartment, just waiting to be arrested, but it would have made things easier. She wanted this done. This guy needed to be caught. She was almost there. *Almost there, Kent. I know who you are. I'm coming for you, asshole.*

SEVENTY-FOUR

Grace came to in the backseat of a moving car. Plastic zip ties bound her wrists and ankles. The first few moments were total confusion. She couldn't remember anything.

And then, it flooded over her. That man... Kent... she stayed perfectly still, hoping he wouldn't notice she'd woken up. She closed her eyes and practiced slow, even, quiet breaths. *Think, Grace. What's happening? He's taken me. That man. It's the man who killed Lauren. It has to be. Has he seen me before? Is there some connection? Or is this an insane coincidence?*

She barely opened her eyes and could see the back of his head. Fear gripped her heart in its icy claw. He had done some really bad things to Lauren. He tortured her. Cut off her hands. Grace started to panic. Her mouth tasted of vomit. She remembered then. The invitation. Erick's wedding. That assface had the nerve to invite her to his *wedding.* A lifetime of sadness washed over her, circling her, taunting her, and reminding her that she had wished for this. She had wished for death. And she was going to get it. This guy was going to kill her. No matter what. This was not someone who would just let a woman go. This was a killer. No matter what she did, or what she said, in the end, she would be dead.

Tears slid gently from the corners of her eyes. She was going to die, but that wasn't what made her cry. She cried because she didn't care. She wanted to care, tried to care, but she couldn't. She'd have to endure whatever horrible things he had planned for her, but in the end, she would be free.

She left her body then. It was like she was sitting on the seat, looking down at herself, the self sprawled on the backseat with bound ankles and wrists. *What's wrong with you Grace? Come on. Get up. Fight for your life. Get up. Talk to him. Do something. You can't just give up, you fucking coward.*

But she just stayed right there, perfectly still and perfectly quiet. There was no fight left in her. No bravery. The bravest thing she'd ever done in her life was love. And that had been her undoing. No matter what this guy did to her, it couldn't be worse than being all alone, broken-hearted, and abandoned forever, by everyone she'd loved. But then, Natalie. The only person who'd never left her. *Natalie is the only one I hate to leave. Everyone else is already gone.*

This wasn't exactly the ideal way to go. Her stomach turned over with the fear of the unknown horrors that might be visited upon her any minute now. She had no one to blame but herself. She'd gotten her wish. Someone had come along to put her out of her misery. *Be careful what you wish for.* That trite statement was raw with meaning now.

Finally, the physical discomfort motivated her to wiggle around, and then to sit up.

"Where are we going?" she asked Kent.

"Oh, hello there, sleepy head. Sorry about the ties. I just wanted to make sure we had a chance to talk."

"So you bound my hands and ankles? Why not just talk? Did you think I would run away?"

"They always do," Kent said with some bitterness. But there was something else in there too. Sadness. Resolve.

"I won't run away," Grace said. And she actually meant it.

"Everyone runs away," Kent said.

"I'm not everyone, Kent," Grace said as she maneuvered herself into a sitting position and repeated, "Where are we going?"

"I'm taking you some place special. I wanted us to have some time to get to know each other."

Grace tried to get some sense of where they were and what direction they were headed, but everything outside the car was too dark and blurry to clue her in. With bound hands, she rubbed at her sore neck.

"My neck hurts, Kent. The skin is… raw. What did you – "

she stopped herself – "What happened to me?"

"I'm sorry about that. You passed out in my arms. Do you remember? I wanted to bring you somewhere so we could talk, but I worried you might wake up confused, and that it would be best if you were out for a while."

There was a long pause.

"So? Is that it? I passed out, and then what? We aren't in Los Angeles anymore; I can see that, so why was I out so long?"

"We're almost there, Grace. Just be patient. Everything will be perfect. You'll see. We're perfect for each other."

Grace couldn't believe this. She remembered then, that he had told her he loved her outside her apartment. So, that was this guy's game? Love? He thought they were perfect for each other? Was this supposed to be some ironic bullshit? The man she truly loved, and had been so right for her, had dumped her and sent her an invitation to his wedding, and at the same moment, a psychotic killer shows up and claims to love her and tells her they will be perfect together? To say dating in Los Angeles was difficult didn't begin to cover it. Grace laughed, then. Out loud. Why was she laughing?

"What's so funny?" Kent's teeth gritted with thinly concealed anger.

"I'm just thinking about the bad day I had and trying to make light of it. You know what I mean, Kent?"

"Yeah... I guess I do."

He pulled onto a long dark road. He'd allowed her to remain conscious during the last part of this drive. He hadn't put her in the trunk. She knew where they were, which meant he could never let her leave here. He told himself the same lies. That she would love him. That she would stay with him, so it didn't matter. He wouldn't have to kill her. All she had to do was love him back, and he wouldn't have to kill her. When he found a good woman, the right woman, he would let her live. With him.

* * * * *

"We're here, Grace," he said as he pulled the car to a stop in front of a small cabin. He turned around and faced her. "Now, you're not going to scream and yell or anything? I can't have that. It will spoil everything."

"Who would hear me?" Grace said. She already knew the answer to that. *No one. No one will hear me scream.* She'd been screaming her whole life, and no one had heard it yet.

Kent got out of the car and opened the back door and pulled Grace out and picked her up. She should fight, but what was the point? And how? She couldn't kick; she couldn't hit. She could scream a pointless scream. It was so quiet. They were nowhere. They were so nowhere that she could see stars in the sky. There are very few stars in the sky in the big city.

Kent set her down at the door. She struggled to stand with bound ankles, and he held her with one arm while unlocking the door with the other. He picked her up again and carried her across the threshold into a place that she figured was the last place she would ever see. How romantic. She finally gets carried across a threshold, and it's by a serial killer.

Kent set her down on the couch and asked her if she was comfortable.

Grace stared at him, unsure what to say. This must be the part where the games begin. The part where she tries to convince him to let her go. The part where she begs for her life. Should she lie, and say she was comfortable, to make him happy? Honestly, how comfortable did he think she could be after riding in a car with bound wrists and ankles, a sore neck that she could only imagine was burned from a stun gun, and after throwing up in the planter outside her apartment where she lived alone, broke, divorced, childless, and recently dumped?

"I'm thirsty," Grace said, because it was the only thing she could think of to say, and because it was true. Someone would notice she was gone. She'd left the front door to her apartment wide open. She had gone down to grab the mail and never come back.

Kent went to the kitchen and got a bottle of water out of the fridge and brought it back to her. He opened it for her and held it to her lips. She drank some, but it was very difficult. This was ridiculous.

"Do you think you could just untie my hands, Kent?"

"I don't think that's a good idea. I think we should talk a little while first."

He held up the bottle for her to drink more water and then sat down next to her on the couch.

"You're the most beautiful woman I've ever seen, Grace."

A hollow laugh escaped Grace's mouth before she could think to stop it.

"You don't get out much, do you, Kent?" She didn't care if he got angry. Bitterness filled her mouth. The most beautiful woman he'd ever seen. What a joke. Was that his standard line, or did he mix them up for all his victims?

"That's not very nice, Grace."

"I wasn't trying to be mean, Kent. I just don't feel very beautiful these days."

"Well, you are. I could look at you forever."

Grace didn't want to, but she started to cry. She closed her eyes and thought of Erick. She couldn't help herself. She imagined he was the one saying it to her. She was pathetic. He was gone. Off loving someone else, and she was sitting here, in front of a killer, crying, and still bound by the memories of a great love, a perfect love, and yet she had been the only one in it. Erick could not have really loved her. You just can't love someone; discard her like trash, and then immediately fall for someone else. It didn't make any sense.

Kent stared at her. She really was different than the others somehow. She was crying, but it wasn't the same kind of crying. It was not fear. It was the absence of fear. She was… broken. That was it. She was broken. A beautiful, broken angel.

"Don't cry, Grace. Everything is going to be all right."

Grace stared right in his eyes. She didn't want to go through all this. Whatever bullshit he was into, whatever psychological games and physical torture he had planned; she wanted to skip it and get to the end.

"Okay Kent, I know you're going to kill me. Can we just get it over with? Or is there something else first? I mean, what do you do with these women? With us? Are you going to rape me first?"

Kent's anger flared. This wasn't going well. What was wrong with this woman? What game was she playing?

"I'm not a rapist, or a killer, Grace." Kent's voice was ice.

Grace's contemptuous laugh scratched at her throat like sandpaper.

"I'm not!" His voice was fire.

"Then what are you, Kent?"

"I'm a good guy. I'm a gentleman. I just want to be loved. That's all. I want to be loved." He sat down, dejected. Her mockery was scorching. Could that be tears catching in his throat?

"Don't we all?" Grace said. She actually felt compassion for him. It was crazy to feel that. He was a psychopath, a killer, a rapist, a madman. How could she feel compassion for him? She felt something else too, something she'd had a really hard time feeling lately.

She felt grateful. It would all be over soon.

SEVENTY-FIVE

Natalie was surprised Grace hadn't responded to her last text. That wasn't like her. She was worried, but it had only been a few hours. She had texted Grace that morning and was insistent that they meet for dinner. Grace was hiding out and not eating enough, and she was going to drag her out of her apartment and out of her funk, whether she liked it or not.

But it wasn't like Grace to just not respond at all. Natalie expected Grace to respond with an excuse, and she was all geared up to argue with her, but she was all geared up with nowhere to go. She called Grace and left a message.

"Grace, it's Nat. Come on. Call me. I just want to know you're okay. You don't have to go to dinner tonight if you don't want, but call me. Or text me. Or e-mail me. Send a carrier pigeon. Anything. Just let me know you're all right. I'm worried."

Natalie walked down the hall, passed Erick's desk and avoided eye contact. She hated him with every cell in her body. A few people were gathered around his desk. What a bunch of pathetic sycophants. She overheard some "congratulations" and wanted to scream. What was that asshole up to now?

She caught Claude's eye and waved him over. Claude flounced over to her and she walked him down the hall, away from the hubbub, and asked what was going on.

"He's getting married. Ugh. Breeders," Claude said with feigned superiority.

Natalie stopped. *Oh god. Oh no. Married? What the hell?* Grace must know. She found out somehow. He probably told her, the asshole. Grace might really be in trouble. This could push her over the edge. What if she didn't know? Natalie would have to tell her. Could this get any worse?

"I hate him," said Natalie.

"Ooh really? Tell me more." Claude was a bit of a gossip.

"I can't. I've got to go. I'm taking a break." Natalie went outside and paced around. She texted Grace again, and called her again. Still no answer. Something was wrong. Grace knew about the wedding. She had to know. Would she do it? Would she kill herself? God, she might. Natalie checked the time. It was her lunch hour. Maybe she could just leave for the day. She went back inside and asked Eileen if she could take off early. She was ready to offer some lame excuse, but to her surprise, Eileen just said okay. She really wasn't the same person since Lauren died. An eerie calm had settled over her.

Natalie drove straight to Grace's apartment. Grace's car was parked in the carport. Natalie walked by the row of mail boxes. There was a huge stack of mail strewn about, but she didn't think much of it at first. She went up to knock on Grace's door and stopped cold. Panic and fear gripped her heart. The door was wide open.

Something was definitely wrong.

"Grace?" Natalie yelled into the open apartment. "Grace? Are you in there? Hello? Your door is open; I'm coming in."

As soon as she walked in, she was sure no one was in there, but yelled out to Grace a few more times. A wine glass, with wine still in it, sat on the kitchen counter. She checked the bedroom and the bathroom and there was no Grace anywhere. She wouldn't just leave and leave her door wide open, would she? Natalie took out her phone and called Grace again. She listened to the phone ring in her earpiece, and then there was another ring, and a vibration hummed in the apartment. Grace's cell phone. It was here, in the apartment. Natalie kept dialing and following the sound until she spotted Grace's purse with her phone in the side pocket. There were numerous missed calls and texts. All from Natalie.

Grace was gone. The front door was open. Her purse and cell phone were here. Something was most definitely wrong.

She remembered the mail she had seen out in front of the building. Why was it just lying out there? No one had cleaned it up? She ran outside. A stack of bills, addressed to Grace, lay strewn about. A foul smell hung in the air. Vomit. Someone had thrown up in the brick planter. A lot. Then there, at her feet, a wedding invitation. She knelt down and read it.

The asshole had invited her to his wedding. Grace knew all right. She threw up in the planter. Her keys were on the ground, next to the invitation. She was gone. But where? She hadn't taken her car. Where would she go? On foot? With no phone, no purse? Had she finally just snapped and gone off the deep end? Or had something happened to her?

Natalie called 911.

"911, what is your emergency?"

"I need to report a missing person," Natalie said with a shaky voice.

"You'll need to hang up and call your local police station."

"What? No. Seriously, I think… she may have been abducted."

"I can connect you to your local police station. What is your location?"

"Los Angeles. 90066."

"Thank you. Please hold."

Natalie was on hold for twenty minutes before she gave up. She suddenly remembered that cute cop who had left her his card when he'd questioned her about Lauren. She could call him directly.

Natalie's brain started firing off unsavory possibilities. Had someone like the creep who killed Lauren taken Grace? The same guy even? No. It didn't seem possible. In fact, that was ludicrous. Or, what if Erick was responsible? He knew both Lauren and Grace, and he had turned out to be a creepy asshole. But was he a killer? That seemed unlikely. Perhaps Grace had just wandered off in a daze. But Natalie needed to report it. There were too many suspicious things about the whole situation.

Natalie tore through her purse, hoping she'd come across his card. She didn't want to leave Grace's place. Not with all the mail and her keys just lying around. She called Claude and hoped he was still in the office.

"Cambridge PR, this is Claude Barrows," he chirped.

"Claude! Thank god you're still there. I need a favor."

"Anything for you, my darling."

"Go into my top desk drawer and see if you can find a card for a detective. One of the ones that showed up to question us about Lauren. I think his name was Garza."

"Ooh. What's going on, sweetie?" Claude was either concerned or titillated or both. Natalie was impatient.

"Please, Claude, it's important."

She held on as she listened to Claude rooting around in her desk drawer.

"Here it is. Daniel Garza. You ready for the number?"

"Can you just text it to me… I can't… write it down right now."

"No problem, honey, just promise you'll tell me tomorrow what's going on with you and Officer Latin Sensation."

"Thanks, Claude. Gotta go."

Within seconds, Natalie received Claude's text with Dan's number. She called him with shaky hands and a pounding heart. She sent Grace all the healing light and love she could muster. Grace was in danger.

"Garza," Dan said into the phone. He was exhausted. This case was taking a toll on him, on the whole department, on the city, on his partner, Erin, and on his marriage. Veronica had left him two days ago. He came home late, and most of her clothes and personal items were gone. She'd left a note that said, "I love you, Dan. But I'm out of reasons to stay. Veronica." He hadn't said anything to anyone. Not to his closest friends. Not to his family. Not to Erin. It was always the same thing. One more case, just close this case, and then you will deal with your life. Meanwhile, your life is walking out the door.

"Hi, Detective Garza. My name is Natalie Acosta. I got your card when you came to Cambridge PR about Lauren McLaughlin," Natalie nervously stated. He was going to think she was overreacting.

"Yes, of course. What can I do for you?" Dan hoped he would get some information that could lead them to Kent Clark.

"Well, this might sound weird, but I tried to call 911 –"

"Are you in some kind of trouble? Is there an emergency?"

"No. I mean, maybe. I don't know. Listen, it's just… my friend, Grace. She's missing. The 911 operator transferred me to local police, and I can't get through. I was on hold forever, and I called you because… well; I'm really worried. I think she's been taken."

"Do you have any reason to believe she would have just taken off?"

"Well, she's been upset. You know, a bad break-up. A really bad-break up. But I'm here. At her place. Her car is here. Her front door is wide open. Her keys are just lying in the driveway, and –" Natalie started to cry. The more she talked about it, the more sure she was. Grace was sad, depressed, and perhaps unstable, but she wouldn't do this. *Not to me*, thought Natalie. *She'd reach out to me. She'd talk to me. She wouldn't just leave.*

"Okay, Ms. Acosta, please try to stay calm. Please give me a detailed description of your friend, and her address, and I will send an officer over right away."

When Natalie got off the phone with Dan Garza, she sat on the edge of the brick planter, away from the vomit smell, and waited. She worried. She cried. She waited some more. Please be okay, Grace. Please.

* * * * *

Erin walked up to Dan, just as he was getting off the phone with Natalie.

"What's up? Send an officer where?" she asked.

"I don't know. Maybe we should go. I know we're busy. But... I need to know what you're feeling about this one."

Erin's expectant face kept him talking.

"Got a call from a Natalie Acosta. She works at Cambridge PR, and she knew Lauren. Her friend Grace is missing."

Dan gave all the details to Erin. She stood absolutely still and closed her eyes for a moment. She was tired. She was completely strung out these days. Her sleep was virtually non-existent. She needed a hot shower, a hot sandwich, and a hot fuck. Not necessarily in that order. She wasn't getting any of those things anytime soon.

"I think we should go over there," Dan said.

"Let's go. We've got everyone searching for a place Clark could be taking these women. He doesn't own any property, and we're hoping maybe there's a family member that does and maybe that will help us find him. In the meantime, I say we follow this. If this woman – Grace? – is missing, and she knew Lauren, or even knows someone who knew Lauren, we can't just write that off as coincidence. Do we have a physical description?"

"Yeah, and an address. Her friend Natalie is waiting there."

Dan and Erin left for Grace Elliott's apartment with two

CSIs and another officer. Just in case.

When they arrived, Natalie jumped up to meet them.

"You! You both came! Oh thank you. I remember you from…" Natalie paled and couldn't go on.

"It's okay, Ms. Acosta; we're just going to go inside and take a look around," Dan said in his most reassuring voice.

"Well, here too. I wanted you to see this," Natalie pointed to the stack of mail and Grace's keys on the ground.

They went through everything, and it did look like there had been foul play. For someone – even someone this upset – just to wander off, leaving behind keys, identification, money, credit cards and cell phone, with the front door wide open, didn't make any sense.

"When did you last talk to her?" Erin asked Natalie.

"It was last night. Around 7 maybe? I can check my cell phone and get the exact time. She said she was going to stay in all night."

"Do you know where she was before that? It seems unlikely someone was outside waiting for her, unless he knew where she lived, or had followed her from somewhere else."

"I don't know if she even worked yesterday."

Erin went into Grace's apartment and checked her purse for receipts.

"Looks like she was at Ralph's Grocery store. She has a receipt with 6:41 p.m. on it."

"Okay, so we run a check on all her credit card purchases yesterday," Dan said. "We'll get Ralph's to pull security camera footage from six P.M. on."

Natalie was dazed by everything going on around her. It was so surreal. She was like an extra in a television crime show. She just stood in the background and tried to stay out of the way, but was more and more scared every minute. She peered at Detectives Taylor and Garza closely. They knew. Grace was in serious danger. But they would never say that. Natalie wished they would just say it. She also wished they would lie and tell her everything would be fine. Instead, Natalie melted into the background like old wallpaper, barely noticeable but still present, listening to what wasn't being said.

Grace might already be dead.

* * * * *

Erin and Dan sent Natalie home, assuring her they would call her with any news they got and asking her to let them know right away if she remembered anything else, or of course, if she heard from Grace.

Security footage from the grocery store confirmed that not only did Grace Elliott stand in the aisle looking at chips, but she was approached by a man matching Kent Clark's description who chatted her up, and left the store moments before she did. Erin was sure he followed Grace home. He probably planned to watch her place and stalk her, and he got lucky when she came out to check her mail.

The security camera footage also showed Kent Clark grabbing the bag of potato chips off the shelf and handing them to Grace.

Erin and Dan went back to Grace's apartment once more.

Erin put on her gloves and grabbed the bag of potato chips still sitting out on the counter. She put them inside a plastic bag.

"You never know. Tons of people have probably handled these. But we know she did, and we know he did. Another set of his prints couldn't hurt."

Dan agreed and just as they were about to leave, Erin's phone rang.

"What's going on, Taylor? Is this another one of his?" Captain Jacobs asked.

"I'm afraid so. We've got security footage showing what definitely looks like Kent Clark talking to the missing woman, Grace Elliott. It's still early. She could still be alive."

"Well, we've got something else. Rose Santos – her car showed up. Covered in parking tickets in Palm Springs. Car was about to get impounded, when an officer finally ran the plates and called it in to LAPD."

"Why are we just now getting this information? How many tickets are on there?"

"You know how this stuff is, Erin. Meter maids just slap tickets on the cars. They don't run the plates. So let's just be glad we've got it. No prints in the car, at all. Not even Rose's. But we know the car was dumped in Palm Springs. And we've got blood in the trunk."

"Shit. I mean, good shit. This is good. Palm Springs. He must have been there for a reason. He could have access to a place there."

"Exactly. We are searching every record we can find. We can't figure out much about his family. We can't find a birth certificate for him. It doesn't make sense. He has a social security number, a driver's license, school records, but no birth certificate on file. It's like he was a ghost until he started junior high school. We can't find any family. No parents."

"Well, everyone has parents. Even if they're dead, there should be some record of them. And how in the hell can you get a driver's license and social security number without a birth certificate?"

"You can't. Unless this guy is more of a criminal mastermind than we realized. We'll find it. We'll find him. Keep me posted."

"Always do," Erin said as she hung up.

"So, what do we got?" Dan was dying to know.

"Rose Santos' car was located in Palm Springs. No prints. But blood in the trunk."

"Palm Springs?"

"Yeah."

"So we've got Los Angeles, San Pedro, and now Palm Springs. Why would he abduct Rose and drive her car all the way out to Palm Springs? That's what? Over a hundred miles? Why go that far, unless..."

"Unless you're taking her there for a reason."

"A quiet place. In the desert."

"Yeah, a quiet place in the desert. Where no one can hear you scream."

SEVENTY-SIX

Grace should fight, scream, do something, but what would that accomplish? He wasn't going to let her go. But shouldn't she try? Shouldn't she, faced with her impending death, fight to stay alive? Where was her humanity? Wasn't survival a basic human instinct? If she didn't fight for her life, even if she ended up dead, if she didn't go out fighting, what was she? That was inhuman. It was monstrous. It was… lemony. Only a lemon would just sit here and wait patiently to die.

Grace was suddenly bombarded with images of Lauren. She could barely remember what she looked like. Very pretty, long brown hair. But she remembered the stories. She'd read them. The cuts, the stab wounds, the severed hands. She'd died from an aneurysm or something, but that was from blunt force trauma. He hadn't had to hit Grace in the head. Grace was disgusted with herself. She couldn't even be abducted properly. *Just faint right in the killer's arms why don't you, you idiot?*

There'd been many others. Grace had seen clips on the news of missing women, and it was possible he'd taken all of them. How many women had come before her? If she let him kill her too fast, he would just go out and get another one. And another. Men like this don't stop until they're caught. Maybe she should fight for her life, if not for her own sake, for the sake of buying time for his next potential victims.

How pathetic. Grace searched for a reason to live, a reason to fight and the best she could come up with was someone else's life?

She'd just been sitting, still bound, quiet, as Kent prepared a table with plastic flowers and candles. He opened a bottle of champagne which he poured into two flutes. His face changed. It took on this softness that made Grace's skin crawl. It was as if he learned that was what a "romantic" countenance was, and practiced it. He was mimicking something, someone he'd seen in a movie maybe.

Then she felt it. *Fear.* Ice cold motherfucking fear. Some part of her was relieved to feel it. She was tired of feeling nothing. Tired of being empty, vacant and numb. This was it. The last moments of her painfully disappointing life. What to do with that? What about the women before her? Had they screamed, kicked, cajoled, begged, wept, manipulated? Had any escaped? Probably not, or he would have been caught. So here she was, one of them. She was strangely connected to them. She felt their painful energy lingering about the room, held hostage in the space between her and this monster, their terror embedded in the paint on the walls. Fear had lived and died in this room. She would live and die in this room. He had control over how she would die. But she had control over how she would live in the moments she had left. She let softness and adoration wash over her face.

"Would you like some champagne, my darling?" Kent said softly.

"Yes, my love," Grace said, in all sincerity.

Kent stopped. She'd surprised him, but just a little. In the end, they were all the same. But he wanted to believe one could be different, so he let the lie turn slowly in his head. *She was unlike any other. She would be the one.*

"Would you like to come and sit at the table, in the candlelight?"

"Yes, please." Grace stood shakily, and he rushed to her side and picked her up.

He set her in a chair, and then he sat down in a chair opposite her. She loved him. It was obvious. But she could be faking it. He shouldn't trust her. She was manipulating him, trying to trick him. Her sincerity was all an act. Every bit of it was a lie.

He hadn't had a woman in his kitchen in awhile. Rose had never made it to the kitchen. She was still in the deep freeze in the garage. Trish was the last woman he'd brought into the kitchen. He was usually better prepared than this. He kept fake flowers around for when he didn't have time to get real ones. He kept numerous bottles of champagne in the fridge – just in case he got lucky. But he didn't have a plastic drop cloth for the floor. Maybe it was all right. Perhaps he wouldn't need it this time. They could stay here forever. This one was special. She was good. She wasn't a lying whore like the others. She hadn't once raised her voice to him. She was perfect.

He handed her a glass of champagne. Grace fumbled to hold it with bound hands.

"Wait," he said, "A toast. To us."

"To us," Grace said, as she awkwardly drank some. He set his glass down and helped her.

"Would you like me to untie your hands?"

Grace was shocked. Untie her hands? Would he really let her hands free? Was she gaining his trust?

"Well, I'm sure I'd be more comfortable with my hands free." An image of severed hands ripped through her mind like a freight train. *Oh shit, please wait until after I'm dead to cut off my hands.*

Kent walked over to a pantry and got a small coil of rope. Grace had her back to him and turned to see what he was doing. Rope did not bode well. *Okay, definitely not gaining his trust.*

Her heart was beating loud enough for him to hear it when he put the rope around her waist and tied her to the chair.

He went to a drawer and took out a knife. *Oh no. He's going to do it now. He's going to cut off my hands. No way. He'll kill me first. Please. Please, kill me first.* Grace willed herself to stay calm.

Kent came over and sat down in front of her again. He

held the knife out, gently, next to the plastic zip tie binding her wrists. He made a sawing motion, but with little force behind it. He couldn't do this. He couldn't just let her sit there with her hands free. She could hit him, scratch him, un-tie herself. He stopped moving the knife and leaned back in his chair. He considered putting a fresh zip tie on her wrists, just in case the knife had weakened it.

"I thought you were going to untie my hands," Grace said in her calmest voice. But as soon as she had mentioned her hands, Kent could only focus on them, on their sweet perfection.

"You have beautiful hands, Grace. Perfect. Such slender fingers. Let me touch them."

Icy sweat trickled all over Grace's skin, freezing her veins and bowels. It was not at all pleasant, icy sweat over and under one's skin. She reached her hands out slowly, taking deep, even breaths, and preparing herself for the pain. Don't scream. Just imagine death. This will all be over soon. *This can't go on forever. This can't go on forever.* She repeated this mantra in her head.

Kent took her hands and gently caressed them with his left hand. His right still held the knife. The familiar tingle thrilled him. She was afraid. She must be. He met her eyes. He really didn't want to kill her. Not yet. Maybe not ever.

"Do you love me?" He asked.

"Yes," Grace said, without hesitation. It was sincere. Wasn't it?

"Please don't lie. So many women have lied to me."

"Why would I lie? It wouldn't make sense to lie. Lying won't save me. Have you ever heard the phrase, 'the truth will set you free?'"

"Of course. Didn't John Lennon say that?" Kent asked. He really didn't know, and didn't care. He just wanted her hands on him.

"Actually, I think it's from the Bible," Grace said, "Anyway, I know what you want from me, and I'm going to give it to you."

"No. They all say that. They all lie. Say they love me and, eventually, they get angry and mean, and cold. They're mean to me. All of them. You won't be any different."

"I'm different, Kent, I promise."

"No," was all he said in a broken little boy's voice.

"I am, Kent. I'm different. I know they all said they loved you, but you're right. They were lying. Because they wanted to live. I don't. I don't care. I love you, Kent," Grace didn't believe what was coming out of her mouth. She wasn't thinking of what to say; she was just letting words flow out of her. She loved him. He was going to set her free. She wouldn't have to struggle anymore after this. She wouldn't have to hold down a menial job, or feel like a failure, or miss her parents, or miss her brother, or miss her daughter, or miss Erick, or walk through this hard life alone. She wouldn't have to be a lemon anymore. She could go out with love in her heart.

Kent was stunned. No woman had ever been this convincing before. None of them had been this good at lying. They all deceived him, like whores are known to do. Could this one honestly be any different? Had he finally, really, truly, found The One?

"Do you really love me?" he said, thinking he resonated power, but coming off unsure, like a frightened child.

"Yes, I do, Kent. I can love you. I know what you are. Who you are. I get you. And I don't love you because you're forcing me here against my will. I don't love you in spite of who you are. I love you because of who you are."

Kent didn't know what to do with his confusion and anger. It was beautiful, what she was saying. He wanted to believe her. She couldn't possibly love him because…

Kent stood up and backed away from her. He leaned against the kitchen wall, staring at her with quiet horror on his face. He saw himself in her eyes. Truly saw himself. He was not handsome. He was not charming. He was… ugly.

"You don't love me. You can't love me because… I'm a monster," Kent said it and knew it was true. It had lurked around the edges of his psyche for too long. *But no. It couldn't be true. It was them. These horrible women. These lying little whores.* Now, this woman, Grace, she knew how he felt about her, how much he already liked her, and loved her, so she was toying with him. *No, I'm not a monster. She's the monster.*

"I know you're a monster. So am I. We're perfect for each other," Grace said. They were. A killer and a woman with no will to live. They were soul-mates.

"You're lying. You don't love me," Kent said, but his voice trembled. He wanted her to keep saying she loved him forever. But he wanted to kill her, too. He wanted this all to stop. Something was wrong. There was a cracking noise. A thundering snap. Like the Universe ripping in half.

"What was that?" he yelled.

"What?" said Grace, utterly confused. She'd heard nothing.

"That noise. You didn't hear it?"

"No."

Kent searched her face for signs of deception. She was so beautiful. Her face was impassive now. But like an angel's. Pure. Perfect love. Love without borders. Love without conditions, rules or exceptions. Forever love. Unconditional love, like a mother's love. Like a mother's love *should* be.

"You love me," Kent said it again, still needing reassurance, "Unconditionally?"

"No, Kent, not unconditionally. There is one condition."

Anger swelled in his chest. Of course. Here it comes. The condition of loving him. He would not give it to her, no matter what. She either loved him unconditionally, or she didn't. She would love him unconditionally, or she would have to die.

"You have to kill me," said Grace in a more level voice than she could believe she had right then, saying a thing like that.

Kent was surprised. Actually, totally surprised. He'd seen anger, pain, rage and fear in women's eyes, but he'd never really seen love. He couldn't believe what love looked like. It didn't look like he'd thought it would. And he'd never heard anything like this. Women had begged to be killed once they were being tortured, and those were only the ones that really deserved it; they'd screamed in anger, "go ahead! Kill me motherfucker!" or something to that effect. But never this. Never as… whatever this was. A necessary condition of loving him?

"No! No! Grace, no! If you love me, then you have to be with me. You have to stay with me. You can't leave!" Kent was angry. He began pacing the room. He was actually fighting back tears. Real tears. He couldn't remember feeling like this, since… well, he didn't know if he ever had. Some things are just buried too deep to see anymore. Too deep to know for sure if they ever existed. He wouldn't even know where to start digging. There it was again, the loud crack. He jumped out of his skin. She was calm. She wasn't hearing it.

"I'm sorry, Kent," Grace kept her voice steady. "It's just the way it has to be. Don't you see? Don't you see why I love you? It's because you're going to set me free. I love you because you are my truth. And you will set me free."

Grace was shocked by her words, but it was almost like

someone else was speaking now. Maybe she had finally lost her mind. *There's nothing where your life used to be, and it's finally okay.* She was a monster. She deserved to die. She deserved to die at the hands of a monster.

"Grace, I love you. You can't ever, ever leave me," Kent sat at her feet pleading with her. He couldn't understand what was happening to him. *CRACK.* It was so loud in his brain. *Maybe this is what it's like when you finally just lose it. A psychotic break. It's so loud when you fall apart inside that you can hear yourself crack. You hear it when you break.* Grace's eyes held an image of his dawning horror. *You can see it in someone else's eyes when you break.* He'd brought the wrong woman here. She was showing him something, something he didn't want to see. She could see a monster, and she could love it. She could love him. But where could they go from here? Maybe he didn't want to be loved after all.

He recoiled and practically ran across the floor to get away from her. His body went rigid. His voice was frozen solid when he spoke.

"Aren't you afraid of dying?" His voice dripped venom. He had completely changed. There was no more of that vulnerability there, no frightened child, no needy, lonely man just wanting love. Here he was. The real Kent Clark. The killer. His growing erection throbbed.

Grace pushed aside her terror like the annoying insect it was. *Fuck fear. Be free,* she said inside her mind.

"Yes," said Grace, "A little bit. Only because I don't know what's on the other side. But I deserve to die, because I'm a monster."

Kent laughed. A cold, brittle accusation of a laugh.

"You're a monster? You think so?"

"I know so. I've committed the gravest sin of all. I've killed everyone I've loved. And myself, a few times over."

Kent couldn't understand or care what she was babbling out. He was through listening to this drivel. She was just buying time. Distracting him. It was time. She needed to show him some love, instead of just talking about it. He walked slowly toward her.

It was obvious he wasn't interested in what she was saying, but she didn't care. It wasn't for him anyway. It was for her. This was it. Her last moments to live. She would do something for herself. The truth would set her free.

"I have sinned. I have not loved anyone enough. I have not loved life. I have sinned against life, because I have never, ever once been grateful for it. Not once, Kent. I've never been grateful."

He came and stood right in front of her, their legs touching. He wanted her to shut up. She would soon.

"I've never been grateful, because I only practiced gratitude when things were happy. When things were good, I could do it. I could love life. I could be thankful for things, but when things went bad, I stopped being grateful. I could be grateful for people until they left me, and then I sullied their memories with my ingratitude. I sullied their memories with bitter hatred of my own precious life."

Kent reached out for the knife. Grace willed her brain not to register it.

He held the knife in one hand as he unzipped his pants. Grace didn't care. It didn't matter anymore. She had ruined everything in her short life. But she was thankful now. As Kent put her bound hands on his dick, she was grateful. She would finally get something she had prayed for. So she had to say it.

"Thank you."

Kent stared at her with cold dead eyes. She had just thanked him. She was truly different. She really was special. He would make this one last.

SEVENTY-SEVEN

Erin was in a complete frenzy. She knew damn well that Kent Clark had Grace Elliott captive right now, probably somewhere near Palm Springs, and she couldn't help her. Grace was still alive and Erin wanted desperately to save her. She felt responsible now, more than ever. Even though this asshole was the killer, there was still blood on her hands. Every moment that passed was another moment Grace could be taking her last breath.

Dan was strung-out too, but Erin's energy was off the charts.

"Taylor! You've got to stay calm. We'll get him. We're closing in on him."

"I know. But we still don't know where he is. I don't want to lose another woman to this prick."

As soon as they made their way into the department, an officer approached them and said Captain Jacobs wanted to see them in her office.

Joanna Jacobs was tired too. Erin and Dan came in and didn't bother to sit. They were both too keyed up.

"I've stopped giving the media any more information," Captain Jacobs began. "I know they're going to keep going crazy with this story, but I'm afraid if this guy is watching, and knows we're getting close, and he does have Grace Elliott – or another woman – captive, he may panic and kill her faster. Let's keep ourselves on the 'no comment' track for now."

Just then a female officer leaned in the open door. Erin didn't know her well. She was fairly new to the force and looked so young, but that could be because Erin felt like she was about ninety years old right now, so everyone looked young to her. The officer's name tag said "Yee," on it.

"I'm sorry to disturb you, Captain, but I think we've got something here," Yee said.

"Come in, Officer Yee. What is it?"

"I think we've got this guy's birth certificate. There were two on file at one point. The name Kent Clark was put on a certificate, but the mother did a re-file six months later because she'd said she made a mistake, listing his parents as Kathleen and Peter Clark. She re-filed with the name Kent Clark Murphy, with parents Kathleen Murphy and father unknown. However, when he registered at school, and later got a social and driver's license, the Kent Clark certificate must have been used, even though it shouldn't have been valid. Basically, no one in his family has the last name Clark. Technically, not even him, according to his second, and supposedly correct, birth certificate. It's got to be the same guy. Same birth date in the same hospital."

Erin was excited. This was something. She wanted to run around and dance a jig with Officer Yee. Even so, as usual, she contained herself and let Captain Jacobs take the lead. She was Captain after all.

"That's good work, Yee. What do we have on Kathleen Murphy, the mother? Maybe she's the one with property."

"She's recently deceased, and we're pulling up real estate records on her now."

"Yee!" A loud male voice boomed from the pen. "Come here and get this!"

Officer Yee ran out and came right back.

"We've got it, Captain! Kathleen Murphy. A home address in San Pedro."

Erin nearly jumped out of her skin. "Let's go, Dan!"

"Wait, Taylor!" Captain Jacobs actually raised her voice, "Stay calm. We've got to consider the fact that he may have this woman in Riverside County somewhere. We can't discount the fact that Rose Santos' car was found there. I'm going to send some local officers to check out the mother's house in San Pedro."

"But Grace could be there, in that house!" Erin said. She hoped she wasn't whining. She might have been.

"I know. All the more reason to send officers who can be there in five minutes."

Dan had kept quiet, out of respect for the Captain, but he was itching to get in his car and get down to San Pedro too.

"It absolutely makes sense to send San Pedro officers, Captain, but Erin and I have been leading this. If there's evidence in that house, we need to see it as soon as possible."

"I'm aware of that, Garza. You two just sit tight for a minute. Yee, keep searching. Search Riverside County records for any property belonging to anyone with the last name Murphy. Focus on the out-of-the-way communities, not the large cities. If you can't find anything in Riverside that makes sense, extend to San Bernardino. "

"Yes, ma'am," said Yee as she scurried out.

The Captain picked up the phone. She called Harbor Division's Captain directly.

"Hi, it's Captain Jacobs. We've got an address for Kent Clark's mother. It's coming to you now electronically. We need officers there right away. Use extreme caution. We believe he's taken another woman. It's possible she's there. I'm sending our team down there, too, but contact me immediately with anything relevant."

Captain Jacobs exchanged few pleasantries in times like these. She hung up the phone and addressed Dan and Erin, who stood patiently – or in Erin's case, impatiently – waiting for instructions. The Captain was tempted to tell them to start heading east, out to the desert, but she could always call local officers out there if they ever got an address. Erin and Dan would fight pretty hard for the chance to get inside Kent Clark's mommy's house and pick through the evidence, their way.

"Okay, go ahead and get down there, but it goes without saying; you're married to your cell phones. If we get any better information on a location for Grace Elliott, you turn around and head out to Riverside County."

"Yes, ma'am," said Dan.

Captain Jacobs stared at him. She gave a half-smile. She didn't like being called "ma'am," but she let it slide, but only because it was Dan Garza, and he had a way with the ladies, even hard-boiled police Captains like her.

Erin and Dan made their way to his car. She wanted to drive, but Dan would fight her on it this time. She was in her "high-strung" mode now, and it made him nervous. She considered letting him know he was acting like a controlling man, but maybe it was best to save the lectures. Somewhere out there a woman was being tortured, and they needed to find her. It really didn't matter who drove. She took three deep calming breaths.

Then, she got a feeling that hit her so hard, it made her woozy.

"Taylor, what's up? You okay?" Dan said.

"We've got to go to the desert," Erin said in a dry whisper.

"What? But we've got evidence in San Pedro. The only evidence we have in Palm Springs is an abandoned car belonging to a woman we presume to have been abducted by him."

"Yes, but why else would it be there? He didn't kill her in L.A., and he certainly didn't kill her in San Pedro and then drive all the way to Palm Springs in her car. That makes no sense."

"Erin, we can't even be sure it's him that took Rose. And even if it was, what if he went to some other place far away? What if Palm Springs was a random place to abandon the car? Maybe he knew we would be searching for it, and that was a convenient place to dump it."

"But convenient *why*, Dan? Because he was east of Los Angeles. We might not know how far east, but we should drive that way. We're going to get a call, Dan. I know it. We're going to need to go out there, and if we head south now, we will be even further away from Palm Desert. And the local authorities will be all over it. It's not like San Pedro, that's still LAPD, still our jurisdiction. We need to maintain some control over this investigation."

"I thought you'd be itching to get into Murphy's house."

"I am, Dan. I really am. But I have a really strong feeling about this. We need to head east. Traffic is going to get worse as the day wears on. It will be a bitch to get out of the city. Even with sirens blaring."

"What about Grace? What if she's in that house in San Pedro, right now, Erin?"

"She's not. And even if she is, Pedro officers are going to get to her before we do. If she's there, and she's alive, they can save her before we can."

Erin picked up her cell to call Captain Jacobs. She'd be open to the crazy idea of letting her and Dan drive out to Palm Desert with no address in mind, wouldn't she?

Joanna Jacobs knew one thing about Erin's strong feelings – they were rarely wrong. Erin appreciated that when something overwhelmed her, Captain Jacobs never got all TV cop and irately yelled things like, "You're out of line, Taylor!" She listened, and if it seemed reasonable, she agreed to pursue it. And sometimes, Jacobs was working on a feeling, too. And if she and Taylor had the same feeling, that must mean something.

Dan got behind the wheel. Erin buckled into the passenger's seat. They pulled on to the Interstate Freeway, heading east, out of the City of Angels, and into the desert.

SEVENTY-EIGHT

Kent was enjoying himself immensely. Grace really was special. He might keep her for just a little while longer. His last few attempts at love had proven pretty disappointing. He could rarely find release with any woman until after she was gone, and growing cold, but it could happen any second now with Grace.

Grace kept repeating her mantra, "It can't go on forever," in her mind, and was utterly unaware of her own body anymore; removed somehow from the brutality and filth of this monster, using her hands. She was oblivious to it, but there was peace on her face. In spite of the horrific thing that was happening to her, she looked quite beautiful – no, beatific.

Kent stole a glance at her face and just like that, he came.

Grace snapped out of it when he groaned, and the warm sticky mess seeped onto her hands. She was disgusted, but she would soon be free. He was done with her now. It would be over soon. All men are the same. *They blow their wads, and then you're dead to them. In this case, literally.*

Kent sat back in the chair across from her and stared. She wasn't doing anything. She wasn't crying. She was perfectly serene. The familiar anger began to fill his head. How dare she just sit there, so utterly calm? He'd convinced himself she was special. Damn, he'd been so stupid. She had manipulated him, tricked him into thinking she was different, but she was just an arrogant little bitch. She actually thought she was special? She thought she was perfect for him? Good enough for him? That they belonged together? All those beautiful women out there, just waiting to be loved by a good man, by a gentleman, and she thought she deserved him? What a filthy little cunt.

"Do you still love me now?" Kent snarled.

Grace snapped out of her daze. She'd almost forgotten he was there. Her attention shifted to her sticky hands. She said good-bye to them in her mind. He would kill her soon, and he would keep her hands around for a trophy.

"Yes." Grace said in a whisper of a whisper.

"You lying bitch."

To Grace, an eternity of silence passed. She didn't know what to say anymore, so she just stayed quiet. And she waited.

Kent couldn't stand it anymore. She was so smug. She was either a liar, or she really did love him. It didn't matter. Either way, she would destroy him if he didn't destroy her first. She sat so calmly, so serenely, and it made him sick to see her. He'd break her. He'd make her sorry. This bitch was going to pay for thinking she was good enough for him.

It hurt so badly, because she didn't see it coming. It hurt so badly, because it was filled with the force of such primal rage. Kent stood up and punched Grace hard in the face. The chair she was tied to toppled over. Her body and the chair issued a thud through the cabin. Kent picked the chair up, with Grace still tied to it, righted it, and waited for her to say something. To scream, to cry, anything. But there was nothing. She just sat there, bleeding and staring past him.

She didn't make so much as a murmur. Not because it didn't hurt, but because nothing came out. Her throat was closed up. The left side of her face felt like it had cracked completely open. Her eye began to swell shut instantaneously. Her lip was raw like one of her teeth had torn through it. Her mouth filled with blood. She lifted her hands to wipe at it, and gagged when the cold, clammy semen mixed with the blood on her face. She willed herself not to throw up. There was nothing to throw up anyway. Her last meal, the one comprised of five potato chips, was resting in the brick planter outside her apartment building. Her last supper. Five potato chips, thrown up in a planter. Criminals on death row get a better last meal than that. What would her last words be, and who would even hear them?

Kent couldn't believe she just sat there and took it. She didn't scream. Tears came out of her eyes, but she wasn't crying. It was just the force of him hitting her so hard. She didn't say anything. She didn't look at him either. Kent was so angry. He picked the knife up off the kitchen table and held it to her chest, in the soft feminine place, right above the top of her modest cleavage. Her breath quickened. She was afraid. She was scared of the pain, but she still said nothing.

"Why do you love me, Grace?"

She could no longer remember why she loved him, or why she'd said the things she'd said. The truth was all she had.

"I don't know. I just do."

Kent pressed the tip of the knife into her skin until he drew blood. Grace gasped from the pain, but still didn't scream. She wanted to. But she couldn't. Hadn't he told her how pointless it would be? If a woman screams in the middle of the desert, and no one is there to hear it, would she still make a sound? Apparently not.

SEVENTY-NINE

Dan and Erin rode in complete quiet for the first part of the journey, as if the taut silence would somehow propel them to Grace Elliott in time to save her.

When Erin's cell phone rang, they were both surprised out of their reveries.

"Captain," Erin said, "I'm putting you on speaker so Dan can hear. What did they find in Pedro? Any sign of Grace?"

"No, no Grace. No anyone."

"We got a Palm Desert address?"

"No. Kent Clark's car is sitting in his mother's garage, but he's not there. No one is. His car is going to the lab for detailed search. There are hairs, fibers, and blood in his trunk. There's an Oldsmobile registered to Kathleen Murphy, but it's not parked in the garage. We figure he's probably switched to her car. I put out a BOLO on her license plate, which I'll send to your phone, too. It's a tan Oldsmobile. In the house, they found a trash bag in a closet filled with family photos, and severed hands in the freezer. They were able to lift the prints. The hands belong to the 19-year-old prostitute, Luz Ramos, who was murdered in that motel in San Pedro."

"Shit," Erin nearly shrieked with joy, "that's fantastic. We've got him Captain. It's only a matter of time now." Hard evidence. Luz Ramos' severed hands in Kent Clark's mother's freezer.

"Yeah, I think we do. No matter what, we can nail the son-of-a-bitch for Luz Ramos. And we'll have enough physical evidence to get him for Lauren McLaughlin, and some of the hair in his trunk is blonde –"

"Root attached?" Erin eagerly interrupted.

"Yup, on some of it," said Captain Jacobs.

"So we might be able to nail him for Trish Morris too."

"Exactly."

"Thanks Captain. You know where to find me." Erin hung up. She and Dan were still tense, but beaming. They gave each other a mental high-five. They were going to get this bastard.

EIGHTY

Kent pulled the neckline of Grace's shirt down and ran the knife in a cut deep enough to pain her, in a line, straight across the top of her left breast. Grace did not scream, but she did let out a guttural growl. Kent's pulse quickened at the frightened animal noise that crept out of her mouth on little fear paws. She was pathetic to him now. Like a helpless, little kitten. What did she know of love? What did she know of loyalty? She was worse than all of them. At least, the rest of them told the truth in the end. That they didn't love him. She still wouldn't admit it. He would force her to confess it.

He took the knife to her blouse – the innocent-looking peasant blouse she wore as if she weren't a helpless animal – and he cut it open, from the neckline down.

Grace hated this more than everything he'd done so far. Abducted, bound, abused, hit, and cut, but being undressed was too much. She hadn't counted on that. When they found her body, they would see it all. Only she couldn't afford shame right now. She could merely endure. She repeated her mantra. *This can't go on forever.* And she told herself she only had to be brave for this one last thing. And though she was in agony, she started laughing right then. She was definitely losing her mind. She just laughed and laughed. Kent stepped back in confusion. She was crazy. Truly crazy.

"What the hell are you laughing at?" He demanded.

Grace didn't think she could really say. The laughing turned to tears and then to quiet.

It had just struck her as funny. The horribly, ridiculously fucked-up situations you can find yourself in, and the thoughts that can sneak up on you.

Here she was, about to die, and she was thinking, *at least I won't have to go to Erick's wedding.*

While the question in Kent's mind was: *how long should I bother keeping this crazy bitch alive?*

EIGHTY-ONE

"Where are you now?" Jacobs demanded, as soon as Erin answered her cell phone and put it on speaker.

"Right around Beaumont," Dan offered.

"Wow. You're making good time."

"We could make better time if Dan wasn't a grandma behind the wheel," Erin said, still wishing she'd forced him to let her drive.

"You know speeding is against the law, Erin," Dan winked at her when he said it.

"You two stop farting around. Right now, you have my permission to speed."

There was a pause. Dan drove faster as Joanna spoke.

"Faster, Dan. Don't be a wuss. Okay, so we've got no property anywhere in Riverside County owned by Kathleen Murphy. But, we did find a few cabins just north of there, in Joshua Tree, owned by a man named Roy Murphy. We tried to talk to him, but he's out of commission. He recently had a stroke and is in the hospital. He lives in Torrance with his wife Jackie. She has confirmed that Roy is Kathleen's brother."

"Shit, that's got to be it," said Erin, "Joshua Tree is pretty remote. How many cabins?"

"Three."

"Are they near each other?"

"Well, 'near' by remote desert property standards, not big-city standards. Each of them is on around two to three acres, so they're spaced out. We have to play this carefully. It will be quiet out there. If he hears a car approaching, he could panic and kill her."

"Shit. Have local authorities been contacted?"

"Hell, no. I don't want a bunch of sirens crawling all over

the place. I'm hoping we can figure out which cabin he's in, and then you two can approach quietly – on foot if necessary, and we will call the local PD for back-up. Joshua Tree isn't an incorporated city, and it's San Bernardino County, not Riverside, so that's who we'll contact when the time is right. What I need you to do now is get your asses to Joshua Tree as fast as possible. When you're close, then you can be cautious. Right now, move."

It was time to move fast, sirens blaring, until they closed the distance gap and discretion would be necessary. Dan and Erin focused all their intentions on finding Grace alive.

EIGHTY-TWO

G race wasn't sure if she was conscious anymore. The world had lost all color. It wasn't even distinctly black and white. It was gray; it was haze, and it was pain.

Every time he cut her, she gritted her teeth and repeated her mantra. *This can't go on forever.* Time was an illusion. She'd already been here forever, and yet she had no idea how long that was. Was it forever, or minutes or hours or days, or a nightmare from which she might never wake up? The world had tilted and distorted everything like a funhouse mirror. Her mind raced up and down the halls of this hellish maze, finding only dead ends, and only dead ends, and only... stop. Retrace your steps. Escape. But there is no way out. *This can't go on forever.*

He kept it as dark in here as he could, but she'd seen daylight come once. She didn't think the sun was there anymore. Maybe it was the next night, or maybe the sun was never coming back. Not even the sun could stay; perhaps even it had abandoned her. She wouldn't be able to endure this much longer. She would bleed to death, or he'd get bored and kill her. The cold anger in his eyes didn't even scare her anymore. It meant that he would finish her.

Grace's skin tingled; her bones became heavy, and then the strange illusion of separation, soul from flesh, pulled her free. The heaviness of her form stayed in the chair, as she, Grace – her essence, her soul? – stepped outside of her body. She watched a woman, tied to a chair, her bound hands in her lap, covered in blood and semen. Her torn blouse open to reveal her upper body, her breasts and torso covered in shallow cuts. How many, it was hard to tell, when there was so much blood.

That woman was vacant. She was leaving this world.

But the other woman – the Grace outside – stood beside her and kept watch. She waited for some sign.

The man put down the knife on the kitchen table and put

her bound hands on his dick again, and began stroking himself. He had his head back, his eyes closed. He was in bliss. A state of grace. He could do no wrong. He was good. He was right. He deserved this love.

The woman outside saw the slightest nick in the plastic zip tie, the strain the psychotic man put on it with every stroke.

Tell me, she said to the woman in the chair, *tell me that you want to live.*

Grace looked up for a moment, to follow this woman's voice; she recognized it as her own. *Stay grateful. Stay in the moment, Grace.*

Grace! Think of all the others who died here, at this monster's hands. There is another after you, Grace. She is cute, and young and smart. She has curly brown hair and dimples. She's taking violin lessons, and she has a cat named Fred, and she wants to live. But she's next. What about that? What about –

"Justice!" Grace screamed. It was the only scream she'd screamed for him so far.

EIGHTY-THREE

Dan stopped using the siren and lowered his speed when he got near Joshua Tree. He and Erin put on their best "No, we're not cops" faces.

Dan pulled into a run-down convenience store to feign needing directions.

The man behind the counter exactly fit the description of a man one would envision as the proprietor of a convenience store out in the California desert. Old, white, with hard lines etched in his face, and a few teeth that just hadn't been able to stick around anymore. And, fortunately, he was helpful.

"Howdy there, what can I do you for? You lost?" he asked. It was his standard question. Pretty much anybody who came in here was lost, in one way or another.

"Yeah… uh… my wife and I rented a cabin out here from a man named Roy Murphy, but we're kind of confused about where we're going. This is the road they're on, but there are three cabins down that way, and we're just not sure which one we're supposed to go to."

"Roy Murphy! How is that son of a bitch?" the man boomed.

"Um… well, a little under the weather these days, actually, but –"

"Well, that's too bad."

"So, you know Mr. Murphy? I don't suppose you know his nephew, Kent? I think he might be staying in one of these cabins."

"No, I never knew about any nephew. I really don't know Roy all that well. I mean, I think it's a shame he's sick and all – "

Erin suppressed the urge to scream. This guy was nice, but she wanted to throttle him. *Hurry, hurry, hurry. Stop talking!*

"Listen, we're kind of in a hurry. Long drive and everything. We're really looking forward to settling in for the night. Do you think you could help us?" Erin kept her voice sweet and patient.

"Well, I think one of them cabins is already rented. A couple of hippie kids came in here a few days ago asking for directions too, and they're staying in that first one you'll come to right there when you turn off the main road. So I guess it'd be one of them other two. Probably the second one you come to is what you're looking for though. Nobody ever asks about that third one. Don't think it rents much. It's kind of run-down."

Erin's heart exploded, but she held it in. She had to contain herself. She and Dan issued very heartfelt thanks, and assured their new friend that they'd be back if they got lost.

As soon as they got in the car, they both said it.

"Third cabin."

"Yea," Erin said, "It's got to be. Run down. Don't rent it much. Maybe Roy just lets Kent use it whenever he wants. So, how do we do this? How close are we? And how close can we get before we need to abandon the car and walk it?"

Dan zoomed in closer on the map on his GPS. They peered at it. They couldn't afford to make a mistake.

Erin checked her phone. It was making her nervous to be in this desolate place.

"We could start losing reception, Dan. This is pretty remote. Should we call back-up now?"

"No, it's too soon. But call Jacobs and let her know. I'm pretty sure we've got a solid address. It's got to be that third cabin. It's also the furthest one from 'downtown' – and I use that term loosely – so if he had his choice, I'm sure he'd take a woman there."

Erin called Jacobs, and Jacobs said she'd give it just a few minutes, and then send back-up.

Dan turned down the desert road that would lead them

to Kent Clark and, hopefully, a still alive Grace Elliott. Their hearts and minds raced forward as the car crawled slowly down the lonely desert road.

EIGHTY-FOUR

When Grace screamed "Justice!" it tore through the silence of the cabin and echoed out into the desert. Kent jumped back, surprised. He panicked, as if someone could have heard her, even though he was aware how remote that possibility was. What the hell was up with this woman anyway? He'd really managed to get a crazy one this time. She was becoming tiresome.

Grace's scream reverberated in her mind, over and again. It went on forever, an endless howl for amends. There must be accountability for this man's crimes. He should not be left to roam free, extinguishing life. It was time that he paid for his sins.

Grace could no longer bear to be a monster. Not when there were so many women; shouting their cries for justice, right now, the non-stop repetition of it in her mind; so many women had died right here, wanting sanctuary, wanting to survive. Grace must honor them with a fight. She must dignify herself in battle, even if it was her last; maybe even especially if it was her last. She had lived in blatant disregard of the precious gift of life for far too long. The women's laments rose up from the hushed desert all around her, spirits wailing out, that they had wanted to live, would have given anything to breathe again. If Grace didn't decide right here, and right now, that she wanted to live too, even if she was going to die, then she was disgracing her own existence. She was degrading all those who perished before her and debasing those who would succumb to this asshole after she was gone. Their blood would be on her hands. If she didn't go to war with him, right now, then she *was* a monster. Just like Kent.

She would go out fighting, fighting for all the women whose hopes and dreams and hearts were buried in the desert sand.

She could see from the corner of her eye, the glint of the knife on the table edge. She didn't turn her head, but she knew exactly where it was.

"I don't love you anymore, Grace." Kent said it with such coldness, but couldn't fathom how ridiculous he was. How absolutely pathetic. He said it as if it mattered. He said it as if anyone anywhere could give a shit. He said it as if he'd won.

Grace screamed, but it was not words. There were no words for *this*. This was the place where words were sent packing, where all the things that thought they mattered lived and breathed. He would not hear words, anyway. Justice wasn't a word he would understand. Justice was something that would spill through his hands when he reached for her throat.

It was seconds. Less than seconds, maybe. But there was no such thing as time. Not really. Grace had been here for lifetimes. She had been here for moments.

Kent rushed for her.

Grace yanked her wrists apart as hard as she could.

Kent had his hands on her throat.

The plastic zip tie finally cracked from the slit his knife had made in it, from the constant tension, and from infinite violation. At last, there was this small equity. Grace's hands were free while Kent's were absorbed with finishing her.

For Grace, the air left the room.

Kent felt the rush in her slender neck, underneath his powerful hands.

Grace moved her left hand slowly toward the table.

Kent was the man. Kent was winning. Grace would die.

Grace focused on the last bit of air still in her lungs. Inside her head, the words "It is enough," rang out. The cold blade was heaven on her fingers.

Kent was God. He held the power of life and death in his hands.

Grace grabbed the knife and plunged it deep into Kent's flesh. Into his soft belly, just above his groin.

Kent screamed and his grip on her loosened. He had to hold on; he could kill her if he held on.

Grace twisted the knife hard in his gut before he could think to grab for it. She pulled it roughly to one side, and then out fast.

He released his hold on her neck.

Grace inhaled profound gulps of sweet air. She took in the deepest breath of all breaths. The baby's breath. The breath of the newborn, the reborn.

She held the knife hard and fast in both hands as he clutched the gaping wound in his abdomen. He was unsteady now, losing his footing, and Grace seized the opportunity. She pushed her bound ankles out and forcefully swung at his legs with hers. Caught off-balance, Kent toppled on to the floor with a thud and a searing yelp of agony.

He rolled into a fetal position. There was blood. So much blood.

Sharp adrenalin coursed through Grace as she scooted her chair back, away from him. She kept her eyes only on him as she untied the ropes around her waist. She cut the zip tie from her ankles and pushed the chair away from her, hard. She leaned up against the wall and slid down to the floor, pulling her legs into a cross-legged position. It felt so good. Her ankles had been bound for so long. *This is what gratitude feels like. I am grateful that I can sit cross-legged, right now. I am bleeding, cut up, burned to the ground, assaulted, violated, possibly dying, but I can sit cross-legged.*

Kent moaned at her.

"Grace, please... please... help me... so much pain... help me..." he tried to get up, but he couldn't. Blood was rushing out of him. A pool of it formed around him, ran across the floor. Soon, it would reach Grace's legs.

She could stand up. She could move away. She could take the knife and finish him off. She could put pressure on the bleeding, maybe try to stop it. She could look for a phone and call for help. She could walk, or crawl, out the door. She could do lots of things. But she just sat there.

It was wrong to sit and watch a man die. But he wasn't really a man to her. He was a monster. So was it wrong to watch a monster die? And even though he was a monster, and even though really, the world would be a better place without him, she could still be grateful to him for bringing her to this place. Not this dumpy cabin in the desert. But to this *place*. The place where she would live from this moment forward.

Because she would live. For ten more minutes, ten more years, whatever the Universe saw fit to give her. When it was joyful, when it was painful, she would live. She *could* live.

And she could live with letting Kent Clark die.

"Grace... please... I love you..."

And she could live with making a joke.

"I bet you say that to all the girls."

She sat still. Nothing else. Just still. Never once letting go of the blade in her hand.

* * * * *

Dan drove down the quiet road until the third cabin was in sight. The first one they approached had a Volkswagen van parked outside of it. The second was dark, and had no cars around. The third had very little light inside, but a car was parked outside. It could very well be a tan Oldsmobile, though they couldn't be sure in the darkness.

Dan pulled his car off the road, and he and Erin got out

noiselessly. They didn't even close the car doors. They silently drew their weapons and walked as light-footed as possible toward the cabin.

When they got close enough to see the car, they could confirm it was a tan-colored Oldsmobile with a license plate matching the one registered to Kathleen Murphy.

The cabin was eerily quiet.

Deep concentration lined their faces. Their breathing was inaudible. Every step Erin hoped not to snap a twig or crunch a pebble that would give them away. The silence was so deafening; she was afraid they were too late. In spite of the cool night air a puddle of sweat pooled in her bra.

They approached the porch. They met eyes. Dan nodded toward the window to the right of the front door. Erin approached the window slowly, as Dan stood, ready, just to the left of the door.

The dark curtains were drawn. Erin couldn't make out anything at all inside. She looked at Dan. She looked at the front door. She raised her eyebrows in a question. Was he enough of a bad-ass stud to kick the door in? Then again, the place was pretty run-down. Maybe even the short legs on her five-foot frame could kick in the door.

Dan was, apparently, enough of a bad-ass stud to kick the door in.

Erin radioed for back-up to approach just as the shoddy door splintered and caved in.

The sight was a complete horror show.

Dan called for medics immediately.

Grace Elliott sat cross-legged, leaning against the wall of the kitchen, unmoving. Her face was bruised and bleeding. One eye was swollen shut; the other was open, but didn't register the dramatic entrance. Her blouse was ripped open from neckline to waistline. Her breasts, chest, and stomach were covered in knife wounds, and a tremendous amount of blood. Her neck, wrists and face were badly bruised.

Kent Clark lay in front of her on the kitchen floor in a fetal position. His arms hugged his abdomen. Blood had formed a pool out and around his body and crept toward Grace's legs. It wasn't clear whether he was dead or unconscious.

Erin went to Grace. She was breathing!

"She's alive," Erin said.

Dan had a moment – just a moment because that was all he could afford right now – to look at Grace. She was alive. If ever there was a woman – no, there never was, not like this, not even his wife – that Dan wanted to scoop into his arms and save, it was her. She was like a broken figurine that had been glued back together, and somehow managed to be more beautiful because of it. Someone, maybe she herself, had bothered to pick up the pieces, and rejoin them. He was looking right into the heart of something. Love, he supposed. Love in its purest form, before all human baggage taints it. He suddenly felt stupid, like a typical, big, dumb man for wanting to save her, to rescue her. Here he was thinking he was such a bad-ass because he could kick a door in, and there she sat, covered in knife wounds with her abductor bleeding out at her feet. She was a survivor. She didn't need saving. She had already saved herself.

Dan checked Kent to see if he was still alive. He was, but just barely.

"Grace, are you okay?" Grace didn't respond, but she moved her head ever so slightly and met Erin's eyes.

"Grace, my name is Erin Taylor. I'm a detective with LAPD. You're going to be okay. An ambulance is almost here. Can you talk to me?"

Grace stared at Erin for a moment. She figured she probably could talk, but she didn't know what to say.

Four EMTs entered then and moved quickly.

"He's got a pulse but it's very faint," said Dan, moving away from Kent so the medics could work. Two handled Kent, while the other two went to Grace.

"What's your name?" Grace had no response for the medic.

"Her name is Grace," Erin answered.

"Grace, my name is John. You're going to be all right. We're taking you to a hospital, right now, okay?"

Grace was still and quiet. She was compliant. She was badly injured, but she would live. She would be scarred. But she didn't care. In fact, she would wear her scars proudly. She hoped every time she saw them, she would remember that she wasn't a lemon after all. She was a warrior. She was a fucking survivor. That must count for something.

The medics were carrying her out on a stretcher. Erin's compassion for Grace stunned her. She couldn't fathom the hell she had endured.

"The others. Their hearts are buried in the desert..." Grace muttered.

"Wait, where? Where in the desert?" Erin was as close as she could get to Grace without lying on the stretcher with her.

Grace didn't know what she was saying, or why she was saying it. Utterly delirious, she started to slip away.

"Detective, you can interview her later. We've got to get her to the hospital."

The medics left. Grace began a slow fade. The ceiling of the cabin became the ceiling of the night sky and then receded to nothing as she finally let go and let sweet unconsciousness take her.

The cabin was a madhouse after that. It crawled with CSIs,

local cops and LAPD. Cadaver dogs were used in order to scour the area around the property.

Erin's tension eased. They had caught him, and the evidence against him was staggering. Rose Santos' body was in the deep freeze in the garage. Her hands were in the freezer in the kitchen.

The cadaver dogs would find an area in the desert sand, near a pile of rocks, just northeast of the cabin that made them sit at attention.

Kent Clark's life hung in the balance, but even if he lived, he would die in prison.

You can't bury that many hearts in the desert and just get away with it, Erin thought, relishing the glass of whiskey she would drink in the hot shower she would have as soon as she got home.

EIGHTY-FIVE

Grace pushed her heavy eyes open and faced a brief moment of utter nothingness. In tiny flashes, then little waves, then huge rushes, pieces flooded back.

"You're awake. Oh my god, Grace. I'm so glad you're –" Natalie was standing at the edge of the hospital bed where Grace lay with most of her torso covered in stitches and bandages.

"Natalie... I love you so much," was the best thing Grace could think to say.

"I love you too, Grace. Now, whatever you do, don't laugh, okay?"

"Why? Are you going to tell a joke?"

"No. Because you have a lot of stitches, and it will hurt if you laugh."

Grace laughed. It hurt.

"Nat, you can't tell someone not to do something. Then they're sure to do it."

"I know. I'm sorry, that was dumb. How are you feeling?"

"Great."

"Come on. Tell me. Or don't. I know it's... it's a lot. I'm here though, for whatever you need. But you know that."

"Yeah, Nat, I know. And I'm grateful," Grace said. And she meant it more than ever.

"Me too, Grace. I'm so glad you're okay. I was so... well, I'm just so relieved. I feel horrible. I should have made you come over that night."

"Nat, come on. You can't know these things. And I'm not sorry this happened. I'm really not."

"Grace! It was so horrible though..."

"Yes, it was horrible. It was horrible beyond horrible with shit on top. But it's okay... I don't know how to explain it.

Something happened to me… inside… there was so much dark there… it was so painful… but now… it's like it broke me. And saved me. It's all good… the cracks, when you break… it lets the light in, you know?"

"That's a song or something…" Natalie said.

"Probably. Or Rumi. It's either Leonard Cohen or Rumi," Grace said.

"Well, they're both mystics." Natalie sat on the edge of Grace's hospital bed and smiled a mischievous smile.

"Guess what?" Nat playfully asked.

"Chicken butt?" said Grace, and tried desperately not to laugh. Her stitches hurt anyway.

"Alas, no chicken butt, but I've got something even better."

"Yeah? What?" Grace asked. What could possibly be better than chicken butt?

"You're kind of famous."

Grace just stared at her. She'd kind of forgotten about the fact that the man she'd nearly killed was notorious.

"Ugh," said Grace. "Kind of don't know how I feel about that."

"Well…" started Natalie, "Just think of it as a blessing. All your photographs will probably sell like crazy. Check this out." Natalie handed Grace the newspaper.

NOTORIOUS KILLER KENT CLARK CAPTURED IN THE CALIFORNIA DESERT

By Meghan Stein

The madman Kent Clark, who has been terrorizing the city, a suspect in multiple murders and the recent abduction of another woman, was captured in a cabin in Joshua Tree late last night. The cabin is owned by a family member who could not be reached for comment.

His most recent victim, Grace Elliott, was found in the cabin with him. She had been abducted and held captive by him for more than twenty-four hours. Ms. Elliott suffered multiple knife wounds, but is now in stable condition at the Hi-Desert Medical Center.

The body and severed hands of Rose Santos, of Culver City, were also found in freezers inside the cabin.

Cadaver dogs located a grave on the edge of the property with the remains of numerous women. One has been identified as Patricia Morris of San Pedro.

Authorities could not provide the exact number of women buried there, but forensics teams estimate the number to be at least five, with that being a modest estimate.

Ms. Elliott, during her capture, was able to grab the killer's knife and fight back. Mr. Clark suffered major stab wounds to the abdomen and is in critical condition under high security. If he recovers, he will be moved to Los Angeles to face charges.

He faces arrest for the kidnapping, torture and sexual assault of Grace Elliott, as well as the murders of Rose Santos, Trish Morris, Lauren McLaughlin, and Luz Ramos. As more remains are identified, he could face charges for the murder of those women as well.

Detectives Erin Taylor and Daniel Garza have led the investigation and commented that they are relieved such a vicious killer has been caught and will be facing the maximum penalties for his sadistic crimes.

Detective Taylor also added that she hoped to get closure and justice for the loved ones of the remaining unidentified women found in the desert grave.

She would not make any suggestions as to the identities of the other women, but only said, "We will examine every inch of the property and every piece of evidence we can in the hopes of bringing some peace of mind to the other victims of Kent Clark – those left behind to bury his dead a second time."

Captain Joanna Jacobs of the Westside division of LAPD will be issuing a press conference tomorrow morning to present any further information uncovered today.

For now, the women of Greater Los Angeles can breathe a sigh of relief that one of the most notorious killers our city has seen in years is off the streets.

"That is so surreal to me," said Grace, as she set down the newspaper. "I feel like this couldn't possibly have happened to me. But these other women, so many… my god… I can't imagine how awful this must be for the other women's families."

"Grace, they have closure, which is something they thought they'd never get. It's not as good as having the women alive, but at least they know what happened to them. They don't have to wonder anymore. They can try to find some peace."

"And look at all these flowers, Grace." There were. A lot of flowers. The room was a brightly-colored blur to Grace. She didn't want to lose what Natalie was saying.

"A lot of victims' families are pretty grateful for you, for what you did." Natalie waited quietly as Grace closed her eyes. The exhaustion sank deeply into her battered body.

"They're grateful for me...," said Grace, smiling. "I guess I can live with that." Then she slept. A perfect, deep and dreamless sleep.

EPILOGUE

Additional murder charges were brought against Kent Clark for the murders of Cicily Masters, Diane Ketchum, Leslie Berger, Sharon Rogers, Jennifer Chan, Emma Burke, and Samantha Alexander. These seven women, as well as Patricia Morris, were discovered in the desert grave in Joshua Tree. Including the previously recovered bodies of Lauren McLaughlin, Rose Santos and Luz Ramos, he is known to be responsible for the deaths of eleven women, as well as the attempted murder of Grace Elliott.

Eileen Cambridge and Jillian Morris started a charity, the State of Grace Foundation, to provide resources and outreach to prevent violence against women, as well as grief-counseling and therapy for friends and family members of women who have met with violence. State of Grace Foundation has already raised money and awarded it to citizens who were crucial in the Clark investigation. Among the recipients are local artist and smoothie-maker Shad Meadows, former prostitute Charmaine Tyler and former cleaning lady Yolanda Flores, who recently received her American citizenship and is now working as an international liaison for State of Grace Foundation, providing outreach to at-risk women in Spanish-speaking countries.

Grace Elliott will continue to show her photography exhibits at local galleries and is expected to have a showing of her work in New York City next spring. She is currently single, and very grateful.

Erin Taylor and Daniel Garza were last seen challenging each other to a tequila shot contest. Captain Joanna Jacobs has insisted they both take a much-needed vacation.

Kent Clark died of sepsis three days after being admitted to Hi-Desert Medical Center. His uncle, Roy Murphy, recently released from the hospital after suffering a stroke, said that no services would be held out of respect for the victims of his nephew's heinous crimes.

Mr. Murphy said that he plans to demolish the cabin in Joshua Tree where his nephew was found, and that Kent would be cremated and his ashes would be buried in a desert grave.

ABOUT THE AUTHOR

[Photo by Sam Grant]

Marnie Olson is a critically-unacclaimed actor and playwright, and most recently, a burlesque performer. The web series she co-wrote, *Namaste Bitches*, is available for your viewing pleasure at

www.WatchNamasteBitches.com.

Marnie knows how to sew, wield power tools and drive stick shift. If she's not trying, she can make you laugh, and if she is trying, she can drink you under the table. Turn-ons include fishnet stockings, spicy food and brave souls. She loves fake hair colors and hates fake food allergies. Her phobias include spiders and laundromats. She is anti-violence unless you honk your car horn for a stupid reason or drive an ice cream truck, in which case she will cut you.

Marnie lives alone in Los Angeles, unencumbered by progeny or partner. She doesn't even have a pet. Why bother? It could die.

Grateful is her first novel.